The Presence
of the
Past

The Presence of the Past

A novel,
inspired by real events

Michael Anderson

2017

First Printing: 2017

ISBN: 978-1-7751966-0-0

Michael Anderson
RR 2
Meaford
Ontario
Canada N4L 1W6

Cover illustration: The cross at the crash site.
Photograph by Michael Anderson

To the two most important women in my life, with love and admiration:

Anne Anderson and Pamela Anderson (née Miles)

In Memoriam:

Lt Col WGH (Bill) Miles, Royal Marines, Rtd
January 14, 1886–March 8, 1947

HIS SPIRIT RETURNED UNTO GOD WHO GAVE IT.
REQUIESCAT IN PACE.

Author's note

THIS IS A NOVEL, but one inspired by true events.

Late in the afternoon of March 8, 1947, an RAF Dakota with five crew and eight passengers crashed in heavy fog high on Mount Epomeo, a volcanic mountain on the Italian island of Ischia (pronounced "Ees-kya"), north-west of Capri in the Bay of Naples. Ten of the people on board were killed in the crash. According to Truman Capote, who lived on the island for a short while in 1949, a group of 'goatsherds' stoned to death three people who somehow survived the crash.

The bodies were looted, as was the plane itself. The looters mutilated the bodies to remove jewelry and gold fillings.

All the victims are buried in the Commonwealth War Cemetery in Naples.

The community erected a cross at the crash site in 1948 or 1949. The cross blew down in a storm some time later but was re-erected. It is still there, as the cover photograph (taken in 2015) shows.

Two shepherds were on the mountain on the night of the crash, but uninvolved in the looting. One died shortly afterwards, for unknown reasons. In 2010, a few years before he died, the older shepherd told his story to the son of one of the victims, who passed it on to me, the grandson of another victim. I was also able to talk with the daughter of two islanders who helped bring the bodies down to Fontana from the crash site.

A commemoration service was held in 2007, 60 years after the crash. As part of the ceremony, a plaque with the names of the victims was placed at the foot of the cross. Members of the victims' families attended a second commemoration service in 2012, five years later. I mention the commemoration services here because, even though they do not appear in the book (although the plaque does in a very different context), they show very clearly how much the crash and its aftermath affected the community.

The events surrounding the crash make a springboard for the novel. The story is not about the crash or the people who died in it. Rather, it's about the wholly imaginary Ischians who were involved in or affected by the crash. The story is a modern morality play, an exploration of guilt, and forgiveness, and faith.

Besides knowing about the two shepherds, we know that a young priest did administer Last Rites. However, the characters of Demonte, Paolo and Brother Renato are wholly fictitious, as are all the Ischians in the book. The Ischians I met in 2015 were, without exception, courteous, hospitable, and extraordinarily generous to the grandson of someone who died in a crash that happened before they were born. There was no-one like the people who behave badly in the book.

Ischia in 1947 was poor and primitive; the Ischia of today is modern and vibrant, and I have nothing but good memories of my time there.

We know very little about most of the victims of the crash. Certainly, nothing is known about what happened to individual victims in or after the crash, except for the only woman on board, who did suffer the rather gruesome fate I describe. When they appear as spirits, the victims in the story are all products of my imagination.

So here's the usual disclaimer: This is a work of fiction and any resemblance to real people, alive or dead, is entirely coincidental and unintended.

Michael Anderson
Meaford
September, 2015 – November, 2017

Acknowledgments

IT IS ONLY WHEN YOU WRITE A BOOK YOURSELF that you realise how heart-felt the Acknowledgements are in other books. When authors thank the people who have helped them, they mean it. Writing a book is not for the faint-hearted, and it's impossible for me to imagine doing it without the support of many, many people.

My deep thanks go to the people who've helped me on this journey.

Rosario Caruso, the Mayor of Serrara-Fontana in 2015, for his extraordinary generosity and hospitality to the grandson of one of the crash victims, 68 years after the event.

Fiore Hawryluk, for her translation of Italian source material and her insights into the Italian mind.

Rosa Iacono, the daughter of two Ischians who brought bodies down from the mountain, for sharing everything she knew of the crash and its aftermath, even consulting her mother to check details.

Godfrey Scotchbrook, the son of one of the crash victims, who organized the 2012 commemoration and who spent an hour on Skype with me.

Debra Ginsberg, editor *par excellence*, who guided a first-time author with tact and made many helpful suggestions.

John Barker and Madeleine Callway, beta readers of the penultimate draft, who offered valuable insight, advice and encouragement.

Members of the Tristram Shandy Book Club and good friends all, who urged me on as I tried something new, who commented on an early draft, and who have been wonderful sounding boards for various ideas: Brian Brittain, Bill Casey, Nick Forrest, James Knowles, Herb Koplowitz, Bryan Monkhouse.

And most especially, Anne Anderson, whose support, patience, wise advice and sharp editing eyes kept me going.

"The past is never dead. It's not even past."

William Faulkner
Requiem for a Nun (1951)

Napoli

Vesuvio

Procida

Pompeii

Ischia

Bay of
Naples

Capri

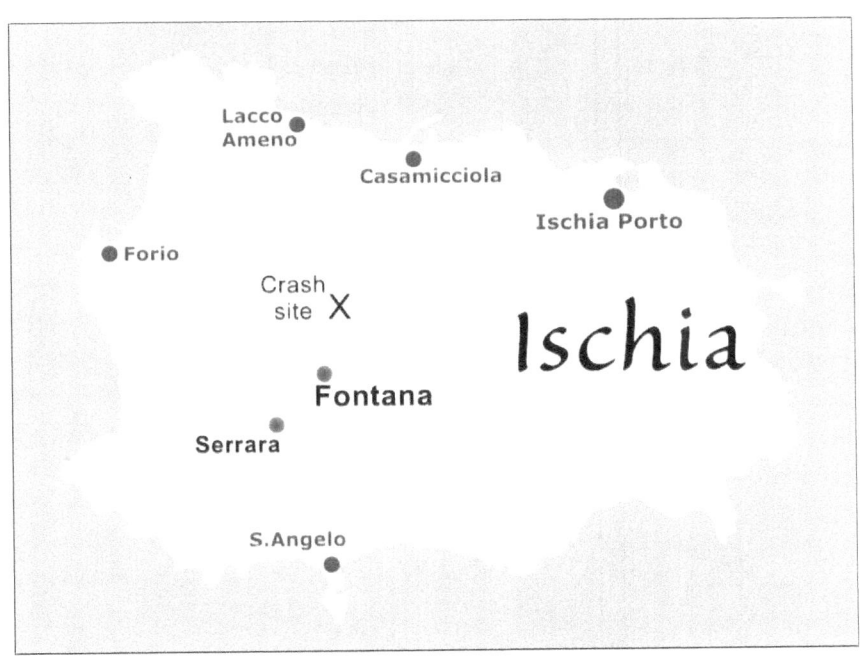

Lacco
Ameno

Casamicciola

Ischia Porto

Forio

Crash
site X

Ischia

Fontana

Serrara

S.Angelo

Cast of characters

Demonte	A shepherd
Paolo	His brother
Adolfo	A butcher
Ulisse	His brother
Tifeo	His brother, a blacksmith
Amedea	Tifeo's wife
Serafina	A spinster, Adolfo's cousin
Cesare	Her brother, a builder
Baldassare	Her youngest brother
Rosabella	Cesare's wife
Filomena	Mother to Serafina, Cesare and Baldassare
Father Giovanni	The parish priest
Brother Renato	A junior priest
Raffaele Cutolo	A Camorra crime boss
Gasparo	A pawnbroker

The presence of the

of the

past

Chapter One

THE LIGHT WAS FAILING as Paolo stumbled back to the small stockade with the sheep. He was cold and wet–the fog had closed in while he was still out, and his worn, much-patched shirt and vest did little to keep him warm. The waterlogged air leaked onto everything it touched. Paolo's hair was wet through and freezing water ran down his back. His cold, damp clothes sucked the heat from his thin body.

He was tired. Alone on the mountain, he'd been daydreaming again, and had lost contact with the sheep. Floating in the clouds, he couldn't decide if the gentle tinkling of their bells was the sound of angels or of the bells used by the spirits of the ancestors to frighten off the Linchetti, the night elves who lived at the top of the mountain. The elves disliked disorder and being surprised, so a bell was included in the coffin when someone was buried so their spirit could warn the elves of their presence. In a small place like Ischia, it was important for everyone to get along.

When he set out earlier, the bright sun had warmed the short March afternoon, taking the chill out of the air. The mountain still wore the widow weeds of winter, had not yet put on the fresh green threads of spring. Paolo found a comfortable place to lie down out of the slight wind where he could see the sheep on the slope below him and hear them as they grazed on the short, winter-dried grass. Comfortable and warm as he dozed, he was unaware of the fog banks rolling in off the Bay, stealthy grey blankets that soon covered the whole island, creeping up the slopes until even the tip of Mount Epomeo was in their dank embrace.

When the fog reached him, he woke up, suddenly cold. Disoriented, he looked around, jumping to his feet when he realized that he couldn't hear the sheep any more. Muttering under his breath, he hurried off in search of his missing charges, who must have wandered off looking for better grass. He knew that Demonte, his older brother, would be furious if he came back without the sheep that they depended on for their meagre livelihood. Nobody who lived on the mountain expected much from life, but things had been especially difficult during the war and they hadn't improved since. Paolo and Demonte relied on the income from selling their sheep to buy the few things they couldn't grow or make themselves.

It was still light enough that he could see the small sheep tracks that criss-crossed the mountain. The sheep would probably have gone to the east, he thought, away from the fenced-in enclosure where they were kept overnight as protection from the feral dogs that roamed the slopes at night looking for an easy meal. Going that way, he chose the lower track, reasoning that lazy sheep would rather go down the slope than up.

Before long, he heard the faint but welcome sound of their bells, muffled by the fog. Hurrying down the path, out of breath and panting, he found the sheep huddled together for safety under a low, stunted chestnut tree.

He couldn't remember how many sheep he had taken out—Demonte had taken some down the mountain to sell to Adolfo, the butcher in town, and Paolo hadn't counted the sheep before he took them out to graze. He carefully counted them several times to make sure he knew how many were there, and concluded that he had them all. Greatly relieved, he started back to where Demonte would be waiting. With any luck, there might even be some warm soup waiting on the stove.

Paolo slipped several times as he hurried in the dark down the muddy, slick paths, anxious to get home and out of the cold fog. At last, he was rewarded by the welcoming light shining through the cracks in the shutters and glowing warmly in the wet air. He shepherded the last of the sheep into the enclosure, then closed the gate carefully behind them; it was old and delicate, and was liable to swing open at the slightest push if not closed properly.

Entering the main room, Paolo was hit by the heat of the fire and the rich odours of sweat, unwashed clothes, and sheep. Demonte would bring ewes in if they were having trouble lambing, and the rank smell of afterbirth and sour sheep's milk hung heavy in the small room. A kerosene lamp on the table was the sole source of light other than the fire.

Paolo threw himself into a chair by the fire, and sighed theatrically.

"Mother of God," he said, "I am cold, and wet, and hungry."

He looked hopefully at Demonte, who was sitting at the only table in the room, nursing a small glass of wine, and then at the stove. But Demonte's expression didn't change, and there was nothing cooking on the stove.

"Don't use that language," his brother said automatically. Paolo just shrugged; he would have worried if Demonte had failed to do his job as the older brother standing in for long-dead parents.

"Adolfo is the son of a whore," continued Demonte after a long pause. He spoke calmly but bitterly. Paolo was unsurprised, knowing that the world was an unfair place, especially for poor shepherds living on a mountain who had to deal with someone like Adolfo.

"He eats his own shit, and he makes other people eat his shit. He has a very small dick, he wanks the priest, and he fornicates with dead goats."

Paolo listened with interest, waiting to hear some new form of abuse, and because he wanted to hear what happened when Demonte had sold the sheep. Adolfo was thought to drive a hard bargain with local shepherds, who had nobody else to sell to.

"I took him four of our best sheep, and he pays me half what they're worth," said Demonte, throwing his hands up in disgust. "What are we supposed to live on?"

Seeing the look on Paolo's face, he asked, "What's wrong with you?"

"I thought you took six sheep," said Paolo. He knew how many sheep were in the flock that morning, had added four to the number of sheep he had counted up on the mountain, and he was two short of the right number.

"How the hell could I do that?" asked Demonte. "You know I can't take more than four at a time. What the fuck have you done?"

Paolo tried to make himself smaller, fearing what was to come.

Demonte rose abruptly and went out of the door, slamming it behind him. The fire and the lamp flickered in the gust of cold air that rushed through the room behind him. The dim light wavered in the corners of the room, the shadows looking like the animal dancers that Paolo had seen in the ceremonies held late at night high on the mountain. He shivered at the memory, and moved the chair closer to the fire.

Demonte came back into the room. "Come with me," he said in a dangerously quiet voice.

They went outside to the sheep pen. "How many sheep are there?" asked Demonte.

"Sixteen," said Paolo without pausing. He knew the number without counting; that was how many he had brought back.

"And how many did we have here this morning?"

"Twenty-two."

"I know you left school when you were still in short pants, but surely you learned something there," said Demonte. The sarcasm was as sharp and biting as the cold. Paolo would have preferred it if he was shouting. "How much is sixteen plus four?"

"Twenty," said Paolo in a very small voice.

"Then where in the name of the sacred Madonna who says she loves us are the other two sheep?" Demonte was now shouting, gesticulating at the sheep with enough energy to create new animals out of the night air.

He cuffed Paolo alongside his head, hard enough to hurt but not enough to damage.

"Brother, I counted them before I brought them back. I thought I had the right number. I thought you took more to the town. I wanted to get back before dark, and I was cold and wet…" Paolo started to cry.

Demonte looked at him, his anger at his little brother competing with affection. When his father was dying, he was in agony–in one of the rare pain-free moments a few days before God took mercy on him and allowed him to die, he told Demonte to look after Paolo, and Demonte had accepted the responsibility. But he could not help

Paolo grow up by being soft on him.

"Paolo," he said. "Two of our sheep are still on the mountain. They will not survive the dogs tonight if you don't rescue them. Go now, and don't come back alone." He turned and went back into the hut.

Snuffling and miserable in the bitter fog, Paolo watched him go. Then he went through the gate, closed it again as he'd been taught, and headed back up the path, climbing the mountain to where he'd found the sheep.

Paolo and Demonte lived higher on the mountain than almost anyone else and they both knew the paths as well as the sheep, well enough that Paolo could find his way in the pitch dark. The fog swirled around him, thick and heavy. He could taste the water in the air and felt it trickling again down his neck. He came to a fork in the path, and paused to listen for the bells or any sound of sheep moving nearby.

Nothing.

He took the right-hand fork, going towards the top of the mountain. He knew there was a rocky outcrop with a few shallow caves carved out by hermits long ago that a sheep could use for shelter. He often took them up there, since it was out of the way for the other shepherds and the grass was not eaten down too much. The outcrop was the second highest point on the island, just west of the main peak of Mount Epomeo.

No one would normally go there at night without company. This was the home of Typhon, son of Zeus, banished to the island and imprisoned under the immense weight of the mountain. Paolo wasn't sure how much to believe the old story, but he knew that the mountain had spewed molten rock long ago when the great castle at Ischia Ponte was still young and that the ground had shaken badly enough in his grandmother's time that the town of Casamicciola had been almost destroyed. "If that wasn't the mountain god, then what was it?" the older people would ask. Paolo didn't have a good answer, so he kept quiet. And like everyone else, he tried not to go up there at night by himself.

As he climbed higher, his unease grew. The wind whispered in the low bushes that dotted the ground, and he could feel the occasional brush of witchnail tendrils on his legs. The fog swirled with the wind, blowing chill and clammy on his face. He wondered if the Linchetti were out and tried whistling to alert them to his presence, to tell them that he had no wish to disturb whatever they were doing on this dreadful night. His whistle was thin and weak, but he persisted. His spirits, already low, sagged even further.

Coming to the outcrop of rocks, he paused again to listen. Maybe he'd be able to hear the sheep breathing or brushing up against the rock, or perhaps they'd recognise his presence and would bleat to let him know they were there. He stood in the middle of the mule track that skirted the outcrop, criss-crossing the island from Forio to Ischia Porto. He held his breath, trying to be as quiet as possible so he could hear the sheep and so the Linchetti would not notice that he was there. But he couldn't hear the sheep and the Linchetti were occupied somewhere else.

In the silence, he gradually became aware of a new sound. It was very faint, a deep thrumming that seemed to come from all around him. He hastily crossed himself—maybe this was Typhon clearing his throat deep within the mountain.

The low rumbling slowly grew louder and more insistent, coming from the south, from the Bay. Whatever it was, it was heading towards him. His legs turned weak and he crouched down beside the rocks. His terror grew as the thing approached. He put his hands over his ears, trying in vain to cut out the noise as it bounced off the rocks and fog.

Then the roaring was right on him, louder than anything he'd ever heard before, a violent assault that filled his head, shook his body, knocked him over. Pinned to the ground, Paolo saw a huge bird with lights shining from its eyes fly right over his head, and he cried out in terror.

A moment later, there was an enormous explosion as the bird flew straight into the slope barely a hundred yards from where he lay. The thunder of the crash battered Paolo, pressing him even harder onto the stony, unforgiving surface of the mule track. The bird shrieked as it slid up the hill, its blinded eyes now without light.

As Paolo slowly raised his head, a fireball lit up the hillside, glowing yellow and red on the swirling wall of fog. It lasted just a few seconds, fading as quickly as it had come, but for that short moment, he looked straight into the yawning mouth of Hell.

And then the silence and dark returned.

Chapter Two

DEMONTE SAT AT THE WORN KITCHEN TABLE, brooding about his younger brother. Although he was only five years older than Paolo, his responsibilities sat heavily on his shoulders. Paolo was willing and he worked hard enough when he wasn't lost in some daydream, but he was a bit simple. Demonte worried about what would happen to Paolo if he wasn't there to look after him.

He took another sip of the thin, acid wine. Soup, he thought, Paolo will need warming up when he gets back. He crossed the hard-packed dirt floor to the cupboard and began getting down some onions and carrots. He put them on the table with the saucepan, and went outside to get some water from the well.

As he went through the yard to the pump, he heard a soft thump from higher up the mountain. He listened for more sounds, but all he heard was the soft sighing of the wet wind moving through the leafless trees. Shaking his head at the strangeness of the world, he filled the saucepan and went back inside.

Demonte had lived on the mountain all his life and knew its ways as well as anyone. Like everyone else, he tried not to go to the higher, more remote places after dark on his own, although he thought that fears of the Linchetti were overdone. And while he enjoyed the stories about Typhon being trapped beneath the mountain, he didn't think that the old god concerned himself much with the insignificant affairs of men. Nevertheless, he didn't like the idea that Paolo was near whatever had made that thump. Or the sheep, for that matter.

He took his warmest jacket from its crude peg by the door and put it on, then pulled a woollen cap over his head. Leaving the saucepan on the table, he checked the fire and went back outside. Hands in his pockets for warmth, he hurried up the path that Paolo had followed earlier.

In the small town of Fontana, the streets were dark except where light spilled out through the cracks in old, wooden shutters. Baldassare walked up the steep street to the north side of town, taking care to avoid ancient bicycles leaning against walls and carts jutting out from alleyways. The cobblestones glinted faintly in the light of his lantern, enough that he could see and avoid the occasional piles of mule droppings. He was on his way to Adolfo's butcher shop, which lay past Ampelio's café, near the top of the street where the town ended and the fields began. It was close enough to the town centre that people could get there easily but far enough away that their delicate noses weren't offended by the things Adolfo did at the back of the shop.

Adolfo specialised in sausages, some stuffed with lamb, others with rabbit. The lamb came from the flocks of sheep that were kept on the mountain. The supply of rabbit sausages varied, depending on the success of Adolfo's rabbit hunts. Both kinds were delicious, although sometimes you had to pick lead shot out of a rabbit sausage, and Baldassare's father loved them. Something had put the old man into yet another vile mood and Filomena, the matriarch in the house, had sent her youngest son out to get the sausages so she could calm her husband down with his favourite dinner. It was an extravagance in these hard times, but a good price to pay if it restored peace.

As Baldassare arrived at Adolfo's shop, he paused before going in. He didn't like his cousin, and he'd heard very quiet rumours about how Adolfo dealt with animals. Ischians relied on mules for transport and for their labour, and on sheep and rabbits for food. People didn't like it when someone treated animals badly, and it was important to end an animal's life cleanly and with honour. Adolfo killed animals for a living but, it was whispered, not always well. However, he was the only butcher in Fontana, and his sausages were very good.

Hesitating on Adolfo's doorstep, Baldassare heard the same thump that had caught Demonte's attention. He was looking in the direction of the mountain, so he also saw a dim flicker of light high up. Baldassare considered himself a modern man, and dismissed the stories about Typhon as being suitable only for children. But as he considered what he'd heard and seen, he decided that something strange and probably bad had happened.

He turned around, ran back to the café and went in.

The café was just large enough to hold a few round tables. Ampelio was in his usual place behind the scratched counter that ran the length of the wall opposite the door. A cigarette hung from his lips and a generous amount of ash adorned the front of his grimy, striped shirt, large enough to hold all the grapes from his brother's vineyard up the hill. He held a glass of Sambuca; his face was flushed and sweaty, so this was probably not his first glass of the evening. A large advertisement for Sigaro Toscana was pinned to the middle of one wall. It was the only decoration.

All the tables were occupied by small groups of men relaxing on their way home from working in the fields. The air was thick with cigarette smoke and the din of people talking at and over each other. Each table held a candle stuck into an old wine bottle. A few people closest to the door looked up as Baldassare entered, but most paid him no attention.

Looking around, Baldassare saw his cousin Tifeo sitting with a friend in the far corner. He pushed his way through the narrow gaps between the tables until he was standing over them.

"Something's going on up the mountain," he said. He had to shout to be heard over the noise. "I think something crashed up there."

"Why, what happened?" asked Tifeo.

Baldassare explained what he'd heard and seen. Tifeo looked skeptical.

"That sounds pretty thin," he said. "We're enjoying ourselves here. You should join us."

"No, I think we should go up and see what's going on," Baldassare insisted. "There might be people hurt."

That got through to Tifeo, who was always concerned about other people and couldn't hurt a fly. He shrugged in resignation, knowing that Baldassare was going up the mountain with or without him. He finished his drink and stood up.

"You should stay here," he said to his friend. "There's no point in all of us getting cold and wet. It'll be miserable up there."

The cold air outside was a shock after the thick warmth inside the cafe. The two men pulled their collars up and started walking towards the dark at the end of the street. Soon they were above the town, barely able to see the low, drystone walls on either side of the track. Their lanterns cast a thin yellow light, enough for them to see and avoid potholes and loose stones. As they climbed higher, the track got rougher and they had to watch their footing. This was not the place or time to strain or break an ankle. The air was even thicker and wetter than it had been in town, and drops of water sizzled as they landed on the glass chimneys of their lanterns.

"How are we going to see anything in this god-forsaken fog?" Tifeo asked after a while.

"We're near the top, I think," said Baldassare. "Let's go a bit further. If we don't see something soon, we'll head back down."

Their progress slowed as their energy and enthusiasm sank under the sodden weight of the fog.

"Who's that?"

The question came at them out of the dark ahead, a voice that none of them recognised.

"Baldassare Greco," called Baldassare. "We've come up from Fontana. What's going on up here? Who are you?"

Two people suddenly appeared in front of them, emerging from the fog like two ghosts.

"I'm Demonte," said one of the ghosts. "This is Paolo, my brother. We're shepherds, we live down there." He gestured into the blackness behind him. "Paolo saw something crash, just up from here." He pointed up a small track that led off to the left.

"Ah. I heard something and saw a light," said Baldassare. "We came up to see what happened."

As they all turned to go up the track, Tifeo's lantern went out, drowned by the dripping air. "Shit," he exclaimed. "We can't see a thing without these. Does anyone have a match?" No one did, so they left the useless lantern beside the fork in the track, and headed up to where Paolo said he'd seen the crash.

"It was just below the rocks at the top," said Paolo after a few minutes of clambering up the steep track. It was the first thing he'd said. His voice was thin and frightened.

They stopped and looked where Paolo was pointing. In the dim light of the remaining lantern, they could just see the hillside rising steeply beside them. Low, thick vegetation covered the ground.

Demonte looked at the two men from Fontana. They were both larger than average and wearing town clothes. His little brother, on the other hand, was small and light, and could clamber about on the bushes like a monkey.

"Paolo," he said, "you'd better go up there and find out what's going on. We'll wait for you down here."

"Do I have to?" Paolo asked. "It's dark up there, and I don't know what's…"

"You're the best person to go up there," said Demonte. "I'm too heavy, I'll go through the bushes. These gentlemen aren't dressed right. Just go up, have a quick look, and come straight back down. You'll be fine." He gave Paolo a reassuring pat on the back.

Paolo reluctantly clambered up onto the bushes and started pulling himself up the slope, going diagonally away from them so he could follow a gentler incline. Within seconds, he was out of sight, although they could hear his progress as he fought his way across the bushes.

"He's a good lad," said Demonte a little defensively, "even if he's a bit soft in the head. He'll do better when he grows up some."

They heard Paolo cry out in the dark above them as he lost his grip and began sliding down the hill. The noise of his falling stopped, and then Paolo screamed.

"Mother of God," said Demonte. "What the fuck is going on?"

They all hurried up the track to where they thought Paolo would be. In the dim light of the lantern, they could just see his boots, hanging almost straight down.

"I'll hold your feet," called Demonte. He reached up to provide a foothold for Paolo. Paolo slid down, resting on Demonte's hands, until he stood in front of them, panting and shivering. Small pieces of broken branches stuck to his clothes and were caught in his hair. His face was scratched.

He gulped air several times before he could speak. Demonte put a hand on his shoulder.

"I slipped—and fell—." His voice trembled. "My eyes were shut, but I reached out to grab a branch—when I opened my eyes—and saw it…"

There was a long pause.

"What was it?" asked Demonte gently.

"A head," said Paolo. "A head. It was looking right at me. But there was no body attached to it."

Chapter Three

"SHIT," SAID DEMONTE, "now we'll never find those sheep."

Later, he regretted saying that. He should have said something more serious, something more suitable after finding a severed head caught in the bushes. But he was a shepherd. He depended on those sheep, regardless of the unfortunate circumstances of heads becoming detached from their owners.

The others all understood perfectly that a man had to put his own wellbeing first. The war had been very difficult, as had the time before that.

Tifeo spoke first. "There must be other people up there. Maybe some of them are still alive." He didn't have much hope; surely everyone would have died in a crash bad enough to tear bodies apart. "Is there another path we can use?" he asked. "Isn't there a flatter area above this slope?"

"Come this way," said Demonte. He turned, leaning into the hill and holding a low branch to keep his balance on the narrow path, and headed back the way they'd come. The others followed in single file, Paolo bringing up the rear. Just past the spot where Baldassare and Tifeo had met the shepherds, Demonte turned left up another track, even narrower. Their remaining lantern threw out just enough light that they could find small footholds in the rocks sticking out from the hard earth. The track finally levelled out before twisting between two huge blocks of tufa, left over from the last time Mount Epomeo spewed molten rock.

They paused beside the tufa to catch their breath.

"This is near where the bird hit the ground," Paolo said. He hadn't spoken since the horror of finding the head.

"This wind is good," said Demonte. "It should blow the fog away before long."

Paolo hunched up and moved behind one of the blocks, trying to keep out of the wind.

"There's a rocky outcrop just ahead," Demonte said. "Perhaps we'll find something there."

They hurried up the path, hardly more than a thin ribbon of flattened grass between low shrubs. Within a minute of leaving the tufa, Demonte suddenly stopped. "What's that?" he asked, pointing to his right. A gust of wind blew the curtain of fog to one side and for a brief moment they could see the tail of an airplane lying on the ground. Leaving the safe footing of the path, they began fighting their way through the vegetation towards the plane. Baldassare cursed as he tripped on a root and fell heavily.

The fog swirled again and then was gone, swept away back towards the Bay. A full moon cast a cold, white light on the hillside as the wind chased the fog down the slope. Tifeo blinked in the sudden bright light, trying to take in the chaotic scene before him. The plane had obviously hit the ground further down and had skidded up the slope until stopped by the rocks rising to the peak. The fuselage was tilted up, as if the plane had tried to climb the hill. Its metal skin was peeled back like a banana. Scattered debris covered the ground on either side of the channel chewed out as the plane tore through the bushes. Suitcases, seats, strange things made of metal; they lay on top of the vegetation like children's toys casually tossed across a playroom floor.

"Look," he said. "Those rocks down there tore off the wings and ripped open the side."

The broken wings lay on either side of two large rocks, mangled and blackened by fire. The fuel in their tanks must have been ignited by sparks as the plane scraped between the rocks. The engines were on the ground beside the wings, clicking and ticking as the hot metal cooled.

And then the final horror. As Tifeo looked closer, he saw several bodies scattered here and there among the debris. The nearest was a tall thin man sprawled on the ground, blood covering the misshapen side of his head. His right arm had been torn off at the elbow and Tifeo could see white bone sticking through the bloody stump. He wore an extravagant gold watch on his other wrist. Tifeo wondered briefly what manner of man would flaunt his riches like that. But despite his wealth, the man was very dead.

On the other side of the thin man, he could see a woman lying on her back. He went over to see if she was still alive. Instead, her eyes were open to the sky, overflowing with rain. Blood covered her from head to toe and stained the ground dark the full length of her body. Her dress had been ripped open right down the front and her entrails had spilled onto the ground. Her white thighs were spread lewdly apart. Tifeo carefully closed her legs and pulled down her dress to preserve what was left of her modesty. One of her shoes lay on the ground beside her foot.

Tifeo turned away and retched. He tasted thin, metallic acid, and spat into the bushes. Wiping his mouth on his sleeve, he went back to the others. Paolo sat on the ground, rocking gently, holding his head and looking at his feet. The others stood silently, shocked at what they saw.

"We must tell people what's happened," Tifeo said. "Demonte, I think Baldassare and I should go down to tell the police."

He took the shepherd by the arm.

"Can you and Paolo wait by the main track?" he said. "Whoever comes up from town will need help in knowing where to go. You can't see the crash from down there."

Demonte nodded. Of all the group, he was least affected by what he'd seen. Killing sheep was something he'd grown up with, and he had been skinning rabbits and preparing them for the pot ever since he could hold and fire his own shotgun. And he'd seen plenty of dead people. Life on the mountain tended to be hard and short.

"We'll keep an eye on things," he said. "Just don't take too long, Paolo will die of cold before too long."

"He can take my coat," said Tifeo. "I'll come and get it later."

"No, no," protested Demonte. "This is far too good for us shepherds."

Ignoring him, Tifeo took off his coat and draped it over Paolo's shoulders. "That should keep you a bit warmer," he said, touching Paolo gently on the shoulder. Tifeo was a big man with the broad shoulders of a blacksmith, and the coat swamped Paolo's slight frame. To Demonte, Tifeo said, "We'll get people up here as soon as possible. It's good that the fog has lifted, they'll be able to see where they're going."

He took another look at the chaos and carnage on the hillside, and shook his head. No one could survive that, he thought. At least it was quick.

"Let's go," he said to Baldassare, and the two men headed back along the track, hurrying to raise the alarm in town.

Demonte watched them go with mixed emotions. It was good of Tifeo to offer his coat, and Paolo was very cold. But Demonte took great pride in being able to look after himself and hated being dependent on others. Now he owed Tifeo, an obligation made more complicated by being indirect, through Paolo.

Even worse, Demonte did not like being responsible for other people. Looking after Paolo was bad enough, but he was family, and family always came first, whatever private feelings a man might have. Tifeo's casual order to wait by the path had made Demonte responsible, not only for the ignorant townspeople coming up the path, who would undoubtedly be hopeless on unfamiliar paths in the dark, but also for all these dead people as well. Even though corpses couldn't protest at how they were handled, Demonte accepted that they had to be treated with respect. But he didn't like the feeling that whatever happened on the mountain later that night would somehow be his responsibility.

His attention turned to Paolo, who continued to rock on the ground.

"Come on," he said. "We'd best get down to the track. It wouldn't do to let those people get lost."

Paolo said nothing. It was as if Demonte hadn't spoken. Demonte shrugged his shoulders. "Very well," he said, "you stay here and I'll go and wait by the path. Make sure the dogs don't come near. Can you do that?"

Paolo kept rocking, his head moving gently from side to side.

Demonte knelt in front of him, and looked straight into his face. Paolo's eyes were unfocussed, unseeing. Demonte tapped him on the arm, softly, then harder. Slowly, Paolo came back from wherever he'd been. He pulled Tifeo's coat tighter around his hunched shoulders, shivered, and said, "I'm cold." It was a little boy's voice, weak and tremulous.

"Come and sit up here," said Demonte, and led Paolo gently back up the path to a level patch of ground beside a large rock. It was out of the wind but had a good view in the moonlight across the hillside and the bodies and wreckage strewn across the rough ground.

"Keep the dogs away," Demonte said again. Leaving Paolo there, he scrambled back down the narrow path to the main track and settled down to wait.

Tifeo and Baldassare arrived back in Fontana breathing hard from hurrying down the mountain. The fog in town had gone, banished by the chill wind, and the lights from the houses nearest the road shone clear and sharp. The comforting smell of wood smoke hung in the air.

They stopped outside Adolfo's butcher shop.

"I should go in and get the sausages," said Baldassare. "My mother will be wondering what happened, and Papa will be even angrier than usual. I completely forgot about the sausages after I heard the crash. I can take them home on my way down to the police station in Serrara."

He pushed open the door to Adolfo's shop and went in. Tifeo hesitated for a second, then followed.

An old picture of a sheep hung on the wall, its body carved by dotted lines showing the different cuts. The sheep was smiling slightly at some internal ovine joke; Tifeo always thought it looked remarkably content, considering its imminent dismemberment. A few lonely salamis hung from a steel rod beside the sheep. A curved marble counter ran across the shop, supported by ornate pillars. The weighing machine at one end looked as if it had sat there since before the Great War–its white enameled finish gleamed, and the red arrow of the pointer rested precisely and reassuringly on the zero mark of the scale. An empty display case stood at the other end of the counter, spotlessly clean. A single sheep carcass hung from a hook attached to the ceiling by the back wall. The remaining hooks were empty, a reproachful and unwelcome reminder that food was still very scarce, four years after the war had supposedly ended. The floor was covered with small square tiles set diagonally, white patterns on a blood-red background.

Adolfo was just emerging from behind the counter, wearing a long white apron, a cap over his thick, unruly hair. He was drying his hands with a red towel. He looked at Baldassare and Tifeo with surprise. "What brings you here?" he asked. His voice was not friendly. "We're just closing."

"I need some sausages," said Baldassare. "The kind that Papa likes especially."

"You're too late," said Adolfo. "You know when I close. I was just going to have a drink with Ulisse and Cesare." He pointed at the small table across the room. Ulisse and Cesare, Baldassare's older brother, were sitting there with small glasses of grappa in front of them. The chequered tablecloth matched the floor tiles.

"I came here over an hour ago," said Baldassare. "I was about to come in, when I heard and saw something up on the mountain." He paused, shaking his head at the memory of what they'd seen. "Tifeo and I went up to see what had happened. There's been a terrible crash... an airplane flew into the mountain, almost at the top... there's bodies and luggage and parts of the plane scattered all over the place."

Adolfo's barely concealed hostility at their arrival suddenly changed to interest. Ulisse shifted in his chair, which seemed far too small for his bulk, turning his flat, black eyes to look thoughtfully at Baldassare. Even Cesare, who rarely said much in a group, showed some interest.

"A crash? What kind of plane?" Adolfo asked.

"What kind? A passenger plane, I suppose," Baldassare said. "We saw some bodies lying on the bushes, they must have been thrown out by the crash. It was hard to see much, the fog was really thick. But I did see white rings painted at the back of the plane."

He didn't see Ulisse stiffen at the mention of the rings.

"I'm going to go down to Serrara to find the police. So, if you have those sausages, I'll buy some and take them home on the way."

Adolfo shrugged and went to the back of the shop. Wrapping the sausages, he said, "We should go up before anyone else arrives. There'll be pickings for whoever gets there first. Besides, I've never seen a plane crash before."

Tifeo lifted a hand, about to protest, but Ulisse spoke first. "You're right," he said. "Let's see what we can find. If the people up there are dead, they won't need it any more." He laughed without humour. "God knows we need all the help we can get these days–if He sent the plane to crash on our mountain, we'd be foolish to refuse the gift."

Baldassare took the package from Adolfo and said, "Not me. I've got to get home with these sausages before Papa has a fit. Then I'm going down to Serrara. And I don't want to take things from dead people."

After the door closed, Adolfo said, "Cesare, you should come up with us. It'll be quite an experience."

Cesare squirmed uncomfortably. He wasn't entirely happy with the idea of leaving the warmth of the shop to go up the mountain on such a cold night just to see if there any easy valuables lying around. But Adolfo was the eldest of his brothers and cousins and was their unspoken leader. Where he went, the others generally followed. And Cesare was engaged to Rosabella, trying to save some money so they could set up house together one day. It was hard to do that when the whole island was so poor; Cesare managed to make ends meet by a series of odd building jobs, but that was no way for a man to support a wife. His dream was to start a small business building houses. He thought he could make a living doing that now the war was over.

"I guess so," he said slowly. "I suppose there's no harm in seeing what's up there."

If Adolfo was disappointed with Cesare's lack of enthusiasm, he didn't show it. His cousin was a follower and Adolfo knew that he would come with them, if only to not feel left behind.

"Well, I'm staying down here," said Tifeo. "The police will be up there soon enough to take care of things. And what you're saying is wrong. I want no part of this."

"Always holier than thou, brother," said Adolfo, in disgust. "Ulisse is right—God sent the plane as a gift. And if not Him, maybe the god under the mountain, he should be grateful for having a safe home here. Doesn't matter either way, we shouldn't turn it down. It's not for us to understand the ways of the gods, especially when they do us a kindness for once."

"Not so kind for the people in the plane," Tifeo said, heading over to the door.

"Planes like that are the spawn of the devil," said Ulisse. It seemed for a moment that he'd say more, but he fell silent again. Adolfo knew that his brother had had an extremely bad war and didn't press him. He also knew that Ulisse was very aware of being less successful in his start in life than either of his brothers, that he was looking for a way to make some real money and be something more than a casual labourer. Maybe the wealth that must surely be in the plane would help him get something going.

"If a plane crashed on our mountain," said Adolfo, "there was a reason. Life has been hard these last years. Maybe this will do some good." He glared at Tifeo. "Unless you're doing so well playing blacksmith you don't need any help, even from the gods?"

Tifeo shook his head. He had just taken over their father's smithy, and a steady stream of customers kept him busy enough. Fontana was a farming community; people needed tools mended, and horses and mules had to be shod. A blacksmith could depend on more reliable customers and income than a butcher, and even more than casual labourers like Cesare and Ulisse. Tifeo tried not to rub people's noses in his relative success, so it rankled that Adolfo would taunt him like that. And he wasn't playing at blacksmith—he'd been learning the trade since he was big enough to swing a hammer.

"You're going up there, it doesn't matter what I say," he said, managing to hold back an angry reply. "I've got an early start tomorrow, so I'm going home." That was as far as he'd allow himself to go in responding to Adolfo's jibes. And if they wanted to climb the mountain on this bitterly cold evening, that was their business, not his.

"Suit yourself," said Adolfo. "You'll get no share of what we find up there."

After Tifeo left, shutting the door with just enough extra force to show his displeasure, the others finished their aperitivos in silence.

When his glass was empty, Adolfo got up, took off his apron and cap, and carefully hung them on a peg beside the counter at the back of the shop.

"Sanctimonious little prick," he said. "Thinks his shit doesn't stink."

He put on his coat and hat, took the nearest lantern off its hook on the wall, and lit it. "Come on," he said, "let's go see what's up there. Take a lantern, both of you, we'll need the light to see anything."

He wrapped a scarf around the bottom of his face against the damp chill and led the way out of the shop.

Chapter Four

PAOLO WAS A BIT WARMER AFTER DEMONTE LEFT, thanks to Tifeo's coat. Huddled inside the heavy woollen covering, he wondered vaguely where the sheep were. He knew he should be doing something about them but could not muster the energy to go looking for them.

After a while, he slowly realized that the wind had shifted direction and was coming around the rock. The comforting thickness of the coat could not compete with the wind's icy fingers, which stole his warmth away like a pickpocket. Fidgeting was no use. Forgetting the sheep, he shook his head, trying to decide whether he should stay where he was, hoping the wind would go away again, or if he should go home to the warmth of the fire. Or find another rock to hide behind. Going home seemed like far too much effort. The wind continued to move around the rock until he could feel it on his face. The easiest thing would be to just sit there, he thought, and wait for morning and the warmth of the sun that always followed fog.

Relaxing, he leaned back against the rock. A sharp point suddenly dug into his back, jolting him back into awareness. If he stayed there, he realized hazily, he'd die of cold. He had to move. Get out of the wind, he told himself. Get out of the wind.

He staggered to his feet, leaning against the rock. Once upright, he beat his arms as hard as he could to get his blood moving again. Just up the hill, he saw another rock, even larger than the one he was standing beside. He pushed his way unsteadily through the bushes, tripping more than once as his foot caught low branches. Each time, he pushed himself to get up and keep moving. To lie in the open would be to die there.

When he finally reached the rock, he found a place where he could sit out of the wind. He was breathing hard from his exertions and was much warmer. Gratefully, he sank down in the dark shadow of the rock. He was a bit closer to the crashed plane and he could clearly see the bodies and wreckage scattered across the hillside under the unforgiving gaze of the moon. Wrapping his arms around himself again, he settled down once more to wait.

After a while, he heard scrabbling noises from down the path, sounding like small animals coming towards him. The Linchetti, he thought, shrinking even further into the shadows. They had heard the crash and were coming to investigate. Down on the path, he could see several figures moving cautiously towards the plane. One of them was talking, the sound carrying clearly to Paolo. Oh, they were cunning, the one talking sounded just like his older brother. "I left Paolo, my brother, behind that rock," the Linchetti who sounded like Demonte said. "Paolo, where are you?"

Paolo knew from stories his mother had told him how the Linchetti would trick people before kidnapping them. He stayed very still and pulled the coat even further around his face so he couldn't be seen in the shadows.

"He must have gone home," said the Linchetti. "I told him to stay here and keep an eye on things. He was in pretty bad shape, though, he wasn't dressed right for the cold and wet. I should go down and make sure nothing has happened to him. Can you watch over things here? The other gentlemen went down to raise the alarm, they should be here soon."

"Yes, they told us, that's why we're here," said one of the other Linchetti, his voice muffled. "We'll take good care of things. You go and find your brother."

The Linchetti who sounded like Demonte turned and went back down the path. Paolo heard him dislodge small stones as he navigated the steep section before the main track, and then he was gone.

Adolfo, Ulisse and Cesare looked at the chaotic destruction before them in astonishment.

"Mother of God," Adolfo said. "Look at that."

Ulisse spat. "When the British chased us through the desert, they strafed our columns, killed many men, blew up our trucks. Planes like this one dropped bombs on us. The destruction was terrible, bits of bodies, bits of trucks, bits of tanks lying everywhere. Just like this." He spat again. "See the back of the plane–those rings? This is a British plane. Bastards! God has punished them for what they did to us."

They approached the plane, stumbling in the low vegetation and trying to avoid sharp pieces of metal. The wings were torn off right beside the fuselage, a clean break, and they could see the bones of the plane. The circular ribs of the fuselage were bent where the metal skin had been ripped off. The front of the plane was smashed in, pushed right back to the cockpit windows, and the metal under the cockpit was crumpled like paper.

Ulisse kicked the plane viciously. "Fuckers," he shouted. "You fuckers!"

Suddenly he froze as he saw a flicker of movement inside the plane. He climbed up through the space where the fuselage had been torn open. A sharp edge of metal caught his arm, tearing his coat and gashing his forearm. Oblivious to the sudden pain, he stood up on the sloping floor. The inside of the plane was almost as chaotic as the outside. A single row of seats went down one side, pairs of seats down the other. All the seats were empty. The lifeless body of one of their occupants lay on the floor towards the back, broken from being thrown against the seats and walls in the crash. Suitcases had burst open, spilling their contents everywhere.

There was a jump seat on the bulkheads on either side of the passage leading to the cockpit. A red fire extinguisher was attached to the wall above each seat. A small boy, two or three years old, slumped in one, held in by a seatbelt. His face was peaceful and he held a blue coloured crayon tight in his right hand. The back of his head was flattened where it had hit the metal wall behind him and his schoolboy sweater was dark with blood. His colouring book was nowhere to be seen.

A soldier sat in the jump seat on the other side of the passage. He wore a khaki uniform, immaculately pressed, with a single row of ribbons on his left breast. He looked about the same age as Ulisse and he was still alive, barely. His chest fluttered and his leg was twitching–this was the movement that caught Ulisse's attention.

"Help me," he murmured in English. "I'm cold." His voice was a light breath, weighing less than smoke. Ulisse had no English and didn't understand the words, although their meaning was clear enough.

Ulisse glared at the soldier. The sounds of screaming men filled his head, mixed with the dull thumps of exploding bombs. A truck blew up nearby, wheels running away from the convoy. Flying shards of metal cut down his friend beside him. A plane flew right overhead, its machine guns chattering and making little spurts in the dust, men desperately jumping to one side to avoid being mown down. The white concentric rings at the back of the plane stood out against the dun and olive camouflage. Had he ever really left the convoy, this trail of defeated men being chased like rabbits across the desert wastes?

He shook his head to clear out the memories and bent down in front of the soldier, their faces inches apart.

"You bastards," he said distinctly and coldly. "You killed my friends."

"Mummy, help me," the soldier said, his head drooping. "Mummy, please, I'm cold. So cold…"

"Fuck you," said Ulisse.

Very deliberately, he held the soldier's head between his hands and slammed it hard back against the bulkhead. The blow unleashed his rage, and he smashed the head again and again and again, screaming obscenities, his fury all-consuming.

"Enough, Ulisse, enough," shouted Adolfo, his words gradually penetrating. Panting, Ulisse stopped and stood back. The soldier's chin rested on his chest, which was now still. The back of his head was matted and bloody, the brain showing through the broken skull.

Adolfo was standing by the door, looking up at him. "Enough, Ulisse," Adolfo said again. "He's dead."

"Where's Cesare?" asked Ulisse. It was all he could think of to say.

"He wandered off," replied Adolfo. "Didn't want to watch you beat the shit out of the soldier."

Ulisse grunted. He'd always thought Cesare was a bit soft, too inclined to take the easy path, not strong enough in standing up for what he believed in. Whatever that was.

"I'm all right now," he said. "Let's see what else is in this cursed machine."

"I'll look over there," said Adolfo, pointing. "I think there are some more bodies." He started down the hill, leaving Ulisse alone in the plane.

Ducking his head, Ulisse started along the short passage linking the main cabin with the cockpit. He didn't get far before he tripped over luggage on the floor. He pulled it back into the cabin, leaving it to look at later. Going back down the passage, he looked into the radio compartment on the left side. An airman was in there, sprawled dead on the floor. The bloody dent on the radio panel showed where his head had hit. The chair lay on its side. The small luggage compartments on either side of the passage were open and empty.

The door to the cramped cockpit was open. Ulisse squeezed his way in. The pilot and co-pilot were both strapped into their seats, and both were dead. The impact of the crash had snapped their heads forward so hard that their necks were broken.

The pilot had rolled his shirt sleeves back, exposing his wrist watch. Ulisse leant forward and took it off, putting it into his pocket. His face was right beside the pilot's and he breathed into the dead man's ear, a strange and unexpected intimacy. The pilot wore a wedding ring. Ulisse tried sliding it off but it was too tight. He felt in the man's pockets, but found nothing of interest. Then he noticed the pilot's jacket, hanging up in a small compartment behind the seat. A wallet was in the left breast pocket. Ulisse removed the bank notes and put them in his pocket, tossed the wallet on the floor.

The co-pilot's watch was bigger and fancier than the pilot's. His jacket yielded another wallet, more cash. One of the jacket pockets held an almost full package of cigarettes. Ulisse put all this into his coat pocket. Taking a last look around the cockpit, he returned to the main cabin.

The first suitcase he looked at was full of women's clothing. It was neatly packed; blouses with lacy patterns, some skirts, two dresses, underwear, four pairs of stockings still in their package. He dumped the whole lot on the floor, looking for something valuable hidden under the clothes, but there was nothing. He put the stockings to one side, thinking they might come in handy with a future girlfriend.

The next case was full of books and papers. He flipped through one quickly but it was full of complicated diagrams and material he didn't understand. He had no time for this, so it all went on the floor. The next two suitcases were equally useless.

He got lucky on the last case. Opening it up, he saw a jacket, then four spotless white shirts, and beneath them, an envelope. Opening it, Ulisse pulled out a thick handful of large blue bank notes. They had a picture of an old man wearing a white bow tie on one side and a row of soldiers with trumpets on the other. The writing was in a language that Ulisse didn't understand, with strange letters. He didn't care about the pictures or the writing but he liked the 1000 printed at all four corners and in the centre of the front, beside the picture of the old man. Putting the money back into the envelope, he put everything he'd found into the smallest suitcase. The last body yielded a ring on the man's little finger and some cash. After checking that there was nothing else worth looking at, Ulisse jumped to the ground and went looking for the others.

Cesare had left when Ulisse started kicking the side of the plane. He knew Adolfo's brother well, and feared what he might do when in this state. Ulisse had always been excitable, even for an Ischian, but ever since he'd come back from his desert war, a dark, angry undercurrent would show itself whenever he was tense. Cesare liked a quiet life and tried to avoid arguments and confrontation; seeing Ulisse like this made him uncomfortable.

Wandering further down the slope, he could hear Ulisse shouting and banging something in the plane. When Adolfo began yelling at Ulisse to stop, Cesare knew that something bad had happened. Anxious to get further away, he stumbled across the bushes, tripping on rocks and grabbing low branches to keep his balance. He stopped just above a particularly steep slope that fell down to the track they'd walked up from Fontana. Finding his way without falling and breaking his neck had demanded his full attention and he hadn't looked at what else was around him.

To his right, he could see the trail of debris cast off by the plane as it slid along the ground, a silver carpet in the moonlight. A darker form caught his eye and he went closer. His legs gave way when he saw what it was and he sank to his knees.

A large, rather corpulent man sprawled on his back, his arms flung open, one leg folded beneath the other. He wore an expensive-looking suit, a gold watch chain looped across the waistcoat. A flamboyant silk handkerchief spilled out of the breast pocket of his open jacket. Immaculate white shirt cuffs peaked out from the jacket sleeves, held together by gold cuff links. A ring gleamed on the little finger of his right hand, made of heavy gold with a stone set in the centre. This had been a man of substance, of wealth.

Cesare stared at the ring, thinking that it cost more money than he earned in a year of hard labour and trying not to look at the rest of the body. He looked down the slope towards Fontana, wishing that he hadn't come on this foolish trek up the mountain. The appalling death and destruction all around him proved that people were right to avoid coming up here at night. No god ever provides a free gift, he thought, there's always a price attached.

Eventually, he could no longer avoid looking at what he'd seen when he first approached the body. The man's shirt and jacket were stained dark with massive amounts of blood. Cesare could see the white bone of the man's spine sticking out from the neck. He looked frantically around for the missing head, hoping to reunite it with its owner but it was nowhere to be seen. The body lay there, headless but peaceful despite the violence that must have thrown it from the deceptive safety of the plane's cabin.

Cesare sat quiet for a few moments, collecting himself. It's just another dead man, he told himself. Few people lived long in Fontana; poor sanitation, not enough food, and hard work all saw to that. There was a doctor further down in Serrara, but he was ignorant and clumsy, with bad breath. Cesare wouldn't have been surprised if the old man used leeches to treat headaches. But all the dead bodies that he had seen still had their heads attached. He wondered what kind of head it was. Large or small? Grey hair, white, or dark? A full head of hair, or bald? Moustache? Well, the morning would tell, when the head was found.

Feeling a bit light-headed, Cesare looked back towards the plane, to where he'd left Adolfo and Ulisse. He could see the plane but they were nowhere to be seen.

He leant forward, carefully removed the watch from the waistcoat pocket, unhooked the chain from the button hole on the other side, put the watch and chain into his own coat pocket. The cufflinks were next. He cleaned the blood off by wiping them on the man's sleeve, and put them into his coat pocket with the watch. The cufflinks were easy to remove but, try as he might, he could not get the ring off the thick finger, so he had to leave it.

The jacket fell open as he struggled with the ring, and he saw a long, thin box tucked into an inside pocket. He took it out and opened it. Several necklaces lay on top, made of thick strands of gold woven together into a thick yellow rope. They were all the same. He picked one up and raised his eyebrows at its weight. Beside them were some rings, all gold, each with a gemstone, all in plain settings. At the bottom of the box was an envelope. He shook it upside down and six diamonds fell into his open hand, shining bright in the moonlight. They looked like small lumps of glass but he knew at once what they were.

Quickly, he put the diamonds back into the envelope, put everything back into the box, and closed it. He still couldn't see Adolfo or Ulisse.

He checked the other jacket pockets and found a passport in one, full of strange, swooping writing, and a wallet in another. He put the passport and most of the cash from the wallet into the narrow box, which he carefully tucked into a pocket deep inside his jacket. The rest of the cash went into his coat pocket with the watch and cufflinks. The dead man's pockets held nothing else of interest, so Cesare stood up and headed back up the slope towards the plane, where he'd last seen his cousins.

Adolfo was crouching over another soldier's body when Ulisse found him. He looked up as Ulisse approached.

"Don't worry," he said, "this one was already dead. Didn't have much money, though." He waved a small wad of cash.

"I found more stuff in the plane," Ulisse said. "You should put that money with the rest of it in this case. We can share it out later."

"There's a body over that way," said Adolfo, pointing behind him. As they went over, Adolfo stumbled on a rock, putting out his hand to grab Ulisse and regain his balance.

A few steps away, they saw the body of another man, past being young but not yet old, lying stretched out on his back. He must have been cold in the airplane, because he had wrapped a long black cloak around himself. The hood of the cloak was folded around his head, casting his face into shadow. His hands were folded across his chest. He looked like a monk. And he was still alive, his hands slowly rising and falling.

"Sweet Jesus," Adolfo said. "What do we have here?"

At the sound of his voice, the man's eyes flickered.

"My wife," he whispered. He spoke in English, and neither Adolfo nor Ulisse understood him. "My wife," the man whispered again. "I don't want to die, it's too soon…" The faint voice faded away, lost in the wind.

"He's a priest," said Adolfo, his voice rising in anger. "He's a fucking priest!"

"If this is a priest," said Ulisse, unmoved by Adolfo's reaction, "he's unusually wealthy. Look at his shoes."

The shoes were indeed quite beautiful, shining with a deep black lustre. They looked oddly defenceless, sticking out from under the cloak.

"They're all rich," said Adolfo. "You've been in their houses, seen what they have. They're so high and mighty, they think they can do what they want to us. But you know what? They shit like us, sin like us, pick their nose like us. I hope they rot in Hell!"

"You know I love them no more than you," said Ulisse. "They did nothing for us in the desert. And God abandoned us."

Adolfo rejoiced in seeing how helpless the priest was. For once, he had the power. A tidal wave of pure, cleansing rage surged through his body, overwhelming him, washing away the compassion he felt when he first saw the man. Picking up a large rock in both hands, he raised it high.

"You arsehole," he shouted, and smashed the rock into the man's forehead with all his strength. The man's legs shuddered, and finally were still.

Adolfo considered the dead man, his face blank. Carefully, he put the rock, glistening with fresh blood, on the ground.

"Cursed priests," he said. "Now there's one less."

He spat on the cloak. Meanwhile, Ulisse had been looking more closely at the dead man. "He's wearing a ring," he said.

Adolfo bent over the man to take a closer look. He tried to remove the ring but it was too tight and would not slide over the knuckle. As he fiddled with the ring, he pulled the sleeve back, revealing a watch. He took it off and passed it to Ulisse to look at. "Have you ever seen a priest wear a watch like that?" he asked.

"This cost a lot of money," replied Ulisse. "It'll get a good price in Napoli."

Ulisse leant forward and tried pulling at the ring to get it off, without success.

"Here, let me," said Adolfo.

He always carried a knife on his belt. It was extremely sharp, suitable for all the reasons that a man needed a knife. The blade was narrow from being sharpened many times over the years. His father had given it to him when he turned twelve. "You're old enough for this," the old man had told him. "My father gave me this knife when I was your age, now it's your turn to have it. Use it carefully and with respect, and only when you have to. When you have your own boy, you give the knife to him, like I'm giving it to you now. Just make sure he understands that the spirits of his ancestors are in it."

Adolfo pulled the knife from its sheath, remembering his father, who died soon after giving him the knife. He was confident that the ancestors would approve of what he was about to do—family always came first, and the ring would put food on the table. The man was dead, after all. The ring was no use to him now.

He carefully took the man's hand, palm up and the fingers slightly curled back, holding it as gently as a lover. He pulled the ring finger back, straightening and stretching it. Carefully, he inserted the point into the joint at the base of the finger where it joined the hand. With a sudden twist, he dislocated the joint, then cut through the skin and tendons, separating the finger. He slid the ring off the severed finger, held it up for Ulisse to see, grunted with satisfaction.

"Sometimes it helps to be a butcher," he said. "That's how you separate a lamb's leg. With a bigger knife, of course."

He passed the ring to Ulisse, who put it into the small suitcase with the rest of their scavenging.

"We should keep the finger," Aldolfo said. "It's not wise to refuse something as powerful as this, if the gods choose to offer it to us."

"What about the other fingers?" asked Ulisse. "Should we take those as well?"

Adolfo thought about this for a moment. "Only the ones with rings," he said. "The rings will mark the fingers the gods want us to take."

Ulisse accepted this decision without comment. Adolfo was his older brother, and wiser.

As Adolfo carefully wrapped the finger in a cloth and put it in his pocket, Ulisse opened the cloak and felt inside the jacket. "Aha!" he exclaimed, pulling out a fat wallet. The main pocket held cash, which went straight into the suitcase. There was nothing else of interest in the wallet and Ulisse threw it on the ground.

Turning back to the body, Ulisse prised the dead man's mouth open.

"What are you doing?" asked Adolfo, obviously wanting to move on to the next body.

"Just looking," said Ulisse, holding his lantern close and peering into the mouth. "Good, there's one!"

He pushed his own knife into the open mouth, twisting it back and forth. After a minute, he reached deep into the mouth–when he withdrew his hand, a bloody tooth lay in his palm, the gold filling glinting in the moonlight.

"Are there any more like that?" asked Adolfo, interested despite his disgust with what Ulisse was doing.

Ulisse looked into the mouth, carefully moving the lantern so he could see into every corner.

"Here's another one," he said, and stuck the knife in again to extract another tooth.

He stood up and gave the teeth to Adolfo, who put them into the cloth with the finger before putting the package back in his coat pocket.

"I don't think he was a priest, after all," Adolfo said, looking down at the body. "He's not wearing priest clothes, and priests don't carry that much money, or wear wedding rings. It was that cloak…"

He shrugged and held his hands out, palms up, as if to say, "What can I do?"

"Well, it's too late now," he said. "What's done cannot be undone, and there's nothing we can do about it."

He kicked gently at the body, trying to get the attention of a dead man.

"Thank you for your gifts," he said with the same formality he used when thanking a sheep for the gift of its life. "I don't know why the gods sent you or what you've done to deserve this, but we thank you."

Ulisse cleared his throat, a little too loudly. He'd lost any sentimentality he might have had about dead people in the desert, where corpses swelled up like black balloons if the scavengers hadn't got to them first. When you killed a man there, it was because you wanted him dead before he killed you. Family didn't come into it. Not at all. And talking to people you'd killed was something you only did inside your head when navigating the uncertain, spirit-filled world between wakefulness and the relief of sleep.

"Come on," he said to Adolfo's back, "let's see what else we can find. We'll be up here all night otherwise."

The two brothers started back across the slope, over to where the wreckage seemed most concentrated.

Cesare saw them coming toward him and paused, waiting beside a large bush of Spanish broom. In a few weeks, the bush would be rich with bright yellow flowers hanging down like paper lanterns–but in early March, the branches were bare fingers reaching for the sky.

"We've done well," said Adolfo as they approached. "What have you got? I saw you bending over something down there."

Cesare held up the pocket watch by its chain. It swung slightly from side to side, glinting in the moonlight.

"This and a tie pin," he said, "and some money in his wallet. He had a small book with funny writing, but I left that."

"Anything else?" asked Adolfo.

"Not really," replied Cesare, trying not to think of the thin box buried deep in his jacket. "I tried to get his ring, a big fat one, but it wouldn't come off."

"Show Ulisse," Adolfo said. "He'll get the ring for you."

"And his head had been cut off," added Cesare. "You can see his spine. I don't know where the head went. Maybe it went down the slope, it's very steep there." His voice was only slightly strained, as though finding headless bodies in the middle of the night was a routine matter and nothing to get too excited about.

Adolfo said, "No head? This is a strange night, no mistake."

"He must have lost his head when the plane crashed," said Ulisse, enjoying his own joke.

"While you're down there," Adolfo went on, "see if there are any other bodies. I'll go the other way. Let's meet back here as soon as possible."

Ulisse and Cesare hurried back to the headless body, stepping over the scattered bits of the plane.

"Maybe it's down there," said Cesare, pointing down the slope.

"No matter," replied Ulisse. "We won't find jewelry or cash with it."

He pulled out his knife. It wasn't a family heirloom like Adolfo's, but it was razor-sharp and very serviceable. Leaning over the body, he pried it into the bottom joint of the man's ring finger, just as he'd seen Adolfo do it. Cesare looked away as Ulisse dislocated the finger and cut it loose.

"Here," said Ulisse, holding out the ring. "Put it with the other stuff you've got."

He put the severed finger into his jacket pocket and stood up as Cesare carefully put the ring into his coat pocket.

"Let's see what else is down this way," Ulisse said and went off without looking back.

While Ulisse and Cesare searched the hillside for other bodies, Adolfo had found the thin, armless man that Tifeo had seen earlier. He whistled when he saw the watch, hefting it as he took it off and put it carefully in his pocket. He found more cash inside the man's jacket, which joined the watch. Looking inside the man's mouth, he could see several gold fillings. Clearly, this had been a man of means. Using his father's knife again, he prised the teeth loose and put them away.

He went over to the dead woman nearby, and looked at her carefully. Even with the rip down the front, he could tell that her dress was not particularly expensive. He wrinkled his nose at the smell coming from her intestines–he was used to the stink from butchering sheep but still found it unpleasant. He bent down and took a good look at the cheap wedding ring on her left hand, resting in the blood of her dress. Part of him recoiled at the thought of taking a ring from a woman who had been torn open so destructively; it seemed one defilement too many. But the ring drew him in. She doesn't need it any more, he told himself, sliding it easily off her finger. He couldn't bring himself to search her clothes, so he left her, following her outstretched arm to find other bodies.

But this part of the hillside was empty of bodies. All he could see were rocks and hundreds of small bits of metal and glass, scattered across the tops of the bushes. No suitcases.

Time to go, he thought, the police will be here soon.

Calling out to Ulisse and Cesare, he returned to where he'd left them. Before long, they came up the hill, panting from the unaccustomed exertions.

"How did you get on?" asked Adolfo. "I've got a bit more, not too much."

Ulisse hefted the small suitcase, demonstrating how heavy it was.

"A decent haul," he said. "Two more soldiers down there. They were good enough to share their rings and money with us. And a couple of cases. They busted open when they hit the ground, but there was still some jewelry tucked away. Curious, they had men's clothing in them. The rings and stuff were probably gifts for their women. Anyway, we have it all now. And I went back into the plane. The pilot had a ring he didn't need any more. And a finger."

"That's a good night's work, then," said Adolfo. "Let's get back down to the shop and see what we've got. If we stay up here any longer, we'll run into the police. That case would be hard to explain."

From his hiding place beside the rock, Paolo watched them leave. He didn't move until the last sounds of scrabbling down the path had disappeared. Then he slowly stood up, stretching out the knots in his body. He'd been too frightened to move while he watched the three men go from body to body. He shivered, but not from the cold. He had heard the violence in the airplane and had seen and heard everything that happened on the hillside. Terrible things had been done to the dead people lying there and he'd been unable to do anything to stop them. It dawned on him that this was not the Linchetti doing this, but people from the town, even though he recognised none of them. Somehow that made it even worse.

Paolo felt enormously tired as he leaned against the rock. His head hurt as he tried to decide what to do. Where were the sheep? He tried to concentrate on the question, but possible places to look slid sideways out of his mind the moment they entered. Surely the sheep would have found their own way home by now? The thought was fuzzy, barely formed.

Was that the Linchetti he heard, that rustling? His heart started beating wildly, trying to escape from his chest. Had they come to find out more about the machine that had crashed so rudely into the world they ruled? Not knowing what to do, Paolo shrank back against the rock, making himself as small as possible.

An eternity later, he peered cautiously around the rock. Nothing moved. Cautiously, he moved out, looking anxiously in all directions. He felt as if he was swimming in thick air as he moved down to the path. Once there, he tried to decide which way to go. The plane lay to his right. Should he go there to see if anyone needed his help? The thought of seeing more dead, damaged bodies was more than he could bear, so he turned the other way slowly and hesitantly and started down the mountain, drawn by dim thoughts of warmth and comfort.

Behind him, he heard the excited yipping of wild dogs, a sound the pack only made after a kill.

Chapter Five

THE NEXT MORNING ARRIVED BRIGHT AND CLEAR. The pale, washed out sky was innocent of clouds, and the early sun shimmered on the smooth waters of the Bay of Napoli. In the far distance to the south-east, Capri rested on the horizon like a smudge of smoke. No trace of fog remained in the air, although the ground glittered with countless bright jewels, sun reflections off the water left behind by the sodden air.

The sun had barely showed itself when people began walking up the mule track out of Fontana. Word of the crash had spread quickly and everyone wanted to see what had happened for themselves. Life on Ischia followed regular and predictable rhythms, day to day, week to week, season to season. Any break from routine was something to savour, something to examine from every possible angle, something to break the monotony of the long dark evenings when entertainment was hard to come by. The excitement of an airplane colliding with their mountain promised a rich harvest of wonder and speculation and nobody wanted to hear about it second hand.

Cesare was among the first group to leave the town. He walked hand in hand with Rosabella, enjoying being so close to her. Their engagement was only a few weeks old, and he hadn't yet become used to their new status. The older men would make lewd jokes, sometimes to his face but more often behind his back; he didn't know whether to be offended or proud. Rosabella was slender and almost as tall as he was, with rich chestnut hair that flew wildly about her face. Cesare couldn't quite believe his luck when she agreed to marry him and harboured a secret fear that he wouldn't be man enough for her when the time came. He squeezed her hand as they walked along and was rewarded by her swift, conspiring smile.

Serafina, Cesare's older sister, walked in silence with Adolfo, her sallow, thin face pinched in her customary look of disapproval. Cesare didn't understand what had happened to her since she'd come back at the end of the war after staying with relatives in

Napoli. She'd always been concerned that things should be done just so, but now she was shrewish, pouncing on the slightest wrong and condemning people for any deviation from what was right and proper. She'd become worse than Father Giovanni, thought Cesare, as if that was possible. The parish priest was known for his moral uprightness and uncompromising application of Catholic doctrine to every aspect of life in Fontana. While his undoubtedly strong faith was noted and respected by his flock, he was not loved. Nor was Serafina. Beside her, yet somehow far away, Adolfo looked as if he was enjoying himself, as if an early morning stroll up the mountain was a rare and welcome change from his work as a butcher.

Ulisse was nowhere to be seen.

Cesare's cousin Tifeo brought up the rear of the small group, in deep conversation with Amedea. Tifeo was a huge man, but gentle, with the biggest hands Cesare had ever seen. His blacksmith business was doing well enough that he could afford to marry Amedea. Beside him, she seemed tiny, though she wasn't much shorter than most of the women in Fontana. She certainly didn't have much trouble handling her man despite her size, thought Cesare, with another twinge of uncertainty about how people might see him and Rosabella.

Behind them, a growing stream of people were making their way up the mountain. Most of them spent all their time in Fontana or in the towns closer to the coast, so venturing this high was an adventure. The sound of conversation and laughter carried easily up the track to Cesare and his group. Disliking the carnival atmosphere and knowing what they were going to find, Cesare grew quiet and let go of Rosabella's hand. He hadn't wanted to go up the mountain again, but hadn't been able to think of a good reason to stay behind as everyone else left the house.

The chatter swiftly died away as people clambered up the last stretch of steep path and saw the crash site. Some were panting from the unaccustomed effort of climbing the hill, and there was the occasional curse as someone realized that their shoes were quite unsuitable for the rough path. Each group did exactly the same thing with their first glimpse of the airplane–they stopped. Because the path was so narrow, they became a plug, preventing the next group from moving up to level ground. Annoyed shouts of "Move along," and "What's going on up there?" rang out as newcomers tried to keep their balance on the loose rocks underfoot.

Under pressure from behind, people in the plug then moved forward, spreading out beside the plane. Before long, a small crowd was staring at the plane, silenced by what they were seeing.

Cesare knew what to expect but he was still horrified by the chaos and violence of the crash. It was bad enough in the moonlight of the night before, but now every detail was laid bare by the merciless sunshine. What were we doing up here, he thought, no good will come of this.

Suddenly a cry went up from the back of the crowd. "There are bodies over here!"

Cesare and Rosabella were caught up in the crowd as it surged away from the plane and started spreading out across the slope.

"Here's another one," someone cried. "And over here," called another. Cesare recognized Adolfo's voice. That's clever, he thought, act like this is all new to us as well.

Soon, the crowd was spread out across the hillside, finding more bodies. Cesare didn't see who first took a piece of clothing, but within minutes, people were carrying jackets and shoes, pushing to get at the best items. Then someone realized there were bodies inside the plane and there was another rush as some of the crowd went over to investigate.

Cesare stayed glued to Rosabella and was with her when she discovered the body of the dead woman.

"Oh, no," Rosabella said, putting her hand to her mouth in horror. "The poor woman!"

It was not surprising that no one had stripped the body, which looked even worse in daylight than it had the night before.

"She must have been cut when she was thrown out of the plane," said Cesare. He didn't like what he was seeing, but he felt curiously detached. He looked at the body and back at the plane, trying to imagine the sequence of events as the plane crashed, the metal skin was peeled back by the rocks, and the body torn open as it flew across the jagged metal.

"I think the dogs have been here," he added, looking at the entrails. They were not whole, and he could see teeth marks around the bitten-off ends.

Rosabella stepped a few feet away to avoid looking at the dreadful sight. She sank to her knees, pressing her knuckles hard into her mouth. Then she pulled back as she saw something else.

"Oh, no," she said again. "Sacred Mother of Jesus, what is this?"

Cesare went over as she reached under a bush and gently pulled something out. It was a very small baby, covered with blood, with its umbilical cord still attached. The placenta was nowhere to be seen, but there was a clean bite on the umbilical cord. Cesare guessed that feral dogs had feasted on rich and easy pickings. The baby had been hidden under the bush and might never have been found had Rosabella not knelt down beside it.

"The poor thing," said Rosabella, starting to cry as she slowly stood up, holding the baby in her arms. "She never had a chance."

Cesare saw Amedea standing with Serafina a short distance off. They both looked stunned by everything going on around them.

"Amedea," he called, "we need you over here!"

Amedea walked over, carefully picking her way around the bushes.

"What is it?" she asked as she arrived. "We've got to stop people, it's dreadful what they're doing."

Rosabella turned around, and Amedea turned pale as she saw her rocking the baby.

"I always wanted a baby," said Rosabella through her tears, "but not like this."

Amedea started crying as well, and put her arms around Rosabella. Cesare hesitated before holding the two women in an awkward embrace. The three of them stood there, the two women crying and Cesare wondering what he was supposed to do. He'd never experienced anything like this before and was incapable of rational thinking. Then inspiration arrived.

"We should take the baby back to her mother," he said. "That's what we should do."

Rosabella looked at her man gratefully, and nodded. "Yes," she said, "that would be good."

Amedea took off the shawl that she had brought for warmth and held it out. Rosabella carefully folded it around the baby so the only thing Cesare could see was her puckered face, eyes tightly closed against the horrors of a world she'd never had a chance to visit.

They went back to the torn body of the mother and laid the baby at her breast.

"Where's Serafina?" asked Rosabella.

They all looked around the hillside, but Serafina was nowhere to be seen.

"Listen to those animals," said Amedea. It was clear from the clamour that people were still actively looking inside the plane and down the slope. "Have they no respect for the dead? Have they no honour?"

"They'll take whatever they can," said Rosabella. "It's just the way things are. You can't always expect poor people to behave well."

"I don't like it," said Amedea. "I don't care how poor people are, they shouldn't behave like that. We have to stop them."

"And how do we do that?" asked Cesare, exhausted after his brief display of leadership.

"We could gather all the bodies together," suggested Amedea. "Collect them by the plane, then stand guard over them. Cesare, can you carry this poor woman by yourself? And where's Tifeo when we need him?"

Cesare hesitated, then pushed her intestines back into the mother's body before picking her up in his arms. He tried to ignore the blood and mess on his hands.

On the way to the plane, they saw Tifeo standing with Baldassare, both of them looking disgusted.

"What have you got there?" Tifeo asked. His face softened as he saw the body and heard the story. "I agree, let's get all the bodies into one place. Cesare, you and I should collect the bodies; Amedea and Rosabella can look after them once we've brought them here."

Cesare carefully laid his burden on the ground under the plane's nose, out of the sun. He arranged her dress as best he could, trying to cover the mess of her insides, then took the baby from Rosabella and put her on her mother's breast. He looked at the two of them for a moment, not satisfied with what he saw. Finally, he crossed the woman's arms so she was holding her infant, the two of them reunited in death.

"Good," said Tifeo. "Baldassare, can you tell the people out there to clear the hillside? The entertainment is over. Cesare, let's stop the looting in the plane. Then we can bring the bodies out."

Baldassare went down the hillside, shouting at people to leave. He was respected enough in the town that people obeyed him and began to make their way back down the path to Fontana, many of them clutching onto shoes and pieces of clothing. Meanwhile, Tifeo clambered into the plane and glared at the people still there.

"It's time to leave," he said in a loud voice. "You've taken what you can, now go!" He had to stoop under the low ceiling, and Cesare thought he looked huge and threatening in the small space.

There was some muttering, but people saw the look on Tifeo's face and started leaving. When the plane was empty, Tifeo and Cesare picked up the body of a middle-aged man at the back of the cabin and brought it carefully to the open door. The small boy was next, followed by the soldier in the other jump seat against the forward bulkhead. Finally, the crew were brought out from the very front of the plane and laid out beside the others.

The two men climbed out of the plane and carried all the bodies to the front, laying them beside the mother and baby. As each body was brought in, Rosabella and Amedea arranged them as best they could.

"Excellent," said Tifeo. "Now let's get the bodies from outside. Baldassare can help."

As he said this, they heard some more people arriving up the path. Fearing that more townsfolk had come up to see what they could find, the two men went down the path, only to meet three carabinieri coming toward them, sweating in their heavy uniforms. Tifeo recognised one of them.

"Salvo," he said, "what brings you so far from civilisation on this beautiful day? There's no coffee up here, you know."

"Eh, Tifeo, no smart-ass remarks today," replied Salvo, whose normal patrol area included Fontana. "This is serious stuff." Remembering his manners, he said, "Good morning, ladies and sirs."

One of the other carabinieri, apparently the most senior, said, "You know these people, Sergeant?"

"Of course, sir," said Salvo. "They're all good people, living in Fontana."

"What are they doing up here, then?" asked the senior man sharply. "This is a crash site and has to be protected. Civilians should not be here."

"Well, sir," Tifeo said in his politest voice, "we knew about the crash last night. Someone went to your offices in Serrara to inform you. We thought we'd find you up here this morning."

"We were all in Forio last night," said Salvo. "We didn't get the message until this morning. We've come straight up." The senior officer glowered. It seemed to Tifeo the officer was more concerned that the people from Fontana might think him inefficient than he was about the crash.

"A lot of us came up at first light," said Tifeo. "Unfortunately, some things have been taken from the bodies. We stopped that, and were just bringing all the bodies to one place to make it easier to look after them properly."

"Looting!" said the officer. He began puffing up, preparing his next pomposity. Like a toad, thought Tifeo, who was a full head and shoulders taller and completely unimpressed.

The carabiniere was about to continue when they heard yet another person coming up the path. They all turned to see Brother Renato, the new assistant priest in town, coming quickly toward them. Short and a little rotund, he wore a long cassock and flat priest's hat, and was breathing heavily from hurrying up the hill. As he approached, he took in the scene–the crashed plane, debris scattered all over the place, bodies lined up under the plane, the carabinieri, and five people from the town.

"I came up as soon as I heard," he said without introducing himself; everyone knew who he was. "What can I do to help?"

"There are many dead people from the crash," Rosabella said. "We're bringing them to one place, under the plane."

"Is there nobody still alive?" asked Brother Renato. He did not sound hopeful.

"Not that we've found," said Rosabella. Cesare looked at his feet, remembering the shouts of rage and the sickening sound as Adolfo's rock smashed into the man's forehead. I should have stopped them, he thought, feeling the first flickering of shame. Tifeo turned to the senior carabiniere.

"If I might suggest, sir," he said, his voice as smooth as honey, "My friends and I can continue to bring bodies up to the plane. Perhaps Brother Renato can do what he can to ease their passage to a better life? That will free you up to do your duty."

"My very thoughts, exactly," said the officer. "Sergeant, you should secure the site with Officer Bazzoli. Don't let anyone else come here. In the meantime, I will go back to the station and use our telephone to contact the office in Napoli. The authorities there must be told about this as soon as possible."

"Excellent, sir," said Salvo, keeping a straight face, "you can count on us."

"How many bodies are there?" asked the officer. "They will want to know."

Tifeo and Baldassare considered the question. They could see the six bodies brought out of the plane, lying beside the woman, but they had not counted the other bodies on the hillside.

"Nine, maybe ten?" said Tifeo. "We haven't had time to look further down the hill."

Cesare continued to find his shoes immensely interesting, and said nothing.

"Good," said the officer, bursting with self-importance. "I shall report that, together with the numbers I see at the back of the air machine, 'K122'."

After the carabinieri had left, Brother Renato went to the bodies collected under the nose and knelt beside the first one to pray. It was the pilot, his unlined face calm and unsurprised. Rosabella and Amedea stepped away to give the priest some privacy.

Tifeo, Cesare and Baldassare watched for a moment before heading off to find more bodies. Tifeo was the first to return, carrying the thin man, his torn arm hanging limply. Brother Renato paused in his prayer as Tifeo gently laid the man down beside the other bodies.

"I couldn't find the rest of his arm," said Tifeo, regretfully. "Maybe the dogs took it."

Leaving Rosabella and Amedea to contemplate this, he went back down the slope.

Before long, the three men returned, each carrying a body. Cesare and Baldassare brought two young men in uniform, struggling a little with the weight; Tifeo bore the man in the cloak with ease.

As Tifeo put the body down, he noticed the man's left hand.

"What happened here?" he asked. "His finger has been cut off."

"I regret to tell you that this has happened also to the pilot," said Brother Renato.

"And to these two soldiers," said Baldassare, holding up their hands in turn. Everyone considered the hands in question. In each case, the ring finger had been cut off cleanly at the bottom joint, leaving a bloody gap where the finger was supposed to be.

Cesare said nothing, remembering the surgical precision with which Adolfo and Ulisse worked.

"What else have they done?" Tifeo asked. Bending over the man with the cloak, he peered into his mouth. "They cut out his teeth," he exclaimed with disgust. "What kind of animals can do something like this?"

Baldassare said, "Unbelievable." He was about to continue when Cesare cut in. "Terrible," he said, hoping he conveyed the right amount of manly disgust. "Just terrible."

But the effort of maintaining the appearance of innocent outrage was too much. "I'll see if there's anyone else left out there," he said, unable to stand there any longer, and hurried off.

"What's got into him?" asked Baldassare.

Then he saw Bazzoli standing on the stub of the wing. The policeman was leaning back against the fuselage, striking a pose and holding his rifle across his chest. He looked as if he'd personally shot down the plane.

"Get down from there!" Baldassare shouted. "Salvo, can't you policemen show more respect?"

Salvo emerged from the other side of the plane, waving his arms and yelling at Bazzoli to come down from the wing. The unfortunate policeman clambered down, looking shame-faced.

"I'm sorry, Sergeant," he said, "I was only having a little fun."

"Well, don't," replied Salvo. "This is not a time for joking. Your job is to guard the site and stop people coming here. Do that, no more, and don't upset my friends here."

He was about to say something else, when Cesare appeared from below them.

"Down here," he called. "There's another body!"

"Dear God," said Brother Renato, crossing himself, "how many more of these poor souls are there?"

"I'll go," said Tifeo and went down to join Cesare. Together, they clambered down to where the corpulent man was waiting for them. Tifeo whistled in surprise as he took in the headless condition of the body.

"This is how I found him," said Cesare, truthfully but ambiguously. "I don't know where his head is." That was also true.

"It must be around here somewhere," said Tifeo. "We haven't seen it further up."

The two of them looked around the body, seeing nothing. Then Cesare leaned over the steep slope beneath the body and immediately saw the head. It was lying on top of some bushes, a few feet above the mule track from Fontana. The tops of some of the branches were broken off, as if a large animal had clambered across the bushes.

"Can you get down there?" asked Tifeo. "I'm far too heavy."

Cesare managed to negotiate his way down to where the head rested against a bush that was a bit taller than its neighbours. Without that, the head would have rolled right down to the path and then even further downhill. He picked up the head and, holding it in one hand, reached back up to grasp Tifeo's outstretched hand and scrabbled his way back up.

When they got back to the plane, the others looked at them in surprise. Tifeo was carrying the headless body easily; Cesare walked beside him, casually carrying the head under one arm as if he was taking a football to practice.

"I think this is the last one," he said. He was a bit light-headed with the strain of keeping up the pretence of seeing the bodies for the first time. It helped that everything looked different in the bright light of day.

Tifeo laid the body at the end of the row. Cesare considered placing the head on its chest and then, thinking better of it, put it where it belonged against the open neck.

"It's mid-day," said Baldassare. "We should get these people down somewhere."

"I know most of the farmers who work the slopes below here," said Tifeo. "I'll organize some wagons to bring them down."

"We should take them to the cemetery," said Rosabella. "The gravedigger keeps a few coffins there. I'll see if he has enough, or if he can make some more for us to use."

"I will stay here for the moment," said Brother Renato. "There are more prayers to be said. The good policemen and I can keep guard."

There seemed little to add to all this, so the five townspeople made their farewells and set off, leaving the policemen to their sentry duty and Brother Renato to his prayers.

Chapter Six

THAT EVENING, CESARE WENT TO ADOLFO'S SHOP. He was exhausted after spending the afternoon putting bodies into coffins and then loading the heavy boxes onto carts. At the cemetery in Fontana, he had helped Tifeo unload the coffins and lay them out in a neat straight line. Tifeo didn't show any signs of fatigue, but Cesare's back and arms were aching from the unaccustomed effort.

The corpulent man with no head was much larger than most Ischians and was a tight fit even in the biggest coffin provided by the undertaker. There was just enough room to squeeze the head into the space between the shoulders and the top of the coffin, and Cesare was able to tug the shirt collar up to hide the thick red necklace where neck met head.

The other bodies were easier to handle, although their limbs were rigid in death and had to be forced into position. Cesare was very aware of the gaps where fingers had been cut off. Two of the men had open mouths, too stiff to close, and he could see where teeth had been removed. Tifeo had said nothing, his face grim.

Walking up the hill to the shop, Cesare couldn't erase the images of Adolfo and Ulisse callously killing, cutting off fingers, hacking out teeth. How could they do that, he wondered, reassuring himself that his own actions were harmless by comparison. Taking jewelry and money from dead people was one thing–killing them in cold blood and mutilating them was something altogether worse.

It had come as a relief to put the dead mother into her coffin. Despite the terrible damage to her body, at least she hadn't been despoiled by people he knew, although he had noticed the absence of a wedding ring. Cesare had carefully arranged her clothes to hide the worst damage, then placed the baby, still wrapped in Amedea's shawl, back in her mother's embrace. They both looked peaceful, as if they were sleeping.

After depositing the last coffin in the cemetery, Cesare had walked through the church to the street, when he felt eyes on his back. He spun around but saw no one behind him in the empty church. Then he saw the huge painting of the Madonna hanging on the wall behind the altar. Her dress was indigo blue, the colour of the evening sky, and she held the Christ child in one arm. With her free hand, she pointed straight at Cesare. "I know what you did," she seemed to be saying. Indeed, both Mother and Child were looking deep into his soul. Judging by the expression of mild disappointment on their faces, neither of them cared for what they saw.

For a moment, Cesare was pinned to where he stood exposed in the centre aisle of the church. After what seemed like an eternity, he broke away and stumbled out of the church to the small square in front of the main door. He could feel the curious gazes of small groups of people as he stood there, sucking in the cool evening air.

A narrow street curved uphill from the square, its cobblestones worn smooth by the years. Shutters were closed against the spirits and perils of the coming night, their once-bright colours subdued and peeling. On the other side of the square, a tall building stood almost as high as the church. Long ago, its facade had been painted a flagrant, erotic scarlet, quite unsuitable for being so close to a place of worship; now the wall was mottled like an old woman's skin, pale and discoloured in some areas, blotched with dark red the colour of dried blood in others. The colonnades and trim were the off-white of old bone.

Cesare's thoughts tumbled over each other as he looked at the familiar buildings. He couldn't deny the excitement of going up to the crash in the dark. It had been like playing corsairs of old with Adolfo and the others when they were all children, made more so by the treasure that they had brought back. But the dead bodies in their games had not been real, and they did not have missing heads, or fingers, or teeth. He knew that mutilating and looting the bodies was wrong, but hadn't known how to stop it. And once on the mountain, he was committed, not strong enough by himself to prevent his cousins doing dreadful things to the helpless victims of the crash. He didn't know what was worse—the blind killing fury or the dispassionate care with which they'd cut off fingers and removed teeth. No one could have stopped them, he told himself; his being on the mountain didn't make any difference to what had happened.

Anyway, his share of the looting would be a nice little nest egg for setting up a home with Rosabella, so some good would come out of all this. Ah, Rosabella. He felt sure that that she'd disapprove of how he came by the money, if by any ill chance she ever found out. Still, he was glad they'd been together through the day. At least she'd seen him helping out.

Ulisse was at his usual seat in the shop when Cesare arrived. Adolfo was behind the counter, cleaning up after the day's work. The counter top was already immaculate. "I just need to deal with the weigh scale," said Adolfo, polishing the pan. Cesare nodded, knowing that Adolfo would not do anything until his obsession with keeping the shop spotlessly clean was satisfied. He sat by Ulisse to wait.

Eventually Adolfo was satisfied that the scale was as immaculate as it could be. Going behind the counter, he washed his hands, glancing occasionally at his reflection in the ancient mirror that hung over the sink.

"I hear you did well today," he said to Cesare. "Bringing down those unfortunate people was a good thing to do."

Cesare was surprised. He didn't think Adolfo would have the slightest concern for the victims, not after the way he had violated their bodies. He tried to think of something to say as Adolfo kept scrubbing away.

Ulisse grunted dismissively. "Unfortunate?" he asked. "What was all that bullshit about 'gift from the gods' you gave us last night? And I didn't see you worrying about using that knife of yours."

"Of course the crash was a gift," said Adolfo. "It would have been foolish not to accept it. As well as being disrespectful to the gods. And those people were dead when we got there —"

Cesare cut him off. "The two that you and Ulisse killed were still alive," he said.

"They were as good as dead," Adolfo replied as calmly as if he was discussing which pasta to serve with his sausages. "All we did was hasten what was inevitable. Merciful, really."

Cesare knew as well as any of them that being merciful was the last thing on their mind. Still, if that's how Adolfo wanted to deal with it, he'd go along with the story. Anything to avoid a confrontation.

"Anyway, what's done is done," said Adolfo drying his hands at last and taking a final look in the mirror. "We were lucky to get up there before the others got a chance to take it all. You saw how they were this morning."

"I still feel sorry for those people," Cesare said.

"Their misfortune was to be in the wrong place at the wrong time," Adolfo said. "Our good luck was to learn of it first. Anyone would have done what we did last night. Anyone."

Cesare wondered who Adolfo was trying to convince. Certainly not Ulisse, who appeared quite unconcerned about the looting and mutilation; even the brutal killing of two helpless people didn't seem to bother him in the slightest.

"Let's see what we've got," Adolfo continued, bringing the suitcase over and emptying it on the table. He stacked the cash neatly on one side. Rings, tie pins, the jewelry from the plane formed another heap, with a small pile of teeth beside it, the gold fillings glittering in the dim light. One of the teeth rolled onto the floor, and Cesare and Ulisse spent several minutes scrabbling under the table before they found it.

"There's a haul for you!" said Adolfo. "Divide that three ways, and we each get a tidy sum."

"How much do you think it's all worth?" asked Cesare. He was trying hard not to think of the slim box he'd put under his mattress when he got home the night before. "There's some strange money there, I wonder where it's from?"

"Maybe a million lira or more," said Adolfo, answering the first question and sounding surprisingly confident. "We won't know until we've sold it all. And that *is* strange money, I've never seen that kind of writing before. We'll have to change it all to lira."

Cesare contemplated the huge amount of money that Adolfo

spoke of so casually. He'd never seen that much in one place, and the idea of having even one third of it took some getting used to.

"That makes it worthwhile, going up the mountain last night," said Ulisse after a long pause. "I thought I was going to die of cold."

"I could build a house with my share," said Cesare.

"And have enough left over for a proper marriage bed," said Adolfo. "You'll need a strong one if you're going to make lots of babies."

Cesare blushed and tried to look casual about the compliment to his virility.

"We should wait for a while," Adolfo went on. "Let the excitement die down a bit. Then we can go over to Napoli, turn this stuff into money we can use. I know a couple of places that will give us a good price. We can all go together, stay at my friend's house overnight, have some fun while we're there. Go to some clubs, show my cousin and good friend Cesare what a woman looks like without her clothes on."

He laughed, and Cesare tried to laugh along with him. All his life, Cesare had looked for Adolfo's approval; being on the mountain with him and then being invited to a few days innocent debauchery in Napoli was a high level of acceptance, one he'd do nothing to risk.

When Adolfo stopped laughing, he turned serious.

"Here's something we don't have to go to Napoli for," he said, producing a small cloth bundle. Unwrapping it, he carefully put four severed fingers on the table in front of Cesare and Ulisse. The cut ends were the same dark red as the floor tiles and the cuts of meat hanging along the opposite wall. Grey and pallid, the fingers were the most disgusting things that Cesare had ever seen and he quickly looked away. Ulisse regarded them with polite disinterest.

"These fingers have power," Adolfo said. "Not as much as the relics of saints, unless these people were unusually holy. They provide a link to the world of spirits and gods. Especially the Linchetti living on the mountain, since that's where they came from."

"You may believe in relics and spirits," said Ulisse. "I don't. I got those fingers because you asked me to, but I have no use for them."

"How about you, Cesare?" asked Adolfo.

"I'm a practical man," said Cesare. "I can work with my hands, but I don't think about spirits and such. And I don't go up the mountain unless I have to."

"The gods up there are real enough," said Adolfo. "They brought the plane to where we could reach it. If it had hit a little further over, everything would have fallen to the bottom of the cliff, and we'd never have found anything in the dark. We should thank them for their help."

Cesare continued to look doubtful. "I don't know what I'd do with them," he said. "Maybe it would be better if you looked after all of them."

"Suit yourselves," said Adolfo. "I've got a small box to put them in. The best place to keep them is on the mountain, so the Linchetti know they are there. I know of a small crevice that is big enough to hold them, but impossible to find by accident." He began wrapping up the fingers in a fresh piece of cloth.

"Some would say that these relics are more important than all the money and valuables in that suitcase," he said, "because they provide a path to the place where the gods and spirits live. When you have your children, Cesare, we will use the fingers to petition the spirits, that they may keep them safe and healthy."

"Old wives' stories," said Ulisse, dismissively. "Fairy tales. Keep the fingers to frighten small children, but don't expect me to believe any of this nonsense."

"Be careful, Ulisse," Adolfo replied. "These are dangerous times, and we need all the help we can get. It's only prudent to respect the gods and the spirits so they protect us. If we offend them, they will allow bad things to happen."

"Spending all that time with the priest has made your brain go soft," said Ulisse. "Enough with all this, anyway. It's getting late, and I need a drink."

"You know where to find it," said Adolfo, obviously upset with Ulisse for bringing up the priest and for questioning the undoubted power of the fingers.

Cesare was embarrassed for the brothers, almost coming to blows over something as intangible as gods and spirits. "What will you do with your share, Adolfo?" he asked, to change the subject.

Adolfo took a slow breath, recovering his composure.

"I want to start a restaurant one day," he replied. "I think tourists will start coming here soon, like they are to Capri already. A good restaurant in Forio could make a lot of money."

"What about you, Ulisse?"

"Put it somewhere safe," said Ulisse, bringing a fresh bottle of grappa and three glasses back to the table. "Keep it for a rainy day. There's not much point in making big plans, stuff keeps getting in the way."

"That's my brother speaking," said Adolfo, accepting a glass of aperitivo and raising it in a silent toast to Ulisse. A peace offering, thought Cesare. After a short pause, Ulisse raised his glass to Adolfo, then to Cesare.

Cesare took a sip of his own drink, relieved that harmony had been restored. An hour later, he took his leave of his cousins, who loudly declared their intention of drinking another bottle together.

As he got ready for bed, he checked that the box was safely tied to the bed frame. Reassured, he fell asleep with the comforting thought that he was a wealthy man.

Chapter Seven

BALDASSARE SAT ON THE STEPS BY THE TOWN HALL, waiting for the English officers to arrive. Nervously, he took deep drags on his cheap Nazionale cigarette, the rough smoke burning his lungs. Beside him, Ugo Artigiani, the Mayor of Fontana, smoothed his thinning hair and then his jacket over and over. In honour of the occasion, he wore his best suit, bought second-hand in Napoli when he won the election the year before. The wide sash with the green, white and red colours of Italy flowed across his ample stomach, proclaiming his exalted status as mayor. Baldassare didn't own a suit, so had to make do with his cleanest, least-darned shirt, with a coarsely-woven jacket and cloth cap for warmth on this cool March morning.

Word of the visit had spread in the mysterious way that important news is known simultaneously throughout a small town. People knew that British soldiers had used the island as a break as the fighting moved past Monte Cassino towards Rome, but that had been at Casamicciola, on the other side of the mountain. A live English officer coming to Fontana was yet another excitement in an already memorable week and everyone wanted to see things for themselves.

At long last, they heard the unfamiliar sound of a jeep laboriously making its way up the steep track into town. No motorized vehicles had ever been seen in Fontana before, and every face in the crowd turned towards the entrance to the square, people at the back stretching to get a better view. Parents held up their children so they could see over the crowd.

Baldassare and the Mayor stood up as the jeep turned the corner and stopped suddenly to avoid running into the people filling the square. After a short pause, the jeep slowly moved forward like a boat moving through water, the crowd parting in front and closing in behind it. The occupants looked straight ahead, their stiff necks the only sign of their anxiety at being surrounded by so many curious but unfamiliar people.

The jeep pulled up in front of Baldassare and Artigiani, who stood by themselves on the bottom step. The driver turned off the engine and for a moment there was a deep hush in the square as people held their breath to see what would happen next. A child at the back cried out, "I can't see!" and everybody laughed, the tension broken.

The driver climbed out of the jeep and stood in front of the mayor.

"Signor Artigiani, I presume," he said, holding out his hand for the Mayor to shake. "I am Flight Lieutenant Calder, and this is my colleague Pilot Officer Drake. Thank you for coming to meet us."

Adolfo was standing near the front of the crowd with Ulisse. Leaning over, he said loudly, his heavy Ischian accent impenetrable to outsiders, "He speaks Italian like a northern peasant!" The people nearby heard the remark and laughed quietly. If Calder heard the comment or the reaction, he showed no sign of it. It seemed that he was more occupied by the need to extricate his hand from Artigiani's enthusiastic grip.

"We are glad to be here," Calder continued, "but we're very anxious to see the crash site. Can we go straight there?"

Artigiani reluctantly let go of Calder's hand. He was enjoying being the centre of attention, savouring the opportunity to show his people how wise they were to elect him.

"We have a small reception arranged for you," he said. "Perhaps you would join me and my colleagues for some refreshment after your journey?"

"I regret that will not be possible," said Calder. "We have very little time and much to do. We really should go to the crash site as soon as possible. I believe you have someone who can show us the way?"

After some more polite you-really-shoulds and no-we-cants, Artigiani conceded. It was agreed that Baldassare would guide the two officers to the crash site and that Artigiani would be honoured to host them for luncheon on their return. With that, the two officers got back into the jeep with Baldassare in the back seat.

He guided them through the crowd and out of the square, up the winding, narrow street past Adolfo's shop, and out of town toward the Restaurant Bracconiere. Once beyond that, the track narrowed even further, becoming steeper and rougher. Calder was forced to slow down to a walking pace, putting the jeep into four-wheel drive to maintain traction on the loose gravel. At one point, they had to squeeze between two trees growing on either side of the track with only a couple of inches between the mirrors and the trees. The scratches and dents on the bark showed that not every cart made it through without incident.

Finally they came to a flat area close to the top of the mountain.

"We stop here and walk," said Baldassare.

He needn't have bothered, as Calder had already pulled the jeep over. The two officers got out, staring at the wreckage on the slope above them. The fuselage lay at the top of the deep channel gouged out of the bushes. Below the fuselage, the wings lay crumpled and twisted on the bushes behind the large boulders that had torn them off like so much cardboard. Black soot covered the wings and boulders, the result of the fireball caused by sparks igniting the remaining fuel in the wing tanks. The surrounding bushes were scorched by the brief but intense heat.

Baldassare pointed up the track. "We go up there a little way," he said. "Then there's a smaller path on the left that goes to the site. It's a little steep and rough, but not too bad." He looked at the other man's brightly polished shoes, which were far better suited to the parade ground than a remote Ischian mountainside.

"What are those people doing?" asked Calder abruptly, pointing at a small group bending over beside a bush.

That's a stupid question, thought Baldassare. It was blatantly obvious that they were scavenging. He hesitated, trying to find a way to say this politely, when Calder suddenly started hurrying up the path, his assistant close behind. Baldassare shrugged and set off after them.

When he got to the plane, Calder and Drake were standing there, sobbing for breath, hands on their knees. Calder's shoes were now dusty and scratched. He must have fallen on the steep section at the end, because his trousers had a rip on one knee. He was short for an Englishman, about the same height as most of the Ischians, and overweight. His face was red from the exertion and Baldassare wondered briefly if he'd have to carry him back down.

They all turned around as someone climbed down from the plane. Baldassare recognized a local farmer who grew fava beans and grapes on a few small terraced fields above Fontana. He wore a heavy leather jacket with a sheepskin lining and was holding several instruments in his arms. It was clear that he'd unscrewed them from the control panel in the cockpit.

"What do you think you're doing?" shouted Calder. His face had gone even redder and he shook with rage. "That jacket doesn't belong to you!"

The farmer just looked at him. "I found the jacket yesterday, in a cupboard in the flying machine," he said calmly. "Now it's mine."

Calder barely understood him—his normally fluent Italian faltered under the force of his fury, and the farmer's strong Ischian accent didn't help. He took a step towards the farmer, raising his fists. Drake quickly put a hand on his shoulder. "That's not going to help, sir," he said. "Best to calm things down, I think."

Calder spun around to face Baldassare. "What the hell is going on here?" he asked, struggling to regain some control. Baldassare thought Calder's head might explode with the pent-up pressure.

"Things are difficult here," he replied quietly. "People are very poor, and there's not enough to eat." He pointed at the plane. "When something like this happens, they naturally try to…"

"Steal," interrupted Calder, still speaking loudly. "The pilot of this plane was a good friend of mine, and this man has stolen his jacket. And those people down there are stealing whatever they can find. Are you all thieves? Do you all scavenge like dogs sniffing out rubbish? Have you no honour?" His voice had risen to a shout, and the group down the slope stopped what they were doing to watch them.

Baldassare was embarrassed. He disapproved of the looting, but he also understood how desperately poor people would do anything necessary to survive.

"Honour is a luxury that starving people cannot always afford," he said, looking at Calder's waistline.

"Nonsense," replied Calder. "Without honour, you people are no better than animals."

"Maybe it's time to inspect the plane," suggested Drake, anxious to move the conversation to safer places.

But the damage was done.

Baldassare had felt something click in his mind. He was standing on *his* mountain, on *his* island, *his* home just a short walk down the hill. He would join *his* friends and *his* family later on to chew over the strange things that had happened during the week. And this short, fat, rude English with his torn uniform and ridiculous accent would be long gone. What right did a foreigner have to criticize him and his people? Calder had abused a privileged position as a guest, becoming an outsider to tolerate for the least time possible. The sooner he finished his business here and left, the better.

"Go," he said to the farmer. "Take the jacket, and those things you're carrying." Then called to the people down the slope, "Come back later, this is not a good time for you to be here."

Calder seemed to be satisfied that something was being done to recognize his outrage. "Let's look inside the plane," he said to Drake, and they both climbed inside.

Baldassare waited outside, glad of the quiet and the chance to gather himself. Finding a place to sit in the sun, he allowed himself to relax. In front of him, the passage of the plane through the bushes led his eye straight to the purple smudge of Capri. It must have come straight in from there, he realized. Across a small depression to his left, hardly worthy of being called a valley, the ground rose again to a ridge that was level with where he sat. The peak of Monte della Guardia lay over his left shoulder, not quite as high as Mount Epomeo, the highest point on the island. Behind him and on the other side of the small peak, cliffs fell steeply. If the plane had been only a little higher, and flying only a little to the west, it would have cleared the mountain completely. What would have happened then, he wondered. Still, when the gods determined that the sands of your life had run out, what could a man do?

A gentle breeze gently stirred the tips of the shrubs, murmuring softly. Spring would arrive soon, bringing warmth and blossoms of cyclamen and violets, helping people forget winter for another year. The bushes of Spanish broom would turn yellow with their big, globular flowers carpeting the hills high above the towns along the coast, and the fennel would release its delicate scent. Maybe this year the tourists would start coming to Ischia, bringing the same wealth that they did to Capri. Baldassare went to Capri once. He had thought it not as beautiful as Ischia, and was glad to get home.

His peace was disturbed by the sounds of the two English officers emerging from the plane.

"This is disgraceful," Calder was saying to Drake in English. "Stripping the plane like that—seats gone, half the instruments removed. We shall have to complain to the Embassy. No one has the right to scavenge a plane of the Royal Air Force!"

Baldassare pointed at the sea. "That's Capri on the horizon," he said. "The plane must have come from there."

"Obviously," snapped Calder. "Even a blind man can see the track where it hit. It's abundantly clear what happened. The real question is how he got so lost. What was the weather like that night?"

Baldassare chose again to ignore the other man's rudeness. "It was dark," he said, "late in the afternoon. It was very foggy, across the whole Bay. The fog normally just sits on the water, but this time it came all the way up the mountain. We have no electric lights in Fontana, so he would have seen nothing. Nothing at all."

For some reason, it was important that the English understood how pitch black it had been.

"I noticed that the switches for the landing lights were set to On," said Drake. "Maybe he came down to see where he was."

"He was a damn good pilot," said Calder, sounding defensive.

"What the hell did he think he was doing? He must have had a good reason to be this low." He took a deep breath. "I don't think we'll ever know."

"Have you seen enough here?" asked Baldassare, thinking that the pilot was maybe not as good as the English might wish to believe.

"Oh, yes," said Calder. "I've seen where my friend died, along with the others, I've seen how much respect has been paid to the site, and I've seen that the plane has been looted. Yes, I've seen more than enough."

Baldassare had nothing to say in response to that, so he merely gestured to follow him, and started back down the now-familiar path. He walked briskly to the jeep, leaving Calder and Drake to make their way down the stony track as best they could.

Half an hour later, Calder pulled the jeep up beside the steps of the Town Hall. The square was now empty and the sound of the jeep's engine echoed off the peeling, pastel walls of the houses around the square.

Driving down the mule track had demanded Calder's full attention, leaving no room for fury or recriminations. As he stood beside the jeep, he seemed almost calm again. Looking at his watch, he said to Drake, "We can spend no more than an hour at lunch. I want to see the bodies before we leave, and we need to check the arrangements for getting them out of this God-forsaken place."

Baldassare hid a smile as he thought about Artigiani's reaction to a one hour lunch. Even in impoverished Fontana, Italian hospitality to guests demanded no less than three hours for a proper lunch. There would be many courses and much wine. Cutting the meal short would be unthinkable.

Much to his surprise, Calder and Drake emerged from the Town Hall just over an hour later. Drake looked sorry to leave a good meal; Calder's mouth was a thin, tight line, as if he'd swallowed sour milk.

"We should drive down to the cemetery," Baldassare said. "You won't want to walk back up the hill afterwards."

As they drove down the twisting, narrow streets, more suited to mules than to jeeps, Baldassare explained that the bodies had been brought down by several people from the town. "I've asked some of them to come to the cemetery, I thought you'd like to meet them." Calder just grunted, concentrating on navigating the turns without hitting anything. At one particularly sharp bend, he was forced to back and fill several times, swearing under his breath as the steep slope threatened to pull the jeep through a small archway. Drake sat rigidly in the passenger seat, his face an expressionless mask.

The cemetery was on a levelled patch of ground on the edge of the town, down the hill a short way from the church. Umbrella pines lined the perimeter, casting shade over the neat rows of graves. A few of them looked quite fresh, with small bouquets carefully placed over the bosoms of the grave's occupants. The older graves were shabbier, the low concrete walls around them stained and cracked, the small headstones leaning over like old men who'd lost their way. The richer dead occupied the mausoleums that stood against the side of the hill rising sharply up to the town. Apart from having more spacious quarters in which to spend eternity, their affluence also entitled them to the spectacular view across the cemetery and over the deep blue waters of the Bay of Napoli. Capri lay in the far distance, a boastful, unwelcome reminder that wealth was relative and that Ischia had come off second best.

The coffins were arranged in a tidy row near the entrance at one end of the cemetery. Baldassare knew most of the people standing in a small group waiting for them, not too close to the coffins, that would be disrespectful, but close enough to be a suitable welcoming party. Tifeo stood at one end, towering over Amedea. Beside them, Rosabella and Cesare held hands. Baldassare thought, not for the first time, that she was wasted on him, even though Cesare was his brother. But it was too late for anyone else to pursue her now they were engaged. Adolfo and Ulisse were glowering at the back, possibly because Brother Renato was nearby, stroking his crucifix.

Baldassare wondered how his cousins had the nerve to show their faces, here of all places, after what they'd done. He didn't like the looting he'd seen in the days after the crash, despite feeling compelled to defend his fellow Ischians in the face of Calder's rude accusations. But that was as nothing compared to mutilating and robbing dead bodies. They were still warm, for God's sake, he thought. It was made even worse somehow by knowing that Adolfo and Ulisse were family.

The coffins were plain, made of planks of pine held together by nails. The wood was rough, unvarnished. Calder looked at them with disdain. "Is this the best you could do?" he asked Baldassare.

"This is what we use for our own dead," Baldassare replied. "We are poor, and the dead do not need more, once buried." He couldn't resist adding, "And luxury is for the living, not those who have taken their place in Heaven."

"I'm not asking for luxury," snapped Calder. "But these primitive... boxes... are insulting to our people."

Gesturing to Drake to help, he started lifting the covers of the coffins. The small crowd moved forward to see better, but quickly recoiled. The faces looking up at them all had a slight green tinge, and the bodies were just starting to putrefy, despite the cool temperatures. The sweet, putrid smell of death is unforgettable, and not pleasant.

"Why are there bells in the coffins?" asked Calder.

"It is our custom," replied Baldassare. "The dead person rings them to frighten bad spirits away as they go to their next life."

"Bloody heathens," muttered Calder, standing up again.

Two coffins caught everyone's attention. One was half the length of the others. The small boy lay in it, his face as peaceful as it was before the crash that cut his life short. His arms were folded over his chest, one hand still holding his crayon. Beside him was his mother, gently holding his unborn sister on her breast. The crowd sighed, and several of the women wiped away tears.

Calder contemplated the family for a moment, then went back to a coffin half-way along and stood for a long time in front of it.

"This is the pilot," he said. "My friend."

He spoke so sadly that Baldassare felt some sympathy for him, despite the man's ongoing rudeness. "I'm sorry," he said. "I hope your friend is in a better place."

Brother Renato stepped around the coffins to join Baldassare and the two Englishmen.

"Some of these people collected your friend and the other victims," he said. "I assure you, they treated the bodies with great respect. Then they brought them down here, to await your arrival. I have been with them, have said prayers for their souls. I hope your grief is soothed by knowing that God has taken them into his everlasting embrace."

"You stop believing in God once you've seen the things that men can do to each other," said Calder. "Keep your useless pieties to yourself."

As he spoke, he suddenly stiffened. Bending over the pilot's body, he moved the right hand, which was lying on top of the left. Then he quickly stood up to face Tifeo and the others.

"Is this how you show great respect to the dead?" he asked sarcastically, glaring at them.

The townspeople came forward to see what he was talking about. The pilot's left hand lay exposed, and they could see the bloody gap where his ring finger had been cut off. Some of them knew what to expect and barely reacted. Adolfo made an exaggerated show of surprise, repeated by Ulisse. Rosabella gave them a sharp look as the other townspeople began talking excitedly to each other.

Calder worked his way down the row of coffins, looking carefully at each body, getting angrier and angrier as he examined them in turn. Finally, he stood up again.

"You animals," he shouted, his Italian getting mangled by his fury. "Four fingers cut off, and three people have teeth missing! And where are their valuables? Where is their money, their rings? You're even lower than beasts, you're pond scum!"

Most of the crowd had no idea what had happened on the mountain on the night of the crash. What they saw was a furious little Englishman shouting at them. His drab grey-blue uniform was dusty and torn. Authority figures in their lives gloried in truly impressive uniforms, with gilt, and swords, and sashes, and medals covering their chests. They wore helmets with tall, brightly-coloured plumes, and high boots that were polished and immaculate. They quickly concluded that this outsider, with his scratched shoes that had seen better days, was not someone they should be afraid of. And they certainly did not enjoy being called pond scum.

Adolfo and Ulisse appeared to be entirely unmoved by the tirade. They had come to the cemetery out of idle curiosity and listened to the ranting with detachment. People die all the time, thought Adolfo, reassuring himself, and dead people have no need of money or rings; far better that the living got to suffer a little less. It mattered little that some of the living had to be hurried across to the next world, they were going there anyway. He knew that townspeople had gone to the crash the day before, picking over luggage and souvenirs from the plane, good for them, so it wasn't as if his little group had been the only ones taking advantage of the crash.

He looked over to Cesare, who was looking uncomfortably at the ground in front of him, his jaw clenched. Tifeo and the others in the group watched Calder with stony faces.

"Signor Calder," said Brother Renato. "The people in this town are very poor, and suffered greatly during the war. Many struggle to put food on the table for their children. Bad things have been done here, but desperate people do desperate things. I hope you will find it in your heart to forgive them."

"Forgive them?" asked Calder incredulously. "To forgive is to condone, and I will not, cannot condone what has been done here. And if I forgive, I will lose my anger. Anger is the only thing we have in the face of great wrong. If we lose the anger, evil will be all that's left."

"Anger is a heavy load to carry for too long," said Renato. "It will change how you stand–upright, like a true man, or stooped and bent under the great weight you bear."

"I prefer to think of anger as a bright fire burning," Calder replied. "It lights the dark and shows the way forward."

Renato tried again. "If God in his infinite wisdom can forgive great wrongs," he said, "who are we to deny that forgiveness? What right do we poor mortals have to deny that which God gives so freely?"

"What's right is right," said Calder, "and what's wrong is wrong. A decent man knows the difference. An honourable man rejects whatever is wrong, whatever the situation." He pointed an accusing finger at the crucifix on Renato's chest. "What was done here cannot be forgiven."

"What of the good people who brought down the bodies?" asked Renato. "Not everyone in our community behaved badly. Does that not count for something?"

"The good deeds of a few do not excuse the evils done by the many," said Calder. His fury seemed to have made him immune to reason.

He faced the crowd. "Which of you did this to my countrymen?" he asked. "Who cut the fingers off dead men, who cut teeth out of their heads? Who stole their rings and their money? I wish to know these people, so I can look them in the eye and condemn them to rot in hell."

His words fell on stony, unfertile ground.

Adolfo chose to believe that they had followed the wishes of the gods and reassured himself that what they did was no great wrong. Tifeo, Amedea and Rosabella felt that Calder should be thanking them for taking care of the victims and were outraged at his arrogance and ingratitude for everything they'd done. The rest of the crowd had no idea about who did what, although rumours were starting to circulate. But they all understood what people must do to survive, that family came before honour, and they deeply resented an outsider insulting them to their faces.

Cesare was the only person with any qualms about what he'd done the night of the crash, but he felt trapped. If he said anything now, he'd lose Rosabella and his place in the community, and Adolfo would never forgive him. He thought of the box under his bed and how it would help him build a good life, one a man could be proud of. A single word now would destroy all his dreams. So he bit his lip, and said nothing.

Calder scanned the crowd, waiting for someone to step forward.

The crowd stared back at him with stony, unreadable expressions, the look that oppressed people invariably adopt with outsiders. Calder thought that one of them looked uneasy, but he stood between the tallest of the Ischians and a very attractive young woman. Calder was acutely conscious of being short and stout, and didn't want to risk looking ridiculous by trying to force a confrontation and failing.

Drake saved the moment by turning to Baldassare. "You mentioned transportation to Ischia Porto," he said. "Perhaps this is the time to load the coffins, so we can get there by nightfall."

Baldassare welcomed the distraction. He was embarrassed for his community, both for what they'd done and for the way Calder was treating them, losing sight of the good because of the bad. He also felt sorry for Calder and the way he'd lost his dignity in his grief and anger. With relief, he pointed at two carts waiting beside the gate, each harnessed to a patient-looking mule. "We normally use these for taking wine to market," he said. "They'll handle the load without any difficulty."

Drake looked at the carts doubtfully. The wheels were almost as tall as he was, with thin spokes. The carts seemed far too rickety to support the weight of a small child, let alone many barrels of wine. Drake feared for the safety of the coffins on the rough, unpaved roads that lay between Fontana and the port. Before he could say anything, Baldassare and the tall Ischian began putting covers back on the coffins and effortlessly lifting them into the carts. When they finished lashing the coffins down, the drivers emerged from the crowd and climbed up to their perches high above the ground.

"You should leave first," Baldassare said to Drake, "otherwise you'll be behind the carts all the way."

"Thank you," said Drake, quietly. "And thank you for your help this morning. I'm sorry it ended this way."

Baldassare nodded and stood aside as Calder pushed past him without a word. Drake hesitated, then shook Baldassare's hand before going out to join Calder in the jeep. Before the noise of the jeep had died away, the two carts were on the move, passing through the gates and turning down the steep, twisting track to the main road going to Ischia Porto.

Adolfo and Ulisse remained with the crowd, watching in silence as the carts left.

"How did those people ever win the war?" Adolfo asked, as people started moving away. "First they fly their airplane into our mountain, then they send that buffoon to visit us."

"Be silent, Adolfo," said Tifeo, who was close enough to hear the comment. "After what you've done, you have no right to criticize others." Heads turned—maybe there was something to the rumours going around town, after all. Still, it was unthinkable to allow a foreigner to harangue them like that.

Rosabella also heard the comment as she and Cesare walked by, her arm tucked in his. "I don't care for that Adolfo," she said. "I'm glad you're not like him." She squeezed Cesare's arm.

"He's my cousin," replied Cesare. "I grew up with him. He's not so bad when you get to know him."

"And Ulisse," said Rosabella, "he's even worse."

"They're part of my family," said Cesare. "Soon, they'll be part of yours, too."

"Well, I don't approve of cutting off fingers," said Rosabella, making a face. She didn't feel Cesare tense beside her.

"Neither do I," he said, firmly. "Let's go home, it's time we decided who sits where at the wedding banquet."

Having regained safe ground, Cesare steered Rosabella through the cemetery gates and up the steps into town.

Behind them, Tifeo and Baldassare watched them leave.

"I wonder what Cesare did that night," said Baldassare. "You saw him with Adolfo and Ulisse when we told them about the crash."

"Whatever he did, it's done," said Tifeo. "If he was with those two when they were looting… well, I hope Rosabella doesn't find out."

"He's my brother," Baldassare said. "I'd like him to keep his balls—such as they are—for a little longer. I've seen Rosabella lose her temper and it's an impressive sight."

"Come back to the forge," Tifeo said. "I've got some fresh wine there, it'll take the taste of that little man away."

After they left, the cemetery was empty and quiet, the poor lying under their heavy blankets of concrete and gravel, the rich in their mausoleums enjoying the view across the Bay to Capri.

Chapter Eight

DEMONTE SAT IN HIS CHAIR BESIDE THE FIREPLACE, worrying about Paolo. Ever since the night of the crash, Paolo had behaved strangely. Fearful instead of confident, subdued instead of brash, refusing to take the sheep to the better grazing ground higher up. Before leaving with the sheep, he counted them exactly seven times, starting over if a count differed from the one before, which happened often; the sheep insisted on moving around as they were being counted. Demonte wondered if he'd been too hard on Paolo for the number of sheep wrong that afternoon, but this extra counting seemed excessive, especially since they'd found the sheep unharmed the morning after the crash.

Demonte knew about the looting, as did the whole community, but he did not realize that Paolo had been an unwilling witness to what Adolfo and his companions had done. He'd heard the rumours about Adolfo's actions that night, but had not asked Paolo about them. People always talked about Adolfo. But, while Demonte disliked—even despised—the butcher, he ignored the gossip. As far as he knew, the worst that had happened to Paolo that night was getting extremely cold. Finding a head without a body was certainly unusual, but Demonte didn't see how it would account for such a noticeable change in Paolo's normally carefree approach to life.

Too carefree, Demonte thought. Paolo was almost a man, and it wouldn't hurt for him to start acting like one. A shepherd had responsibilities. Paolo couldn't go through life like some sort of *buffone*, a court jester. It was time that Paolo began showing that he was serious about his work and that he could be trusted with more important jobs. Maybe spending half the night on the mountain and almost freezing to death had helped him grow up a bit; maybe his strange behaviour was just his way of getting used to leaving his childhood behind.

As Demonte came to this conclusion, slowly masticating his thoughts like one of the sheep chewing the tough grass of the mountain, Paolo came in, carefully closing the door behind him. The weather was much warmer, bringing a foretaste of spring, and Demonte could smell the changing season on the air that Paolo brought in with him.

"It's Sunday," he said, "we should go to Mass. We haven't been for a while. It would be good to take Communion. And you can return the coat to the gentleman from the town who loaned it to you."

Paolo looked down at his feet and the mud that covered his battered shoes. The pellets of sheep shit pressed into the soles didn't smell much, but he felt certain that the priest would not want it tracked into his church. Expecting his usual day of tending sheep, he wore his least good shirt. An old piece of twine tied around his waist held up grubby trousers. There was a rip in the left knee from when he'd slipped on a wet path and torn the leg on a sharp branch.

"I'd better wash and change," he said, his voice flat. Bringing in some water from the pump outside, he poured it into the battered basin on the counter without bothering to heat it. Stripping off his shirt, he scrubbed at his arms and neck, removing most of the grime. He washed the dirt and shit off his shoes before putting on his cleanest shirt and trousers. Finally, he ran his wet fingers through his hair, trying to tame the thick, unruly locks, as heavy and curly as a sheep's winter coat.

Demonte watched all of this without stirring from his chair. He had already changed and was ready to go.

"That's better," he said. "Good enough for church. You'll be able to go chasing girls afterwards!"

Paolo said nothing. He had few hopes of finding a girl, even at the best of times. Why would anyone be willing to live the hard, lonely life of a shepherd's wife? Oh, he had felt his stomach lurch each time he saw an attractive young woman in town, especially if she gave him a second look, but he had never mustered the courage to approach them. Instead, he relieved the pressure with his right hand, furtively, trying to not make a noise that Demonte might hear. The priest had taught that pleasuring oneself was a sin in the eyes of

God, that moral and physical decay was the inevitable result, but the relief was always so overwhelming that he had no way of stopping what he knew was a vile habit. He had confessed it once and Father Giovanni had reacted so strongly that Paolo thought he'd fallen out of the confessional. He'd never talked about it again, to anyone.

Demonte watched the play of emotions on Paolo's face and decided not to pursue the subject. He had heard the occasional faint, rhythmic sounds from Paolo's bed, understood exactly what was going on, and chose not to make Paolo's life any more difficult than he had to.

"Let's go," he said. "We've time to find a good seat before the service begins. Don't forget the coat."

When they arrived at the square in front of the Chiesa di Sant' Antonio, it was full of people enjoying a few extra minutes of sun and warmth before going into the dark interior of the church. A large white statue of Christ presided over the multitude, his arms outstretched in welcome. The peeling paint on the statue gave the Saviour a leprous look. Stone showed through the white walls of the church, with their pale yellow colonnades, the result of too many years under the brutal summer sky without new paint. The remaining paint reflected the bright morning sun, blinding people in the glare.

Demonte was anxious to get good seats, so he went straight into the church, Paolo behind him. Passing through the high wooden doors, they paused inside to let their eyes adapt to the gloom, only partially relieved by candles lit around the perimeter of the church.

As he had done since he was a child, Paolo went first to admire the diorama against the back wall. It showed Christ's birth, with Mary receiving the wise men. A group of musicians played exotic instruments, some with white faces, others black. They reminded Paolo of a group of American jazz musicians; he'd seen their picture in the local paper when they played in Napoli after the war. On the right of the tableaux, a group of villagers went about their business, oblivious to the holy scene taking place behind them. A few shepherds with their sheep looked from the left at the brightly coloured group clustered around the baby Jesus, clearly wondering what was going on. Angels with red and blue dresses hovered in mid-air above them all, held aloft by immense wings. Several naked cherubs flew just over Mary's head, jostling each other like small children trying to see better. As he always did, Paolo wondered how it would feel to fly like that, watching what people were doing on the ground. What would it be like to be free, released from the burdens of gravity and the hardships of life as a poor shepherd?

He went to join Demonte half-way down the nave, a small shepherd with pieces of sheep shit still on his shoes, pushing unnoticed through clusters of gossiping townspeople dressed in their Sunday best. Behind him, latecomers were slowly entering the church. As Paolo and Demonte had done, everyone paused inside the door, creating a press of bodies behind them. But no one was in a hurry, and the quiet hum of friendly Sunday morning conversation gradually filled the church.

Inside the sacristy, Brother Renato and Father Giovanni were preparing for the service. Two young altar servers sat quietly in a dark corner, their serious expressions reflecting the importance of their role. They were barely in their teens, still fresh-faced and not yet shaving.

Renato was still new to his new position in Fontana, and found the murmuring coming through the thick door to be both alarming and uplifting. All through his time in the seminary he'd longed to be with his own congregation, sharing his faith with them and guiding them on their path to God. He had a good speaking voice and had enjoyed the lessons when he learned to project his voice throughout a church so that even the less faithful at the back would sit up and pay attention, and, perhaps, be led to the Light. He'd found that he enjoyed being a performer, perhaps too much so. When he confessed this in one of the regular weekly confessions that all acolytes were expected to make, his confessor had chastised him for his pride. "You are not an actor in some play," the confessor had said, making it sound as if Renato was lower than a street juggler.

"You are a shepherd of your flock and your task is to protect them, to lead them to a life free of sin, so they may pass easily through the gates of Heaven. It is not to *entertain* them." The word 'entertain' was said with prurient disgust.

"Pride goes before destruction," the confessor had said, "and a haughty spirit before a fall. Proverbs 16:18."

To make sure the lesson was not lost, Renato was told to prostrate himself before the line of his peers waiting to enter the dining hall for the midday meal and to enter the hall last. His penance was for a week.

After thinking about this for a while, Renato concluded that a gift for public speaking was not inconsistent with his faith, but was something to cherish. Surely a God-given talent should be cultivated, not buried in the ground? And how could he share the Gospel if people at the back couldn't hear him or if he sounded weak and unconvincing? He accepted that it was wrong to be proud of his voice, but that shouldn't stop him from using whatever meagre skills the good Lord had seen fit to bestow upon him. But he still got stage fright before going out in front of the congregation.

Lost in his thoughts, Renato didn't hear Father Giovanni speaking to him.

"Brother Renato," the priest repeated sharply. "If you would grace me with your attention…"

Renato shook his head to clear it, and looked at Father Giovanni. "Yes, Father?" he asked, politely.

"I wish to change the first reading," said Father Giovanni. "Several members of our flock have expressed some… reservations… about what happened on the mountain recently. We must set their minds and hearts at rest." He put his hands together, as if praying. "I have prepared a new homily for them, but need you to plough the field before I plant the seed."

Renato noted the use of the word 'our' with interest; normally, the older priest referred to 'my' flock or, when he was annoyed by some transgression, 'the' flock. Whatever the priest had heard, it must be serious for him to bring Renato into it.

"What kind of reservations?" he asked. He thought that what had been done on the mountain was evil and wrong, despite his plea to the RAF officer to forgive the looters.

"It matters not," replied Father Giovanni. "Our job is to help them find peace with God and then with themselves. The reading is Psalms, Psalm 37. I have placed the bookmark in the correct place for you."

Brother Renato bowed his head in submission. It was not for him to question the order of his superior, and he had no choice but to do as he was instructed. His training at the seminary had included reading without preparation, so a last-minute change did not present a challenge. However, he could not remember what this particular Psalm was about, so he was curious how Father Giovanni proposed to reassure the congregation that what had happened on the mountain was not sinful.

Both men turned to look at the clock on the wall as the church bell fell silent. It was one minute before ten o'clock. Father Giovanni insisted on starting Mass precisely on time, and had been known to chastise persistent laggards from the pulpit.

"Come," he said to Brother Renato and the altar servers, "let us begin."

The congregation fell silent as the sacristy door opened and the small procession emerged. The eldest altar boy led the way, carrying the cross. Father Giovanni came next, reciting the entrance antiphon, followed by Brother Renato, also reciting the antiphon. The second altar server brought up the rear.

Tifeo watched them move slowly up the side of the church before turning down the central aisle. The church always seemed dark and oppressive to him, even with the multitude of candles along the walls. He appreciated the ritual of Mass, although he always felt closer to the gods when out on the mountain. It was far better being in the open, the clear sky over his head and the wind from the Bay blowing through and cleansing his soul. The mountain was his real church, somewhere he could be alone, opening his heart and communing in his own way with the beings who inhabit the ephemeral world lying beyond the limited sight of mortal eyes. Still, there was something to be said for the reassuring, unchanging ritual of Mass, and for the feeling of community that came with it.

As Father Giovanni went through the opening greetings and prayers, Tifeo was distracted by seeing Adolfo, who was sitting on the other side of the aisle, several rows in front of him, with Ulisse on one side and Serafina on the other. He nudged Baldassare, who was sitting beside him, and pointed. When Baldassare looked at him, Tifeo raised his eyebrows in comic surprise and raised his shoulders, questioning. Baldassare just shook his head and turned his attention back to the altar.

As he did, Brother Renato stepped to the lectern. His face was lit by the candles on either side of the Bible. He slowly opened the book, deliberately creating a little drama, forcing people to pay attention to him.

"Our reading today is from Psalms," he said. "Psalm 37."

After a short pause, Renato started reading. Tifeo had not heard him speak in church before and was both surprised and impressed by his powerful voice. Brother Renato was not tall, standing only shoulder-height to the lectern, but his words carried easily to every corner of the church. He spoke clearly and slowly enough that the reverberations off the stone walls would not muddy what he was saying. Tifeo relaxed in the cadence of the words, but was startled when Renato read: "The steps of a good man are ordered by the Lord: and he delighteth in his way."

This is going to be interesting, thought Tifeo.

Renato paused again. He seemed to be gathering his strength, knowing what was coming. When he resumed, his voice was quiet and reassuring, but still powerful. "…But the salvation of the righteous is of the Lord: he is their strength in the time of trouble. And the Lord shall help them, and deliver them: he shall deliver them from the wicked, and save them, *because they trust in him.*"

Slowly and carefully, he closed the Bible and in complete silence, walked slowly back to his chair.

Father Giovanni watched him sit down, then got to his feet and walked over to the lectern. His eyes blazed above the deep shadows cast on his gaunt face by the candle light. He was taller and thinner than Brother Renato, more intense, and his white vestments seemed to glow in the light from all around him.

"The steps of a good man are ordered by the Lord," he repeated. He spoke softly, but his rasping voice could be heard by everyone in the deep silence filling the church. "And He asks us to trust Him."

Tifeo could see that Adolfo's dark face was tight with tension, in stark contrast to Ulisse, who sat as easily as if he was having a drink with friends at Ampelio's. Even in the dim light, Tifeo could see Serafina's jaw clenching and unclenching.

Tifeo felt movement along his pew, and leaned forward to look sidewise. Rosabella sat next to Baldassare, with Cesare at the end of the pew beyond her. Tifeo thought he looked most uncomfortable.

"My children," continued Father Giovanni, "We all know about the airplane that crashed on the mountain a few days ago. It is only natural to feel sympathy for the unfortunate victims who did not survive."

That's all of them, thought Tifeo, watching Giovanni hold his arms out as if he could gather thirteen dead people into his arms.

"But we have to ask ourselves," Giovanni said, "how could such things happen with a merciful God?"

He sounded quite reasonable as his gaze travelled across the people seated in front of him. Was it Tifeo's imagination, or did the priest's eyes linger for the briefest moment on Adolfo before moving on? Adolfo certainly seemed to be paying intense attention to what the priest was saying.

"Remember, when God created the world, he looked upon his work and *saw that it was good*. God is not the creator of evil and pointless suffering. He must allow evil and suffering to occur, of course, because that is the only way to open the path to love and goodness. Therefore, there can be but two possible explanations for the crash. Either God allowed it so that some greater good would come from it, because he loves us, or He caused it to punish evil doers."

Another pause, as Father Giovanni let his words sink in. Tifeo saw a few heads nod in silent agreement with the priest's logic.

"None of us is wise enough to know the mind of God," Father Giovanni went on, continuing with the same calm that a teacher might use when explaining why two plus two equals four. "So let us consider both of these alternatives."

Behind him, Brother Renato stirred. So far, he had sat quietly as he listened to his superior speak. But now he sat up quickly, and Tifeo caught a look of profound disquiet cross his face before he regained control of his expression.

"What evil might the people on that plane have introduced to the world?" Giovanni asked. "What sins might they have committed? We cannot know. But we do know that it was a British plane, and that the British did very bad things in the war. They bombed our hospital ships, causing the loss of many helpless lives. Perhaps God caused the plane to fly into our mountain so that British families would suffer the same anguish that Italian families suffered when their loved ones were killed in their hospital beds. Perhaps it was an eye for an eye.

"Or it may be that He wanted you to share the riches on the plane. He knows how much His flock on this mountain has suffered in the last few years, with what fortitude you have borne poverty and misfortune. Wealthy people do not usually give up their riches willingly, so perhaps God gave them a helping hand. And in return, has offered them a place in everlasting Heaven. Think what love He showed them, the chance to spend eternity in His arms in exchange for a shorter life here on Earth!

"We cannot know if the crash was punishment or gift. That is for God alone to know, in His infinite wisdom. Either way, you should feel blessed. If the crash was punishment, then it was divine justice, and keeping the wealth from the plane is part of the retribution. And if it was God's gift, then He meant you to benefit from that wealth. Either way, what happened on the mountain, all of it, was God's will, even if we do not know exactly what His plan was."

By now, Adolfo had relaxed, and he sat in his usual slouch. Tifeo saw more heads nodding in the rows in front of him. If any of those people had helped themselves from the plane, they were now reassured that they had done nothing wrong. More than that, they could go home comforted by the priest's reassurance that they had merely done God's will.

Brother Renato watched Father Giovanni intently, his face immaculately expressionless.

"Remember, God loves us all," continued Giovanni, coming to his conclusion. "He is our strength in times of trouble. He is all-wise, all-knowing, and all-compassionate. Whenever he causes or allows things to happen, it is part of His inscrutable plan for us, and it is not for us to speculate on what that might be. It is enough to trust that God loves each one of us, and carries each of us in His heart.

"I urge you all to hold that thought in your own hearts, and to find your own way to thank God for his love and generosity.

"And now, let us pray."

As Paolo and Demonte walked out of the gloom of the Chiesa di Sant' Antonio into daylight, Paolo looked troubled. He squinted in the bright sunlight bouncing off the church facade, and put up his hand to shield his eyes from the glare.

"What's the matter?" asked Demonte, seeing Paolo's face.

"I didn't understand what Father Giovanni said," replied Paolo. "How can stealing be a good thing?"

"Paolo, people took what they needed from the plane," said Demonte. "You know what it's been like here. If it was God's will that the plane crashed, it would have been wrong to refuse His gift. Besides, everyone was killed in the crash. You can't steal from a dead person."

"But they weren't all killed in the crash," said Paolo. "I saw what happened."

"What do you mean?" asked Demonte, surprised. "No-one could

survive a crash like that."

"No, I was there," insisted Paolo. "I went behind a rock to get out of the wind. I saw everything. At first, I thought it was the Linchetti killing and stealing, but then I realized…" His voice trailed off.

"What did you realize?" asked Baldassare. He had left the church with Tifeo just in front of Demonte and Paolo, but heard Paolo's plaintive voice behind him. Turning around, he faced the two shepherds.

"I don't want to talk about it," said Paolo. He sounded small and frightened, as if he was back on the mountain, shivering behind the rock, seeing dreadful things.

"Come on," said Baldassare, impatiently. "We need to know what happened that night. Someone cut fingers off those people. Did you see who did that?"

"No," said Paolo. "I can't. It was bad. Bad. People did bad things."

Demonte didn't like hearing Paolo talk like this.

"Here, Paolo," he said, gesturing at Tifeo. "This is the gentleman who lent you his coat in the fog so you wouldn't get cold. Give it back to him and say thank you."

Baldassare wouldn't hold back. He was as sure as he could be that Adolfo was involved in the mutilation and looting on the night of the crash, but needed to hear it from someone who had been there.

"Paolo," he said, "what people? What did they do?"

He had raised his voice and heads turned to see what was going on.

"No," said Paolo again. "People did bad things. I don't want to talk about it."

Adolfo was one of the people who heard Baldassare. He moved close enough that he also heard Paolo's reply.

"It doesn't matter what you saw or didn't see," he said. His voice was tense but lower; the last thing he wanted was to attract any more attention. "You heard Father Giovanni, the crash was God's gift to us."

"Bad things," said Paolo, stubbornly. He knew Adolfo from the few times he had been into the shop. Seeing him in his church-going best clothes, Paolo had no idea that this was one of the people he'd seen on the mountain. "Bad things," he said again. "Bad people."

"You're a shepherd," said Adolfo angrily. "Do you think anyone cares what you saw or what you think? And it's not for a shepherd to question a priest."

"I know what I saw," said Paolo, sounding less confident. "I was very cold, but I know what I saw."

"What did you see?" asked Tifeo gently.

"Bad things," Paolo repeated. He looked away from Tifeo and Baldassare. "But I don't want to talk about it. I have bad dreams."

"If Father Giovanni says it was God's will," said Adolfo, "then it was God's will. It's not for us to question."

Tifeo said, "Adolfo, leave the boy alone. He's suffered quite enough without you making matters worse."

Adolfo looked around. The townspeople had drifted away after losing interest in whatever had caused raised voices. Ulisse stood a few yards away, watching them, a sardonic look on his face.

Demonte said, "Paolo, return the coat to the gentleman." He was very aware that Adolfo was the only person who would buy sheep from the shepherds on the mountain and that a major confrontation would be most unwise.

Adolfo nodded to Demonte, an acknowledgment that he had steered the conversation into safer waters, then went over to rejoin Ulisse. The two of them exchanged a couple of sentences, looking back at Tifeo, Baldassare and the shepherds, then turned and started following the townspeople out of the square.

Paolo watched them go, a puzzled look on his face. He shivered as a gust of cool wind blew through the square.

"The coat, Paolo," Demonte reminded him.

Paolo handed the coat back to Tifeo. "Thank you for the loan of your coat," he said politely. "It was good and warm."

"It was nothing," said Tifeo. "I'm glad it helped."

Paolo smiled shyly and turned as if to leave.

Quickly, Baldassare said, "I'm sorry you had to put up with Adolfo. He can be difficult, sometimes."

The two shepherds said nothing. It was clear that they thought 'difficult' was putting it mildly.

"Did you see who was on the mountain while you were there?" Baldassare asked. "Was it Adolfo?"

"Thank you again for the loan of your coat," Demonte said to Tifeo. "It saved Paolo from freezing to death. It was a very difficult night for him, one he does not care to think of too much."

Baldassare finally recognised that he would not learn any more. "Very well," he said. "I wish you both a good day."

Demonte and Paolo touched their caps and headed past the church to the street that led uphill past Adolfo's shop, towards their modest hut high on the mountain, away from the complexities of life in town.

Baldassare and Tifeo walked slowly across the square and sat on the low stone wall that in front of the statue of Christ.

"Can you believe that priest?" Baldassare asked. "That was the most sanctimonious nonsense I've ever heard! And asking for a share of the spoils like that…"

"What did you expect?" asked Tifeo. "He did exactly what he had to."

Baldassare spat on the ground with great eloquence.

"People in the town are divided," said Tifeo. "Some people took things the morning after the crash, some went up too late to get anything useful, others didn't go up but wished they did, and some think that taking anything at all was wrong. If Father Giovanni told us today that taking things from the crash was wrong, the whole community would be at each other's throats."

"Well, it *was* wrong," said Baldassare.

"You and I both know that," replied Tifeo. "So does the young priest, Brother Renato. Did you see his face? But that matters little. Father Giovanni will tie himself in knots to excuse evildoers if that's what he has to do hold the community together."

"That's all well and good," said Baldassare. He understood the need to maintain the appearance of harmony in the town, even if it was as thin and flaking as the paint on the church walls. Life in a small place like Fontana would be intolerable–unworkable, even–if people took offence at every wrong, imagined or real. "But what do you think about Adolfo and Ulisse?" he asked. "You saw them in church, and you've heard the stories."

"They're my brothers, and I loved them once," replied Tifeo. "What am I to do? If I accuse them out loud of what we think they did, what will it do to my family? No, I can do nothing there. And you have your own family to think of, I think Cesare was also on the mountain that night, although I cannot be sure."

"I don't know what Rosabella sees in him," said Baldassare, "even though he is my brother. She's twice the man he is."

Tifeo chose not to respond to the inference that Rosabella had chosen the wrong brother. Instead, he said, "There's something else. That English officer was right to be upset about how the bodies were mutilated and about the stealing, but he didn't have to insult all of us. It didn't take long before the whole town heard what he said. And what was their reaction? They decided that he was an arsehole and that no one had done anything wrong. Father Giovanni had to go along with that."

"So we're stuck," said Baldassare. "We can do nothing, even though we know this is all wrong. Evil was done on the mountain that night. And the next morning."

"What choice do we have?" asked Tifeo. "If we make a fuss, what will happen? Our families will be torn apart, and so will the community. I don't like this any more than you, but what's done is done, and there's nothing we can do about it. Who would listen to us, anyway?"

"So we do nothing?"

"We keep our peace," Tifeo replied, "for the time being. When the time is right, we can do something."

Chapter Nine

THE PIAZZA DI SANTA RESTITUTA WAS HUMMING as Tifeo and Baldassare arrived. Everyone was wearing their Sunday best, enjoying the mild weather that always arrived in May, a welcome interlude between the damp chill of winter and the oppressive heat of summer. Small boys played tag, running around the palm trees that lined the piazza, shrieking with laughter. Their older brothers lounged self-consciously on one side of the square, their sisters on another, each group eyeing the other with careful casualness. Parents and grandparents chatted in small groups, enjoying the chance to catch up with old friends.

Tifeo and Baldassare had crossed the mountain to Lacco Ameno the day before to spend the evening with a distant cousin. Their heads ached, the result of a long evening in a small restaurant facing the harbour. The best chef on the island, so the cousin claimed. Living up to his reputation, the chef produced plate after plate of extraordinary *paranza* fry, sea urchin in one, calamari and squid in another. It was all washed down with copious amounts of Forastera, drunk out of small, brightly-coloured clay tumblers. Despite their sore heads, the two men were in high spirits as they joined the crowd.

"There's Amedea," said Tifeo, as he saw her with several people from Fontana. "I should be with her."

"Go, go," said Baldassare, giving his cousin a gentle push. "I'll catch up with you after the service."

Turning around, he bumped into Adolfo, who was standing by himself watching the crowd. Ulisse was nowhere to be seen.

"What are you doing here?" Baldassare asked, surprised. "You know what people are saying about you. I would think you'd stay away from gatherings like this."

"This day is special," Adolfo replied. "And I have as much right to pay my respects to Santa Restituta as anyone."

"Special or not," said Baldassare, "I'm amazed you can show your face."

"Your amazement can go shit itself," Adolfo said calmly. "I care nothing for it, and neither does anyone else."

Ever since Father Giovanni's homily, the community of Fontana had closed ranks, acting as if nothing wrong was done after the unfortunate English were killed when their airplane flew into the mountain. Should anyone from outside the town be so insensitive as to ask about the crash, they would be treated to expressive shrugs, platitudes about how sad it was for those poor people, and a change of subject.

No one was going to say in public what some thought privately, that the looting was wrong. Adolfo's butcher business suffered a bit immediately after the crash, but it picked up again as people decided that the inconvenience of going down the mountain to Serrara or Sant' Angelo for fresh meat was too great a price to pay for their reservations about what he may or may not have done. It was only a rumour, after all, and his sausages were really very good.

And as people decided not to think about things that made them uncomfortable, they forgot entirely that fingers had been cut off dead people and that teeth had been removed. It was best to put the whole affair out of their minds.

Baldassare scratched his head, remembering that night and the days following. He wasn't sure what Cesare had done, but he was as certain as he could be that Adolfo and Ulisse were responsible for mutilating and looting the dead bodies. But the collective amnesia that was spreading across the town made it increasingly difficult to talk about, except with Tifeo.

"Have you no shame?" he asked.

"For what?" said Adolfo. "What should I be ashamed of?"

Defeated, Baldassare shook his head, feeling unable to take a stronger stand and confront Adolfo directly. Not in public.

Adolfo said, "I'm just here to celebrate Santa Restituta like everyone else. Like you, cousin."

"And will you ask for forgiveness?" asked Baldassare, making a last attempt to get Adolfo to confess what they both knew.

"Why not?" replied Adolfo. "Have you not also done things that require God's mercy? We all have, you know, so stop being so fucking sanctimonious. And stop looking as if you swallowed a lemon, you'll frighten the children."

"I'm amazed you can live with yourself."

"That's something we all have to do. But regardless of all this, I hope I shall see you in the shop soon. I bought some sheep from Demonte the other day, at a good price for him. They will be ready to eat next week."

"We'll see," Baldassare said. "I should join the others, everyone is going into the church."

As he went into the Chiesa di Santa Restituta, he saw Tifeo already sitting with Amedea a third of the way down the church. Light was streaming in from the windows high on the walls, and clusters of candles were burning on every flat surface. A picture of the blessed Santa Restituta hung on the wall above Tifeo and Amedea. The saint was being helped away from a burning boat by two angels. There was no hint that anyone else was in the boat–every time Baldassare saw the picture, he wondered if the saint managed to sail the boat by herself. Or, assuming there were sailors on board, what had they done that made them unworthy of being rescued? Then an impious thought–those were surely very incompetent angels, since the saint was dead when she landed at San Montano.

Normally, a statue of the saint sat in an alcove below the picture. However, today was her saint's day, so the statue sat on a gold-painted sedan chair at the front of the church, wearing a tall crown and glorious green and gold gown. Sketching a quick cross on his chest, Baldassare sat beside Tifeo and made himself comfortable.

Once the service started, he allowed himself to be carried along by the familiar ritual. The cardinal leading the service gave a short homily in which he exhorted everyone to love and respect their Santa Restituta, not least because she would keep the sea peaceful for the fishermen who risked their lives daily on its uncertain waters. Calm days were her handiwork, he explained. Storms were the devil's children, let loose to play when people did not pray sufficiently or when they strayed from the straight and narrow path that leads to Heaven.

After the homily, a small procession entered at the main door and made its way down the aisle from the door to the altar. Father Giovanni and Brother Renato led the way, with Mayor Artigiani bringing up the rear. He was wearing his mayoral sash again, together with his usual public look of overbearing self-importance. With ostentatious care, he carried a large glass vessel containing oil.

The cardinal placed the vessel on the altar beside a large gold cross and several chalices.

"A thousand thanks," he said, turning to face the congregation. "It is a fine tradition, each community patiently and humbly waiting its turn to contribute holy oil to us, the Church and home of the blessed Santa Restituta."

His voice was smooth, unctuous.

"As you all know, this is the holy oil that we will use over the coming year. Blessings will surely follow from your sacred gift. Harmony and prosperity shall be your reward."

Like everyone else in the church, Baldassare, Tifeo and Amedea received Communion. Baldassare viewed it as a necessary, sometimes comforting ritual, something that linked him to his community. Amedea didn't care much for the spiritual aspects, but participated because she didn't want to cause trouble.

Only Tifeo had serious qualms about being part of a rite that he found faintly ridiculous. Was he really to suppose to believe that a piece of bread had magically turned into the body of Christ? Tifeo preferred his ceremonies to use real sheep. Sacrificing a carefully-chosen, living animal, taking its life to propitiate the spirits and gods was more genuine and respectful than what he thought of as an infantile pretence. Nevertheless, he was part of this community, so he kept his misgivings to himself and, when it was his turn, obediently stuck out his tongue to receive the host from the soft, scented hand of the cardinal.

Demonte and Paolo were among the last to enter the church and among the first to leave. Sitting on the low wall surrounding the fountain in the middle of the piazza, they watched as people left the church. Adolfo was in a knot of strangers, just in front of Baldassare and the others.

"I don't like him," said Paolo. "I think he is not a good person."

"You don't have to like him," replied Demonte. "But you do have to do business with him."

"I still don't like him," repeated Paolo.

"What part of this do you not understand?" asked Demonte. He was becoming more and more exasperated by Paolo, who was getting more withdrawn and taciturn by the day. The carefree boy was long gone. Keeping his voice calm, he said, "You know that we depend on him to buy our sheep. Going down to Serrara or, God forbid, to Sant' Angelo, will take far too long. And Adolfo gave us a good price for the last sheep he took. I don't know why, but I wasn't going to complain."

Paolo said nothing. His eyes flickering, he watched Adolfo as he strolled casually across the square, leaving on the street that led to the small harbour. After Adolfo had disappeared, he asked, "Do you think about that night, Demonte?"

"No, why would I?" replied Demonte, once he'd worked out when 'that night' was. He was surprised. Paolo rarely initiated a conversation any more.

"It flew right over me." Paolo said. "It was like a big bird. Then it hit the ground. It screamed before it blew up. I think about it often. And I dream about it. Bad dreams. I wish they'd go away, I don't like them. It was very cold."

"I'm sure the bad dreams will go away," said Demonte gruffly. He was more comfortable talking about sheep than he was about feelings. Awkwardly, he put an arm around Paolo's thin shoulders. Paolo shook it off and moved slightly away.

"The dreams aren't going away," he said. "They're getting worse. I can't help thinking about all those dead people. They had their fingers cut off. I wonder if I could maybe have stopped them, but I was too cold. I thought it was the Linchetti, but…"

"But nothing," interrupted Demonte. "There's nothing you could have done, so stop being so hard on yourself." Despite himself, he was getting annoyed with Paolo's constant harping on bad dreams and bad people. He was also feeling more than a little uneasy because the worst looting had happened after he'd promised the big blacksmith that he would watch over things. How much of this was his fault, he wondered, and his discomfort made him gruffer than he might have been otherwise.

"Sometimes things just happen," he said. "Anyway, it's in the past, there's nothing you can do now. You've got to let it go. Forget it."

Rebuked, Paolo sat beside him in sullen silence.

"Look," Demonte said, more gently, "it's a warm day. Let's sit and relax here for a while. There's nothing else to do until the parade starts. A rest will do you good."

Paolo always enjoyed parades. Although he liked his quiet, solitary life tending sheep on the mountain, the noise and confusion of a good parade made a welcome and exciting change. Being small and obviously a shepherd, he was invisible to people from the town, giving him an opportunity to lose himself in the crowd and be an observer, the role he preferred.

He was glad to hear the sound of music as the band marched into the square. There were only fifteen musicians, but they included several fifes, clarinets and cornets, enough to carry the tune, some horns and trombones, and a satisfyingly large bass drum. A tall, gangly man with cadaverous cheeks led the band, obviously enjoying himself. He wore a uniform of startling blue, with a magnificent red sash across his chest. Some of the bandsmen marched upright, very conscious of their appearance—others were teenagers, untrained in the finer art of marching in step, and oblivious to the impact of their threadbare, hand-me-down uniforms, often too short for their rapidly growing limbs.

As the music filled the square, the various parts of the parade began to gather. Officers of the local carabinieri clustered together in their best uniforms, braid glittering in the sunlight. Small girls with angel wings attached to their shiny, pastel dresses chased each other around the square, squealing with excitement, their newly-polished shoes now covered in dust. A young Franciscan friar wandered out from the church, his brown robe cinched at the waist by a white rope, his hood pulled over his head. The friar reminded Paolo of a picture he had once seen of medieval monks in the monastery attached to the great castle at Ischia Ponte

Finally, a small procession of priests emerged from the Chiesa di Santa Restituta, led by an altar boy carrying a large, ornate gold cross with a crucified Christ, another altar boy swinging a thurible, the thick smell of incense spreading across the crowd. Father Giovanni came next with Brother Renato at his side. Priests from the other churches on Ischia followed. The cardinal was at the back, resplendent in his maroon cape and skullcap, benignly making the sign of the cross to the crowd on either side. Finally, the saint herself emerged from the church, carried in her litter by eight strong young men, two at each corner.

Without anyone actually directing things, the parade assembled itself into the correct order. The band was at the front, followed by the group of clerics, the saint resplendent in her litter with the friar by her side, the mayors of the various communes on the island walking behind the litter, the carabinieri behind them.

Paolo couldn't tell when the signal was given, but the band seemed to decide that the parade was ready, and struck up a sprightly military march. They moved off, carving a path through the crowd and around the periphery of the square, dragging the rest of the parade in their wake. Every now and again, the bandmaster would look over his shoulder and, if the parade was lagging too badly, stop the band so everyone else could catch up.

Paolo and Demonte were in the middle of the crush at the back of the parade, shuffling along in the press of bodies and trying not to get separated. Behind them, Tifeo and Amedea walked with

Baldassare. Cesare and Rosabella were further back, Serafina watching them for any signs of impropriety. Paolo could see Adolfo and Ulisse walking behind the carabinieri.

People joined and left the parade, a spontaneous and fluid exchange of marchers, spectators, friends and family. Walkers waved and called out to familiar faces in the watching crowd. The chatter of relaxed voices rose above the throng, the sound of a community enjoying a fine May evening and taking the opportunity to celebrate their saint with friends, neighbours and kin.

Once around the square, the band led the way to the Via Roma, heading towards the small harbour. Candle-lit lanterns hung from the trees beside the road, swaying gently in the light breeze coming off the water. Shop owners had used the occasion to fill their windows with the best they had to offer, hoping that some of the crowd would be tempted to return when the parade was over.

The eight litter-bearers seemed to be carrying their load easily, although the litter swayed alarmingly when one of them stumbled on the rough cobblestones, almost knocking over the friar. Something began stirring in Paolo's mind, something malign and dark, but it pulled back as soon as he tried to examine it. He shook his head hard in frustration, trying to jog the thought loose to where he could see it. But it stayed hidden in the shadows, just out of sight.

Giving up for the moment, Paolo saw that the front of the parade had turned onto the stone pier that jutted out into the harbour. He could see their destination tied up at the end—a two-masted boat used to transport kegs of wine to the market in Napoli. The boat began sounding its foghorn in greeting as the parade came into sight. Mournful bellows echoed off the buildings along the seafront, drowning out the music that the band was still trying to play.

The flat deck was large enough to hold the saint's litter, together with the entourage who would accompany her to Casamicciola, the next town along the coast. Paolo yearned to go with her on her annual trip around the island, visiting each of the towns in turn to bring blessings and good fortune for the coming year. Being a sea-going saint, it made sense for Santa Restituta to make the trip on water. Paolo saw the Bay of Napoli every day from high on the mountain but he'd only been out on it once, with a school friend whose uncle owned a fishing boat. Going with the saint would be fun, he thought wistfully.

He saw Adolfo stumble on the rough stone surface of the pier, almost falling over before grabbing Ulisse beside him and regaining his balance. Once Adolfo was upright again, Ulisse punched him gently on the arm, a gesture of reassurance and friendship.

The dark thought stirred again. He had seen someone stumble like that before.

The memory sprang to life, emerging from its hiding place, and Paolo was back on the mountain, cowering beside his rock, hiding from the bitter wind, watching again as Adolfo pounded a rock onto the head of the man he thought was a priest. Over the roaring in his ears, Paolo could dimly hear Adolfo screaming at his victim. He was right, there were no Linchetti on the mountain that night, just Adolfo and his brother. Was someone else there as well? He couldn't think clearly enough to know, his head filled with the sight and sound of a defenceless man being slaughtered.

Sobbing, he pushed his way from the safety of the crowd to the edge of the pier. Leaning over the edge, he vomited into the water. Wiping his mouth with the back of his hand, he stood up shaking, barely aware of two mothers hustling their children away from him, disapproval rigid on their faces. Shivering in the warm May air, he wrapped his arms around himself, just as he had behind the rock.

The crowd had stopped moving as they watched the crew lash Santa Restituta's litter carefully but securely to the deck. When that was done to everyone's satisfaction, the saint's companions joined her on deck while the crew made preparations for their departure.

Paolo stumbled along the edge of the pier back to solid land. Finding a bollard, he sat on it, putting his head in his hands. The bile tasted acid and thin in his mouth. After a minute, Demonte joined him.

"What happened?" he asked. "I looked around and you'd disappeared."

Then, seeing Paolo's miserable face, he said, "Are you alright? You look terrible."

"It was Adolfo," said Paolo. "And Ulisse. They were the ones. They did those bad things."

"Oh, for God's sake," said Demonte, his voice rising, "grow up and be a man. When will you stop this snivelling? I've already told you a thousand times, we can't afford to piss off Adolfo, we depend on him to buy our sheep."

But he was troubled. It had been very dark that night, and the men coming up from Fontana had dressed warmly, their faces and voices muffled. He had no idea who they were; he wouldn't have recognized his own mother in the foggy blackness. And he'd shown them the way to the crash.

Shit, he thought, why does Paolo have to be obsessed with this? This was nothing but trouble for them. They were shepherds, Adolfo bought their sheep and, starting not so long ago, at a reasonable price. They were poor enough, but they'd be even worse off without Adolfo. Fuck, what a mess!

Making his choice, he knelt beside his little brother.

"Paolo," he said, speaking as gently but firmly as he could, "Maybe you're right, maybe they did those things, I don't know. But it's best if we say nothing of this. Not to anyone. It's too dangerous for us. Without Adolfo, we can't make enough money from our sheep. We have to stay quiet, keep it this between you and me. All of it, you hear?"

"But what they did was wrong," said Paolo. "It was bad." He sounded young and disconsolate.

"I know," Demonte said, "but anything we do will only make things worse. We can't change the past. All we can do is live with it. You've got to forget about all this."

"Wrong, wrong," Paolo said, almost to himself, and Demonte couldn't tell if he was talking about what he was asking him to do or what Adolfo had done.

Standing up, he patted Paolo gently on the shoulder.

"Let it go for now," he said. "Enjoy the fireworks instead, like you always do. We'll talk more in the morning, get it all sorted out."

Paolo nodded numbly.

"You watch the show from here," Demonte went on. "I'll be along the road a little way. When it's all over, I'll come back and get you, then we can walk home tonight. How does that sound?"

Paolo nodded again, too miserable to say anything. He watched listlessly as Demonte made his way along the road, past a group of excited teenagers, and out of sight.

The boat carrying Santa Restituta was moving slowly towards the harbour mouth with a small flotilla of sightseeing boats following in her wake like ducklings straggling after their mother. All around him, people were settling down for the show. Paolo watched what was happening on the water, unaware of Tifeo sitting nearby with Baldassare and the others.

Once beyond the stone breakwater protecting the harbour, the flotilla came to a halt. A gentle breeze was coming from the west, off the open water, and the boats all turned into it, their engines running gently, enough to hold their position. The light was starting to fail and Paolo found it difficult to see some of the boats against the water.

The sky over the harbour suddenly lit up as the fireworks began. Startled, Paolo was jolted upright. The first salvo was meant to get people's attention; a dozen rockets went up at once, trailing graceful arcs of sparks before mushrooming into huge white spheres that filled the sky. A heartbeat later, a series of booms rolled over the crowd, echoed back from the mountain behind the town. In the short silence that followed, a small child cried. Paolo sat, frozen.

A barrage of rockets erupted into the sky, each one exploding before Paolo could absorb the one before. Light scattered in front of the crowd, white, blue, red, yellow, continuous and confused. Some rockets blossomed into gigantic flowers, others dripped white strands down to the water. The harbour was as bright as midday in summer. Smoke began drifting across the water, white to Paolo's left, red as blood in front. Most of the rockets made a deep boom that he could feel in his chest, others screamed as they fell out of the sky.

The noise was deafening, a violent assault that battered Paolo, driving him to his knees.

Tifeo saw him slide to the ground, clutching the bollard to stop the turmoil blowing him away, but still unable to tear his eyes away from the violence over the harbour. He nudged Baldassare beside him and pointed at Paolo.

"Look, the shepherd," he shouted over the din. Baldassare looked over and raised his eyebrows as if to say 'what's wrong with him?'.

An errant rocket went off right over their heads, producing a thick shower of yellow and red sparks falling in front of them on to the pier. The thunder of the explosion was the loudest yet, an enormous sound that left no room for thought or feeling.

Tifeo laughed delightedly. He loved fireworks. The bigger, the louder, the brighter, the better. This was the best send off for Santa Restituta he could remember.

So he was surprised when Paolo staggered to his feet and pushed past him, away from the harbour. The crowd behind Tifeo parted to let Paolo through, but their attention was fixed on the fireworks show and they paid Paolo no regard at all.

Then he was gone.

DEMONTE STORMED INTO THE HOUSE, slamming the door behind him. The room was empty. Dirty plates sat on the table, the remains of their quick breakfast that morning.

"Paolo," he shouted. "Where are you?"

Silence.

Demonte looked into Paolo's room. Finding nothing, he went back outside.

"Paolo, where the fuck are you?"

More silence.

Demonte had enjoyed watching the fireworks by himself. Spending all day with Paolo was getting tiresome with his constant fussing about whatever Adolfo may or may not have done.

Where did they find the money for this, he had thought, as the show reached its over-excited climax, the whole sky lit up and explosions bouncing around the harbour. He sat for a few moments, letting his eyes and ears recover from the cacophony, before returning to where he'd left Paolo on the bollard. Tifeo and the others were just packing up.

"Where's Paolo?" Demonte said.

"He left about halfway through," replied Tifeo. "He seemed in a big hurry."

"Did you see where he went?"

Tifeo shrugged. He preferred watching an entertaining fireworks show to following a shepherd he barely knew through the crowd.

Throwing his hands up in despair, Demonte walked back and forth along the sea front, threading his way among spectators going home. Paolo was nowhere to be seen. Defeated, Demonte started home, cursing Paolo under his breath. His lantern was where he and Paolo had left them in the morning, knowing they'd be needed to find their way back in the dark. Paolo's lantern was gone.

Learning that Paolo had headed home did nothing to improve Demonte's temper. He started up the narrow mule track that crossed the mountain between Lacco Ameno and Fontana, his lantern throwing off just enough light that he could avoid the potholes and dung. The moon rose as he walked, its yellow face hanging low in the sky over his shoulder. Before long, the moonlight was strong enough that he extinguished the lantern.

Despite his anger and anxiety, Demonte enjoyed the walk. The sweet scent of orange blossom lay heavy on the air, and it was still warm enough that he sweated slightly in his church-going clothes. For a while, he put Paolo out of his mind and opened himself to the refreshing feel of spring on the mountain.

Demonte's good mood lasted until he got home and saw that there were no lights shining through the shutters. Where was that damned boy?

Once he knew that Paolo was not at home or anywhere nearby, Demonte went back inside to consider his next steps. The problem was that Paolo could be anywhere. He had plenty of places where he liked to take the sheep and could have gone to ground in any of them. Demonte had no chance of finding Paolo in the dark. Best to wait until morning, he thought. Paolo would come home of his own accord, most likely to feed his adolescent appetite.

The moon was now high in the sky, a reminder that the night was well advanced. Worried about Paolo, but reassuring himself that the boy wouldn't come to any great harm on the mountain that he knew so well, Demonte decided to get some sleep. Morning was not far off, and the new day would bring whatever the gods chose.

Paolo had been warm and out of breath when he got home after rushing up the mountain as fast as he could. Standing on the path just above the small hut and breathing deeply, he realized that he didn't want to go in. Demonte would be back soon, he'd be angry, and would shout at him. This was the only home he'd ever known, but tonight he felt that it would be confining, almost a prison. He didn't want the cosiness, he wanted to be outside, free of walls, constraints, and shouting.

Turning away from the house, he took the path that went up the mountain, his feet leading him higher and higher. By the time Demonte got home, Paolo was lying on his back, watching wisps of cloud float gently across the moon. He was in the small hollow under the low chestnut tree, one of the few places left where he felt safe. His mind drifted with the clouds, drained of thought and feeling. Warm and comfortable, he relaxed for the first time in weeks, and slept.

When he woke, the eastern horizon was bright with the approaching sun. Paolo yawned and stretched. He could see the shadowy dips and hummocks of the shrubs leading downhill in front of him, their round yellow blossoms glowing like Chinese lanterns in the growing light. Beyond them, the waters of the Bay were calm. The fresh green leaves of the tree rustled gently.

Paolo sat up, listening hard. There were voices in the wind, calling to him. Try as he might, he couldn't make out the words. He shook his head to clear it, then listened again. There it was, a faint murmuring of light voices, whispering truths that were not meant for human ears. The Linchetti, he thought, maybe they don't know I'm here. But the voices were not threatening and he felt unafraid.

He got to his feet. The voices paused, then continued, inviting him to join them. Come this way, they said, seducing him, pulling him up the mountain. You're safe with us, they said, and he gratefully accepted their assurances, climbing the familiar path ever higher, up to where he would be free of his troubles.

Squeezing between two large boulders, he arrived at the crash site. Most of the plane was gone, cut into pieces and taken away as souvenirs. The scene was peaceful, with no sign of the horrors he'd seen the night of the crash. He walked straight past the boulder that kept him safe, past what was left of the plane, following the voices.

Beyond the plane, he negotiated the narrow path, twisting and turning through the jumble of rocks on either side. Arriving at the peak, a flat area of rock the size of his tiny bedroom, he stood in front of a cliff that dropped straight down for several hundred feet to the treetops. Tall grasses waved gently beside him. Looking past the cliff edge, he could see across the forest to Forio and its small harbour. The town lay quiet in the shadow of the mountain.

Standing well back from the drop, he sank into the profound silence that lay beyond the soft wind and the whispering voices. The quiet had its own being, its own life force. Paolo had no idea that the complete absence of sound could be so powerful, and surrendered himself to it without reservation.

He felt his consciousness flow beyond his skin, seeking to become as one with the silence, the wind, the whispers. He longed to be part of the vastness of the mountain, the sky above his head, the huge expanse of deep blue water reaching to the farthest horizon.

But his clothes were in the way, a barrier to the complete merging of his being with everything beyond. Quickly, he removed his clothing, until he stood there with every inch of his skin exposed and open and porous. The soft air stroked him and drifted through his body as easily as it did through the trees below.

Now there were no boundaries to separate him from all that he loved. The mountain, the sky, the air… they were part of him, just as he was one strand in the rich weaving of life. The rightness of it all filled him with a deep, quiet joy, leaving him at peace for the first time in his short life.

A movement caught his eye. Without moving his head, he knew the Linchetti were with him, swaying in the breeze, watching. These are spirits, he realized, not elves.

I don't have to be afraid of you, he thought, nor does anyone else.

You can join us, they said, become one of us; travel on the breeze, travel with us.

I can't, he said sadly, I don't know how to ride the wind.

To answer him, a Linchetti swooped up in front of him, carried up the cliff on a thermal, his white arms outstretched, his eyes watching him, unblinking.

You can fly if you want, the Linchetti said, floating effortlessly above the cliff edge. Ride the wind like me, free to go wherever you will. Your cares will be left behind on the ground and you will be as light as the air itself.

I can't leave my brother, he said.

You won't, you will stay on the mountain like us, and one day he will join you. Then you will be together until the end of days.

Paolo thought of the angels and cherubs in the church and how much he had always wanted to fly like them. Were they Linchetti that had been blessed by Heaven, given the honour of welcoming Jesus to this life?

Then he was filled with the absolute certainty that he could fly, that he could indeed be weightless, riding the wind, soaring over the mountain. Never before had he felt so confident of anything. His troubles fell away from his narrow shoulders, leaving him calm and serene, and he knew deep in his bones that he would fly as lightly as the puffy seeds that drift across the hillside in spring.

I can do this, he said to the spirits, I can do this.

Come, come and join us, they replied, swaying in unison.

Paolo took a step back, ran across the flat rock as fast as he could, and launched himself into the welcoming air, arms stretched out in ecstasy. And as he rode the wind at last, his soul left his body for good, joining the spirits waiting to greet him, becoming one with the breezes that caress the mountain.

Chapter Eleven

"IT'S TIME WE WENT TO NAPOLI," said Adolfo.

He stretched out his legs, relaxing with Ulisse and Cesare at the table in one corner of his shop, their usual aperitivo in front of them. Even at the end of the day, the stifling heat of August lay like a suffocating blanket across Fontana, forcing the elderly to retreat indoors from their chairs in open doorways. People who were normally even-tempered found themselves snapping at friends and family over trivial disagreements. Adolfo had opened the door and windows at the back of the shop in a vain attempt to bring in some cooler air from the shadowed alley. The three men were all uncomfortably warm in the turgid air.

"Everyone has forgotten about the crash," he went on. "We can tell people that we're going to see my friend Angelo in Napoli for a few days. There are several places near the port that will know what to do with the... with what we have."

Ulisse glanced curiously at him but said nothing.

Cesare said, "I can go whenever you like. I'm waiting for some wood to come across from Napoli, this would be a chance to talk to the supplier there. Maybe hurry him up a bit."

He thought about the box still stashed under his bed. The wealth hidden there was worth far more than what he was sharing with Adolfo and Ulisse. He wondered if he should tell the others about the box. It would be difficult to explain why he'd kept it secret for so long, but he felt sure that they'd forgive him once they saw how much more they'd get. He opened his mouth to say something but his brief moment of virtue passed as Adolfo spoke again.

"Let's meet here next Monday," he said. "First thing, so we get an early start. I'll send a note to Angelo."

The boat ride from Lacco Ameno to Napoli terrified Cesare. The *Vincenzo Monti* appeared to be nearing the end of a long and difficult life. She sat low in the water beside the dock, weighed down by large kegs of wine, crates of dried fish and chaotic piles of miscellaneous, unidentifiable bits and pieces scattered wherever there was spare space on deck. The boat rocked gently in the swell entering the harbour, banging rhythmically against the wooden piles. She badly needed a new coat of paint and one window of the small wheelhouse was broken. Black smoke drifted from her stack, lying heavy on the water.

"Find some seats over there," the skipper called out as they gingerly stepped down from the dock, pointing at a slightly less crowded part of the deck, aft of the wheelhouse. He was a small, wiry man with a face like a wizened monkey. "We'll be off soon," he said, "we just need to load a few more things." Cesare looked around, but couldn't see room for anything else to come aboard. He followed the others and managed to make a seat for himself by shifting some crates.

Adolfo saw the unease on Cesare's face and said, "He makes this journey every day." Cesare was only slightly reassured. Ulisse had somehow made himself comfortable and sat with his face in the morning sun, eyes closed.

Eventually, they cast off. Moving beyond the breakwater, the *Vincenzo Monti* immediately began rolling viciously. A strong north wind tore the tops of the waves to shreds, and whitecaps stretched as far as Cesare could see. He turned away from the wind to avoid the spray being blown into his face, only to see water sloshing on to the deck and flowing across the faded planks before draining from the scuppers.

"Relax," shouted Adolfo above the noise of the wind and the engine. "I've been out with Nicola in far worse than this. He's sailed here since he was a kid. This boat was originally called *Rondine*, but Nicola renamed it after his father when the old man died in the first war."

Cesare appreciated Adolfo's attempt to reassure him, but failed to see the connection between Nicola, his father, the name of the boat and his safety. Instead, he became increasingly distracted by the state of his stomach. Before he disgraced himself, the *Vincenzo Monti* passed through the gap between Ischia and the adjacent island of Procida into relatively calm water. The rolling eased, and he felt his insides consider moving back to their usual location. Hugging the shore to stay out of the wind and the occasional German mine that still swam in the centre of the Bay, the skipper pushed the throttle open to coax as much speed as possible out of his poor old boat.

Looking back along their wake, Cesare could cover the full extent of Ischia with his hand. Even with the heights of Mount Epomeo clearly outlined against the sky, the only home he'd ever known seemed very small. At the east end of Procida, they passed the severe square walls of the castle, once a cardinal's palace and now a prison looking down on the town below. Cesare thought the grim building far less impressive than the Castello Aragonese at Ischia Ponte and felt reassured. Ischia had a long and rich history and was a good place to build a life, despite being rather remote.

Adolfo followed Cesare's gaze to the prison. But, unlike Cesare's, his thoughts were uneasy. Part of the trouble was having no one to talk to. He loved Ulisse, but would never have described his taciturn brother as someone with whom he could hash out life's problems. Cesare seemed not yet fully grown up, and perhaps not completely reliable. Going to either of the priests was unthinkable–he knew exactly the response he'd get from one and had no idea how the other might react.

Why did the little shepherd have to throw himself off the mountain like that? The question had been like a stone in his shoe ever since he'd learned of the naked, broken body found at the bottom of the cliff. Paolo had committed a mortal sin by taking his own life, and Father Giovanni had refused to allow the shepherd to be buried in the cemetery, despite Demonte's entreaties. "Let him make his peace with God if he can," the priest had said. "My faith will not allow me to save his soul when he defied God's will by taking his own life. He was a manifest sinner. Compassion and forgiveness have nothing to do with it."

In the end, Demonte and Tifeo buried Paolo in the small hollow beside the chestnut tree, high on the mountain. Demonte couldn't afford a headstone and the grass had grown back remarkably quickly. Now the sheep grazed there again, as they had done for centuries.

How much did the little shepherd know, wondered Adolfo. Had he seen Adolfo and his companions on the night of the crash? What had he told Demonte? Or anyone else, for that matter. What legacy of trouble had he left behind?

And that damned plane! How could anyone not miss the mountain, for God's sake? Adolfo suspected that the loot was going to be more trouble than it was worth, all because of a most incompetent pilot getting lost in fog and then flying stupidly low.

He shifted uncomfortably on his hard seat, feeling sorry for himself as he looked at the prison high on the cliff, and shivering in the cool air coming off the water. Despite his protestations to Ulisse and Cesare, he feared there might be a stain on his soul. Smashing a rock into someone he thought was a priest felt wonderful at the time, a release of some sort, but now he wasn't so sure. If any good was to come out of all this, it was from the looting. Father Giovanni's homily helped Adolfo for a while, but he knew a whitewash when he heard one. And if God meant him to remove wealth from dead bodies, why did he feel so unsure of what he'd done? His self-respect was destroyed, and he had no idea how to restore it.

If it really was God's will, he should use the money well. Take some of his share and do good with it. Not all of it, he needed some for himself, but enough that God would notice. Then, when the time came to weigh his soul, his sins would surely be counterbalanced by the good he'd done.

By the time he'd reached this happy conclusion, the *Vincenzo Monti* had crossed the narrow channel between Procida and the mainland. The prison was now behind them, and Adolfo found himself looking instead at the lighthouse on Capo Miseno. Comforted by this sign, Adolfo relaxed, resolving to enjoy the rest of the trip. Get the money first, he thought, have some fun before heading back to Fontana. Deciding how to save his soul could come later.

Cesare was dozing fitfully as the *Vincenzo Monti* proceeded past the lighthouse and started across the mouth of the large bay tucked in behind the cape. He woke suddenly and unpleasantly, jolted upright by the renewed rolling of the boat.

"Not again," he complained, looking at the broad expanse of whitecaps between the boat and the shore, which seemed a long way off.

"This won't last long," said Adolfo. "And it's not too bad here, not as rough as further back."

Cesare held tight to the rail, praying that his stomach would remember its place. He was relieved and deeply grateful when the *Vincenzo Monti* finally turned into the harbour at Napoli. Waves exploded against the long breakwater, throwing up bright showers of spray, but the water inside was calm, and he felt safe for the first time since leaving Lacco Ameno.

The port overwhelmed Cesare, who was accustomed to the more manageable harbours around Ischia. Ocean-going freighters lay beside wharfs that seemed larger than the whole harbour at Lacco Ameno. A small fleet of fishing boats huddled together in one of the many basins, with fishermen on their decks working on nets and other equipment. A ferry passed them on its way out to sea; Cesare thought the passengers on its upper deck might be some of the tourists who were starting to visit Capri, and wondered why they were waving at him.

As the *Vincenzo Monti* steamed straight at a dock, Cesare stood up, gaping at the sprawling confusion before him. A row of buildings, five stories high, stood on the other side of the road that ran around the harbour. Behind them, a sprawl of more buildings climbed the hill up to the massive castle that dominated the skyline. He thought that the apartment buildings beside the port were big enough to house the whole population of Ischia. Only the sacred Madonna knew how many multitudes lived in the huge city.

Ulisse had slept the whole way from Lacco Ameno, seemingly oblivious to the wind and waves. Now he regarded the scene without expression, rubbing his eyes.

"Good, we're here," he said. "I'm hungry."

Seconds before the *Vincenzo Monti* collided with the dock, she turned sideways into an impossibly small space behind another small cargo boat and kissed the dock. Bare-chested men on its deck were tossing huge crates ashore under the watchful eyes of a tall, well-dressed man. Even in the August midday heat, he wore an immaculate double-breasted suit. The magenta handkerchief tucked in the breast pocket matched the tie perfectly. A stylish fedora shaded his face. Cesare thought he looked magnificent, and was painfully aware of how shabby his own clothes must look.

Seeing the boat tie up, the man walked casually over, swinging his walking stick gently in one hand.

Nicola clambered up to the dock to meet him. After the two men exchanged a few words that Cesare could not hear, Nicola reached into his pocket and put something into the man's outstretched hand before sketching a quick, furtive salute. The tall man tilted his head in acknowledgment, then beckoned to some of the men working at the other boat, who came over to start unloading Nicola's cargo.

"What was that all about?" Cesare asked Adolfo.

"Keep your voice down," said Adolfo. "That's a Camorrista. Nothing happens on the dock unless he says so. Now it's our turn. Don't say anything until we're out of the harbour."

Adolfo climbed up to the dock, followed by Ulisse and Cesare. They had to take care to avoid dirtying their city-going clothes on the grubby ladder. The Camorrista waited patiently for the three men to approach him.

"What brings you to Napoli?" he asked. Cesare thought it a friendly question, but then noticed how closely the man was watching them.

"We have some small goods to deposit at Gasparo, the pawnbroker," said Adolfo.

"And then?"

"We are staying with my friend Angelo, on the Rua Francesca."

The man thought for a moment. "Angelo Russo?" he asked, "Or Nuvoletta?"

"Angelo Nuvaletta."

"A good man. And how long are you here for?"

"Just a few days, then we have to get back to Ischia."

The Camorrista's nostrils flared, just a little. It was clear to Cesare that he did not think much of Ischia.

"Welcome to Napoli," the Camorrista said. "I hope your visit is enjoyable. And peaceful."

"We thank you for your time and kindness," said Adolfo, pressing some coins into the man's hand.

"Yes, yes," said the elegant man, pocketing the coins so quickly that Cesare barely saw his hand move. "Now, if you'll excuse me…"

A few minutes later, Cesare, Ulisse and Adolfo were walking up Via Duca di San Donato into the maze of modest shops and bars that grow like barnacles around any port.

"Gasparo's place is here," said Adolfo, turning into a small alley, barely wider than a mule track on Ischia and without even the pretence of a sidewalk. Clothes hung from metal balconies, faded from the sun and many, many washings. The narrow alley lay in shadow but the air was heavy and humid, with no hint of breeze for relief. Cesare's nose stung with the thin, sharp tang of rotting garbage.

Gasparo was clearly a cautious man. An iron grating guarded the square window that opened into his shop. The opening cut into the grating above the counter was just large enough for the exchange of cash and small objects. A hand-painted sign—USURAIO—hung crookedly above the window. The plaster on the wall had been scraped away to reveal the original brickwork, on which was painted 'MONEY LIBERALLY ADVANCED ON JEWELLERY, OLD GOLD, SILVER, ETC. MUSICAL INSTRUMENTS, BICYCLES, GUNS, MISCELLANEOUS PROPERTY, FURNITURE, AND OTHER EFFECTS. PURVEYOR OF THE HIGHEST QUALITY'. Cesare could hardly read the faded writing.

Gasparo himself sat on a stool behind the opening, leaning on the counter at the bottom of the window. Deep laughter lines cut into his generous, open face under a thatch of thick white hair. He wore a clean white shirt, collarless, and wide scarlet suspenders. Cesare liked him immediately.

"What can I do for you boys?" he asked as the three stopped in front of him.

"We have some things for you to look at," said Adolfo. "We want to sell them, not put them in hock."

Gasparo looked at them more closely.

"I don't believe I've seen you here before," he said, a question in his voice. He was quite accustomed to his role as unofficial banker to a poor neighbourhood, accepting pawned goods as collateral for a loan. But when people brought things to sell, they were either desperate or they had acquired the items under dubious circumstances. A man in his profession had to take some care to avoid unnecessary complications.

"Our friend Angelo suggested we come here," said Adolfo. "Angelo Nuvaletta. We came over from Ischia this morning."

"Angelo did come to see me," Gasparo said. "Ischia, you say? We don't normally see people from there." Another query.

"Some of the items are a little… unusual," said Adolfo. "Foreign money, for example, some small lumps of gold."

"Unusual items are sometimes worth nothing," Gasparo said. "Or they may fetch a good price. Ischia… Didn't an English plane crash there a little while ago?"

Adolfo shrugged. "Yes, they got lost in fog," he said, "and flew into the mountain. It was very sad." His voice was calm and matter-of-fact.

"That's what I heard," Gasparo said. "News travels, even between Ischia and Napoli." A warning, delivered with a friendly smile.

"It does indeed," agreed Adolfo. "Even in our small town, we have heard that Gasparo will give us a fair price and that we can rely on his discretion."

Gasparo beamed at them, delighted that a mutual understanding for their business together had been established so easily.

"Well, then," he said, "you should come inside so I can see what you have."

The Taverna Paradiso was anything but idyllic.

The entrance to the bar was jammed in between a grocery shop selling tired vegetables and a second-hand clothing emporium. Customers entered through a door that had long since lost its paint, before going down steep steps that had tripped many inebriated customers on their way out who had reached for a railing that wasn't there. The cellar had once been occupied by a wine wholesaler, and the musty fragrance of old wine and oak casks still lingered in the air.

Adolfo, Ulisse and Cesare sat together in one of the arched alcoves that led off the main room.

"This is a dump," Cesare said. "We can do better than this."

"This is where Angelo told us to meet him," Adolfo said.

Ulisse said, "Cesare's right. But the drinks are strong and cheap. We should wait until Angelo gets here, then we can decide what to do."

They had to shout to be heard over the din. Most of the other customers seemed to be sailors, although a few women with hard faces sat among them. They were all talking at the tops of their voices. The noise and smoke from many cigarettes filled the small room.

A young woman came down the narrow staircase at the far end of the room. Long black hair flowed like smoke to her waist, and her full lips were painted ruby red. Her dress was cut very low, showing off the generous curves of her breasts. Threading her way between the close-set tables, she joined a somewhat older man at a small table by the bar.

Cesare stared at her, fascinated. Women in Fontana simply did not dress like that. Seemingly unaware of his stare, she put her elbows on the table as she leaned forward to talk to her companion, making her breasts swell out even more. Adolfo was saying something, but Cesare didn't hear a word.

Ulisse turned his head to see what had captured Cesare's attention so completely. He just had time to admire the ample charms on display before the man grabbed her wrist and started squeezing. She tried to pull her hand back but his grip was too strong. She grimaced in pain as the man spoke angrily to her.

Ulisse shook his head. This was none of his business, but he was old-fashioned and didn't like seeing women being hurt like that. Adolfo had his back to the drama playing out behind him, so Ulisse tapped him on the shoulder and pointed. Adolfo turned around to see what was going on. The movement caught the man's eye; he looked over to see Ulisse still shaking his head and Adolfo with a disapproving expression on his face.

Slamming the woman's arm onto the table, he got up and lumbered across to them. The woman rubbed her wrist, looking frightened. The man was big and paunchy, with eyes set too close together.

"You got a problem?" he asked loudly, putting both hands on the table and leaning over Ulisse. His breath smelled of garlic and stale wine, and he obviously hadn't washed since Jesus was rocked in a cradle.

Ulisse held his hands up without saying anything. He wanted to keep the overpowering smell at a distance. More than that, he wanted to placate the man.

"What the fuck is the matter with you?" said the man, his voice rising. "You got a problem, or not?"

Ulisse recognised the futility of trying to calm him down. He'd been in enough bars like this to recognize a drunken bully when he met one. He also knew that confrontations with bullies rarely ended peacefully.

"You shouldn't treat a woman like that," he said. "It's wrong."

"I treat her any fucking way I want," shouted the man. "She make a mistake, I fucking punish her."

Around them, heads had turned. The noise level gradually subsided and people began to edge away cautiously, knowing what was coming. The young woman watched the developing catastrophe in dismay.

Cesare was bewildered. One minute he'd been admiring a gorgeous woman just a few feet away, imagining what she'd look like with no clothes on, and now a fight was about to break out.

"She's my woman," shouted the man, his voice even louder in the now quiet room. "She work for me. So you mind your own fucking business."

Ulisse shook his head in despair.

"Stand up," the man said more quietly, still glaring down at Ulisse. He moved back a little, bunching his fists. "I show you who is boss here. Stand up!"

Ulisse looked around. It was obvious that the entire room expected a fight. They wanted him to stand up and get beaten to a pulp. Then, when the entertainment was over, they could get back to serious drinking. The only person who seemed indifferent sat by himself at the back of the room. Better dressed than the sailors, he watched the proceedings with no more than mild interest.

Ulisse was sitting beside the table, facing the pimp. He pulled his feet back as if preparing to stand up. Without warning, he kicked up as hard as he could. The point of his toe went straight into the man's groin. The man sank to his knees, his hands covering himself. He made a strange keening sound, the only sound in the room.

Ulisse regarded him thoughtfully for a moment, stood up, took an empty wine bottle from the next table and hit the man hard at the back of his head. The man stopped keening. He fell forward, face down.

Ulisse rolled him over, grabbed his hands, and effortlessly pulled him upright. The man's nose was bloody from hitting the floor. Ulisse lifted him onto his shoulders. Carrying the unconscious man like a sack of grain, he made his way to the door and up the steps to the alley outside. He put the man down against the wall, next to the fading palm tree painted under the Taverna Paradiso sign, carefully positioning him so he wouldn't slide sideways.

The room was still totally silent when he returned.

"What a bag of shit," he remarked to the sailor at the next table, and sat down.

Conversation soon picked up as people decided the show was over. Some of the sailors looked disappointed–instead of a prolonged, enjoyable brawl, the one-sided execution had lasted less than ten seconds and had no more drama than the spectacle of someone peeling potatoes.

The young woman shook her head in stunned disbelief. Her eyes darted nervously between the open door, Ulisse, and the quiet man at the back. Cesare could see that she was terrified of what might happen when her pimp came back. He began to get up to go over and reassure her, but stopped when Adolfo put his hand on his shoulder.

"Wait," Adolfo said. "She'll be alright."

A short while later, the well-dressed man came over to their table, bringing a fresh bottle of wine.

"You handled him well, my friend," he said. "Where did you learn to fight like that?"

"In the army," Ulisse replied. "Many of the bars in North Africa were like this one. Most were worse. I learned quickly that bar fights are best kept short. You get hurt in long fights, and they attract the police."

Cesare looked at him, surprised. He'd never heard Ulisse say as much in one breath before.

"True, true," agreed the man. "It's never a good idea to attract the wrong kind of attention."

He turned to Adolfo.

"And how did you get along with Gasparo?" he asked. "Did he treat you fairly?"

"He was fair," replied Adolfo, not surprised that the man knew about their business with the pawnbroker. "Not overly generous, but fair. What we heard of him in Ischia was accurate."

"Good," said the man. He sat quietly, then said, "My name is Raffaele Cutolo. I represent the owners of this establishment. I'm sure they'll be grateful that there was no greater disturbance this evening."

"What about that idiot outside?" asked Ulisse.

"He should have been taken away by now," said Cutolo. "It will be explained to him that he cannot operate in this part of the city any more. He can go elsewhere, and we shall say nothing of this if asked, but his time here is finished. People like him bring us into disrepute."

"And if he returns?" asked Ulisse.

"Then he will be banished from Napoli," said Cutolo. "However, there will be more final consequences should he foolishly persist. We understand that we are all fallible, but severe transgressions of our rules cannot be forgiven. People must have faith that we will take care of them, that we see all and know all, that good behaviour will be rewarded and bad punished."

"And the girl?" asked Cesare, finding his voice.

"She is safe from him," said Cutolo. "He would be most unwise to see her again. But she will have to find someone else to look after her. I may be able to help in that regard."

"She looks very frightened," Cesare said.

"Indeed," Cutolo agreed. "Perhaps you could go over and give her my assurance that she will be well protected from that buffoon."

Cesare needed no more encouragement. He quickly went over to sit with the young woman and began talking earnestly to her. She looked over at Cutolo, enquiring. He gave her the slightest of nods. A few minutes later, she got up and went up the stairs, closely followed by Cesare.

"She'll make a man of him," said Adolfo. "About time, too."

Cutolo poured another glass of wine for himself and the two Ischians. "This has turned out to be a more interesting trip than perhaps you expected," he said. "Allow me to make it even more interesting."

Adolfo and Ulisse sipped their wine cautiously.

"We have an unexpected vacancy," went on Cutolo. "A promising young man, we thought, but he forgot that his first loyalty must be to his chief and his clan. Alas, he is no longer with us."

His face had turned hard.

"When you join the Camorra, you must be... chaste, as it were. No one, not even your wife and family, can come between you and your fellow Camorristi. Our vows require this. You understand?"

Ulisse nodded.

"I very much liked how you dealt with an awkward situation. It's possible that you might enjoy taking the place of the recently-departed young man. The work is interesting and varied and, as a Camorrista, you will enjoy a degree of status and respect that are perhaps less available on Ischia. Does that appeal to you?"

Ulisse nodded.

"Then tell me, when you were in the Army, did you ever kill a man?"

Ulisse nodded again. "Several," he said. "I cannot say that I enjoyed it, but it was my duty."

"Only a sick man enjoys it, and we do not want men like that," said Cutolo. "Are you married?"

"No."

"Would you like to live in Napoli?"

"Of course."

"Would you have any reservations about belonging to the Camorra?"

"Of course not!"

"Would you be able to maintain discipline as required, even killing a man when ordered, should that be necessary?"

"Yes. I learned discipline in the army."

"You understand that once you join, there is a period when you or we may decide that our relationship is not to our mutual benefit? If so, you may go your way with no hard feelings. But after that, there is only one way to leave."

"I have heard that, yes. It seems reasonable."

"Everything we do is reasonable!"

"I meant no offense—"

"And none taken. But you must be careful, Ulisse, in how you speak. People look for meaning where there may be none, and see ill will when none is intended. Neapolitans are quick to take offence, and slow to forgive."

Ulisse looked away.

"And what plans do you have?" Cutolo turned his attention to Adolfo.

"I think I will open a restaurant," said Adolfo. "Tourists will start coming to Ischia soon and they will want places to eat."

"You should come and see us if you want investors in your restaurant," said Cutolo. "Ischia is close to Napoli, and we are always looking for suitable business partners."

"Thank you," Adolfo said, and Ulisse could hear the rejection under the politeness. That's fine, he thought, it's time we went our separate ways.

The three men chatted casually as they finished the bottle of wine. Cutolo was about to get up when Cesare and the girl came back. She saw him to the table, then went back upstairs. With careful nonchalance, Cesare sat down.

"Is there any more wine?" he asked.

Adolfo laughed, and punched him on the arm. "That's my man," he said, with just the slightest stress on the last word.

Cutolo stood up. "This has been a most rewarding evening," he said. "Ulisse, I will meet you back here in two weeks. We will find some suitable accommodation and start your introduction to your new duties. I hope you all enjoy the rest of your stay."

He looked at his watch. "Angelo should be here soon," he said, and left.

Unbidden, the bartender brought another bottle of wine.

"Wait a minute," said Ulisse, and went up the stairs leading to the street.

The pimp was gone.

Chapter Twelve

ADOLFO HEARD SOMEONE ENTER THE SHOP as he picked up a knife. The body of a freshly-slaughtered sheep hung from a hook, the head with its dead, staring eyes swinging gently at waist height. The skin lay on a table at the side of the room, ready for cleaning. Adolfo needed the razor-sharp knife to disembowel the sheep before butchering the carcass into various cuts for display in the shop. His apron was stained from the blood of the two sheep he had already killed and skinned that morning.

Leaving the sheep hanging, he went through to the shop. Brother Renato stood just inside the door, looking around curiously. Water dripped off his flat hat, the result of being caught in an early winter rainstorm.

"Yes?"

Adolfo kept his voice as neutral as he could, just managing to suppress most of his habitual hostility. Father Giovanni never came to the shop himself, sending his housekeeper whenever they needed meat. This was the first time that Brother Renato had come in, and Adolfo wondered what was going on. Still, anyone entering the shop was a potential customer.

Adolfo held out his arm to shake hands, realized that he was still holding a bloody knife and that waving it inches in front of a priest might be misunderstood, and awkwardly moved it to his other hand. He wiped his right hand on his apron, but it was still the unmistakable hand of a butcher, so he half-raised it in greeting.

Renato's round face was open and friendly. He said, "I would like to buy some meat. We're providing a meal for the poor after Mass on Sunday."

Adolfo relaxed a little. He said, "I have fresh sheep in the back. Most suitable for you, I think."

If Renato thought there was anything incongruous about serving mutton to members of the Church's flock, he kept it to himself.

"Come with me," Adolfo said. He led Renato behind the counter and through the door to the workroom at the rear of the store. Waving a hand to banish the flies that were congregating on the sheep, he asked, "How much do you need?"

"We expect thirty or so people," Renato replied.

"Most of a sheep, then." Adolfo pointed at one of the carcasses on the table. "I've made a start on this one already. Finishing it off won't take long."

Gripping the ankle of one leg, he carefully cut through the muscle at the top of the thigh. Adolfo always enjoyed feeling his hand and a sharp knife working as one, finding the best path through the meat and cutting cleanly with a minimum of waste. He grunted with satisfaction, put down the knife and picked up another, much heavier than the first. Angling it down, he pushed the tip into the joint at the base of the leg, where it joined the hip. With a hard twist, he dislocated the joint, then cut through the meat and tendons, separating the leg. He held it up for Renato to admire.

"You've done this before!" said Renato with mock surprise, clearly congratulating Adolfo on a job well done.

"Even a butcher may take pride in his work," said Adolfo. "If that's not a sin."

"Only when taken to excess," said Renato, looking slightly uncomfortable. "When can you have this ready?"

"Come back tomorrow morning," said Adolfo. "And consider it alms for the poor. A penance for my sin of pride, perhaps."

"You're supposed to confess before making a penance," Renato said. "But your offer of alms is generous. I'm sure the poor will appreciate it."

Adolfo was very conscious that Renato was looking at the white bone of the exposed hip. He gestured at the rest of the carcass. "There's more than enough here for what you need," he said.

"It would be good to see you in church again," Renato said. Adolfo could hear the hope in his voice. "Perhaps you would like to come to confession?"

Adolfo shook his head ruefully. "That would need a month on my knees," he said, making light of it. He looked up as a thought appeared to strike him. "But perhaps I could make a large contribution to the church. God would look on that with favour, would He not?"

Seeing Renato flinch, Adolfo hurried on. "That was common in the past, I think. People would give the Church a suitable amount of money, no? The indulgence would spare them the horrors of Purgatory and Hell. I'm only a simple butcher, but I can afford something like this."

Before Renato could say anything, someone knocked at the outside door. Adolfo spun around and opened the door. Demonte stood outside in bright sunshine, peering into the darkness inside the room.

"Come in, come in," Adolfo said, showing only a little of the surprise and none of the relief he felt at being rescued from Renato's furious look.

Demonte had kept to himself since his brother had thrown himself off the mountain, coming into town only to buy essential supplies. This was the first time Adolfo had seen him since Paolo's death.

Everyone in Fontana knew about Paolo, although no one wanted to discuss it. The connection between his suicide and the plane crash was too close for comfort. Rather than talk about difficult things, the whole town had collectively and silently agreed to ignore the whole sorry story and act as if there was no crash, no looting, and no shepherds hurling themselves off the mountain. It was as if Paolo had never existed.

But here was Demonte standing in his workroom, looking at the slaughtered sheep, his bloody apron, his equally bloody knife. And at Brother Renato.

"Brother Renato is here to buy some meat for the church," Adolfo explained. He felt curiously defensive about having a priest with him and the slaughtered sheep. "They're having a meal for the poor. After Mass. On Sunday."

Demonte nodded. "I have some lambs ready for you," he said to Adolfo. "Three of them. When would you like them?"

They quickly agreed on a day and price for the lambs. Renato waited quietly, his evident anger at Adolfo subsiding as he listened.

Demonte stood at the door ready to leave when Adolfo spoke again. "I was sorry to hear about your brother," he said. "Please accept my condolences."

"And mine, also," added Renato. "I hope he is at peace."

Demonte glared at him. "How can he be at peace?" he asked. "He was buried in unconsecrated ground and without the blessing of the Church. My innocent brother was in Purgatory already in this life, then you condemned him to spend the rest of eternity in Hell. You think he's at peace there?"

Renato flinched at the raw anger in the shepherd's voice. "That was… regrettable," he said. He felt trapped; he had to support Father Giovanni in public, even when he thought the older priest had done the wrong thing. 'Regrettable' was the best he could do.

"Regrettable!" Demonte's contempt was scorching. "I don't know how you can live with yourself."

He turned his back on the young priest. "I think I know what happened on the mountain," he said to Adolfo. "Paolo talked to me before he died. So your condolences mean nothing to me. Nothing! He would still be here were it not for you."

He paused, breathing heavily.

"But you and I need each other, so we will say no more of this. I will bring the lambs to you next week, as we agreed. You will pay me, as we agreed. And life will go on."

Adolfo just nodded at him, unwilling to provoke another outburst by saying any more.

After Demonte had left, Brother Renato cleared his throat. "That is a very angry man," he said. "I know why he is angry with the Church, but why should he be angry with you? What did you do after the crash?"

Adolfo shook his head. "Some things are better left unspoken," he said.

"Not so," replied Renato. "God sees all, knows all. If you have sinned, you must repent before the gates of Heaven will be open to you. Come to me in the safety and sanctity of the confessional, and confess your sins before God. Only then can He forgive you."

Adolfo shook his head. "Father Giovanni told us the crash was God's will," he said, "part of His plan for us. So tell me, how can what anyone did afterwards be a sin?"

"But you're not certain, are you?" asked Renato. "Why else would you be asking about indulgences?"

"That's in case God changes His mind," said Adolfo, trying to make light of it. "And if he doesn't, perhaps I can be forgiven any future sins."

"You cannot wipe your soul clean with money," said Renato. "It's not like cleaning shit off your arse with yesterday's newspaper."

Adolfo, shocked into silence by Renato's unexpected and unpriestly coarseness, waited as Renato collected himself.

"To be forgiven in the eyes of God," the priest said more calmly, "you must first confess your sins before God. That means to a priest. You know this as well as I do, so why do you fight it?"

"To a priest," repeated Adolfo. He took a deep breath. "And what if the priest is a sinner himself?"

"We are all sinners, priests included," Renato replied. "We are born in sin, we live in si–"

"Oh, spare me," Adolfo cut in. "I know the words. My question is a simple one. If a priest sins, his relationship with God is damaged, no? How then can he hear confession and be a reliable go-between with God?"

"Priests make their confession like everyone else. They repent, and pay penance. Like everyone else."

"And is God the only one who can forgive sin? What about the people sinned against?"

Renato felt the question press against his chest. He was angry with Adolfo, for his obstinate refusal to face up to whatever it was he had done. But for the first time, he also began to sense the hurt beneath the defiance, even if he didn't know the cause.

"It is for God to forgive mortal sin, acts that distance someone from His grace. But He also asks us to forgive those that do us wrong. 'Forgive us our trespasses, as we forgive those that trespass against us.' The hard truth, Adolfo, is that we cannot be forgiven until we have forgiven."

"I'm starting to understand the English officer," said Adolfo. "The one who said that anger is the right thing when evil has been done."

"He was wrong," shouted Renato, furious again. "Anger and hate are padlocks on your heart. You can never be truly free until they are unlocked and thrown away."

"But you're angry with me now, aren't you?" said Adolfo. "How can you help me when you're like this?"

Shocked, Renato stared at him for a long moment. Then he started laughing helplessly. How fitting, that the object of his anger should prick the balloon of his wrath so casually. He'd been aware of his growing pomposity as they talked but had been unable to control it. Adolfo's simple question pricked that balloon as well.

Still laughing, he reached out to steady himself and put his hand on the bloody head of the sheep lying dead on the table beside him. The glassy eye looked reproachfully at him. Is that a blessing, it seemed to ask, or am I just something to lean on? Renato quickly pulled his hand back and turned to face Adolfo, who was regarding him with some amusement of his own.

"Here," Adolfo said, handing over a wet towel, "you'll want to wash before you leave. A priest with blood on his hands? That will give people something to talk about!"

Still laughing, Renato cleaned his hands.

"I'll come back tomorrow for the meat," he said. "And thank you again for giving it as alms. I shall remember you in my prayers."

Adolfo watched Renato walk down the narrow alley to the main street. I like the pain and anger, he thought. I'm alive as long as I feel the pain. It's all I know. What would be left in its place if the pain went away? And anger is not a padlock, it's a burr under the saddle, something to propel you forward, something that gives purpose to a life.

Something to embrace.

Chapter Thirteen

BROTHER RENATO WHISTLED AS HE WALKED BRISKLY along the Via Roma, heading east out of Fontana. It was another glorious day late in spring. The early morning sun had not yet burned off the dew, and his sandaled feet barely stirred the dirt on the track. The air was clear and tangy with the scent of lemon blossom, birds were singing, and the Bay shimmered slightly, bright shards of light startling his eye. The sound of a man calling to his mule rose easily from far down the hill.

He thought that 'Via Roma' was a very pretentious name for a humble mule track, hardly wide enough for two carts to pass each other, heavily travelled as it was. Carved into the hill, the track followed the contours of the mountain, sliding gradually down towards the sea, a long way down. Once out of town, the track was lined with dry-stone walls, barely waist-high. Every now and again, the ground flattened out enough that small fields could be cultivated on either side of the road. Taking advantage of a cool morning, men and women who had worked these fields all their lives stooped over pulling up weeds by hand, just as their ancestors had done.

Occasionally a farmer looked up and, seeing Renato striding along in his cassock, raised a hand in salute. Renato was too new a priest to be comfortable with this, let alone expect it, so he responded to the greetings with an awkward wave. He knew that none of the farmers expected him to stop and talk.

A short way out of town, he turned up Via Epomeo, a smaller track that forked off to the left, going uphill towards the peak of the mountain. Trees crowded in from both sides, forming a refreshingly cool, dark green tunnel.

Still whistling, he soon arrived at his destination, Tifeo's forge. Through the open door, he could see that Tifeo was already hard at work, despite the early hour. Amedea was there as well, pumping the bellows that fed the fire, her sleeves rolled up above her elbows. Smoke billowed from the chimney with each stroke of the long handles. As Renato entered the smithy, the heat struck him in the face like a blow from the hammer dangling from Tifeo's left hand. In his other hand, he held a long pair of tongs, preparing to place a horseshoe over the anvil.

Waiting for Tifeo to finish what he was doing, Renato looked around at the strange implements neatly arranged on the walls. Growing up as the son of a lawyer in Siena, he had always been bookish, removed from how people made a living with their hands. His ignorance made him uncomfortable with his own clumsiness with the tools that some of his friends used so casually. But he was much better at schoolwork than they were, and liked helping them out with homework. Joining the priesthood had been an easy choice, combining what he was good at with what he enjoyed.

But his father had been bitterly disappointed when Renato told him of his decision. What's wrong with being a lawyer, he'd asked, not good enough for you? Disappointment turned into a feeling of being abandoned when Renato went to Ischia, an insignificant island at the other end of Italy, with none of the glory and history that was Siena. When will we see you again, his father had asked, and Renato, being young and full of excitement at going to new places, did not understand his father's real question and had failed to respond adequately.

Some years later, the newly-ordained Brother Renato finally admitted to himself that he was ambitious, that he wanted to rise high in the Church's hierarchy. Even later, he realized that he also wanted to prove to his father that he'd made the right decision in joining the Church, that you didn't have to be a lawyer in Siena to be successful and respected, that an acorn could only grow strong and healthy beyond the shadow of the oak.

Lost in thought, it took him a few moments to realize that the hammering had stopped and that Tifeo and Amedea were politely waiting for him to speak.

"I do apologize," he said, clearing his throat. "I am reminded of some of my friends when I was a boy."

Tifeo and Amedea remained silent and expectant, allowing

whatever was troubling their visitor to pass.

"You are making horseshoes, I see," said Renato. It was an idiotic thing to say–of course they were making horseshoes, the still-glowing evidence was right in front of him.

Tifeo helped him out by saying, "There are over fifty mules in this area, and they all need shoes. As long as there are mules, there will be work for a blacksmith."

Renato smiled, grateful. "It is because you are a blacksmith that I am here," he said. "There is an idea I should like to talk to you about."

"Well, then," said Tifeo. "We should sit outside where it is more comfortable."

He led the way through the back door to a small area under the trees. Several chairs and a small table were arranged in a welcoming group in the shade, facing a chaotic pile of metal scrap, some of it blackened by fire. Raw material for a blacksmith, thought Renato as he sat down, and then realized with a shock what he was looking at.

"Are those pieces of the crashed airplane?" he asked Tifeo.

"Some are," replied the blacksmith. "Others are pieces of scrap from all over the place. People know I need metal, so they sell it to me."

"The plane–" Renato began.

"You know the British came back to take what they wanted from the wreckage," interrupted Tifeo.

Renato nodded.

"They left much of it behind," continued Tifeo, "what was too heavy and not worth the effort. Since they did not want it, I saw no reason it could not be put to good use."

"I have heard that many people have taken small pieces as souvenirs," said Renato. "They have put these… mementoes… on their mantels. I must confess, I find that distasteful."

"As do I," said Tifeo. "But the material here can be used in many good ways, even for horseshoes. Imagine, pieces of a flying machine connecting mules to the ground." He smiled, enjoying the thought. "Nothing we make here is frivolous, or useless."

He went over to the pile of metal, returning with a small piece of machined steel.

"This was from one of the engines," he said. "You can see how well it was made."

As Renato admired the part, Amedea emerged from the smithy carrying steaming mugs of hot chocolate. She put mugs in front of the two men, took one for herself, and sat down.

"Many thanks," Renato said to her, giving the engine part back to Tifeo and taking an appreciative sip of the chocolate. He was touched–this was a real luxury so soon after the end of the war. Even a blacksmith with regular work would not normally drink this.

"I'm ashamed of how people behaved," said Amedea. She had clearly heard the conversation. "Looting like that, keeping pieces of the plane to look at…"

"You know that I agree with you," said Renato. He had to tread carefully here, he could not be seen to contradict Father Giovanni. First Demonte, now these two, he thought. "That is why I came here this morning."

"…and cutting up the bodies like that," continued Amedea. She was obviously determined to speak her mind. "What kind of animals could do that?"

Renato looked at her with admiration. He was a young man and, despite his vows–or maybe because of them–very aware of how his body responded to desirable women. Amedea's face glowed from the heat inside the smithy and the force of her indignation. Her thin shirt clung to her skin and he found it easy to imagine the soft weight of her breasts. Her dark hair, cut unfashionably short, was tucked behind her ears, exposing her neck. A most attractive woman, and strong. Tifeo was a lucky man, he thought, not without a pang of envy. Something for his next confession, perhaps.

"We should do something," said Amedea, who seemed completely oblivious to the effect she was having on their guest. "We can't just pretend it never happened. Those poor people in the plane–it's as if they never existed!"

"That's why I'm here," repeated Renato. He realized that he had to take control of the conversation before Amedea worked herself into such a fury that she couldn't stop. A year later, and she was still incensed.

"We need a memorial," he said, now that he had their attention. "Something that will last, something that will preserve the memory of the victims."

"What are you thinking of?" asked Tifeo.

"I'm a priest," said Renato. "The only kind of memorial I can think of is a cross. A large cross, placed where the plane crashed, where those unfortunate souls met their Maker."

Amedea crossed herself. Exactly, thought Renato, watching Tifeo anxiously.

"That's a wonderful idea," she said. "Tifeo, don't you think so?"

"Brother Renato," Tifeo said, the slightest emphasis on Renato's title. "You know that my views on spiritual matters are somewhat different than yours. But we do live on the same mountain, even if in different parts."

He paused as Renato nodded to acknowledge and respect what he'd said.

"Like you and Amedea, I hate what happened that night. A memorial is the right way to respect the victims. But I have no symbol to offer as potent as yours. I agree that a cross would be the best solution."

Renato relaxed a bit, relieved that the first bridge had been crossed. He knew very well that Tifeo came to church only as a social obligation, and had been unsure of how his idea of a cross would be received by someone whose opinion mattered in the community.

"How do you suggest we do this?" asked Amedea.

"I was hoping you could tell me that," replied Renato. "The most durable material I can think of is metal, so…" His voice trailed away.

"…so you'd like me to make a cross." Tifeo finished the thought.

"That would be a wonderful thing."

"I can do that," Tifeo said. "My thoughts have been made uneasy by what has happened. When I walk the mountain, I can feel lost spirits all around me, crying out for recognition and a proper departure from this world. If you think a cross will help, I will make one for you."

"I am most grateful," said Renato. The second bridge was behind him. The idea of spirits roaming the mountain, troubled or otherwise, did not fit easily with what he was taught at the seminary. But he would say nothing of that if the cross would set Tifeo's mind at rest. And he was reminded every day that things worked differently in this remote part of a remote island.

Amedea looked worried. "How will the town react to this?" she asked. "People there would prefer not to have their conscience disturbed. No one talks about the crash any more, and there's no sign that anything ever happened now the plane has been removed. If anyone feels any guilt about what they did, silence is their best defence. A cross–a large cross, you say–would force them to remember something they'd rather forget."

"I agree with you," said Renato. "But to shed your guilt, you must first confront it. Only then can you atone. What happened is what it was, but it must not be forgotten. Our cross will be a reminder that great sin was done on that mountain–and once people have made their peace with God, then it will be a symbol of His grace and forgiveness, as always."

Tifeo said, "To pretend a crime never happened would be to condone it. Let's put up the cross to remind people of what happened, both the bad and the good. We should not forget the good because of the bad."

Renato watched Tifeo turn the engine part over in his huge hands.

"There will be some people who might need persuading," he said. "The mayor, for example. I will speak to them before we make any further plans. But I did not wish to discuss this with anyone else until I had talked with you. I am very glad that you have agreed to do this."

Finishing the last of his hot chocolate, he said, "I wonder if you could make the cross out of pieces from the plane? That would be appropriate, don't you think?"

After Cesare and Rosabella were married at the end of the previous summer, they assumed responsibility for the regular family Sunday lunch. Preparing a large meal was too much to ask of his mother after Carlo, her irascible but sausage-loving husband, dropped dead one day. He had rushed to a window to yell at some children who were making too much noise; when he turned away from the window, he clutched his chest and keeled over, dead as a lump of tufa before he hit the floor. Now he lay in unaccustomed peace in the graveyard with his father and his father's father, while Filomena, dressed in widow's black, spent her time at church preparing her soul for its final journey. When not on her knees, she sat in a chair carefully placed in one corner of the kitchen, complaining about her arthritis and the deplorable state of the world. Cesare and Rosabella thought that she would soon be reunited with her husband, and felt vaguely uncomfortable for hoping she'd do so without waiting too long.

On this Sunday morning in spring, Rosabella had hurried back from church to finish preparing the main course. Entering the kitchen, she was greeted by the rich smell of rabbit, rosemary and garlic. She had bought two rabbit *di fosso* from Adolfo the day before—bred in deep holes cut into the tufa up the mountain and fed on herbs and greens, the rabbits were a delicacy, perfect for Sunday lunch. Slow-cooked in an earthenware casserole while everyone was at church, the tender meat would fall off the bone. And because they were bred especially for eating, she didn't have to check the meat for lead pellets placed there by shotguns.

Putting on her apron, Rosabella took three round loaves down from the shelf and cut a circular opening at the top of each one. Scooping out the soft bread in the middle, she carved out three bread bowls. While she was doing this, Amedea entered, a little out of breath.

"You walk too fast," she said, putting on her own apron. "What can I do?"

"Let's lay the table before the others get back," said Rosabella. "We can finish in here when everyone is ready to sit down."

The two women chatted casually as they laid the table and put out the wine. Friends since their earliest schooldays, they enjoyed these times together.

A clattering from the front door signalled the arrival of the men, who had to walk more slowly to accompany Filomena. Cesare stuck his head into the kitchen and was promptly shooed out again. Neither Rosabella nor Amedea thought men had any useful role in a kitchen.

"Time for pasta," said Rosabella. "The *lumaconi*, I think." She liked how the rich juices collected inside the shell-shaped pieces and squirted into her mouth as she bit into them.

While the pasta was cooking, Rosabella washed the rabbit livers, mashed them with red vinegar, and added the mixture to the casserole. Finally, she took some of the juices from the casserole, combined them with enough loose bread to make a heavy broth, added some pasta, and filled each of the bread bowls with the thick, steaming mixture. The rest of the pasta went into the casserole.

Calling to the others to take their places at the table, Rosabella and Amedea brought all the food out to the dining room. The room quickly grew quiet as everyone gave their full attention to the food. Meals like this followed the tradition of centuries on Ischia. Rich or poor, people ate the same meals of simple food that came from the land around them, with fish on Fridays. Women went to extra lengths on Sunday, if only to make up for impoverished meals provided the rest of the week.

As plates were pushed away one after the other with satisfied sighs, Rosabella looked around the table. Cesare, her still-new husband, was at the other end, looking handsome and boyish. She knew his weaknesses as well as anyone, but felt that she could manage him and make him a better man, someone who would give her and her children the life she craved.

Baldassare sat beside Filomena, a dutiful youngest son taking care of his mother. Serafina sat on the other side of her mother, next to Cesare. Her dark grey dress sucked all the colour from the air around her. What a shrew, thought Rosabella, she's as sour as month-old milk. I'm glad she keeps house for her cousin Adolfo rather than living here with me and Cesare.

On the opposite side of the table, Cesare's cousin Tifeo sat with Amedea. They had started joining Cesare and Rosabella for Sunday lunch after the wedding. Ulisse had disappeared to Napoli for some mysterious reason; Adolfo was still unmarried and had become quite withdrawn in recent months. Rosabella didn't like Adolfo much, and thought that a wife would do him good.

Filomena was still determinedly mopping up the last drops of rich gravy as Cesare passed the wine around so people could fill their glasses.

"I have some good news," he announced. "We've bought some land on the road down to Forio, just before the Via Crescenzo Mattera. It's almost at the bottom of the mountain, but high enough that you can see over the roofs. We're going to build a house there and sell it. This is the beginning of our building business."

Serafina sniffed. "Who's going to buy a house down there?" she asked. "It's in the middle of nowhere. You'll build it, no one will buy it, and you'll be stuck." She adored Cesare, but her instinct with any new idea was to find fault with it.

Cesare glared at her. Rosabella could tell that he wanted people to congratulate him, not question his business judgment. Deciding to take the plunge had been difficult for him and she had worked hard to make him less anxious about what he was taking on. Criticism was the last thing he needed.

She stepped in before Cesare could say anything he might regret. "Houses down there are selling quite well," she said. "This is a nice piece of land. You can't build behind it because of the mountain, and it catches the breeze so it will be cool in summer."

"You won't get enough money to make it worthwhile," said Serafina.

"I think it's a wonderful idea," Amedea said. "I've heard that people are starting to buy again."

"Tourists," said Tifeo. "They'll start coming here soon, and they'll want somewhere to stay."

"Why would anyone come to Ischia?" asked Serafina. "There's nothing here except the mountain."

"Not so," said Tifeo. "We have beaches and hot springs. People will come for their health, just like they've done since the time of the Greeks. And we have the old castle."

"That's just a ruin. Who wants to see a pile of rocks growing out of the sea?"

"People are already going to Capri," said Baldassare. "There's nothing there to look at except a small cave. You can't even see that without taking a boat. If they can attract tourists, so can we."

"Well, I don't want tourists here. They'll spoil everything, make a mess. Things are perfectly fine just as they are."

Baldassare's patience ran out. "Serafina, can't you ever say anything good? You're always down at the mouth, you do nothing to help, and you always criticize people who are trying to do something useful."

"Well, if you don't want my opinion…" said Serafina. She dabbed at her eyes delicately with a small piece of lace. It had small pink and yellow butterflies embroidered around the edge. Baldassare snorted in disgust.

Tifeo said, "I agree with Amedea, this is a good thing to do, and a good time to do it. A group of Americans and English are living in Forio now. They're spending enough to feed the entire town, even though they're mostly artists and writers."

Rosabella said, "There are also rumours than an English musician has bought the old quarry outside Forio. He's going to build a house there, I can't think why."

"I've heard the same story," said Tifeo. "Amazing that a musician can afford that." Turning to Cesare, he asked, "Something I was curious about–how are you going to pay for the land and this house?"

"I've borrowed money from Adolfo," Cesare said without

hesitation. "His shop is doing well, and he's looking for other things to do with his money."

"I didn't know he was doing that well," said Tifeo. "A year ago, he was almost broke. But I suppose you can never tell when or why things change."

"He told me the other day that he's also thinking of opening a restaurant in Forio or Sant' Angelo," said Cesare, reinforcing the picture of Adolfo with money falling from his pockets.

"Cheaper in Sant' Angelo, but most tourists seem to stay in Forio," observed Baldassare. "How will he decide?"

Cesare shrugged. He said, "We're going to start building in a couple of weeks. The crew is all ready to go, we just need to get some supplies over from Napoli."

"That's wonderful," said Amedea. "This is going to be a big success."

Serafina raised her head to say something, caught Baldassare's eye, and subsided again. She glared at her lap, her lips pressed together in a thin, tight line.

"We'll start with just one house," said Cesare. "Build another with the profit, then another. We can make a good living at this, I think."

Rosabella said, "If there really are going to be a lot of tourists, maybe we should be thinking of guest houses where they can stay. Or even a small hotel."

"When the tourists start coming in big numbers, there'll be all sorts of money to make," said Tifeo.

Cesare was fidgeting with his wine glass. He said, "Let's take this one step at a time, shall we? We'll start with one house, see how it goes before we make any more big decisions."

Amedea said, "You'll never guess who came out to see us a little while ago. Brother Renato."

"Better him than Father Giovanni," said Rosabella. "He's a dried up old stick. But I must say, Brother Renato is quite good looking, even if he is a bit chubby. It's a pity about his vows…"

She looked down the table at Cesare, who gave her a mock scowl. He said, "He needs the vows to hide behind, he couldn't deal with the competition otherwise."

"It would be fun to find out how strong those vows are," said Rosabella, taunting him a bit more. Somewhat to her surprise, she had discovered that she liked sex and was good at it. Cesare was an enthusiastic if not yet skillful lover and she enjoyed discovering new ways to make their bed a more interesting place. Keeping Cesare on edge would pay off later in the day when everyone had left.

"Rosabella!" Amedea pretended to be shocked. Tifeo said nothing, remembering how Renato had looked at Amedea. Serafina gripped her handkerchief even more tightly and looked at her lap.

"Why did he want to see you?" Baldassare asked.

"Amedea, we shouldn't say too much about this," said Tifeo.

"Oh, nonsense," said Amedea. "We're with family here."

"Stop tantalising us," said Rosabella, reluctantly ending her game with Cesare. "What did he want?"

"You all have to keep this to yourselves," began Amedea. Without waiting for their consent, she went on. "He wanted to talk about the crash."

"What crash?" asked Serafina.

"The airplane crash, last year," said Amedea, impatiently. "All those poor people died, and there's nothing to respect their memory. He thinks we should put up a memorial to them, a cross."

"That's a terrible idea," said Serafina immediately.

"Why?" asked Amedea. It was her turn to feel aggrieved that a good idea was being attacked.

"It was their own fault for flying into the mountain," said Serafina. "Why should they get a memorial?"

Cesare said, "The tourists won't want to be told that such a terrible accident happened here. They won't come."

"If it's at the peak where the crash happened," Tifeo said, "tourists won't even know it's there. It's a long, steep climb from the coast and there's no reason to go up so high. They'll prefer lying on the beach or being at one of the hot springs."

"What about the people in town?" asked Cesare. "They won't want to be reminded of what happened."

"Brother Renato thought of that as well," said Amedea. "He thinks they should be reminded whether they want it or not. Terrible things were done, all that looting and mutilation, and no one has owned up to doing it. He hopes that putting a cross there will make people confess and repent."

"But Father Giovanni said the looting was the will of God."

Now it was Tifeo's turn to lose patience. "Cesare," he said, "you know that's rubbish as well as we do. Whoever was on the mountain after the crash is in terrible trouble. Looting, cutting up dead bodies, it's all a violation of what's right and proper. The people who did that should look to their souls. And so should the people who were looting the next morning."

"But we were all on the mountain then," said Cesare, "helping bring down the bodies. I was sorry Father Giovanni didn't mention that."

"True, but people were still looting when we were there. I can understand that, even if I think it was wrong. But what happened the night before was much worse. I cannot believe that God condones cutting fingers off a dead person."

"It's a good thing that none of us were involved in *that*," said Cesare. His voice was strong and sincere. "But why did Brother Renato come to you about all this?"

Tifeo said, "He wants me to make the cross. With steel that came from the plane, I've got plenty of it stored behind the forge."

Rosabella said, "I still have dreams about finding that poor baby. Caught under the bush like that, the poor little thing. Having a memorial up there is a lovely idea."

"Babies are lost to mothers all the time," said Serafina. "Why should this one be treated any differently? Why do you play God like this?" Her voice was fierce, demanding.

Surprised, Rosabella said, "She was ripped from her mother's body, Serafina. That was not normal. And none of us is playing God."

"How do you know it was a she?" Serafina seemed glad to seize on a small, unimportant detail.

"The usual way. We saw that it was a girl, before we wrapped her up. Why does that matter?"

"It doesn't." Serafina sounded tired. "Do what you want with the cross, none of it means anything to me."

Rosabella turned to Tifeo. "Did you agree to his request?"

"Of course," he replied. "Brother Renato has to talk to other people first, but I said that I would make him a cross."

Cesare said, "That's settled, then. When will you know to go ahead?"

"When he gets back from Napoli, I think," said Tifeo. "He's going there in the next week or two. In the meantime, I've started to collect pieces of the plane to use. The cross will be nearly three metres high, so I need a lot of material."

Filomena had followed the conversation with a friendly but vacant smile on her face, turning to whoever was talking. She was very deaf and found it hard to understand what people were saying at the best of times. A rapid conversation with raised voices, echoing from the high ceiling and tiled floor, was beyond her. But she knew one thing for certain—that lunch was not yet over.

She said, "Is there any dessert?"

Chapter Fourteen

CESARE FELT UNCOMFORTABLE every time he went to Adolfo's shop. He knew that his family wanted nothing to do with his cousin, believing the rumours and innuendo about the crash. Baldassare and Tifeo made it very clear how much they disapproved of what they thought he'd done, and Rosabella just didn't like him.

But Cesare grew up with Adolfo. His cousin had been like an older brother, showing him how to set a snare for rabbits and how to skin and dismember the ones they actually caught (not many, but enough that they kept on trying), and looking out for him in the schoolyard. Serafina was very much the older sister and far too quick to correct him when he did something wrong. Cesare knew from experience that she'd report any major transgressions to their parents, constraining the natural exuberance of a small boy. Baldassare was the youngest child, his mother's pet, and rather serious. Not interested in playing with either of his siblings, Cesare had gravitated to his older cousins, who welcomed him into their small group.

The sun was still warm on his back as Cesare walked up to the shop for his usual end of day drink with Adolfo. The stone walls glowed honey-warm, and the doorways were full of old folk soaking up heat and warming their fragile bones after the cool, damp winter not long past.

The smell of fresh hay wafted down from the fields just above town, the first cut of the season. On just such an evening long ago, Cesare remembered, he was out in the fields with Adolfo and his two brothers, bursting with energy on a beautiful day in late spring. Finding an empty wine bottle at the side of the mule track, they balanced it on top of a dry stone wall and took turns throwing stones at it. Ulisse easily won the contest, so Adolfo, Tifeo and Cesare jumped on him. Tussling like squirming puppies in the newly-cut grass, they were soon dirty and scratched from loose stones on the ground. Tired of wrestling, Cesare pulled away. "Look," he cried, "we're surrounded!" It was true. The stooks of freshly-stacked hay looked like Bourbon soldiers standing threateningly around them. "We have to do something," cried Tifeo. "Attack!" He leapt to his feet and ran headlong at the nearest soldier, knocking it flying. The others joined in without thinking and before long, the four comrades in arms had overcome their foes, all of them vanquished and scattered on the ground. Lying on their backs and sobbing with laughter, they didn't hear the farmer coming up the track.

"What the fuck are you stupid kids doing?"

Scrambling to their feet, the boys were confronted by a stocky man, looking with appalled fury at what they had done to his neatly piled stooks. "What in the name of the sacred Madonna and all the saints did you think? Have you no respect?" The farmer looked as if he might attack them with the scythe he was holding.

"We thought they were sol—," began Cesare, still thinking it was all a huge joke.

"Shut up, Cesare," said Adolfo. Then, to the farmer, "Our game got out of hand, sir. We apologise."

"Apologies won't restack my hay," said the farmer. He pointed at Cesare. "I know your parents. What do you think they'll do when I tell them about this? Do you think they want their son undoing the work we farmers do up here?"

Cesare finally realized that he was in serious trouble. "Oh, no," he said, "please don't say anything to them." He was only seven years old and this was all too much for him. He began crying.

"For God's sake," said the farmer. "Crying won't get you anywhere."

"It wasn't his fault," said Adolfo. "I started it. But we didn't mean to... to do this." He waved at the destruction on the field. "Please forgive us."

"Forgive?" the farmer said. His voice rose with indignation. "First you apologise, then you ask me to forgive you. That's not nearly good enough, not when my hay is still scattered on the ground. That took me all afternoon to stack."

"We'll re-stack it for you," said Adolfo. "We've done it before, we know how to do it."

"If you've done it before, you should have known better than to knock it all over."

"You're right, sir, we should. But we didn't know when to stop. We're truly sorry."

"You're old enough to understand what you were doing." The anger had drained from the farmer. Now he was just tired at the end of a long day. All he wanted was to go home and have a glass of wine with the supper waiting for him. "I have to come by here at first light tomorrow morning," he said. "The hay must be stacked properly by then. If it is, we'll say no more about this. But if it's not…" The unspoken threat hovered in the air like a swarm of hornets.

"We'll get it done, sir," said Adolfo. "And we promise not to do anything like this again."

"Well, then." The farmer looked at the position of the sun. "You'd better get to work, you don't have much time."

The incident had cemented the bond between the four boys. Getting into and out of trouble together had been frightening but exhilarating, especially since they'd survived the shared danger. Cesare knew that he would have received a good thrashing if his father learned what had happened; his uncle would have delivered an even worse beating to the others. As the eldest, Adolfo was their natural leader, a position that was reinforced by saving them from both the farmer and their parents. Cesare knew that he could rely on all of three of his cousins for protection.

He had been sorry when Adolfo became an altar boy at the urging of his deeply religious mother. It must have been the intense exposure to Catholic doctrine, because it only took a few months before Adolfo became more serious and somewhat withdrawn. Or maybe it was the changes brought about by adolescence, and meeting his father's expectation that he would soon take over the family butcher's shop. Either way, he was not nearly as much fun to be with.

But the bonds established in those early, carefree days had lasted, until Tifeo had become alienated from Adolfo soon after the incident with the stooks. Cesare never understood what the problem was, and didn't know how to walk this tightrope, his loyalty to Adolfo and Ulisse on one side and that to Tifeo and the rest of his family on the other. It was like the log they once used to cross over a deep stream–any betrayal meant falling one side or the other from the log down to the cold water and rocks below.

After Ulisse left to work for the Camorra in Napoli, Cesare found it awkward to maintain the routine of going to Adolfo's shop at the end of the day for a small aperitivo. Ulisse usually didn't say much, but his presence at the table was a reassuring continuity for Cesare and he missed him. But Adolfo had insisted, so Cesare still made the daily walk up the hill to the shop once he'd cleaned up after a day building the house in Forio.

Adolfo was cleaning the counter when Cesare came into the shop. This was his unvarying ritual at the end of the day, and Cesare knew that his grappa would have to wait until Adolfo was satisfied that the counter was immaculately clean.

Eventually, Adolfo finished washing his hands, another habit, and came over to the table carrying two full glasses. They chatted casually for a while, then Cesare asked how Ulisse was doing in Napoli.

"He says well," replied Adolfo. "But you'll soon be able to ask him yourself–he wrote to say he's planning on coming back for a few days later this month."

"That's good news," said Cesare. "I'd like to see him again."

"If you can drag yourself away from Rosabella," Adolfo said. He sounded resentful, bitter.

"Adolfo," said Cesare, trying to be conciliatory, "You know I have family obligations now. And the house business is going well, that's taking a lot of time. But why don't you join us for Sunday lunch? I'm sure everyone would like to see you there."

"Are you joking? Your wife would like to feed me rat poison, and my little brother Tifeo gets on his high horse every time he sees me. So does Baldassare. I don't know which of them is worse."

"No, no," protested Cesare. The log over the stream was getting more treacherous by the minute. "We're all family. Rosabella doesn't know you like I do, she'll come around in time. And she's told me several times she'd like the whole family together for Sunday lunch."

"And holier-than-thou Tifeo and Baldassare? What do they think?"

Cesare knew very well what Tifeo and Baldassare thought of Adolfo, and why, but had no idea how to reconcile their differences.

He said, "Tifeo was at our house for lunch on Sunday. Brother Renato has asked him to make a cross as a memorial to put up where the plane crashed. Tifeo said yes, said he'd use metal he's salvaged from the plane."

"That's a terrible idea! Why can't they let sleeping dogs lie? People are starting to forget all about that damned crash. This will just bring it all back."

"I don't like this any more than you do. I spoke against it, but everyone thought it was a good idea. Except Serafina, but no one listens to her."

"You couldn't even persuade water to run downhill," Adolfo said, throwing up his hands in disgust.

Cesare flinched. He said, "You know that no one can argue Tifeo out of something once he's made his mind up."

"That fucking plane," Adolfo said. "It's all in the past, now. If we just gave it time, people will stop caring about what happened. Why must that stupid priest keep reminding everyone?"

"He fears for our souls, apparently. That's what Amedea said."

"After Father Giovanni told us it was all God's will? That young priest had better be careful."

"Maybe, but Tifeo agreed with him. They're convinced that... taking things was wrong, all of it." Cesare couldn't bring himself to say out loud what they both knew.

"Let them think what they like. I'll take care of my own soul, it's none of their business. And you take care of yours."

Not if that meant confessing to the priest, Cesare thought. He had no intention of doing anything that might draw unwelcome attention to his involvement. So far, accusing fingers were pointing at Adolfo and Ulisse, away from him, and he wanted to keep it that way. If people knew what he'd done, Rosabella would never forgive him and neither would the rest of the family. What would happen then to his new house-building business? And he was terrified of what Adolfo and Ulisse might do if they found out about the locked box now hidden in his workshop.

After Cesare had left, Adolfo poured himself another aperitive and sat brooding. Despite his bravado with Cesare, his growing doubts about what they had done troubled him. Hiding behind Father Giovanni's cynical reassurances about God's will was all very well, but didn't help him sleep. Staring into the darkness late at night, he kept seeing teeth with gold fillings, and rings, and money with strange writing, and severed fingers. Other memories he kept in the shadows, where they belonged. And now the new priest in town seemed determined to make his life even more difficult.

Why wouldn't Brother Renato accept his offer to make a substantial contribution to the church? It was as close to atonement as Adolfo could get, a down payment on redemption for the next life, and the priest threw it back in his face. Wasn't it his job to smooth the rocky road to Heaven?

Adolfo wanted nothing to do with Father Giovanni and now he realized that the younger priest was just as bad, quite willing to substitute his own judgment for those of the God he was supposed to represent. And hypocritical, by the Madonna, saying that Father Giovanni's refusal to bury Paolo was 'regrettable'. This was just another example of priests refusing to help people in need of spiritual assistance.

Despite his unease about his actions after the crash, Adolfo consoled himself with the thought that he'd never knowingly harmed other people. The people on the mountain were dead and could take no offence, something that the two priests could not claim for their victims.

But this small moral victory didn't make him feel any better. Instead, Adolfo felt sorry for himself, being tormented by forces beyond his control. Brother Renato and Tifeo would put up their damn cross and there was nothing he could do to stop them.

Brother Renato enjoyed getting to know Tifeo. The blacksmith was the only person in town with whom he could relax, forget that he was a priest, and have a real conversation rather than exchanging banal small talk. He'd been surprised the first time this happened, not expecting a blacksmith in a small village to be intelligent and well read, but now he realized that Tifeo was both and relished their time together. He knew that Tifeo was considerably more pagan that he should tolerate, but he could sense the reverence for the mountain, and felt confident that he was with a good man. He'd seen Tifeo in church, and clung to the faint hope that maybe he could bring him around to a truer faith.

It was another beautiful late spring morning as they walked up the hill, leaving Fontana behind them. More and more, Renato looked for opportunities to get out of town. He always felt cleansed and closer to God when walking the mule tracks high on the mountain.

He was glad that Tifeo was coming with him on this occasion. He knew very well that Demonte was angry with him and the Church and hoped that the shepherd would be reassured when he saw someone he knew and trusted.

Passing Adolfo's butcher shop, Tifeo said, "Adolfo came to see me the other day. He wanted to pay for the cross."

"What did you tell him?" Renato asked, wanting to understand more about how things were done in this small, primitive town.

"I refused, of course. He'd be paying with dirty money, and we want no part of that. It would tarnish the cross, dilute its power to remind and heal. The victims and the mountain deserve a better memorial than that."

Renato remembered Adolfo's clumsy attempt to buy an indulgence. Was this something covered by the confidences required by confession, he wondered. Hesitating, he said, "He tried something similar with me. I also turned him down. His understanding of theological matters is—inexact."

Then, to obscure what might be seen as an indiscretion, he hurried on, "But he does seem very troubled. I can say this, even though he has not come to me for confession."

Tifeo laughed briefly, with no hint of humour. "He has much to be troubled about," he said.

"About the crash?"

"Indeed."

"Are you sure of this?"

"As sure as I can be. He was involved in the looting and, I think, the mutilation. So was Ulisse. I don't know about Cesare—he's weak, but I don't think he's capable of cutting fingers from a corpse. He's still family, so I take care not to enquire too closely."

"You're quite open about Adolfo and Ulisse." A question.

"Yes, but only with people I can trust. They're my brothers, so things they do reflect on me. If they succeed at something, people feel better about me. And if they do something bad... But I'm the youngest brother, so nothing I do changes how others may think of them. Cesare is a cousin, people can separate us more easily."

Renato walked on in silence, trying to absorb this. He was considerably shorter than Tifeo, and had to hurry a bit to keep up.

"This is a small town on a small island," Tifeo continued. "Many things here change very slowly. People who lived here several hundred years ago would think nothing had changed if they were to come back. We farm the same way, mules shit—sorry, relieve themselves—in the streets the same way, our houses look the same. Even the church is the same. Our oil lamps may be more modern and the cobblestones in town are only one hundred years old, but we have no electricity, no motor cars, no cinema... The modern world has not yet arrived here. So why should we be surprised that people still see each other in the same way? People are poor, and rely on their family above all. Without family, we are like dead leaves being driven by the wind."

Renato said, "Then should not forgiveness start within the family?"

"He has not harmed me. I have nothing to forgive."

"Not directly, but perhaps he has hurt your family's reputation, stained your honour? Is that not something to be forgiven?"

"Renato, please stop beating a dead horse. Forgiving Adolfo is not something I give much thought to and, with respect, neither should you."

"I'm sorry," Renato said. "It's just that divine forgiveness is such an important part of my faith."

Tifeo stopped abruptly in the middle of the track. They were now high above town, surrounded by open stretches of low shrubs, with large boulders scatted across the hillside like a giant's marbles. The landscape around them was wild, hard, and very beautiful. The low morning sun moulded the humps and hollows with clear, warm light. Renato was panting a bit from the exertion of keeping up with Tifeo and took several deep breaths to recover.

"Look around you," Tifeo said. "Like life in town, this hasn't changed very much in hundreds of years. People may go to your church, but they still believe that gods and spirits live up here. You and I can be friends, but you have to accept that I answer to different, more ancient gods than yours."

"And do your gods forgive the way mine does?"

"My gods are slow to forgive, and think yours too quick and too generous."

My God gave us his only son, Renato wanted to shout, what gives yours the right to criticize mine? He beat down the urge to yell in Tifeo's face.

"Why is that?" he asked as calmly as he could.

"Because something that is given so freely, at such little cost to your god or the sinner, is worthless. Your god forgives all sins, be they great or small, with equal alacrity. And he says that his forgiveness is infinite. That alone makes it worthless.

"People think they can confess to the priest, do their penance, and the slate will be wiped clean. Then they go out and sin all over again, as if nothing happened. But the harm they do to themselves and others cannot be undone so easily. The stains build up and harden, and soon cannot be scraped off like old paint. Forgiveness is more complicated than simply going to weekly confession."

Renato was finding it hard to breath. Such blasphemy was hard to take, especially from someone he would have as a friend. This was different from arguing at the seminary, when you knew at least that everyone shared the same faith. He was very aware that the next few minutes would determine how his new friendship would turn out, to say nothing of his ministry in Fontana. If he had to swallow this bitter potion, so be it.

He realized that Tifeo was waiting for his response.

"And what would your gods say?" he managed to ask.

Tifeo nodded, clearly appreciating the effort Renato was making. He said, "My gods were roaming these hills long before yours appeared, and their roots go deep. If we mortals harm each other but do no disrespect to the gods, they are not interested, except perhaps as entertainment. In such cases, forgiveness is a matter for the victim and the person who did them harm.

"On the other hand, be very careful not to offend these gods. They are quick to take offence and slow to forgive. Their forgiveness is hard-won, and sometimes withheld altogether when they would rather have their revenge. Just like Italians, just like Ischians."

This is neither the time nor the place to have this debate, Renato thought, we should talk of other things.

"I think that Adolfo is much troubled," he said, "and possibly trying to find a way to atone for things he has done. I may have been too hasty in pushing him away, to deny him the opportunity to repent. It was not for me to judge, I should be clearing the path for him, making it easier, not harder, for him to confess his sins before God, repent, and atone."

"Adolfo is too impetuous, too inclined to act before thinking. I don't know if he is troubled, or looking for forgiveness. But he has a big problem if he is, because the people he mutilated and robbed are all dead. There is no easy way to reach them and beg for their forgiveness."

"So what do we do?"

"He did very bad, terrible things, violating the natural order," said Tifeo. "No decent person can say otherwise. As did Ulisse, we shouldn't forget him. They brought disgrace to the community and to their family. Mind you, the community, some of them, also brought disgrace upon themselves. Adolfo and Ulisse aren't the only ones."

"Surely Adolfo is not all bad?"

"Of course not, no one is all bad. He gives bed and board to Serafina, who would try the patience of Santa Restituta herself."

"That seems a generous act."

"They belong together."

"So what do we do?" repeated Renato.

"We should start with the memorial," said Tifeo. "After that, let's see."

"And if I can help ease Adolfo's soul, I will. Let's see whose god can do him the most good."

"If either of them chooses to ask for the help of our gods, they may or may not listen. They might say, if he got himself into this mess, let him get himself out of it."

"I prefer my God to your gods," said Renato. "They sound too temperamental and unreliable, too difficult."

Despite his light tone, he was amazed at the conversation. Where was the bolt of lightning, he wondered, unsure if it should strike him for allowing such heresy to be said out loud, or Tifeo for his pagan beliefs. Best to keep it all from Father Giovanni at his next confession, he thought. The older priest would be appalled at his failure to manage the conversation better. Why then did he feel that he'd made progress in his relationship with the pagan Tifeo?

"Let's move along," he said. "We're losing time here."

They just managed to catch Demonte as he was about to leave the enclosure to take his sheep out to graze. Leaning on the rickety gate, Demonte waited at the entrance as the two men come towards him.

Demonte shook hands with Tifeo, ignoring Renato. "You're up early, and what's he doing here?"

"He wants to talk with you," replied Tifeo. "You should listen to what he has to say."

"What's he got that I should waste my time with? Look at him, he can't even walk up here without having a seizure."

"Brother Renato is different," said Tifeo, "more flexible than his predecessors."

Flexible, thought Renato. Is that supposed to be a compliment?

"Well, priest," said Demonte, his arms crossed. "Tell me why you've come. Then be on your way."

Renato cleared his throat nervously. He was about to do something he'd never done before as a priest and he didn't know if he could do it without making things even worse.

"Demonte," he started.

"I know who I am. Get on with it!"

"When we last met, you were very angry with me. With the Church. I came here to tell you that I think I understand why, and that you have every right to be angry."

Demonte examined Renato with suspicion.

"This better be good," he said.

"I want to apologise to you," said Renato. "Three times. Once for myself, for not being properly sympathetic for your loss. Once for Father Giovanni, who was too unforgiving, too rigid when he refused Paolo a proper burial. And once for the Church, who let you down."

Tifeo raised his eyebrows in surprise.

Renato ploughed on. Now he was started, he had to finish the speech he'd so carefully thought through.

"And I want also to apologise to Paolo," he said, "wherever he may be. Whatever agony made him... do what he did... must have been more than he could bear. He did not deserve to be treated like that."

Now it was done, Renato's first reaction was overwhelming relief. He knew very well that he had missed an opportunity at Adolfo's shop—worse, he had made Demonte's pain worse. Apologising was the first step in undoing that damage.

Demonte's expression didn't change. "Words are all very well." he said, "but they're cheap. According to your precious Church, my Paolo was unfit to be buried properly and will suffer for eternity. But any sins he committed were small, not important. Nothing that would justify being condemned like that. Nothing, you hear? Words won't change any of that. So if that's all, you'd best be gone." Turning his back on Renato, he started walking away.

"What if we can rescue him?" asked Renato. So close! He didn't want to lose Demonte just yet.

"What?"

"All Soul's Day is coming up, the Day of the Dead," Renato said, "a day when we pray for all souls departed this world. We can pray for Paolo, repent on his behalf, pay his debt. God will see that he was a good person, then his soul may leave Purgatory and enter the joys of Heaven."

"You can do that?"

"And will. It's the least I can do. The Church did you and Paolo harm, let Her now make amends."

Renato was careful not to lay too much fault at Father Giovanni's feet. The older priest was his superior and it would not do for Renato to undermine his authority any further. As it was, he felt very uncomfortable with what he was doing. The Church was supposed to be the final arbiter of what was right and what wrong. The Pope's word was infallible, was it not? And did not every priest, from Rome to the smallest parish in the furthest corners of the Church's reach, have to share that moral certainty? Without that, how could their flock be confident in their direction? Acknowledging even the slightest possibility that the Church might not always be right was dangerous. Once people started questioning what the Church taught, where might it lead? Who else could provide and interpret the signposts that pointed the way to Heaven?

I'm a priest, he thought, with the obligation to protect the Church and Her authority. Why, then, was he driven to concede that a mistake had been made?

His answer became clear when he saw Demonte's face. The shepherd's attitude of suspicion and hostility had softened, replaced by growing hope.

"And you think that Paolo's soul can be saved?"

"With prayer and sincere repentance, yes. But we should do this on All Soul's Day, that is the right occasion for prayers for the dead."

Demonte nodded.

"Come to the service in the morning," said Renato. "Then we will go to where Paolo is buried and take care of his soul."

"I could not protect Paolo when he was alive," Demonte said. "Perhaps this will make up for that. We'll see."

On their way back to town, Renato became lost in his thoughts. Eventually, Tifeo said, "You did well, back there. No one dressed as you are has ever apologised before, especially to a poor shepherd."

"Did I? I feel that I have betrayed my Church."

"How can that be, when you restored hope? I don't know if there's a Heaven or Hell, or where Paolo's soul has gone, and I don't know if your god will listen to your prayers. But I saw the look on Demonte's face. Refusing Paolo a proper burial was wrong, this will put that right."

"I am accustomed to feeling guilty for my own actions," said Renato. "I know how to deal with that, how to confess and repent before God. But this is different. Why should I feel guilty for what someone else did?"

"Because it was done in the name of your Church."

Renato groaned. "That does nothing to make me feel any better."

"Renato, this is very simple. You felt guilty about the harm done to Demonte and Paolo. You apologised. You're going to do something that will undo the harm, and Demonte is half-way to forgiving you and the Church. And you did all this without invoking your god. Not once have you spoken about seeking his forgiveness for what was done, perhaps because it was supposedly done in his name."

"I was taught that forgiveness was God's business, his gift to bestow upon us poor sinners. I should have called for His help."

"But gods have nothing to do with this. Guilt and forgiveness are strands in a rope that tie two people together forever. Like marriage, this is a bond that no one else can share, no one, not even the gods. All they can do is interfere, get in the way of two people trying to untangle the rope that binds them. The best thing the gods can do is stand back and let them sort it out for themselves."

"The Church teaches that what really matters is our relationship with God. Everything we do on this earth is directed at salvation."

"I think not. Before we meet our gods on the other side, we must live our lives here. That can be difficult, sometimes. I have to believe that our gods look with favour on those who live good lives, in peace with their neighbours. Unsnarling ropes by themselves, without divine help. If the gods help you resolve your problems, how can you say you have cleaned up your own mess?"

None of this helped Renato one bit. He accepted that the Pope's word was final and infallible. But he was starting to realize that the Church consisted of people like himself, flawed and all too prone to making mistakes. It followed that, just as he erred, so could other priests. As had Father Giovanni.

When a priest made a mistake, especially one that harmed someone, whose shoulders carried the burden of repairing the damage? Surely not God, that would be asking too much of even a benevolent, all-powerful deity. No, it had to be a priest. If not the erring priest, then his brother in Christ, to ensure that the Church could be trusted to safeguard the wellbeing of Her children. The Church had to clean up Her own mess. If that meant relying on his sympathies as a human being to correct an misguided application of Church doctrine, that's what he had to do.

"Tifeo," he said, "I don't know whether I should thank you for showing me new ways of thinking about things, or condemn you as an agent of the Devil. Either way, thank you for your help with Demonte. He wouldn't have listened to me without you there.

"But I must ask one more thing of you. You will appreciate the risks I am taking with this. Father Giovanni would be most displeased to hear about it. He would tell the Bishop if he knew and then I would be in real trouble. So I must rely on your discretion. May I sleep tonight without this worry?"

Tifeo laughed, a welcome sound after the seriousness of the conversation. He said, "You have no idea how little he cares for my opinion. If I told him what you did with Demonte or recounted our discussion word for word, he would dismiss it all out of hand; he'd accuse me of trying to sow discord between two priests and discredit the Church. No, I will not tell him. However, I will speak to Demonte to ensure his discretion. You may sleep well tonight, and tomorrow."

Much relieved, Renato said, "In that case, let's get back to town. It is time for lunch, and this unworthy priest would enjoy a glass of wine with his friend."

Chapter Fifteen

BROTHER RENATO ALWAYS ENJOYED EARLY MORNINGS. High on the mountain, the air was still cool before the stifling heat made the narrow streets of Fontana feel like a bread oven, even this early in the summer. Closing the high wooden door behind him, Renato glanced up. Pale blue and entirely clear of clouds, the sky promised another fine day.

Putting his small bag on the ground, he locked the door. Packing the bag for his trip to Napoli hadn't taken long; some clean underwear and socks, toiletries, his Bible. His belongings were as simple and humble as his room, two narrow flights of stairs above the street. It held his bed with a crucifix on the wall above the head, a small chest of drawers for his clothes, a comfortable chair beside the window where he could read, and a small rug. The rug had once been a vibrant red with a blue pattern around the edge, but was now faded and a little threadbare in places. It had been on his bedroom floor when he was a child and he took it everywhere as his only tangible connection with his family in far away Siena.

Renato carefully put the key at the bottom of the bag and set off up the street. He had more than enough time to walk over the mountain and down to Lacco Ameno before catching the ferry to Napoli. Leaving this soon was not part of his plan, but he had woken early after a mostly sleepless night, and was glad of the opportunity to clear his mind and think things through as he walked.

Setting off towards Adolfo's shop up the hill, he was conscious of the silence, the closed and locked doors, the windows so carefully shuttered against the unseen perils of night air. What secrets are hidden behind those blank walls, he wondered. How can anyone truly know what lies in another man's soul?

He passed the widow Bonome, dressed in her customary black, energetically swabbing her doorstep as if she could wash away all the sins of the world. Surprised at seeing him up so early, she muttered a greeting; distracted by his thoughts, he barely managed a reply. Other than her, the streets were empty.

Leaving the town behind him, Renato lengthened his stride. The air was even fresher up here, and he breathed deeply to clear out his lungs, enjoying the sweet smell of orange blossom. A few sheep grazed calmly behind the stone wall alongside the track, sharing the field with a tethered mule.

As he had done throughout the night, Renato examined the events of the previous afternoon, trying to decide exactly what he'd seen.

Father Giovanni had led afternoon Mass as usual, with Renato assisting in his normal role. One of the altar boys was sick, so the younger boy had to do double duty.

"You had to work hard today," Renato said to him in the sacristy afterwards. "You did well."

The boy smiled shyly. He had only been a server for a few months, and seemed to be getting more serious as he became accustomed to his new responsibilities.

"I'll be off," Renato said to Father Giovanni. "I must pick up my laundry before packing. I'll be back in plenty of time for Mass on Sunday."

"Please give my respects to the Bishop," said the older priest. "And tell him that we miss seeing him, that he is always welcome to visit his flock here."

As Renato went to the door, Father Giovanni asked the altar boy to stay behind a little, to be coached on the right way to present the various objects required for the Eucharist. Giovanni liked each object to be passed to him in a particular sequence and the boy had mixed them up.

The laundress had his clean clothes waiting for him, neatly bundled and wrapped. She liked the small level of prestige that came from washing a priest's clothes, even if it was mostly underwear. Renato could not afford to have his shirts washed and ironed more often than once a week. He did his usual dance with the laundress, politely but firmly avoiding her clumsy attempts to pry some secret from him. He didn't have many secrets–he was a priest, after all–and he knew very well that anything he told her would soon be repeated all over town, with fictitious but salacious detail added for theatrical effect at each retelling.

Back in his room, he unpacked the laundry, putting some clothes to one side for his trip and the rest in the appropriate drawer. Thinking that he had time to read a few verses before going down to dinner with his landlady, he realized that he had left his Bible at the church. Chiding himself for his forgetfulness, he briefly debated just leaving it there until he returned from Napoli, before deciding that he had to go back and get it. Otherwise he'd have nothing to read, and besides, what kind of priest would he be, travelling without a Bible?

The massive door at the entrance to the church made its usual squeal as he opened it. Loud enough for the dead to rise and dance the tarantella, he thought, and resolved to get it oiled after he got back from Napoli, even if Father Giovanni didn't seem to care. He stepped into the cool darkness inside, closed the door behind him—another loud complaint from the rusty hinges—and paused to let his eyes make the transition from bright sunlight. The air in the church was still heavy with incense.

Once he could see again, he started down the side passage, past the diorama of our Saviour's birth, towards the sacristy. To his surprise, he could see light under the door. Before he could open it, the door was flung open. The altar boy—what was his name, Guido?—rushed past him, saying something that Renato couldn't quite hear. Confused, Renato watched the boy run down the church, use all his strength to open the heavy door, and hurry out into the square, leaving the door open.

"What was that all about?" he asked as he entered the sacristy.

"Oh, he realized that he was late for supper," replied Father Giovanni after a short, uncomfortable silence. He seemed distracted and uneasy, looking around the room as if he'd lost something. He smoothed the front of his cassock.

"He's not the most intelligent boy we've had here," Giovanni went on. "I explained that the bread must be placed on the altar before the wine, not after, as he did this afternoon. Christ said, 'Eat my flesh and drink my blood,' did he not? The sequence matters, but the child didn't seem to care."

He shook his head, inviting Renato to share his despair at the challenge of overcoming the boy's lack of interest.

"And what brings you back here?" he asked. "I thought you were packing." He sounded almost accusing.

Renato gestured at his Bible, which he had picked up from the table where he'd left it. "I forgot this," he explained. It was obvious that the older priest wanted him to leave as soon as possible. "I should be getting home myself, supper will be on the table."

Giovanni nodded, seemingly relieved that he would have the sacristy to himself again.

As Renato reached the highest point on the track before it swooped and snaked down the other side of the mountain, he felt bewildered by what had happened. Why did it take so long to explain the reasons for putting bread on the altar before the wine? Why had Guido left in such haste? Being late for supper didn't seem enough to warrant such hurried confusion. Did the boy say, "We did nothing" as he rushed past? Or was it "I did nothing"?

The only reason for all this that Renato could come up with was so distressing that he couldn't hold it in his head for more than a brief moment, preferring to hope that there was another, simpler, more innocent explanation.

He paused before heading down to Lacco Ameno and his ride to Napoli. The rising sun warmed his back as he enjoyed the view laid out below. Green treetops tumbled down the steep mountainside, leading to small fields and then to the chaotic red roofs of the town. Beyond the port, the deep blue waters of the Bay lay quiet.

Despite his troubled thoughts, he was content to be out in the open, the clear sky above him seeming like a window to Heaven. The new day was young enough that it held only promise, another reason that just after dawn was his favourite time of day. I should enjoy being out here, he thought, and thank the good Lord for the privilege of being alive on such a wonderful morning. Resolving to put his dark thoughts to one side, he set off again, new energy in his step.

Cesare was hot, tired and angry when he arrived home that afternoon. The electrician he'd hired for the new house on Via Crescenza Mattera didn't know his arse from his big toe, something that quickly became apparent when Cesare asked him about the cat's cradle of wires in the small utility room. In a rare demonstration of common sense, the new Electricity Committee for Ischia had chosen Forio as one of the first towns to be electrified on the island, reasoning that this would further encourage foreigners to stay there. Seeing the opportunity to increase the value of the house, Rosabella had persuaded Cesare to risk installing electric lights. His foreman, a pugnacious little man who'd been building houses on Ischia all his life, thought he was crazy, and said so. We've been building houses the same way for a hundred years, he said, we know what works. Why change? Were the old ways not good enough any more?

Caught between his wife and his foreman, Cesare had been forced to choose. Now he had a new foreman, someone who wanted a job more than he wanted to be right. Having chosen, Cesare showed complete commitment to introducing modern innovations like electrical lights, but he was getting tired of fighting conservatives and incompetents every day. Paying someone to learn a new trade was just one more cross to bear. At the end of another long day, he wanted nothing more than to clean up and then head up to Adolfo's for a quiet drink.

Going upstairs to the bedroom, he found Rosabella packing his case for his trip to Napoli the next morning.

"Hard day?" she asked, seeing his face.

"The usual shite," he said, stripping off his shirt and throwing it in the corner. "Jesu, those people wear me out."

"You mustn't say things like that," she said, coming over and ignoring his dismissive shrug. Wrapping her arms around him, she pressed her breasts against his bare skin, breathing in his musky scent. Cesare could feel himself getting hard, pushing against her stomach. She kissed his chest, then licked his nipples, slick with sweat.

Cesare said, "This is the wrong time of month," trying to resist the urge to throw her on the bed and fuck her silly.

"It's the right time, if you want to make a baby," she replied, her voice husky.

"Oh, no," he said, pushing her away. "We've been over this a thousand times." His voice began rising. "We have to wait until the business is up and running."

"And when will that be?" she asked angrily. "'We have to wait', you keep saying. Until when? When will you decide to become a father?"

"When I don't have to spend every day making sure the idiots who work for me don't screw up everything they touch." His anger rose, fuelled by frustrated lust and the resentment and self-pity caused by his useless workers. "If it wasn't for me, nothing would ever get done, or done right."

"So you hired the wrong people," she shouted. "Whose fault is that? And why does it mean I can't have a baby?"

Downstairs in the kitchen, Serafina stood rooted to the floor, able to hear every word of the fight. The door to the house was generally unlocked during the day, and she'd come over to borrow some flour for the limoncello cake she wanted to make as a treat for Adolfo.

Listening to Cesare fight with Rosabella was an unexpected but welcome bonus. She'd never really cared for her sister-in-law, thinking that she wasn't good enough for her younger brother. Too flamboyant, and just look at that flaming mass of red hair, always looking uncombed, you'd think she'd crawled backwards through a hedge. And how she dressed! Bright colours, even on Sundays, and showing far too much bosom. Which, Serafina also thought, was too large.

But what Serafina really resented was Rosabella's very vocal enthusiasm for sex. Several times she'd come over to the house to borrow something, only to stand shocked in the kitchen as the sounds of very active lovemaking came down the stairs. Serafina knew that sex was dangerous. Something to endure, she thought, not enjoy. So she hated hearing Rosabella tell Cesare to do this, or do something else harder, or softer, and, Oh Dio, can you do that again? But she'd learned when they liked to have sex, which was far too often, and, despite her repeated resolutions to avoid those times, kept coming back, a small piece of her shrivelling and drying up each time.

And now this talk of babies! Did Rosabella not realize the problems that having a child would bring, even if she survived the messy, painful and dangerous process of hosting and growing a living thing in her belly and then pushing it out from between her legs? But no, she seemed to think that producing a squalling infant would make her complete as a woman. Serafina couldn't bear the idea of a baby in the family, and the thought of smug, self-satisfied Rosabella suckling one with those big udders made her want to retch.

The fight upstairs seemed to have run out of air.

"I'll only be gone for a few days," Cesare was saying. "It will be safe again when I get back."

"A few days," said Rosabella, "an eternity without my big, strong Cesare." A little girl voice, making Serafina wince.

"Think of what we can do afterwards," said Cesare, and Serafina could hear the small boy bragging inside the grown-up voice. "We'll give that bed a good workout."

Serafina moved quietly to the door, then paused as Cesare continued.

"With any luck," he said, "I'll bring back news that will help us grow the business to something really big. Then we can talk again about babies, I promise."

That was enough for Serafina. She opened the kitchen door, then closed it noisily. "Is anyone home?" she called. There was a sudden silence upstairs, followed quickly by the sound of Rosabella hurrying down the stone steps.

When she went home with the borrowed flour, Serafina was

invisible to people enjoying the late afternoon warmth. She hurried along the shadowed side of the street, her thin shoulders drooping inside her drab grey dress with its high neck, her face hidden under a floppy hat with a melancholy, fading flower pinned to one side. No one paid her any attention. It was if she didn't exist, had never passed by.

The Very Reverend Ottavio Acquaviva d'Aragona leapt to his feet as Brother Renato was ushered into his office. Beaming, his arms outstretched in welcome, he met Renato half way across the huge expanse of deep carpet lying between the high double door and his desk.

"Welcome, welcome," he said, reaching up to embrace Renato and kiss him on both cheeks, before showing him to an enormous chair on one side of the fireplace, which was wider than Renato's bed was long. The Bishop settled himself into the other chair and carefully arranged his cassock, his small feet just reaching the floor.

"Will you join me in a glass of wine?" he asked. "You must be tired after your journey."

Renato was neither thirsty nor particularly tired, having slept on the boat, but he knew how to handle himself in situations like this.

"You are too gracious, Your Excellency," he said. "That would be most refreshing."

The wine appeared with astonishing speed. Waiting outside, thought Renato, the Bishop runs a tight ship. Be careful.

Sipping his wine, the Bishop said, "I hear things are going well on Ischia."

It seemed like a question. Renato said, "Indeed they are, Your Excellency. Crops are doing well, and people seem content. They are good churchgoers, and follow the teachings of the Church and Our Lord in their daily lives."

The Bishop chuckled. "Our humble role in the Church is merely to bring the word of the Lord to our flock, is it not? The teachings are one and the same, no?" He treated Renato to a benign smile, as if they were two simple churchmen chatting over wine. But Renato saw the sharp look that preceded the smile.

"Indeed they are, Your Excellency. I meant nothing otherwise."

"Excellent, excellent." The Bishop seemed relieved, as if they had successfully avoided a tricky theological trap laid by Satan himself. "I hear you are doing good work with our flock. Father Giovanni speaks kindly of you."

"He is too generous, Your Excellency. I am but a poor priest doing his best." Was that laying it on too thick?

"Aren't we all?" said the humble but Very Reverend Ottavio Acquaviva d'Aragona, sitting under the large portrait of a supercilious-looking man dressed in ornate red robes. "Aren't we all?"

From the brass plate, Renato could see the portrait was of Cardinal Virgilio Rosario, the Bishop's 16th Century predecessor, who ended his career in Rome as the illustrious and very rich Vicar General for Pope Paul IV.

The Bishop took another sip of his wine, which Renato thought was really very good.

"Now, is there anything I can do for you?" he asked. Renato relaxed, just a little. He had negotiated the first turn.

"Your Excellency will undoubtedly remember the tragic crash in March last year," he began. "A British plane flew into Mount Epomeo, and everyone on board was killed."

"Of course, of course, a most unfortunate event. The British buried everyone here in Napoli, you know. They weren't considerate enough to invite me to the funeral, unfortunately."

"Most regrettable, Your Excellency," Renato agreed.

"And how does that affect our very pleasant conversation this afternoon?" asked the Bishop. He rang the bell for more wine.

"Thirteen souls went to meet their Maker too soon," said Renato, "including a two-year old boy." He had to take the next corner very carefully. "Many of the townspeople feel that we should do something to mark their memory, to show respect for their untimely departure from this world."

"How do they propose doing this?"

Renato saw that the Bishop was only mildly interested, so he waited until the wine had been poured before responding.

"They asked me if a cross would be appropriate," he said. "To show that they have been gathered into the welcoming arms of our Lord. Naturally, I said that I thought this was a generous and appropriate gesture, worthy of our God-fearing community."

"Who would pay for this?" the Bishop asked. The mention of generosity seemed to have caught his attention.

"There would be no cost, Your Excellency. A local blacksmith has collected suitable parts from the plane and has agreed to fashion them into a cross. A most fitting idea, do you not think? He is a devout man and has offered to donate his services."

"Most commendable," said the Bishop. "What does Father Giovanni have to say?"

Renato had been waiting for this question.

"Father Giovanni has spoken eloquently about the tragedy," he said. "In fact, he gave a most moving homily at Mass shortly afterwards. He expressed great sympathy for the victims and their suffering. And in none my conversations with him has he expressed any concern with the idea of a memorial."

He watched the Bishop absorb all this. Timing it perfectly, he added, "And if I may make a modest suggestion for Your Excellency to consider… I think it would be most appropriate for you to lead the Mass when we bless the cross. Father Giovanni did ask me to extend an invitation to you to come to Ischia, and this would be the perfect occasion."

There, he'd done it. Everything he'd said was true, and he felt only slightly guilty for leaving out minor inconveniences in the cause of a greater good. What the Bishop didn't know wouldn't hurt him. He kept his face calm and his hands still in his lap as the Bishop ran through the political calculus of lending his authority to an event like this.

"You are most eloquent," the Bishop said, and Renato knew he had it. "Ask your blacksmith to make the cross, and I would be pleased to celebrate Mass with you. Make the necessary arrangements with my secretary. And I will ask the British to send someone to join us. Someone senior. This is a good occasion to teach them some manners."

"May I offer my deepest gratitude, Your Excellency?" asked Renato. "Your generosity of spirit is truly inspiring, and I know our congregation on Ischia will be humbled by your presence."

"As you said earlier, my son, we poor priests must do what we can. Now, is there anything else?"

Here it was, the last turn on this perilous racetrack. There was nothing like the thunder of hooves in the Palio race in Siena, but this quiet room was just as dangerous.

"Your Excellency, there is one other matter on which I would appreciate the benefit of your wisdom. It is a question of considerable delicacy, and I lack experience in situations like this. I hesitate to raise it, but…"

"Well, what is it?" The Bishop showed a hint of his irritation at the lengthy introduction, even as he preened a little under the naked flattery.

Renato coughed slightly, to emphasise how difficult this was for him. "I had to return to the church the other day to collect my Bible, which I had forgotten. My return was unexpected. When I arrived, the altar boy ran from the sacristy, past me, and out of the church. He seemed distressed. I was wondering—"

"Don't tell me Giovanni has been at it again," the Bishop snapped. He had started tensing when he heard the word 'unexpected', and now he was leaning forward, glaring at Renato.

"Your Excellency?" Renato had intended merely to ask how he should approach the boy, the safest question he could think of, but it seemed his words had triggered something much larger.

The Bishop collected himself, visibly reining in his emotions.

"Father Giovanni was sent to Ischia because of his history of… of having… inappropriate relationships with boys. It was felt that being in a small backwater like that would… constrain his activities. Reduce the opportunity, it was thought, reduce the consequences."

Renato felt sick. 'Reduce the consequences?' To whom? He must have been blind, not knowing that something dark and evil was going on right under his nose. In a desperate attempt to cling on to something rational, he resented the Bishop casually referring to Ischia—an island he was becoming rather fond of—as a backwater.

He breathed in deeply, trying to maintain his composure.

"He was told in no uncertain terms that his actions were an affront to decency," the Bishop continued, his voice tight. "He was instructed to desist."

Renato's first reaction was that calling it an affront to decency trivialised the harm that Giovanni must have caused over the years. And what about an affront to God, he wondered. Keeping his face scrupulously sincere, he asked, "What can I do, Your Excellency? What should I do?"

"Nothing. Nothing at all."

The Bishop looked up at the portrait for inspiration. The long-dead Vicar of Christ stared back, one hand resting on a globe, the other caressing a large crucifix hanging on his chest. Renato waited, unable to anticipate what advice might be offered.

Eventually, the Bishop tore his gaze from the unresponsive portrait.

"Father Giovanni talked to me recently about the possibility of being released from his pastoral duties. He has bought a small vineyard outside Fontana. Apparently he wishes to pass his remaining days growing grapes and making wine. A strange desire, I thought that was something only monks did."

"Is he ill?" asked Renato. Giovanni seemed not old enough to be retiring.

"Not that I know of. But I think his request should be granted. When he is a winemaker and not a priest, he will have no further access to these boys and can do no more damage. Yes, it would be best to let him go quietly, without making a fuss."

"What about the boy? What should I say to Guido?"

"Guido? Who is this Guido?"

"The altar boy I spoke of, Your Excellency. I fear he has been deeply harmed by Father Giovanni. Should we not be helping him?"

For the first time, the Very Reverend Ottavio Acquaviva d'Aragona looked troubled. "Brother Renato," he started saying. "Brother Renato, your sympathy and desire to help this unfortunate boy are to be commended. But the interests of the Church must take precedence over those of a single child. What happened to him is undoubtedly... regrettable. But that is as nothing compared to the harm that would be done to the Church if people knew about these unfortunate incidents. How can the flock rely on the shepherd who fails to protect them? If we lose the trust of our flock, how can we lead them, how can we save their souls?"

Regrettable, thought Renato, remembering how he had used that word himself when confronted by an angry Demonte. It was a grossly inadequate word then, as well. And how could a priest who did this to defenceless young boys possibly be trusted to save anyone's soul?

Renato's face must have shown something of his feelings, because the Bishop hastened to add, "Speak to the boy if you must. Tell him whatever you like. But he must be told to keep his silence. The people of Ischia must never learn of the isolated actions of a single straying priest. This will protect the Church, will ensure that their trust in the Church–and in you, Brother Renato–will not be challenged. Their ignorance is for their benefit, you understand?"

"Indeed, Your Excellency. I understand you very well."

"Good, good, I thought you would. I'm glad I have no need to remind you of your vows of obedience. Now, I have to ask you this: do you have any similar... preferences?"

"Indeed not!" Renato was affronted by the question, and let it show.

"You can never tell these things," said the Bishop, vaguely.

"I took a vow of celibacy when I became a priest, Your Excellency, as we all did. It is an inviolable commitment before God." Was that a look of pity he glimpsed on the Bishop's face?

"I am reassured." The Bishop leaned back, relaxing once the difficult part of the conversation was behind them. "But we should look to the future, not dwell on past unpleasantness. When Father Giovanni retires, it strikes me that his position on Ischia will become vacant. A replacement will be required. Since you are already there and, I'm sure, beloved by your congregation, you would be well placed to take Giovanni's place. You should consider this, I think."

Astonished, Renato said, "I'm not sure if I am ready, Your Excellency."

"Based on this conversation, I think you are. But there is no hurry. Pray to God for guidance, and reflect on it. You might be a little young to lead a parish, but Ischia is a good place to start assuming more responsibility. After that, who knows, hmm?"

"Your Excellency is too kind," said Renato. Having crossed the finish line without falling off his horse, he was exhausted, and wanted nothing more than to escape and think about everything said, and not said. Even the sharp recognition that he was sorely tempted by the offer could not keep him in this room.

"Not really," the Very Reverend Ottavio Acquaviva d'Aragona said lightly. "You handled yourself well today. I can see why Father Giovanni spoke so highly of you, despite his deplorable… tendencies. It's getting late, and our time together is over for today. But before parting, I must impress on you the seriousness of all this, and remind you that on no account are you to speak of the matter, most especially not to Father Giovanni."

"I understand completely, Your Excellence."

"Good."

The Bishop held out his hand. Renato knelt and kissed his ring. A few minutes later, he stood alone on the street outside the palace, his hands shaking uncontrollably.

Walking up from the port of Napoli through the confusing tangle of narrow streets, Cesare savoured the bustle and crowds. He knew he'd be glad to return to his quiet life in Fontana, but a short dose of excitement and energy was a welcome change. It helped that the ride across the Bay to Napoli had been much smoother than before, almost something to enjoy.

Everything looked different in daylight, making it difficult to find his way. He took several wrong turns before ending up on a street he recognised. Seeing the alley he wanted on the other side, he started crossing without looking. A hand reached out and pulled him back, just as a tram sped by inches in front of him, its bell clanging furiously.

"If you want to get killed by a tram, do it somewhere else!"

Safely on the other side, he went up the alley, turned left, and saw the Taverna Paradiso, looking no more heavenly in the bright sunlight than it had on his previous visit. The palm tree beside the door seemed even more faded, and bags of rubbish were piled haphazardly beside the wall.

Inside, the bar was dim and almost empty. It still smelled of old wine and cigarette smoke. Pausing to let his eyes get used to the dark, he saw Cutolo sitting by himself at the same table at the back. The Camorrista wore an elegant blue suit with an extravagant handkerchief tucked into the breast pocket. A small glass of wine lay untouched on the table in front of him.

"Will you join me for a glass of wine?" he asked. He waved a languid hand, inviting Cesare to sit with him.

Cesare wasn't particularly thirsty, but he wanted to impress Cutolo and thought it would be unwise to seem ungrateful. "Thank you," he said, "that would be good."

Cutolo nodded to the barman, who hurried over with a fresh glass.

"I understand your new house is going well," said Cutolo.

"Indeed it is," replied Cesare, not surprised that Cutolo had taken the trouble to find out. "There are some teething problems with the new electrical systems, nothing we can't handle. The house will be ready for sale in less than a month."

"That's good progress." Cutolo sounded genuinely impressed. "And how long do you think it will take to sell?"

"I've already put out feelers. More and more people are buying holiday homes on Ischia, some foreigners, many from Napoli, some from Roma, even. We designed the house to be very attractive to them. For example, there is a big terrace overlooking Forio. The people who sell houses tell me there is already interest and that it should sell very quickly. I hope so, then I can use the profits to build something bigger."

"That's what I wanted to talk to you about," said Cutolo, taking a small sip of wine. "A business proposition."

"I'm always interested in business propositions," Cesare said with careful nonchalance. He'd been expecting this, ever since Ulisse had spoken with him on his recent visit to Fontana. "Signor Cutolo wants to see you," Ulisse had said. "He didn't tell me what about."

Well, here he was, even if he did feel a bit intimidated.

"It is important that this discussion stays between us." Cutolo looked hard at Cesare. "I must have your solemn word that it goes no further."

"Rosabella, my wife, is a very strong woman," said Cesare. "I have no secrets from her. Other than her, you have my word."

"Other than her, then. You do understand that we take promises seriously, do you not? Very seriously."

"Yes, I do understand that." Cesare forced himself to look calmly back at Cutolo, despite wondering what he was letting himself in for. Whatever it was, the profits would be immense, well worth the risks involved in working with the Camorra.

"Good." Cutolo paused to take a small sip of wine. "As you must know, we have many business interests. Our work in taking care of our community costs a lot of money, and these businesses raise the necessary funds. Regrettably, while the government tolerates our activities in keeping the community safe–it's cheaper for them, after all–they are less sympathetic when it comes to our other activities. Frankly, it's shameful how they want to tax the fruits of our labours. Fortunately, there is a solution that benefits many people, even the government. That's where you come in."

"Me?" asked Cesare. "I'm just a small builder on Ischia. How can I possibly help you with a problem like this?"

"You've already shown us that you're a good businessman and a capable builder. We wouldn't be talking to you otherwise. How would you like to expand your business, many times over?"

"Of course I would," Cesare said. "But I'd need significantly more money, to buy land, buy more equipment, build more houses before I've sold them."

"We can provide that capital, Cesare. These business interests produce a lot of cash, and idle money is like idle hands–it attracts trouble. Our proposition is that you set up a new building company. We'll invest in it, and we'll help you get supplies at a most desirable price. The company will build hotels, they have good profit margins, perhaps also some houses to sell, or holiday villas. Naturally, there will be profits arising from all this. You keep some, we keep some. Two thirds for you, the rest to us. The company pays enough tax to keep the government off its back and everyone is happy. How does that sound?"

Cesare was stunned. This was everything he wished for, an opportunity to make a lot of money, get the status he craved in the community, and make his brothers and cousins concede that he was as good as they were. They thought he was weak and not as clever as them; this would prove that he was neither. And it would show Rosabella and her idiot family that he was a worthy husband, a man who could provide her with everything she wanted, and more.

Cutolo watched as Cesare submitted to the temptations laid out before him. "All you have to do," he said, "is agree to the terms and conditions in the contract we'll give you. We'll help you get set up, then you're off and running."

Cesare took a deep breath, aware of the cliff in front of him and the irrevocable decision he was about to make.

"Thank you," he said. "You won't regret this."

"I'm sure we won't," Cutolo said. "You know what you're doing, and there's no limit to what we can achieve together. Just make sure this conversation stays between us. Now, let's celebrate with a glass of this new wine that just came in. Tell me what you think of it."

As they sat chatting about the latest political scandal, the young woman whose pimp had been banished came in and sat by herself at a table across the room. Her dress was cut even lower, and she had a flower in her hair. The barman brought her a small glass of limoncello.

Cesare couldn't help staring. Rosabella liked wearing dresses that were a bit daring by Fontana standards, but they only showed the beginning swell of her bosom, nothing like the generous expanse of rounded skin on display in front of him. After what seemed like an eternity, she realized that Cesare was looking over at her and gave him a small smile of recognition.

"There's more than one way to celebrate a new business relationship," said Cutolo, seeing his reaction. "Would you like to renew your acquaintance with the young lady?"

Cesare hesitated, thinking of Rosabella pressing her breasts against him. But she was in Ischia, and he had just made the deal of his life. Did he not deserve some reward? Surrendering to temptation with only a flicker of guilt, he went across the room and was soon deep in conversation with the whore. He did not see Cutolo giving her another small nod, or watching him with a thoughtful expression as they went upstairs.

When Cesare returned to the bar later, the room had filled up considerably with sailors looking for a cheap night out and women intent on parting them from their money. The air was thick with cigarette smoke and noise. Cutolo was nowhere to be seen. Instead, Ulisse sat in his place, another small glass of wine in front of him. The sailors and their whores kept their tables slightly further away from his table than from the others, as if they feared being contaminated by being too close.

Cesare could feel eyes watching him as he worked his way between the tables. He clearly didn't fit in here, and people were wondering who he was, a bit suspicious. Then, as he approached Ulisse, chairs moved slightly to give him more room. As Ulisse stood up to greet him, Cesare was surprised—and impressed—by how much his cousin had changed. The rough, worn clothes Ulisse normally wore on Ischia were gone, replaced by a dark blue pinstripe suit almost as beautiful as Cutolo's. The double-breasted jacket had wide shoulders and wide lapels, tapering to a narrow waist. Ulisse always had an air of confidence about him, even as a child, but now it was quieter, and because of that, more menacing.

"How did your discussion with Signor Cutolo go?" Ulisse asked.

Another change. The old Ulisse would have made at least a token effort at pleasantries, asking how things were going, or enquiring after Rosabella's health. This one was all business, getting right to it.

Cesare said, "Very well. He wants to go into business with me, building houses and hotels on Ischia."

"Did you accept?"

"Of course I accepted. The offer was far too good to refuse."

"Do you realise what you're getting into?" asked Ulisse. "These are not gentle people."

"Thank you for your concern." Cesare spoke stiffly, offended by the implication that he didn't know what he was doing. "I think I can handle things."

Ulisse shrugged.

"You need to watch how you behave," he said. "Don't try anything stupid, and conduct yourself with the greatest care. The Camorra don't like it when people draw attention to themselves. And they're very moral. For example, that whore was a mistake. Once is acceptable, but you'd be wise not to do it again."

"Going with a whore is a mistake?" Cesare was surprised. Most of the men he knew, married or not, talked openly of an occasional visit to a brothel. As natural as cleaning your teeth, they said. If a man was truly a man, he'd get urges that his wife couldn't always satisfy, especially at certain times of month. Relieving those urges with a whore was a perfectly reasonable thing to do.

"Family is very important for the Camorra," Ulisse said. "The Camorra clan comes first, always, but they also expect their members to treat their own family with utmost respect and honour. They would think that fucking a whore is disrespectful to Rosabella."

"But she'll never know about it," protested Cesare. "What she doesn't know won't hurt her."

"That's beside the point." Ulisse was starting to get annoyed with

Cesare's failure to understand. "They expect you to do the right thing, even if no one is looking. And don't think they won't know what you're doing on Ischia, because they will. They seem to know everything."

"Well, I won't do anything stupid," Cesare said. "I want to build a business and make a lot of money. Nothing is going to get in the way of doing that."

Ulisse said, "Just be careful."

Chapter Sixteen

ADOLFO SAT BY HIMSELF ON THE LOW WALL across from the Chiesa di Sant' Antonio. The statue of our Saviour stood high behind him, his arms stretched out in welcome.

Nobody paid Adolfo much attention. Life in Fontana meandered along at the same leisurely pace that it had enjoyed for hundreds of years, and the sight of someone taking his ease in the shade, perhaps waiting for a friend, was nothing to warrant a second look. People knew that life was hard and short, and thought it better by far to appreciate the sunshine, good food and wine whenever they came your way. Cherish your family and friends while still alive before spending Eternity in whichever destination God chose for you.

Lost in his thoughts, Adolfo almost missed Father Giovanni as he left the church. Jumping to his feet, he waved to attract the priest's attention. Giovanni took a moment to realise that someone wanted to talk with him, and was even more startled when he saw who it was.

"Adolfo," he said as he sat down and adjusted his cassock. "This is a most welcome surprise." His manner was unctuous and smooth, if a little uneasy.

Adolfo mumbled something incoherent. Now that the priest was sitting beside him, a bit too close for comfort, he didn't quite know how to begin what he'd come here to say.

"We miss you in church," said Father Giovanni. "As I recall, we've seen you there only once in many months. A good shepherd always worries when a member of his flock has strayed. Should I be anxious for your soul?"

Adolfo shook his head. He had no wish to discuss the state of his soul with anyone, least of all the priest. He felt adrift, that he was the helpless victim of malicious forces beyond his control. His sleep was being disturbed more and more often, his thoughts tumbling over each other, unasked-for memories of what he'd done on the mountain. Looking at himself in the mirror when shaving that morning, he had seriously considered running the razor across his throat to end his misery. Then he'd remembered how the man sitting beside him had refused Paolo a proper Christian burial, and had carefully put the razor down.

"You look troubled, my son," said Father Giovanni. "Are you sure there is nothing I can do for you?" He smiled invitingly, showing uneven teeth stained yellow and brown from years of smoking cheap, hand-rolled cigarettes. Adolfo still said nothing, shifting uncomfortably on the hard stone. Giovanni went on, "It was no coincidence that brought you to the church when I spoke of the crash. I know that many people from the town carried a weight on their conscience because of their actions then. A needless burden, as I told everyone, but still. Are you perhaps one of them? If so, I would encourage you to come to confession, that I might help."

"Thank you for your concern," said Adolfo. It would take a team of mules to get him into the confessional with Father Giovani. He was very conscious of the priest looking hard at him with avaricious eyes, the apparent concern on his pinched face not quite hiding the desire to learn and hoard more secrets.

"I came on an another matter," he said, steering the conversation away from the delicate matter of his compromised soul. "You know there's talk about a memorial for the people killed in the crash?"

"Memorial?" asked Giovanni, reluctantly accepting that he wouldn't be seeing Adolfo at confession. Clearly, the idea of a memorial was news to him. "That shouldn't be necessary. Those people are buried in their own cemetery in Napoli and they were not from here. Why should there be a memorial?"

"I asked the same question. Apparently it's so we don't forget what happened… don't forget the crash."

"Most people in Fontana would prefer to forget," said Father Giovanni. "What's done is done. A memorial will do nothing to bring those people back, and they weren't even Catholic. How could a perpetual reminder of those unfortunate events possibly do anyone any good? A memorial might make people think they did wrong, they'd forget what I told them, and then where would we be?"

Giovanni's agitation was getting the better of him. He stood up and turned to face Adolfo, who was sitting in the long shadow cast by the giant Jesus. "We really must paint that statue," the priest said distractedly, "it looks awful."

A thought struck him.

"Why are you telling me this?" he asked. "What kind of memorial is being proposed? And who is behind this wicked idea?"

Adolfo hesitated for a moment. He didn't mind identifying Brother Renato but Tifeo was his brother. He thought briefly about how Tifeo had grown distant when they were at school together, then hostile more recently. Adolfo didn't know why this happened and didn't care any more. His own protection from intrusive questions was more important than keeping family secrets.

"Tifeo is making a cross, apparently. I don't know if this was his idea or Brother Renato's, but they're both involved."

"Tifeo? That pagan heretic? He's got no business making a cross!" Father Giovanni was furious and didn't attempt to hide it. He either forgot or didn't care that Tifeo was family for Adolfo. His voice rose. "How dare he commit this blasphemy? And what is Brother Renato thinking, getting mixed up in this? He should know better!"

He looked up at Jesus for support but the Son of God was hiding his thoughts behind his coat of scabrous paint.

"Renato gets back from Napoli tomorrow, and I'll see him then. We'll soon put a stop to this nonsense."

Adolfo felt pleased as he walked home. Brother Renato would be severely chastised by his superior and left in no doubt about the error of his ways. Maybe he'd be less inclined to interfere in things that were none of his business after that. And there would be no cross. No permanent reminder of the crash, its victims, or what happened afterwards. No awkward questions.

Soon the town could leave the whole episode behind, in the forgotten past, where it belonged.

Renato entered Tifeo's smithy just as the blacksmith took a glowing piece of metal from the coals and placed it on a huge anvil. Holding one end with long pincers, he hit the metal several times with a heavy hammer, then rotated it and hit it again and again as if he was trying to punish the metal for some dreadful crime. Renato covered his ears to protect them from the deafening noise. The metal seemed to be stretching where Tifeo was hitting it, getting longer and thinner.

When the metal had cooled too much to be worked, Tifeo pushed it back into the coals.

"This is the last rod," he said. "You've come at a good time."

There was no greeting—it was as if he was expecting Renato to walk in at that precise moment.

Amedea smiled at him as she began pumping the bellows to feed oxygen to the fire, but said nothing. Her skin was slick with sweat, glowing in the red light of the fire. In her thin shirt, she might as well have been naked but, to his surprise and later remorse, Renato found himself unsurprised and accepting. She looked like some elemental creature, entirely natural, dancing in front of a fire.

Tifeo was shirtless, sweat running down his chest and leaving streaks of soot behind. Still wearing his travelling cassock, Renato felt distinctly out of place.

Taking off his flat priest's hat, he said, "I came straight from Lacco Ameno to tell you. The Bishop has agreed to come to Ischia and consecrate the cross when we put it up."

Amedea smiled again, but kept pumping. Tifeo said, "That's good to hear. You will have an interesting discussion with Father Giovanni, I think."

Renato said, "We'll see about that tomorrow."

He said it lightly, but he did not think that his superior would react well to what he'd done and he was not looking forward to the discussion. Rather than get into that, he asked, "How is the cross coming along?"

"We're almost finished this piece," said Tifeo, "then we can start joining bits together. Stay and watch, if you like."

A short while later, Tifeo declared himself satisfied. The metal had been drawn into a rod as thick as two of Renato's fingers and as long as his two outstretched arms.

"This is where things get interesting," Tifeo said, putting more coals onto the fire. Amedea pulled down a new bellows, as long as she was tall, placed the end into a slot beneath the coals, and resumed her pumping. The forge was soon hotter than ever. Red light flickered on the walls as shadows danced their erotic dance in the corners. The fire roared.

Tifeo put one end of the long rod into the fire, then selected a shorter piece, the length of Amedea's forearm, and added it to the fire. Renato watched the rods change colour, mesmerised. The dull black quickly turned dark maroon, reddened, then became yellow. When the two ends reached a pale, creamy yellow, the colour of Parmigiano cheese, Tifeo nodded at Amedea, who put down the bellows, picked up a pair of pincers and grasped the short rod, placing the hot end on the anvil. Tifeo picked up the longer rod and laid the hot end at right angles on top of Amedea's piece. With his other hand, he hit the joined ends as hard as he could, several times, until the metal had cooled to a dull red.

Tifeo said, "The trick is to get the metal as hot as possible before joining them. Then the two pieces flow into each other when I hit them. It's as if they wish to become one."

The blacksmith seemed very tall to the much shorter priest. His breathing was slow, even after his strenuous efforts with a heavy hammer. Renato thought he looked like Hephaestus, the Greek god of blacksmiths who forged thunderbolts for Zeus to hurl from the heavens when he was displeased. But that would make Amedea the equivalent of Aphrodite, Hephaestus' consistently unfaithful wife, and Renato didn't think that was likely.

"The cross will be made of two hollow boxes," said Tifeo, "each box framed by these rods. The pieces we just welded together will be part of the cross-piece. Now let's do another."

"Perhaps I could help with the bellows," said Renato. He wanted to be part of this arcane, primitive process, so far removed from the refined, spiritual world he was used to.

"Of course," said Tifeo. Renato rolled up his sleeves, took the bellows from Amedea, and started pumping vigorously. The fire roared again, a throaty, animal sound that seemed to emerge from the ground itself.

Tifeo watched the fire intently, his eyes reflecting red splinters of light. Looking up at the blacksmith from his labours, Renato had the impression that Tifeo was worshipping the fire, engaging in some ancient pagan ritual. And what does that make me, the priest wondered, his acolyte?

With flames licking red across the coals, and the heat, and the noise, the forge seemed more like the inside of a volcano than the contemplative interior of a church. What manner of gods live in a volcano? Is this how you worship them? He shook himself free of the heretical thoughts as Tifeo placed another two pieces into the fire with the same loving care that Renato used when placing the sacrament on the altar.

Working the bellows was harder than it looked and Renato was soon drenched in sweat. Seeing Tifeo's amused look, he kept pumping as hard as he could, watching the rods begin to change colour. His arm muscles burning, it wasn't long before he was panting like a dog lying prostrate in midsummer heat.

"Enough," said Amedea, "enough. We'd like you to live a little longer."

Gratefully, Renato let her take over the bellows. He took the glass of water being held out by Tifeo and drank it without pausing. Without apparent effort, Amedea picked up the pace, and soon the two rods were the pale yellow that Tifeo wanted.

By the time he left, Tifeo and Amedea had built the complete box for the horizontal part of the cross. The box was hollow, twice as long as Tifeo was tall. The rods sketched just the outline of a box, the slightest of gestures showing where the box began and ended. It looked as light as the air it contained, yet Tifeo and Renato had to strain when they carried it across to a bench at the side of the forge.

"We'll do the rest tomorrow," said Tifeo, "it's getting too late to start the next piece now."

"I'm impressed," said Renato, "and grateful. This will be a most fitting memorial, whatever other people might say." He almost mentioned Father Giovanni but thought better of it just in time.

"I'm glad you approve," said Tifeo. "And I'm glad you could help us make it." He was too polite to suggest that Renato had made only a very small, negligible contribution. Amedea spontaneously leaned over and gave him a quick, innocent kiss on the cheek, leaving a small smudge of soot that she immediately wiped away.

Renato suddenly felt very tired after a long day. He had travelled back from Napoli, walked over the mountain, and helped make a very large cross. Nevertheless, he had a big smile on his face as he walked down the hill to Fontana and his bed.

His good mood lasted until just before dawn, when he woke with a start, his legs tangled in the thin sheets. Grey light leaked into the room through thin cracks in the shutters, closed out of habit rather than a fear of night spirits. He was a modern Catholic, after all.

Confused thoughts chased each other like ill-behaved children playing in the street, running in and out of shadows. An image of Amedea half-naked, a pagan goddess. The Very Reverend Ottavio Acquaviva d'Aragona offering him inducements in return for his allegiance to the Church, like Satan tempting Jesus. His squirming awareness that he found the prospect attractive. Shamed remorse at his simple acceptance of Amedea's nakedness and her kiss–he should have remonstrated with her or, at the very least, looked away. Darkest of all, knowing that Father Giovanni, his superior and someone he should look up to and learn from, was a monster, a disgrace to his vocation.

Unable to go back to sleep, he got up, washed his face, and dressed. It was too early to go down to the church, so he opened the Bible at random, hoping that he would find calm and solace there. But the words blurred and meant nothing.

He sat beside the window for a long time. One hand rested on the open Bible in his lap, the other on the cross on his chest, but he gazed quietly out of the window, listening to the familiar, reassuring sounds of the town waking up. Eventually he stood up and went slowly downstairs for his usual simple breakfast.

The church was cool and peaceful when he arrived. Going to the front, he crossed himself before the altar before sitting in a pew directly in front of the chair that he normally used during Mass. What can the person who sits in that chair do to be a better priest, he asked himself. What must he do to tend his own soul, that he might take better care of his flock?

Do what you do best, came the answer. Spend your talents wisely in the service of your fellow man. How else can life be worthwhile?

A deep calm settled on him as he sat there. Freed of his internal struggle, he looked around, enjoying an unfamiliar view of familiar objects. The replica of the boat that brought Santa Restituta, the blue trim on the altar candlesticks that matched both the blue of the water under the boat and the blue of Mary's robe. A painting of Jesus healing a leper by placing His hands on him. Another painting of Adam and Eve being evicted from the Garden of Eden, watched by a self-satisfied looking snake coiled around a half-eaten apple.

He jumped as the door to the Sacristy opened and Father Giovanni entered the church. The older priest looked haggard and gray as he hurried up the side aisle, not noticing Renato.

"Father Giovanni," Renato called out.

Giovanni stopped and spun around to see who was there.

"Ah, Brother Renato," he said, walking back to where Renato was waiting for him. "Returned from Napoli to grace us with your presence, have you?"

Renato was astonished. Father Giovanni had a sharp tongue, but had never spoken to him like that before.

"I returned last night," he said. "Father, is something the matter?"

"The matter?" hissed Giovanni. "The matter? Oh, no, nothing's the matter. Not unless you think that erecting a cross without my knowledge or permission is a matter we should be discussing."

"I am sorry you did not hear this from me," said Renato, carefully. "I was hoping to talk about it with you today."

"Today is several days too late." Giovanni was standing right in front of him, just inches away, his back to the altar and the tortured body of Christ dying on the Cross. "I learned about it the day you went to Napoli, and have had much time since to wonder why you would disobey me."

"Disobey, Father? I do not recall you saying anything about a cross."

"When I spoke…" Giovanni paused to cough, a dreadful hacking, liquid sound that sounded as if he had the Bay of Napoli in his lungs. "When I spoke of the crash," he went on when he had recovered, "I thought I made it perfectly clear that people were not to concern themselves about it any more. Was that not clear enough for you?"

"You certainly relieved them of any possible guilt for what they did."

"Why do you wish to erect a cross, then?" Father Giovanni was close to shouting now, his voice echoing in the empty church. He wiped spittle from his chin with a once-white handkerchief.

Renato said, "It seems an appropriate way to remember the thirteen people who died that night. And an unborn infant."

"Thirteen Protestants," spat Giovanni. "They'll spend eternity in Hell for their apostasy. The child was not baptised, so cannot go to Heaven."

Despite himself, Renato couldn't help looking at the painting of Jesus and the leper.

"And why did you ask Tifeo to get involved?" Father Giovanni went on, still angry.

"He's the only blacksmith we have. Who else should I ask?"

"He's pagan, a disbeliever, he cannot be allowed to do this. He never had a Christian thought in his life. Having him make a cross– the very symbol of our Lord's suffering and forgiveness–is heresy. The cross will be tainted."

"He showed great compassion when we brought down the bodies after the crash," Renato said. He forced himself to stay calm and not lower himself by shouting at this man, this molester of children. "He may not share our faith, but…"

"But nothing, Brother! You cannot please God without faith
Without unquestioning faith, we cannot be saved. Tifeo will end up
in Hell because of his pagan beliefs."

Renato said nothing, torn between knowing that Tifeo was a
good man and accepting that Father Giovanni was theologically
correct, even if the milk of forgiveness and tolerance was running a
little thin on this occasion. Taking his silence for uncertainty,
Giovanni said, "Do not allow Satan to poison your mind with doubt,
Brother Renato. Doubt is the enemy of faith, just as evil is the enemy
of Godliness. An uncertain faith is no faith at all, and God cannot
forgive faithlessness. Now, enough. You will not proceed with this
cross."

"That may be difficult," said Renato.

"I don't see why. Just tell Tifeo to stop. What else is there to do?"

"Before I left for Napoli, you asked me to invite the Bishop to
visit us in Ischia. I followed your instructions, by asking if he would
come here to consecrate the cross. He saw virtue in the idea of a
memorial and was gracious enough to accept the invitation. It would
be difficult now to… uninvite him, as it were."

"You did what?"

"If I did wrong here, it was with the best intention," said Renato.
"I beg your forgiveness."

"My forgiveness? You'll never get that." Giovanni was shaking
with his fury. "Instead, you should prostrate yourself and do your
begging of God."

"And what should I say to Tifeo?"

Before Giovanni could answer, he was convulsed by another bout
of coughing. Doubled over, he held his handkerchief to his mouth.
Alarmed, Renato put his hand under Giovanni's elbow. "Please, sit
down," he said, helping the older man to the pew. "Have you seen
the doctor about this?"

"It's just a bad cough, no need to bother him," said Giovanni,
gasping for breath. "It will soon clear up."

He wiped his chin again. Renato saw to his horror that there was blood on the handkerchief.

"Father, I really think you should consult the doctor. This looks more than a cough."

"Stop interfering," said Giovanni, pushing Renato away. "You've done enough of that already."

"Will you at least rest a while? I can take Mass on Sunday, to give you more time to get over this."

"I shall go home now." Giovanni suddenly sounded terribly tired, his fury fading away. "We will talk more about your cursed cross tomorrow."

Alone once more, Renato sat again in the pew. The tortured figure of the crucified Christ looked very small on the huge cross. How could the symbol of divine forgiveness create such conflict, he wondered. Surely God would appreciate the compassionate intent behind the memorial, regardless of whose hands fashioned it.

Finally, he confronted the serpent writhing in his mind. Was he in danger of losing his soul by his reluctance to condemn other beliefs, by enjoying the opportunity to learn about new and unfamiliar ways to worship the divine? Perhaps he should strive to be more like Father Giovanni, not less, and protect his faith with battlements of uncompromising certainty.

He remembered how his lawyer father loved to entertain himself at dinner by plucking a topic out of thin air with a courtroom flourish and then arguing both sides with equal ferocity and eloquence. Renato had rolled his adolescent eyes at the time, preferring the clarity of finding the single right answer to even the most complex of life's problems. Later, he'd found relief when his seminary teachers showed him a single road to follow, when he could surrender himself to unquestioning faith in the boundless benevolence of God.

But he was now starting to realise that he had absorbed more of his father's 'on the one hand this, on the other hand that' approach than he thought. The apple of curiosity had fallen not so far from the tree after all and, it seemed, unwavering belief did not come naturally to him.

Needing help, he prostrated himself in front of the altar, and asked for God's guidance. But God had apparently decided that he should solve this problem on his own, because He remained silent.

Brother Renato lay there for a long time with his troubled thoughts, unable to resolve the conflict between belief and curiosity, between certainty and doubt. When he finally rose to his feet and dusted his cassock, his cheeks were wet with tears and his heart felt as if it was full of stones.

Chapter Seventeen

FILOMENA WAS LUCKY–AND CONSIDERATE–ENOUGH TO DIE quietly in her sleep. She had joined Cesare and Rosabella as usual for supper, then sat in her chair beside the fire, snuffling from a heavy cold and contemplating whatever it is that old people think about. Surely not the future, for there were very few grains of sand left in her hourglass. Rosabella asked her once if she ever thought about dying. "Oh, no," Filomena had replied, "I'll worry about that when the time comes. After that, I'll be in Heaven. So there's really nothing to think."

Once Filomena was safely in bed and supper cleared away, Cesare and Rosabella finished a bottle of wine as they discussed plans for the new hotel he was going to build with Cutolo's money. It was only a few months since he'd seen the Camorrista but in that short time Cesare had found and bought a spectacular site overlooking Sant' Angelo, with a remarkable view over the small harbour and across to Capri. He just needed to navigate the Byzantine path to getting the necessary permits and he could start construction. Builders on Ischia were normally quite casual about inconvenient paperwork, but Cesare thought it more prudent to avoid unwelcome attention from the authorities.

By the time they went upstairs, Cesare was relaxed, cocksure about his business acumen and the wealth and status waiting once the hotel was built. Satisfied with her progress, Rosabella had continued her slow and careful seduction in the bedroom. An accidental touch as she brushed past him, then she made sure he could see her as she undressed in the bathroom. It all ended most satisfactorily in bed; Rosabella was sated, and Cesare fell heavily asleep in moments, comforted by the thought that he was Fontana's most accomplished lover. He had either forgotten or no longer cared that this was Rosabella's fertile time of the month.

Filomena's room felt different the moment Rosabella went in the next morning to help her get up. Normally, she'd be aware of the sparrow-light figure stirring in bed as she opened the shutters. Not hearing anything, she'd bent over the still shape of her mother-in-law and saw at once that Filomena had departed. The sunken, grey face was empty and diminished, looking like the old farmhouse that Rosabella passed when collecting berries, once full of bustling, cheerful life but now empty and deserted as if no one had ever lived there.

Rosabella's first reaction was one of overwhelming but guilty relief. Caring for Filomena was time-consuming, and Rosabella could feel growing resentment of the old woman disrupting the life she was trying to build with Cesare. This feeling was coloured by a different kind of relief, that Filomena was released from the many discomforts of the last few years. Then, sadness. Despite the minor physical complaints of an old woman and the occasional nagging, Filomena had been a good mother-in-law and Rosabella had enjoyed her company. The house would be quieter and less interesting without her.

Both Rosabella and Cesare were surprised by the number of people who came to the funeral. Most were from Fontana, but older people also came from further away, notified by the posters put up in surrounding towns ('She has serenely gone out like a candle,' they read, before giving the date and time of the funeral.) The funeral director from Forio had justified his rather steep price, because Filomena looked almost young as people bent to kiss her in the open coffin.

Later, as people at the graveside tossed handfuls of earth onto the coffin, Rosabella wondered what Carlo, Filomena's recently-dead husband, would have thought had he known his wife would be lying on top of him for all eternity, even if she wasn't face-down. She suspected he would have preferred it the other way around.

Friends and neighbours had been more than generous before the funeral and there was a mountain of food left over for the reception at the house. Rosabella, Amedea and Serafina bustled back and forth between the kitchen and the living room, trying to keep the flow of food and drink moving.

The talk was somewhat subdued to start with, in keeping with the occasion. Naturally, people wanted to commiserate with each other and to tell stories about Filomena but without mentioning her name, in case her spirit heard and refused to leave. After a while, the noise level gradually increased as the food and wine freed tongues to indulge in less morbid forms of conversation. Soon people were shouting just to be heard above the din.

Cesare had seized the opportunity to trap Mayor Artigiani in a corner. The Mayor looked as if he'd rather be far away without this builder towering over him.

"Signor Mayor," Cesare yelled, "my permit applications have been in your office for weeks. We're ready to start building, but we need those permits. When will they be ready?"

Artigiani was affronted. He liked being Mayor, liked the ceremonies and public rituals that went with the job. Permits were much less interesting unless they came with cash attached. Cesare's bluntness was a rude challenge to the status of his position.

"This is hardly the right occasion to discuss permits," he shouted back. "Come to my office next week, and we can…"

"We need to start as soon as possible to be ready for tourists next year. This will be a beautiful hotel, very desirable. Signor Mayor, think of all the tourists, all the money they will bring."

"How many tourists will the hotel accommodate?" Artigiani asked, to be polite and to calm Cesare down. He had not even looked at the permit applications.

"There are twenty rooms. My associates and I think that two to three hundred wealthy visitors will stay there each year."

"Associates?" Artigiani's interest rose, just a bit. Associates could mean there was serious money behind this project, some of which might stick to his fingers.

Cesare bent down to speak more quietly in Artigiani's ear.

"My associates are based in Napoli," he said. "My main contact is a Signor Raffaele Cutolo, perhaps you know of him. My cousin Ulisse, over there, is now working with him."

Mayor Artigiani was astonished, and alarmed. He knew Cutolo's name and reputation and had heard rumours that someone from Fontana had joined the Camorra. He pulled out a small notebook and made an elaborate pantomime of consulting it.

"It seems my luncheon tomorrow has been unfortunately postponed," he said, looking studiously at a blank page. "Perhaps you'd care to join me and we can discuss this matter more thoroughly. And I will speak to my assistant to ensure that your permits are approved without delay."

Watching from the other side of the room, Rosabella saw the exchange and Cesare's agreement with whatever the Mayor had suggested. Ridiculous little man, she thought, pleased with Cesare for getting what he wanted.

Behind her, Tifeo was talking with Brother Renato, something noted with considerable concern by the more faithful in the room. Serafina, in particular, found it hard to look at the two of them without pursing her lips in disapproval. Brother Renato had done a good job at the funeral in Father Giovanni's absence, they all agreed, but what was he doing being so friendly with that pagan? Granted, Tifeo had attended the funeral service for his aunt, as he should, and had the good taste to not take communion, but still. And where was Father Giovanni, anyway? He had been sick for some time now, but the nature of his illness was a mystery.

Rosabella heard Tifeo say, "Look at them, Renato, they fear for your soul, as if I might contaminate it."

Moving further into the room, she saw Adolfo in a corner by himself. Not wanting any of the guests in her house to be ignored, she navigated her way through the crush to him.

"The funeral went well," she said, "you must be pleased."

"Yes, it was a good service." Adolfo seemed reluctant to talk at all.

"You really should join us at Sunday dinner," persisted Rosabella. "It would be good to have the whole family together." Part of her role, she felt, was to be the family peacemaker.

Adolfo looked at her suspiciously. "I doubt that Tifeo or Baldassare would agree with that," he said. "They think I cohabit with the Devil."

Rosabella put her hand to her mouth, pretending to be shocked. "Oh, no," she said, "I'm sure they don't. Your sausages are much too good. You must have help from Heaven."

Adolfo rewarded her efforts with the faintest glimmer of a smile.

"Speak to Tifeo," he said. "My little brother would rather not see me again. The feeling is mutual, I assure you."

"And is there nothing that will close the gap between you?" asked Rosabella. "I'm sorry to see you so far apart."

"We've been distant since we were boys," Adolfo said. For the first time, Rosabella thought he sounded sad about Tifeo. "I don't know how it started. But I wish he would stop criticizing me to anyone who will listen."

Rosabella opened her mouth to reply, when Adolfo said, "Rosabella, you must excuse me, I wish to speak to the Mayor now your husband has finished with him."

Mayor Artigiani sighed when he saw Adolfo coming towards him. He knew that meeting members of the community was inevitable when he was obliged to attend events like this, but that didn't mean he had to enjoy it. All they ever did was bring more problems. By the look on his face, Adolfo was going to be no exception.

"Signor Artigiani, why are you allowing this cross to be erected?" This family was nothing if not direct, thought the Mayor, although he was puzzled.

"What cross?" he asked.

"What cross? Why, the one that's supposed to be a memorial to the English who died in the crash. I thought you would have known all about it."

Artigiani shrugged elaborately. How can I be expected to know absolutely everything, the shrug suggested, although he generally tried to do just that. "Tell me about it," he said.

When Adolfo finished explaining, Artigiani said, "I agree with you. People are just starting to forget about the crash. They do not wish to be reminded that they participated in what happened afterwards. We can't change anything, best to let it go."

"Since it was God's will, as Father Giovanni told us," said Adolfo, "their consciences should be clear." He was anxious to remove any doubt about the morality of removing wealth from dead bodies. "It won't help to cause any anxiety on that score."

"There is another reason," said Artigiani. "I am doing everything in my limited power to help your cousin Cesare build his hotel. It will attract many tourists, wealthy ones. The last thing they will want is to hear about is an airplane crash that killed everyone, let alone the slightest suggestion that the victims were not treated with the utmost respect."

"We are agreed, then. What will you do?"

"Brother Renato is young and new to our island, and does not understand our ways. I will speak to him, help him see that we should leave this unfortunate episode in the past, where it belongs."

On the other side of the room, Baldassare accepted a glass of wine from Rosabella. "I heard the most remarkable thing the other day," he said. "The rumour is true—an English milord, a musician, of all things, has bought a small estate just outside Forio. And when he arrives, he will bring his own car. Imagine! I think this will be the first car to live on the island."

"Where will he drive it, I wonder?" asked Rosabella. "All we have are mule tracks."

"Into Forio, I suppose. There's nowhere else to go. But why he can't walk or take a mule and cart like everyone else, I don't know."

Rosabella laughed. "I can't see an English aristo walking for an hour to buy supplies." Ever practical, she frowned as she thought. "Where will he get his petrol? We have none here."

"He'll have to bring it with him, there's nothing else he can do."

Rosabella shook her head at the crazy thought of bringing your own petrol across from Napoli, just to avoid a long walk.

Beside the door to the kitchen, the Mayor was getting nowhere with Brother Renato. Tifeo watched, an amused smile on his face.

"I could order you to desist from this foolish plan," said the Mayor finally, making himself as tall as he could.

"I think not," Renato said. "The cross will be on common land at the top of the mountain and is a matter for the church, not for secular authorities."

"Very well," said Artigiani, "you leave me with no alternative but to appeal to the Bishop."

"That would be most unwise," Renato said, reluctantly playing his trump card. "I have already spoken with him and he has given his blessing. In fact, he will come to Ischia to consecrate it. As you may know, he is considerably averse to changing his mind once it is made up. I fear he will not welcome your intervention."

Despite himself, Renato couldn't help feeling a small sense of satisfaction in winning the argument with this puffed-up little man. Feeling a bit ashamed, he decided to offer an olive branch.

"The cross will be high on the mountain," he said, "where the plane crashed. Very few people go there, and certainly no tourists. I think it is highly unlikely that the cross—a symbol of forgiveness, after all—will create the discord you are worried about.

Artigiani just glared at him. Losing patience, Renato said, "I'm sure you'll want to attend the consecration. I'll make sure you get an invitation in the next few days."

When Artigiani had left in a state of frustrated fury, Tifeo slapped Renato on the arm. "That was excellent," he said. "But tell me, are you really a priest? That last comment seemed definitely un-Christian."

"Sometimes I wonder that myself," said Renato. He sounded very sad. "I must find Rosabella and offer my thanks for her hospitality. Then I'm going home."

The Very Reverend Ottavio Acquaviva D'Aragona was increasingly sorry that he had accepted the invitation to dedicate the memorial cross. The day was warm and the mountain steep, and he was uncomfortably hot in the mid-summer sun as he led the small procession up the mule track out of town. The sharp-edged pebbles on the track bit through the paper-thin soles of his shoes, which were more suitable for the palazzos and cathedrals of Napoli than they were for this stony ground. And it was a very small procession indeed, no more than a dozen or so people. The Bishop liked addressing people in their hundreds and thousands when he could rely on the majesty and dignity of his presence to create the appropriate impression on his listeners; conducting Mass with fewer people than he could fit into his kitchen seemed a waste of his high office. Brother Renato should have realized that, he thought. It was a pity that Father Giovanni was too ill to organize this event, he would have known better how to accommodate the Bishop. His mood was not improved by the conspicuous absence of the British, who had added insult to injury by ignoring his generous invitation to be part of the ceremony.

The Bishop considered himself a modern man, happily embracing innovations such as motor cars and the wireless. As a senior cleric, he could enjoy the many comforts and conveniences available in a sophisticated city such as Napoli. This was only reasonable, he believed, as compensation for the many burdens of his position. Ischia, on the other hand, was isolated and rural, left behind by the modern world. Why, they didn't even have electricity in Fontana, whereas the Bishop's palace in Napoli had enjoyed electric lights for many years.

Stories of pagan practices continued to find their way across the Bay to the Bishop, another sign of Ischia's medieval isolation. On a bright, sunny day like this, it was hard for him to understand how anyone could seriously think that elves—the Linchetti, he thought they were called—lived up here, but the tales persisted. Father Giovanni had managed to suppress much of this; the Bishop considered the accomplishment a tribute to the priest's uncompromising adherence to strict Catholic doctrine, almost enough to offset his unfortunate predilection for small boys. Troubled by his thoughts of elves and deviant priests, the Bishop's hand crept automatically to the crucifix on his chest, seeking the comfort that came from stroking the heavy silver.

Beside him, Renato was enjoying the walk, oblivious to the Bishop's distress. His thick peasant shoes protected his feet, the sun warmed his face, and birds sang. The grasses in the field beyond the drystone wall stirred gently in the soft breeze. A woody aroma drifted from a soft carpet of rosemary in a sunlit corner of the field. Renato recalled with pleasure the story of the Virgin Mary placing her cloak on the shrub so she could rest–when she got up, the white flowers had turned blue, the colour of her cloak. He breathed deeply and silently thanked God for the privilege of being alive on a day like this. The lack of a Mayor to round out the procession troubled him not even a little.

The Bishop came to a sudden stop when he turned a corner and saw the cross for the first time. The ground rose almost straight up before them, with rocks scattered among the yellow shrubs. The cross stood high at the top of the cliff, the black rods proud and alone against the sky. From here, Renato could fully appreciate the genius of Tifeo's design; the two hollow boxes of the cross had a powerful presence that seemed magnified by the natural strength of the mountain. The result was impressively large, as high as two men, and light as gossamer. Renato felt he could blow it away with a single breath, while knowing very well how strong it was.

"That is quite extraordinary," the Bishop said with genuine admiration. Perhaps he'd been wrong about Brother Renato after all. "Who made it?"

"Tifeo, the blacksmith," replied Renato. "Perhaps Your Excellency would care to meet him?"

Without waiting for an answer, he beckoned to Tifeo, who was at the back of the procession with Amedea. When Tifeo came to Renato's side, the Bishop held out his hand, expecting Tifeo to kiss the episcopal ring. Instead, Tifeo shook it awkwardly, and said, in his thickest Ischian accent, how honoured he was to meet the Bishop. Nonplussed, the Bishop said, "That is a truly inspiring cross you have made, you must have felt God's spirit flowing through you."

"I am but a simple blacksmith, Your Honour," Tifeo mumbled. "I just do the best I can." The Bishop could barely understand him. Amazed that an ill-spoken blacksmith in a primitive backwater like this could produce something so remarkable, he nodded politely and turned back to Brother Renato. "God works in a mysterious way, does he not, Brother Renato?"

A little further up the slope, Renato turned onto the small footpath that led away from the mule track. The group followed in single file, occasionally putting a hand against a rock to keep their balance on the narrow path. Emerging into an open space, Renato stopped again. "This is where the plane crashed," he told the Bishop. He pointed down the slope. "It came from there, from Capri. The pilot must have been very lost."

The ground in front of the two men fell away to the south before rising again to a small rise. A crude shepherd's shelter made of simple stone walls stood at the top of the small valley, almost hidden in the long grass. Yellow flowers waved gently, bright splashes of colour against the dark green shrubs, grasses and ferns that covered the hillside. Rocks lay strewn across the slope, some as large as wine carts, but even they looked as harmless as children's toys scattered on the floor.

The Bishop looked around, trying without success to imagine what had happened. It all looked completely innocent. With some effort, he could see a slight indentation in the vegetation where Brother Renato said the plane had slid up the slope, but otherwise he could see no sign of the violence that must have accompanied the crash. No sign that thirteen people and an unborn child had died here.

Renato said, "Please come this way, Your Excellency," leading the Bishop up an even narrower and steeper path to the cross. On one side of the path, the raw rock of the mountain grew out of the shrubs. On the other, the ground fell sharply away. The Bishop had to lift the skirt of his cassock with one hand to avoid tripping on it. With his other hand, he held his crosier away from the rocks to protect the ornate gold snakes at the top, regarding each other with eyes of red rubies. Turning a sharp corner between two high boulders, the two priests emerged onto a small, flat area with the crash site behind them and a sheer drop in front. Below the cliff and beyond an expanse of forest, they could see the town of Forio, a toy fishing boat heading out of the harbour. The waters of the Mediterranean shimmered, serene and as blue as rosemary all the way to the distant horizon.

The cross was mounted on two large bolts set firmly into the rock. At its foot was a small stone plaque: "AI CADUTI DELL' AERO", it said. "TO THE FALLEN OF THE AEROPLANE."

The Very Reverend Ottavio Acquaviva D'Aragona contemplated the cross and plaque in silence, then turned to look thoughtfully at the crash site. Renato stood beside him, holding back tears. Eventually the Bishop said, "This is a very beautiful place, Brother Renato."

"Indeed. Very beautiful, but also very sad."

"Come," the Bishop said. "Let us celebrate Mass together."

Demonte was among the group waiting for the priests to return. The only person not from the town, he stood a little apart, carefully watching the grasses and shrubs, looking for some sign that Paolo was with them. Brother Renato had followed through on his promise to offer prayers of repentance over Paolo's unmarked grave, but Demonte was of the mountain and he felt certain that Paolo's spirit was still tied to this place. The flat area that now held the cross was the platform from which Paolo had hurled himself into thin air, where Demonte had found the small pile of clothes before looking over the cliff and seeing Paolo's insignificant, pale body draped across the rocks at the bottom like a discarded rag.

Demonte thought of that moment often, despite the intense stab of guilt that always came. The shame of not looking after his little brother, of failing in his promise to their father, was like a stiletto buried in his heart. The guilt lay deep within him, a wound to his soul that he kept fresh by obsessively picking at the scab, night after night. Yet he also welcomed the sharp pain; it meant that Paolo still lived, if only in his memory, the only immortality he was likely to have.

When Tifeo told him about the cross and its location, Demonte was pleased. He liked the idea of a memorial to the people who died in the crash. But in his mind, it was also a memorial to Paolo, who died because of the crash. And if he was the only person who thought of the cross in this way, so be it.

Tifeo could see where Demonte was looking so intently and guessed at what he was thinking. Following the shepherd's gaze, he could see nothing in the grasses and shrubs. But a gathering of this size so high on the mountain was unusual and he could feel curiosity growing around him.

Amedea tapped him on the shoulder and pointed. Over on the other side of the valley, Adolfo sat on a small rock by himself, watching what was happening. Several small caves were set into the low cliff behind him, shallow indentations that must have provided the barest minimum of shelter to the hermits who came up here long ago to find God.

Tifeo felt a familiar flash of anger. He had once idolised his older brother but now felt only shame at being in the same family. Despite what he'd told Brother Renato, he was very aware of what people thought of Adolfo and didn't like being associated with him. But he'd stopped being so vocal about his contempt after Rosabella told him about her conversation with Adolfo at the wake. "I think he misses you," she'd said. "He just doesn't know what to do about it."

Tifeo's feelings of shame and contempt for his brother were complicated by his growing realization that there was a hole in his heart where his brother ought to be. Despite hating what he knew Adolfo had done ("You'll be getting no share of what we find up there," Adolfo had said, leaving no room for doubt about what he intended) Tifeo missed him, missed the easy camaraderie they'd enjoyed when younger.

He wondered if he could have stopped Adolfo and the others. Would they would have listened to him? How much of all this was his fault? Not the deaths, that had already happened, but the rest of it? He thought it strange that he felt as guilty for not doing what he should have been done as Adolfo should feel for what he did do. But things not done must remain undone once their moment has passed, and his only chance for doing right was lost forever.

Amedea sensed his distress and squeezed his hand silently, a reassurance that he was not alone. Tifeo carefully relaxed his tense shoulders, breathed deeply and slowly, and forced himself to watch the priests coming down from the cross.

Across the shallow valley, Adolfo could see the cross clearly where it stood at the edge of the cliff. That fucking cross, he thought, that fucking priest, that fucking brother of his. Making the cross out of bits and pieces from the plane was the last straw, making it impossible to pretend, even to himself, that the cross was just a cross. Instead, it would be a permanent and potent reminder of that terrible night. If only they'd left well enough alone, he could have let the memories fade away like the morning mist. Without the memories, it would be as if nothing had ever happened, and he'd be able to sleep at night.

Adolfo's attention was pulled back by the sight of the two priests returning to the group waiting on the relatively flat and open piece of ground just below the cross. A small altar had been brought up for the occasion. Adolfo recognised Brother Renato in his white alb, knowing that the other figure in red must be the Bishop. But where was Father Giovanni? Adolfo had heard at his aunt's funeral party that he might be ill, but surely not so ill that he couldn't be part of something like this?

The Mass began. The Bishop pitched his voice up to be heard above the rustling of the wind, every familiar word clearly audible across the valley. Adolfo found that he could listen to the words or follow the actions of the priests, but he couldn't do both. Preferring to listen, he gazed unseeing at the grasses swaying in front of him.

"God our Father, your gift of water brings life and freshness to the earth; it washes away our sins and brings us eternal life." The Bishop's voice was clear and true. The emphasis on 'our sins' was delicate but unmistakeable—we have all sinned, he was saying, none of us is clean, every one of us should seek the divine gift of God's water. And then, after the slightest but most intentional of pauses, the reassuring offer of comfort, of eternal life. Surrender yourself to

God by accepting His gift, and all will be forgiven.

You, too, can be saved, Adolfo.

But from what, he asked himself. Was what they did on the mountain really as bad as Tifeo and the others thought? If we hadn't gone up there, he thought, other people would. The result would have been the same. As it was, we're being blamed for doing what anyone in Fontana would have done if they had the chance. Maybe they're just jealous that we got there first.

Who did Tifeo think he was, anyway, setting himself up as the judge of right and wrong? That was a job for priests, not blacksmiths, and pounding red-hot metal into submission was not the same as guiding souls to God's grace.

And Brother Renato was misguided. He was young, inexperienced, and much too close to the precious Tifeo. No, it was enough to pay attention to what Father Giovanni had said in his homily, no need to heed what Tifeo and Brother Renato thought. Or anyone else.

Reassured once more that his soul was not in mortal danger, Adolfo relaxed, pushing his doubts back into the shadows where they belonged.

The Bishop's voice faded to a dull murmur, lost in the breeze. Light gusts blew up the valley, successive waves undulating smoothly across the grasses and shrubs. The round heads of yellow flowers bobbed up and down, looking like drowning swimmers. Mesmerised by the continual, shifting motion, seeing patterns appear and dissolve, appear and dissolve, Adolfo lost himself in the ceaseless swirl of light and dark. Unable to tear his eyes away from the flowers, he leaned back, resting his head against the huge rock behind him. The rock seemed to grow out of the ground, as rooted in the soil as a tree, just as massive, just as alive.

Adolfo floated, adrift in the waves moving across the valley. The solid rock against his head was not enough to stop his mind wandering with the wind sighing through the grass.

The Bishop's voice cut into his reveries. "My brothers and sisters," he said, "to prepare ourselves to celebrate the sacred mysteries, let us call to mind our sins." What sins was he talking about? Whose sins?

What if Father Giovanni was wrong about the crash being God's will? The thought was unbidden. Adolfo knew better than most that the priest was human, just as capable of sinning as the next man. '*Our* sins', the Bishop had said, twice. Surely that meant that Giovanni– and the Bishop as well, for that matter–were human, as flawed as he was. And if they were sinners themselves, how could they be trusted to truly represent the voice of God?

Adolfo groaned aloud as he realized that the once-solid ground beneath his feet was no longer safe. He could feel his certainty, born of self-protection, crumbling before the forces of doubt.

The grasses in front of him opened and he saw the face of the man from the plane, the one he thought was a priest. Beneath the hood of his cloak, the man's forehead was crushed and bloody, and when he opened his mouth to speak, Adolfo could see the gaps where there had once been teeth.

You killed me, the spirit said.

No, cried Adolfo, you were going to die anyway. You cannot blame me for this.

You cut short my time. We have so little, every second is precious, and you stole the last few moments left to me.

It was a mercy, to end your suffering.

I was far beyond suffering, the spirit said, and it was no mercy. Because of you, I could not prepare myself for death, nor could I bid farewell to my wife.

It was God's will, I meant no harm.

How could this possibly be God's will? What kind of God wills what you did?

Across the field, the yellow heads of the other spirits nodded in agreement. We are tethered to this place, they said, until you atone. Only then will we be free to leave, to find our ultimate destiny.

Atone, asked Adolfo, how can I atone when I seek atonement for myself?

Dark shapes writhed in the farthest recesses of his mind,

dangerous shadows of memories which he had always tried to push out of the sunlight but which never quite went away. Even on good days, he knew they were there, waiting to emerge and wreak havoc on the precarious balance of his life. Now they were squirming like snakes in a pit, pushing against his fading will and self-control.

And at last, the darkest, most shameful memory of them all slowly crawled out from the shadows. Adolfo tried to push it back into the dark where it belonged, but no longer had the strength.

He was with Father Giovanni in the sacristy. The priest smelled of stale cigarette smoke and bad breath. "I know your father would be proud of you," he was saying. Adolfo thought his dead and not particularly religious Poppa would have been horrified at what he was doing. Becoming an altar boy was his mother's idea; she thought he needed a father figure to guide him through his approaching adolescence.

"You seem tense," Father Giovanni said. "Allow me." He stepped behind Adolfo and started massaging his neck and shoulders. It felt good, and Adolfo could feel himself relaxing. "This is God's grace," Father Giovanni said, "working through my fingers. Be grateful."

After a few minutes, the massage stopped. "Thank you, Father," Adolfo said. "Don't thank me," replied Father Giovanni. His voice sounded a bit strained. "Give thanks to God for the relief He brings you."

The next time Adolfo was alone with Father Giovanni, he received another neck massage. It felt just as good as the first one. When it was over, Father Giovanni patted him gently on the backside and told him to go through the church and tidy up the pews.

"Do you do this for all the altar boys?" he asked before opening the door.

"Only the ones like you, who wish to be closer to God," answered the priest. "But God is more generous with his gifts to those who strive harder. I think you might be one of those."

Adolfo was anxious to please, and the neck massages did feel good. So he worked hard in the church and faithfully followed Father Giovanni's instructions.

"You're doing well," Father Giovanni said after a few weeks. "It seems that God wishes to thank you for your efforts. Remove your shirt and lie down over there and I will see what I can do." He pointed at a padded bench beneath a stained glass window showing Jesus washing the disciples' feet.

Adolfo felt a flicker of discomfort but did as he was told. His unease grew as Father Giovanni massaged first his neck and shoulders, then worked down his back. His eyes squeezed shut, he could hear the priest's breathing becoming ragged, and felt the slightest trembling of his hands as they reached his waist. He stopped breathing altogether when Father Giovanni pushed his thumbs under his trousers and then the worn elastic of his underpants, and fondled the cleft at the top of his buttocks. He must have made a sound, because the hands paused. Adolfo tensed, and the hands quickly withdrew.

"Turn over," said the priest. "I should rub your shoulders from the front."

Adolfo lay on his back, eyes shut tight, as Father Giovanni massaged his shoulders and under his collarbone. "Can you feel God's power flowing through my fingers?" the priest asked. Adolf said nothing. "Maybe this will help," Giovanni said, and slowly moved his hands down Adolfo's chest, gently stroking the skin all the while. Once again, his hands moved under his trousers and underpants, stroking his stomach. It felt terribly wrong and wonderfully good at the same time. His confusion grew to breaking point when he realized that his *cazzo* had become stiff.

He must have sobbed, because the stroking paused. Adolfo sat up quickly, forcing the priest to pull his hands away. "I should get home, Father," he said, his voice shaking, "my mother is expecting me soon."

Father Giovanni looked disappointed. "Very well," he said. "But God's gift is not yet complete, we can continue another time."

His mother was making supper when he got home. "That's nice, *carissimo*," she said after he told her about the massage. "It's good that he wants to help you. Now, can you please wash your hands and lay the table?"

Adolfo felt helpless to say no when Father Giovanni next asked him to lie shirtless on the bench. "Is this really what God wants?" he asked, his arms clutched tightly against his chest. "Oh, yes," replied Father Giovanni, sounding reassuring. "He sees all and knows all, and understands when boys need comfort, as you do. When I rub your back, you will feel His goodness and grace flowing through my hands into you."

Instead, all Adolfo could think of was how rough Father Giovanni's hands were and how wrong they felt around his waist. He liked the neck rubs, they relaxed muscles that had been tight ever since his beloved Poppa had been taken too soon to meet his Maker. But now he felt taken advantage of and it was becoming obvious, even to an innocent like him, that the older man was enjoying himself far too much. He was just a tool that Father Giovanni used for his own pleasure. Defenceless, increasingly terrified of what might happen next, and totally alone, he finally realized that this was deeply wrong and that Father Giovanni was a monster. And he had no idea of how to save himself from whatever else the priest was intending.

Biting his lip, he slowly undid the buttons on his shirt, then took it off. Before he could put the shirt on the chair, he heard voices in the church. Looking up at the clock, he saw that it was much later than either he or Father Giovanni thought. The voices were members of the choir arriving for practice.

"Quick, put your shirt back on," hissed Father Giovanni. "No one must see you like this."

Fingers fumbling in his haste, Adolfo put his shirt back on as quickly as he could. He had just tucked it into his trousers when there was a knock on the door and the choir master stuck his head into the sacristy. Did his eyes rest just a moment on Adolfo? "Are you ready for practice, Father?" he asked. "We will work on the Agnus Dei for Sunday's Mass." Father Giovanni paused for a moment, then hurried through to the church, leaving Adolfo on his own.

When he came out, the choir was concentrating hard on their singing. The glorious music rose to the rafters of the church, joining earth and Heaven with a shimmering ladder of sound. 'Lamb of God, who takes away the sins of the world…' The only person who paid him any attention was Demonte, the eldest son of the shepherd high on the mountain, who smirked knowingly when he saw Adolfo emerge by himself from the sacristy before scuttling up the side of the church.

He was crying by the time he got home.

"What's the matter?" his mother asked.

"I don't like Father Giovanni, Mama," he said. "He wanted to do bad things to me."

"You must have misunderstood. He's a priest, he won't do bad things."

"He's a bad man," protested Adolfo. "He wanted to rub me in bad places."

His mother was tired after a long, hot day, and her temper was frayed. This was the last straw. "Don't you ever talk about Father Giovanni like that," she shouted. "He's a good man, you need him now your father isn't here." She slapped Adolfo hard on the cheek. "Go to your room! I don't want to see you until dinner is ready."

Dinner was eaten in silence. Ulisse and Tifeo both knew that something was wrong but were wise enough not to pry. The last thing Adolfo wanted to do was talk about Father Giovanni again, least of all with his brothers listening. And judging by the force with which she banged pots around in the kitchen after dinner, his mother was still furious with him for questioning the actions of a priest.

But she didn't argue when he said that he didn't want to be an altar boy any more. And the next time he saw Father Giovanni, the priest took one look at his face, bent down and said firmly, "No one will ever believe you," and walked quickly away, saying nothing further, then or ever.

Many years later, Adolfo felt the familiar heat of shame and humiliation as he sat by himself on the mountainside. His life had never been the same since that day. Despite his skill with sausages, he knew himself to be worthless, a victim of malicious forces beyond his understanding or control.

The spirits were still watching him, waiting. Addressing the man he killed, he said, I thought you were a priest. Or a monk, they're all the same. It's not my fault you looked like that.

Is this a place where men habitually kill priests?

The spirit seemed mildly surprised.

Adolfo could say nothing. He felt enormously tired. He had managed to contain the memory of that dreadful time for all these years, but now the cage was wide open, and he feared he would never be able to capture the beast again. And now the beast had a companion, the sickening recognition that what he did after the crash was deeply wrong. The pretence that he was merely following God's will was just a paper-thin mask, too flimsy to hide behind forever.

He wept. He wept for the things that Father Giovanni had done to him, for the things that the priest had taken from him, for the things he had done himself. He wept for what was, and what might have been, the person he could have been, the things he could have done. The loss of his family, the burial of his self-respect under a mountain of shame.

He wept, and the spirits watched in silence.

Across the valley, the Bishop was preparing to give communion. "Deliver us, Lord, from every evil, and grant us peace in our day," he said as Brother Renato placed the sacraments on the altar.

Deliver us from every evil? thought Adolfo, his cheeks wet. What hypocrisy is that? Father Giovanni is one of you, and look at the evil he has delivered. You are the people who did evil, what possible right do you have to pray for deliverance? Misery turned rapidly to anger as he thought about the terrible things done to him.

I must hold on to this anger, he thought, it's only right in the face of such evil. Anything else would be to condone it, act as if it had never happened, forgive the unforgivable.

What about us, asked the spirits. Are we not also entitled to our anger? Look at what you took from us.

You had already lost what we took, said Adolfo, startled by their question. You were dead, and had no further use of material things.

Not so, they replied. You took our dignity and impoverished our families. And Paolo joined us too soon because of what he saw you do. Think of the long life he could have led but for you. You have much to answer for.

I meant you no harm, he cried.

Perhaps not, but look now at what you've done. Your deeds tie us here and we cannot leave until you untie the knots.

I am trapped, Adolfo thought. Father Giovanni on one side, these spirits on the other. Is there no escape?

He groaned again and leaned forward, putting his head in his hands.

For the last time, the Bishop's voice broke into his thoughts. "Go in peace to love and serve the Lord," he said, coming to the end of Mass and giving blessings to the small group standing in front of him.

Peace, thought Adolfo, what peace? I don't know what that means any more. And love? I have no one to love, and there is no one who loves me. Certainly not the Lord, who abandoned me in His own house when I needed Him most.

He looked for the spirits, seeking their sympathy—or at least their understanding—but they too had abandoned him, leaving behind only the waving grasses and mocking yellow flowers.

He wept again, tears of rage, remorse and self-pity running down his face. Sobbing, he rose clumsily to his feet and stumbled towards the path that led down to Fontana and his shop, the only place he felt safe.

Chapter Eighteen

ULISSE LOVED NAPOLI.

He loved the bustle and crowds, so different from the placid pace of life on Ischia. He could sit in Fontana's main square and meet everyone he knew before the sun had reached its peak–in Napoli, he could walk the streets in the centre of the city for days without running into any familiar faces. In Fontana, the gossip today was indistinguishable from that of yesterday. But here, life was rich and complex, and event followed unpredictable event with chaotic exuberance, providing an endless and infinitely varied supply of topics for conversation over a glass of prosecco.

Most of all, he loved the opportunity. Men in Fontana were born, followed in their father's footsteps, and died. Neapolitans could choose that life if they wished or they could make their own path, pursuing greater dreams, taking larger risks perhaps, but doing so in the hopes of reaping even larger rewards.

Ulisse knew that he would be scratching out a living as a labourer had he stayed in Fontana, building houses for someone else. Maybe even for Cesare, God forbid, a life as rewarding as that of a mule pulling ploughs in the fields outside town. Instead, he had money in the bank and a small but comfortable apartment on the Via San Giovanni Maggiore Pignatelle, a side street whose name was longer than it was wide, with the great advantage of being just a two-minute walk to the table kept reserved for him at the Pizzeria San Gennaro. The staff knew who he was and who he represented, and took great care that he was well looked after.

Sitting there one warm evening in early autumn, he idly watched a muddle of small boys playing soccer in the square. Several small dogs, barely larger than the football, ran among the boys, yapping excitedly. The waiter rushed out to shoo the boys away whenever the game veered too close to the tables outside the pizzeria. The game would drift away towards the other side of the square, flowing like water around the statue at the centre and then, inevitably, would drift back again.

A particularly scruffy little urchin kicked the ball as hard as he could, apparently trying to make an impression on the larger boys. Instead, the ball skidded sideways and flew through the air straight at the waiter carrying Ulisse's pizza Margherita and an open bottle of wine on a small tray. Ulisse stuck his hand out in an automatic reflex and, much to his surprise, caught the ball.

The boys ran over to retrieve their ball but stopped when they recognised, with the age-old instincts of all street children, someone to be afraid of. They gathered in a semicircle, watching warily as Ulisse casually bounced the ball up and down. The dogs milled around in confusion, wondering why the game had suddenly ended.

"Signore, signore, please accept my apologies." The waiter had put the tray on the table and was hopping up and down in his agitation. "Those children are a menace, we can do nothing to keep them away…" His voice trailed away as Ulisse pointed at the boy who kicked the ball and crooked a finger at him. One of the older players pushed the terrified urchin out of the group. The boy hesitated before slowly coming over to stand in front of Ulisse, his head hanging. The sound of the bouncing ball echoed around the square, now silent as everyone watched the unfolding drama.

"Look at me," said Ulisse. His voice was stern and the other boys sighed, expecting the worst. The boy reluctantly raised his head, his eyes brimming with tears.

"What's your name?"

"Giampiero," the boy said in a whisper.

"You don't kick very well, Giampiero, do you?" asked Ulisse. Giampiero shook his head, looking down again at his feet.

"Are you sorry for what you did?"

The boy nodded, his head bowed.

Ulisse bounced the ball a few more times, then held it out to the boy.

"You need to practice more," he said. "This time, I forgive you. Next time, you won't be so lucky. Now go, before I change my mind."

Giampiero turned and scampered back to safety, clutching the football.

"You boys need to be more careful," Ulisse called out to them. "Stay away from the tables, you hear? If anything like this happens again, there'll be trouble. You understand me?"

The boys all nodded, the older ones more vigorously. They recognised how narrowly they had just escaped.

"Bugger off," said Ulisse, waving his hand in dismissal. "I want to enjoy my supper in peace."

The waiter watched as the soccer game resumed on the far side of the square.

"With respect, signore, you were too lenient with them," he said. "They will soon be back, causing more trouble."

"Perhaps," said Ulisse. "But now they've learned that forgiveness and retribution are brother and sister. We should all remember that, do you not think?"

About to protest, the waiter suddenly remembered who he was talking to. "Of course, signore," he said. "I hope they learn their lesson and remember your kindness."

His pizza finished and the plate removed, Ulisse relaxed with his wine. The soccer game continued safely on the other side of the square, boys coming and going as their energy and mothers allowed. It was a perfect Neapolitan evening, the last light of the sun bouncing off walls on the east side of the square, warming the dull gray stone of the surrounding buildings. Families casually strolled together around the square, chatting with friends and enjoying the open air. The square hummed with the buzz of a community that preferred to live outdoors, the sound of people content in the moment, regardless of how hard their life might be otherwise.

As he finished his bottle of wine, Ulisse saw Cutolo making his way across the square, coming to join him. Waving to the waiter, he ordered more wine.

He had rapidly gained Cutolo's trust since joining the Camorra, reliably applying their particular doctrine of tough love with discretion and firmness. Most of the disputes he dealt with were minor, generally arguments between neighbours or family members. Quite often, all he had to do was show up and people who were about to kill each other suddenly became best friends.

More severe situations required a stronger hand; the previous week, he had learned of a foolish young man who was considering setting up a street corner betting operation in direct competition with the Camorra's own man. When Ulisse went to see him, he found it necessary to lift the would-be sinner off the ground, pushing him against the wall. "You would be most unwise to do this," he said. "We'll drive you out of Napoli, away from your family and friends." The young man's eyes, full of naïve defiance, showed that he expected this threat and was unmoved by it.

"Of course," Ulisse went on in the same calm, quiet, frightening voice, "should you persist in this foolishness, we have more extreme measures. You should not think you'd be the only one affected—your family will also suffer. And your girlfriend, Paloma, isn't it?" Now the young man's eyes flickered, so Ulisse allowed him back on his feet. "There is only one path to the future you seek," he said, "and that's to accept our protection. Trust us and work within our rules, and you can do well. Take another path and I promise you it will end badly. But your ambition is impressive. Come and see me next week and I'll introduce you to someone who can help make your dreams come true." Under the circumstances, the young man found the offer to be both attractive and magnanimous, and quickly chose to join the faithful host of small entrepreneurs working under the guidance and protection of the Camorra.

Cutolo sat down on the other side of the small table, refusing the offer of pizza from the waiter who had rushed over as he arrived. Ulisse poured him a glass of wine. The two men watched the peaceful scene in the square with the satisfaction of two shepherds overseeing a flock of content sheep.

Eventually, Cutolo sighed. "We have a problem," he said.

Ulisse transferred his attention from a young woman who was being closely chaperoned by her parents, much to the frustration of several potential suitors hovering nearby. He waited for Cutolo to continue, knowing that the other man hated to be rushed.

"What do you know about Giordano Bruno?" Cutolo asked after a long pause.

"I've heard some rumours, no more."

"They're true. He's been going around the bars in La Sanità trying to persuade people there that we cannot protect them, that they'd be better off with the 'Ndrangheta. They'd like to take over our operations in Napoli and Bruno has decided to throw his lot in with them. The Madonna only knows what he thinks he'll get out of upsetting arrangements that work perfectly well."

"Have any of the bars chosen to believe him?"

"Not yet, but we know of two that are tempted. Bar Gamberoni, and the Gran Caffè Nilo."

Ulisse knew that Cutolo wasn't just passing the time with this conversation. "What do you want me to do?" he asked, confident that he'd earned the right to be that direct.

"Several people have talked with Bruno. He thinks our time has passed, that families like the 'Ndrangheta are the way of the future. He will not listen to reason. He even has the nerve to accuse us of being corrupt, as if the 'Ndrangheta were not. Threats have no effect. He's convinced that he's right and that the 'Ndrangheta offer better protection than we do. We only have one option left. And it must be exercised in a way that demonstrates to these bars and everyone else that they must look to us and not to these Calabrian upstarts."

Ulisse nodded. "You'd like this problem to go away."

"As soon as possible."

Cutolo left soon afterwards, leaving Ulisse to finish the wine.

As the light faded, he decided to go down to the two bars right away. He always found action preferable to thinking and this situation didn't seem to require much thought or planning.

The bars were close together on the edge of La Sanità, normally an area loyal to the Camorra. Making a quick stop at his apartment and picking up his small car, he drove first to the Gran Caffè Nilo. He could see everyone who was there from his table at the back of the room but Bruno was not among them. When he'd nursed his drink long enough to be polite, he got up and went to the Bar Gamberoni. The bar was one street over, half-way up a small, dark alley that was full of garbage and graffiti.

He saw Bruno the moment he walked in. The heretic sat with a small group at one side of the bar, their glasses of grappa on the red and white checked tablecloth. Bruno saw him and stiffened. Ulisse ignored him and found a table where he could watch the door without looking directly at his prey. The noise level returned to normal levels as everyone in the bar decided that he was there to have a quiet drink, not to cause trouble.

His drink finished, Ulisse casually walked to the door, conscious of eyes watching every step. Outside, he found a doorway between the bar and the street and stepped into the shadow to wait. Bruno would emerge eventually, on his own or with the others. Either option was fine with Ulisse.

An hour or so later, Bruno came out of the bar with his friends. It seemed they were the last customers to leave; Ulisse heard the door being locked behind them. After loud farewells, his friends went the other way, leaving Bruno alone in front of the bar. He looked up and down the now empty alley, then began walking quickly towards the street. Foolish, thought Ulisse, but convenient. He stepped out behind Bruno and hit him hard at the back of his head.

By the time Bruno came around, Ulisse had tied him to a very old and uncomfortable wooden chair. Ulisse was smoking a cigarette and watching him, his eyes dark as wet stones.

Bruno said, "You can do whatever you like to me, but the 'Ndrangheta will win in the end."

"You cannot break faith with the Camorra without consequences," Ulisse said.

"My concern is for the people who live here," replied Bruno. "The 'Ndrangheta will take better care of them than you do. I would rather betray the Camorra than my friends and family who live here. You have family, I know—surely you would do the same for them?"

"When I joined," said Ulisse, "I swore a blood oath that the

Camorra were now my family and that my loyalty to them was absolute, more so than to my family on Ischia. You swore the same oath. But you have betrayed your Camorra family and must pay the price."

"Is there no room for doubt in this loyalty?" asked Bruno. He sounded genuinely puzzled, more interested in the question than in the certain fact that his arms and ankles were tightly bound and the equally certain fact that very bad things were about to be done to him. "No room to wonder if there might be a better way?"

"None." Ulisse's tone was final. "Doubt is the enemy of loyalty and cannot be allowed to poison people's minds."

Bruno sagged as he realized that Ulisse was closed to argument. He turned his head to look up and down the alley, but it was empty. There was no one to help him, and angels and miracles were rare in this part of town.

Ulisse pulled out an old pallet from a nearby pile of garbage and put it in the middle of the alley, opposite the door to the Bar Gamberoni. He lifted Bruno and the chair without any effort and placed them in the middle of the pallet. A pile of discarded cans of cooking oil lay to one side of the garbage, beside wads of discarded newspaper. Ulisse distributed the paper under and around the chair, then emptied the cans over them, over the pallet, and over Bruno, shaking them to get the last drops of oil out. Bruno's eyes were closed. Finally, Ulisse went back to his doorway, returning with the jerry-can he'd brought from his car. He emptied the can, pouring petrol over Bruno, soaking his clothes, then over the pallet and newspaper.

"You don't have to do this," whispered Bruno, opening his eyes as the horror of what was about to happen to him sank in. "Please don't…"

Ulisse said, "I must. My oath requires it." He took a deep drag on his cigarette, tossed it into the petrol-soaked newspaper, and calmly walked away. Behind him, he heard the whoomp as the petrol suddenly exploded into flame. As he turned into the street, doors and windows were flung open up and down the alley as people rushed out to see who was screaming.

Adolfo rang the bell at Father Giovanni's front door, then stepped back. To his left, the street sloped down sharply under the archway that linked the back of the church to the priest's house. Adolfo had never been in the house but he knew that the rear looked over the graveyard, down the slopes beyond, the trees now bare of leaves, and then across the water to the pale reminder of Capri in the far distance.

The front of the house was freshly plastered and painted a lustrous shade of deep yellow. A man of substance lived here, the façade announced, someone important. The other houses around the small square opposite the church were not as well kept–patches of plaster and paint had peeled away from the walls, exposing the crude clay bricks underneath.

Adolfo had been busy since the Mass to consecrate the cross. Business was good; he always had fresh lamb for sale, even this late in the year, and people seemed to like his new recipe for sausages. If he was a touch more taciturn than usual, people did not notice or, more likely, were too polite to say anything. And to his great relief, there were no comments, pointed or otherwise, about either the Mass or the cross. The people of Fontana appeared to have decided that some things were best left undiscussed.

Cesare came to the shop for aperitivo less often these days, claiming that he was too busy building his new hotel down in Sant' Angelo. Adolfo was accustomed to the feeling of being abandoned by people close to him and did not feel offended. But his anger at Father Giovanni simmered, a constant undercurrent that disturbed his sleep and interrupted his thoughts at unexpected moments.

Late one evening, he was on his own in the shop after locking the door and decided that it was time to tackle a long overdue clean-up of the whole place. Swabbing down and scrubbing one surface after another, he nurtured his anger until, by the end of a week's work, the shop and workrooms were spotless and immaculate, and his fury at

Father Giovanni had become a hot flame at the centre of his chest.

At first, he relished the feeling. Now the beast was released, he had something–and someone–to blame for the darkness that never seemed to lift from his soul. Knowing that he was the victim of forces beyond his control was liberating; it meant that he didn't have to face up to the consequences of his actions.

But by the end of the week, he was forced to the conclusion that he had to do something.

In his zeal to clean, he had finally turned his attention to a large cupboard in a back corner of the room where he slaughtered sheep. Assorted pieces of old equipment lay forgotten on the floor in front of the cupboard, making it hard even to approach the door. Looking at the cupboard early one evening after the last customer had left, Adolfo couldn't remember what was inside, although he was sure that everything would be old and unpleasant to handle. Only one way to find out, he thought, and began clearing a space in front of the door.

By the end of the evening, he was hot and tired, but satisfied with his efforts. The floor was clear and almost all the cupboard contents had been placed in a pile outside the back door, ready to be taken to the dump. The most surprising thing he found was his old altar boy robe; years ago, he'd used it as a cloth to wipe his knives clean. After removing everything else and cleaning the inside of the cupboard, he had hung the robe, stiff with the dried blood of long-dead sheep, back on its hook.

Before replacing the robe, Adolfo had held it tight, thinking about how Father Giovani had changed his life in those few weeks. Since then, he had been alone, buffeted by forces he could neither see nor understand. As he remembered the night of the crash, even the decision to go up the mountain had been made with virtually no thought. Why not go and see what had happened? Maybe there'd be some money lying around, God knows we need it. Let's go up before other people get there, why not?

And what did it bring? Nothing but trouble. If he could only undo the deeds of that night, he'd willingly give up the money they'd taken. Then he wouldn't have to be on the receiving end of all this guilt and unspoken criticism that he felt everywhere he went, a price that was far too large compared to what they took.

Once the blood-stained robe was safely back in the cupboard, Adolfo focused again on his anger, but it was no longer a source of comfort. Instead, it ached continuously over the following days, an ongoing and unpleasant reminder of the wrongs done to him. Father Giovanni had much to answer for, he thought. Why should he be allowed to live out his life in comfort without being forced to acknowledge the harm he'd done? Adolfo knew that other boys had been treated the same way, although none of them had spoken out. Maybe it was time that someone confronted the priest and forced him to admit that, yes, he had done great wrong.

And so it was that Adolfo stood in front of Father Giovanni's door late on a cool November morning, waiting for it to open. He reached out to ring the bell again but paused when he heard someone coming. The door slowly opened, and the housekeeper looked out.

"Yes?"

Adolfo knew her from her frequent visits to his shop to buy meat and thought she was one of the ugliest women he had ever seen. Small dark eyes peered at him suspiciously, like currants set above her doughy cheeks. A huge purple birthmark ran down one side of her face, from her scalp into the high neck of the shapeless black dress. Her name was Viviana, although he couldn't think of anyone less full of life.

"I am here to see Father Giovanni," he said. "He's expecting me."

"He's not well."

"He asked me to come at this time. I would be sorry not to see him."

Viviana looked at him as if he was a piece of meat she might have to throw out, then reluctantly opened the door to let him into the pitch-black entrance hall. He waited politely for her to close the door before following her down the dark corridor to the back of the house. The only illumination came from light leaking under closed doors and reflecting off the polished tile floor. Adolfo could feel his energy drain away with every step.

She knocked on the door at the far end of the corridor, opened it, and said, "The butcher is here to see you. He says you're expecting him."

Adolfo couldn't hear the response but she turned and waved him in, her ostentatious sniff making it abundantly clear that she thoroughly disapproved of his presence. He squinted as he went in, temporarily blinded by the intense light pouring in through the huge window. The room was large and airy despite the heavy wood furniture against the walls.

Father Giovanni sat in a shadowed corner, dwarfed by the huge chair. A faded dressing gown swaddled his emaciated body, his thin, bare legs emerging from the bottom. His grey hair was long and lank, and thinner than Adolfo remembered. The pink, scabbed scalp looked liked the skin of a badly-skinned sheep. A Bible lay on his lap, one claw hand holding it open, the other marking his place as he looked up. A bloody handkerchief lay on the table beside the chair.

Adolfo said, "Thank you for agreeing to see me."

"I'm dying," Giovanni said. His tone was matter-of-fact, if faint. "In a few weeks, no more, I shall be with my Maker. Sit, sit." He gestured at the chair on the other side of the window.

Adolfo thought that Father Giovanni looked dreadful. He was quite accustomed to death, confronting it every time he led a sheep into the slaughter room, but this was different. Shocked by the hollowed-out skull in front of him, he could say nothing as he sat down.

"Naturally, I am contemplating the fate of my soul," Father Giovanni continued. He gestured at the Bible, his hand shaking a bit. "As should you, my son."

Without warning, he bent forward as he was seized by a violent, uncontrollable bout of liquid coughing. Adolfo watched, appalled. When the coughing eventually subsided into a wet gurgle, the priest reached out for the handkerchief and wiped the bloody spittle from his chin. He winced as a spasm of pain hit him, and rubbed his chest.

"You and I both know that your soul is stained," he went on, as if nothing had interrupted his thought. "You desecrated the bodies of the people from the plane, before you stole from them."

Adolfo was taken aback. He had asked to see Father Giovanni in a state of moral certainty and fury. And yet he was the one being accused before he had a chance to deliver his prepared speech to confront the priest with his acts.

Taken aback, he said, "I did no wrong. It was God's will, you said so yourself."

"So it was you," said Father Giovanni, "I thought so."

"Many people stole from the plane," Adolfo said. "You know that."

"But not all of them removed fingers or teeth. I knew it was you the moment I saw those cuts. Only a butcher could sever a joint that cleanly."

Adolfo sat in conflicted silence, his hands clenched. He wanted to hurl Father Giovanni's sins in his face, not be forced to account for the ones he knew were his.

"My comments in church were not for you," the dying man continued, "and you should not take them too literally. They were for the rest of my flock, who needed solace and comfort. But you have a different problem. You know you did wrong."

This was more than Adolfo could tolerate. This sanctimonious, wicked priest was the last person on earth with any right to lecture him.

"I did nothing wrong," he shouted. "You said so in front of everyone. Everyone, the whole town! And they believed you. How could you tell us it was God's will if you didn't believe that yourself? None of us did anything wrong."

Father Giovanni's skeletal hand casually brushed the point aside as if it was a pesky fly resting on the Bible.

"When you asked to see me," he said, "I assumed it was to make your peace before God. I hoped it was, I would like to help you confess your sins, repent, and gain His forgiveness." His voice was a hoarse whisper.

"Confess? Confess?" This was the opening that Adolfo needed. With relief, he abandoned the last of his restraint, knowing that he was in the right, feeling the cleansing rush of justified anger and outrage surge through his body. "How can you, of all people, invite me to confess?"

"I'm a priest," said Father Giovanni. "Of course I can take your confession. Why would I not?" He sounded genuinely surprised.

"After what you did to me, you have no right to condemn me. Or hear my confession." Adolfo's voice was tight.

"What are you talking about? I did nothing to you."

"Nothing? Was it nothing, putting your hands where you did?"

"I do not recall whatever you are thinking of, but my motives have always been pure. 'To the pure all things are pure, but to the corrupt and unbelieving nothing is pure; their very minds and consciences are corrupted.' I can only think that I should never have asked you to be an altar boy."

"I wish you never had. I trusted you, and you repaid that trust with your depravity. All that bullshit about God's love flowing through you, all you wanted was to get your filthy hands on me."

To his shame, Adolfo was weeping, something he'd vowed not to do. But now the tears were streaming down his face. He wiped them away furiously, smearing them across his cheek.

"You're the one who is depraved, my son, thinking that anything I did was less than pure. There was no harm done. All I ever wanted for any of my boys was to show them God's love. But you refused that precious gift. How do you think I felt after that?"

"What about your vows of chastity? Molesting me and the others means that you broke your vow."

"Chastity?" asked the priest, surprised again. "What does it have to do with anything? That forbids congress with a woman, and I have never broken that vow. Never."

He sounded so reasonable, his faint voice so calm, that Adolfo had to pause to collect himself.

"If I'm depraved," he said eventually, "it's because of you. You made me what I am. You disgust me, and when you die, I hope you go straight to Hell."

"Before I draw my last breath," said the priest calmly, "I shall make my final confession and Brother Renato will administer the Last Rites. I shall show our Good Lord that I repent of my sins, such as they are, and with His divine forgiveness, I shall be welcomed into everlasting Heaven. I await the inevitable with serenity."

"And I shall curse you and your memory until I go to my grave. You will never have my forgiveness."

Father Giovanni looked at him sadly. A faint pulse beat in his forehead and the faintest blush warmed his sallow cheeks.

"It grieves me to see such anger," he said. "I shall pray for you, that it does not eat you up. But your forgiveness will not decide the fate of my soul. That is for God, and God alone, to decide in his infinite wisdom and charity to those who love him. As I do."

"And what about me?" cried Adolfo. "Does my pain count for nothing?" He wiped his eyes again.

"Your pain is yours. I cannot help you with that. Until, that is, you decide to rejoin the rest of us who worship the one true Lord. He will forgive you your sins, as you must forgive those who have committed sins against you–real, or imagined. Once you have regained His grace, you can pray that he will relieve you of your pain."

"God abandoned me when He allowed you to use His name. He should have struck you down."

"You and I were only together in His house. Let us suppose for a brief moment that what you say is true, He would hardly strike me down there. And here I am, many years later. He has not struck me down, in His own house, or mine, or anywhere else. Apparently He did not take the same offence that you have."

Adolfo felt exhausted, defeated. He could still feel the anger but now it was suppressed, roiling away far below the surface. Suddenly, he wanted nothing more than to get out of this light, bright room, with its painting of Jesus blessing the children in one corner and evil in another.

"Come back, when you are ready." Father Giovanni's voice was a little stronger. "If I am able and still here, I would be glad to take your confession."

Adolfo walked to the door with as much dignity as his distress would allow. Turning, he looked across the room at the miserable creature who had ruined his life. "That," he said, "will happen only when men walk on the moon." It was the best he could do.

The housekeeper was doing something noisy at the back, clearly unaware of his departure. He managed to navigate the dark passage to the front of the house without walking into any of the furniture along the walls. The atmosphere was suffocating and he was glad to open the door into the street and fresh air.

Brother Renato was standing on the stoop with his hand outstretched toward the door and was forced to step aside as Adolfo pushed past him without a word into the small square outside. He watched curiously as the butcher hurried up the slope to the corner, turning left to get to his shop.

When Renato entered the living room at the back, Father Giovanni was reading his Bible again.

"I ran into Adolfo on the way in," Renato said, who had licence to come and go as he wished. "Or rather, he almost ran into me. Why was he here?"

"He asked to see me," said Father Giovanni. "I encouraged him to confess his sins, especially about what he did after the crash. He refused, unfortunately. I fear he is lost to the Lord. He used to be an altar boy, you know, until he decided he'd rather play ball and chase girls."

Oh no, thought Renato, another one. How many more are there? But Adolfo, as well?

"He seemed distressed," he said.

"He imagines that I was unkind to him in some way. I cannot understand why, I was very fond of him until he left. I think something was troubling him. I tried to help him, you know, but he turned me away."

Renato wondered how the older priest could live with himself after everything he'd done. But, remembering his orders from the Bishop, he managed to stop himself from asking any further questions. Instead, he opened his battered briefcase and pulled out his notes.

"About the sermon for next Sunday," he said, "I thought I would speak on 'The Means Necessary for Salvation'."

For the next hour, the two priests discussed the sermon and how to link it to Christmas, now only a few weeks away. Father Giovanni seemed energised by the exercise, despite having to pause occasionally to cough and deal with the excruciating pain that seemed to strike out of nowhere. Brother Renato, for his part, was content to follow the older priest's suggestions. To do anything else would force him to confront his doubts about his faith, his Church, and his conscience, battles he was not yet prepared to join.

Ampelio always opened up his outdoor tables in the week leading up to Christmas. Warmed by large paraffin heaters, his customers sat jammed together, enjoying the tradition and watching the bustle of activity on the packed street, calling out to friends as they passed by. Families always started their outing at the church, where children stood in front of the huge, ornate nativity scene with their mouths open in astonishment, forgetting that they'd seen the exact same display only a year before. Their progress up through town was inevitably interrupted and delayed by the urgent need to buy last minute presents at the stalls of tempting seasonal gifts laid out by shopkeepers. By the time they arrived at Ampelio's, the children were buzzing with fatigue, overexcitement and too many sweet treats, and their parents were exhausted. Ampelio's harried staff flew from table to table, bringing hot chocolate and *torrone* for the younger ones, something more substantial for their parents. Ampelio himself presided over the noisy throng with a benign smile and a relatively clean shirt.

Adolfo sat alone at a small table squeezed into one corner, nursing a glass of Sambuca. He had long since sold every scrap of meat in the shop and didn't want to have a drink there on his own, forced to listen to the sounds of the festivities outside. Cesare had not showed up, something that was increasingly common these days. Probably celebrating the season with his crew down in Forio, Adolfo thought, instead of being up here with his cousin.

Brooding on the unfairness of life, he was slow to realize that someone was standing right beside his table. It was Tifeo.

"You don't look too happy," Tifeo said, pulling up a chair that was miraculously vacant and waving at a waiter for attention.

"And what, exactly, am I supposed to be happy about?"

Tifeo said, "I looked in your shop, but it was closed. I'm glad I found you here."

Adolfo said nothing. He wanted to shout at Tifeo, make his brother leave him alone, but he felt trapped in his corner, unable to raise his voice to say what he wanted without heads turning, without people wondering what was going on between the two of them.

Tifeo said, "It's Christmas, Adolfo, a time to celebrate, for families to be together. Amedea and I would be glad if you could join us for dinner on Christmas Eve. A traditional meal, like Momma used to make—seven fish dishes, the works."

Adolfo took a slow sip of Sambuca to hide his surprise. His estrangement from Tifeo had lasted so many years that he couldn't remember the last time they ate together.

"Why would I do that?" he asked, struggling to keep his voice down. "You've made it very clear what you think about me. I'm surprised you think I'd feel welcome in your house."

"It saddens me that we have grown so far apart," Tifeo said. "Is it not time we brought the family back together, closed the gap between us?"

Rosabella, thought Adolfo, she's been talking to him. He didn't know whether to be annoyed that she was sticking her nose where it didn't belong or grateful that someone was taking an interest in him for once. But now he didn't know how much to believe Tifeo. Did he really want Adolfo to come to dinner or was he just asking so he could tell Rosabella that he tried?

His confusion must have shown itself, because Tifeo went on, "You're the head of the family, you should sit at the head of the table on occasions like this."

"I don't need you to tell me what to do," Adolfo snapped.

"Do you not think our difficulties have gone on long enough?" Tifeo asked. "This is a time for us to come together, forgive whatever wrongs have driven us apart."

"I don't know what wrongs you should forgive me for," Adolfo said. "And you're no angel, badmouthing me to anyone who will listen is not the way to bring us together."

"You're right," Tifeo said. "that was wrong, and I'm sorry. I've stopped doing that and will not do it again. I hope you can forgive me."

Adolfo snorted. Words said cannot be unsaid, he thought, and the damage is done. And who knew if Tifeo could be trusted to keep his opinions to himself in future?

"Well, you're too late, in any case," he said. "Ulisse has invited me to join him in Napoli."

"That's too bad. In the New Year, perhaps." Tifeo got up to leave, putting some money on the table. "That should cover my drink," he said. "We'll miss you, but will drink a toast to you and Ulisse. And think about family."

Adolfo watched his brother thread his way between the packed tables. So fuck off, he'd wanted to shout, but just managed to stop before the words passed his teeth. There was no point in letting Tifeo see how angry he was. Angry with Father Giovanni, angry with Tifeo, angry at the world. Angry at himself, for being a victim and not knowing how to break out of the endless circle of shame and guilt. Angry because he couldn't find a way to stop being angry.

For his part, Tifeo was disappointed. He could tell how upset Adolfo was but had no idea why, let alone how to break through to the brother he once had. Still, he'd promised Rosabella that he'd talk to Adolfo and he'd done that. Maybe there'd be other opportunities to get him talking about whatever troubled him so much.

Adolfo always enjoyed making sausages. He liked the physical labour of cranking the handle of the meat grinder, transforming warm lumps of fresh lamb or rabbit into finely-ground meat. Good as that felt, he thought that the true skill of sausage-making came when he used his strong hands to combine ground meat with wine (sometimes honey) and spices to produce a mixture that could be squeezed into casings. The mixture—almost a paste, really—had to have just the right degree of smoothness and the perfect balance of spices.

He considered himself to be an artist, unlike the mechanics elsewhere who churned out the same product time after time. Creating a new batch of sausages was like making a painting; the raw materials might be essentially the same, but his creativity and skill determined the final result. His choice of ingredients depended on his mood, sometimes hotter, sometimes more mellow. Even though his customers never quite knew what their sausages would taste like, they always had confidence that they would be excellent.

Several weeks after Christmas, he still felt sick with fury whenever he thought about his disastrous meeting with Father Giovanni. The accusation that he was the depraved one, with the clear implication that whatever happened was all his fault, was like having acid flung in his face. He wanted nothing more than to rub the priest's nose in his own filth, to exact retribution for what had been done to him. How else was a victim supposed to feel?

Brooding, his mood dark and angry, he savagely added an extra pinch of red pepper flakes. This batch of sausages would be even hotter than usual. About to plunge his hands into the mixture to spread the pepper evenly throughout, he heard the tinkle of the bell on the door to the street.

Cursing under his breath, he grabbed a cloth to wipe his hands and went to see who it was. Viviana, Father Giovanni's housekeeper, stood just inside the shop, seemingly unwilling to venture very far into the room. She looked curiously at Adolfo's hands, which still had red flecks on them. He wiped his hands again. The red pepper was very noticeable on the white towel.

"Yes?" Adolfo had no patience for pleasantries.

"Father Giovanni wants to see you. As soon as possible, he said. He doesn't have much time left."

"I don't want to see him. He can rot in Hell, for all I care."

Viviana flinched at the tone in his voice. She shifted her considerable weight uneasily.

"He thought you might say something like that. He asked me to tell you that this is not about your soul, but his. He wants to clear the slate, that's the phrase he used, before he dies."

"And why is that any concern of mine?"

"I think I know what happened between you," she said. "I couldn't help hearing what you said when you came to see him."

Adolfo looked away, unable to handle the look in her eyes. Who else knows about this, he wondered, the remorseless tide of shame and humiliation surging up yet again.

"When you live in someone's house," she went on, "there are no secrets. I know what kind of man he is, and I think he wants to do right by you. It might be very late, but that is his wish."

Hesitantly, she reached out and patted him on the arm. Adolfo didn't know which was worse: her evident dislike of him, or her pity.

"Please," she said. "It will be good for both of you."

After she left, Adolfo stood for a long time, seeing nothing, absently-minded wiping his hands on the towel. His face felt as heavy and unmoving as a block of wood. How can I face him again, he wondered. But, but… would this provide some comfort? Would Father Giovanni finally acknowledge the harm he'd done?

Remembering his unfinished work, he hurried to the back and, for the rest of the afternoon, lost himself in the reassuring comfort of creating the hottest sausages he'd ever made.

The next morning, he found himself once again at Father Giovanni's front door. Pulling the chain, he heard the bell ringing at the back of the house, followed by footsteps coming down the hall. Viviana opened the door. She looked at him with some surprise.

She said, "I didn't think you were going to come."

"Well, here I am," he said. "I don't know if this is a good thing or not."

"He's having a bad spell," she said. "Can you come back later?"

"It's now or never," said Adolfo. "If I leave now, I don't know that I can do this again. It's hard enough as it is."

"Very well," she said. "I hope he's up to it."

The curtains had been drawn in the room at the back and Adolfo took a few seconds to locate Father Giovanni in the gloom. The priest had been propped up in bed, supported by a mountain of pillows. His chest fluttered up and down as he panted, taking short, shallow breaths. The smell of imminent death hung in the air.

Giovanni painfully turned his head to see who had entered the room. His face had caved in. Adolfo looked at a skull, with dull eyes sunk deep into their sockets.

"You," Giovanni whispered. Adolfo could hardly hear him.

"Sit." Another whisper, with just the hint of a wave towards a chair beside the bed.

Adolfo sat. Despite himself, he couldn't help but feel pity towards the pathetic creature in the bed. Is this what we all come to, he asked himself. Dear God in Heaven.

"Water."

Adolfo found a jug of water on a side table, poured a glass. Leaning forward, he held it to Giovanni's dry lips and gently tilted it back. He poured faster than Giovanni could swallow, and water dribbled down the shrunken chin. He wiped it away, as carefully as he would spilt milk on a baby.

"Adolfo." Giovanni seemed to be gathering his energy.

With no warning, he screamed, clutching his stomach with one hand. He reached out with the other and grabbed Adolfo's hand, holding it with surprising strength. The screaming went on and on, a thin high-pitched screech that cut Adolfo to the bone like one of his knives.

Viviana rushed in. "You need more laudanum," she said, glaring furiously at Adolfo as if the pain was his fault. Giovanni waved her away, saying nothing. With a look of despair, she left the room.

Gasping for air, Giovanni said, "This is more than I can stand.

I'd like to ask you to throw me out of the window. "

"Then there'd be two of us sinners. You, for asking, and me, for doing it. Neither of us would see Heaven."

Giovanni seemed about to reply, but was seized by another agonising spasm. His screams were louder, more piercing, the sounds of a lost soul howling in the wilderness. Adolfo sat frozen, unable to move. Once he had to put down a sheep that got caught in a barbed wire fence, slitting open its stomach and spilling its guts in its struggle to get free. He could still hear its screams in his nightmares, but they didn't shred him like this.

When he'd recovered, Giovanni said, "This is a foretaste of Hell. I'm surrounded by devils already, torturing me with their pincers. I shall experience these pains for all eternity, unless I can be forgiven for my sins."

Adolfo said nothing, waiting for the apology he craved. Once he heard it, he could decide what to do.

"You were angry when you came before, and accused me of hurting you. But look at me now… I beg you, be merciful. In the name of Our Lord, forgive me for any harm you think I may have done to you."

Adolfo sagged. Instead an apology, he was being asked to forgive without any acknowledgement of the damage done, without getting anything in return. And how could this possible clear any slate?

"Why would I do that?" he asked.

"One day," said Giovanni, "you will also need God's forgiveness. But He does not show mercy to those who will not show mercy to others. Show me mercy that you may receive it yourself." He sounded plaintive.

"Are you admitting that you did me wrong?"

"You misunderstood how much I wanted to help you. If that was doing you wrong, then I am sorry. I'm sorry if you feel I hurt you. None of the other boys complained as you have. Now, will you please forgive me? There is so little time left."

The other boys? Adolfo looked at Giovanni with disgust. After all the harm he'd caused, he was reduced to this? A despicable shell of a man pleading for forgiveness with less pride than a beggar on the street. Adolfo knew deep down that he was the better man of the two of them–any sins he might have committed were as nothing compared to Giovanni's.

Adolfo felt certain that a victim's anger was righteous when directed against his abuser. And now, at last, he had the opportunity to put it to good use, restoring the balance between them, wiping out the shame.

He leaned forward, putting his head next to Giovanni's.

"I hope you rot in Hell," he said. "I hope the demons there stick your miserable hide with red-hot pincers. I hope you suffer like this for all eternity, without mercy. Your name is forever cursed."

"No! I didn't mean to hurt you. Forgive me, you must. Don't leave me like this!"

Adolfo went over to the window and pulled the heavy curtains open, letting bright sunshine pour into the room.

"It's a beautiful day out there," he said. "Enjoy it, while you can."

Walking back to the shop, Adolfo replayed the conversation over and over in his head, savouring the sweet taste of revenge. For the first and only time he could remember, he had wielded the power. If the gods in their wisdom saw fit to place the tools of retribution in his hand, it was only right that he used them to punish the priest for what he had done. This was the best way to channel his anger, to slake his thirst for vengeance, no mercy shown. Justice demanded no less.

Filled with self-righteous virtue, he went to the back of the shop. Demonte had brought in two sheep the day before, and it was time to kill and dress them so he could put fresh cuts out for customers before the weekend.

Adolfo took pride in his skill as a butcher and worked hard to kill animals cleanly and painlessly. He knew that some people spread malicious rumours about what happened in the slaughter room, but paid them no attention. Perhaps they were squeamish about seeing live sheep go in one end of the shop and raw meat and sausages come out the other, and used these stories to hide their discomfort. But they still bought the meat; Adolfo mostly overlooked their hypocrisy, charged them a little more, and was content to take their money.

The killing this afternoon did not go well.

Normally, he talked quietly to a sheep before killing it, calming it and thanking it for the sacrifice of its life and the gift of its flesh. But this time the sheep seemed to feel his anger even as he tried to soothe them. They were large and made strong by their lives on the steep slopes of the mountain. Sensing what was coming, they refused to cooperate, kicking and struggling as he tried to subdue them. Their furious bleating filled the room. It took a long time before he was able to stun them with a blow to the forehead before hoisting them up by their back legs and cutting their throats. By the time both sheep were dead and skinned, Adolfo was exhausted and his apron and shirt sleeves were covered with blood and gore. Now silent at last, the two carcases hung from huge hooks, swinging gently.

Washing his hands and arms, he felt none of his fury with Father Giovanni; the distraction and effort of the last few hours had washed it all away. Too late for the sheep, he thought, scrubbing hard at his hands. The abrupt recognition that his anger had caused a bad death for the innocent sheep came as a shock. He had always thought that anger was a good thing, something to focus the mind, something that gave purpose to his life. But not if it caused considerable and unnecessary suffering to animals who had done nothing to deserve it. This was not a white-hot, purifying anger, it was dark, and harmful, and shameful.

Adolfo made sure he had cleaned the last of the blood from under his fingernails and put on a clean white shirt. Pulling the grappa down from the shelf, he poured himself a large drink and drank it standing up. A second drink lasted no longer than the first. Replenishing the glass again, he went over the table in the corner.

The door to the shop opened as he sat down and Cesare came in.

Cesare said, "Drinking by yourself? That's a bad sign."

"It's been a hard day," Adolfo replied, trying not to sound defensive. "Where have you been? I've hardly seen you."

"The hotel," Cesare said as if that explained everything. He poured his own grappa and brought it over to the table. "What made today so hard?"

"Father Giovanni is dying. He asked to see me, so I went down to his house this morning. And then I had to kill some sheep this afternoon. I've only just finished cleaning up."

"Really? Why would he want to see you?"

"I've been thinking about the money we brought back from Napoli," Adolfo said. "What did you do with your share?"

"I used some for the house we built, put the rest somewhere safe, keeping it for a rainy day. Why?"

"Guests at your hotel will want somewhere nearby that they can eat. There's a house just down the road that's for sale. It could be converted easily to a restaurant, somewhere they could walk to in a few minutes. I was thinking of buying it with my share. You can convert it for me, then I could open it soon after the hotel."

"I know the house," said Cesare. "Let's go and look at it together, decide what changes have to be made."

Adolfo nodded. "I want to do something useful with the money," he said. "That was a bad night, no mistake, one I don't like remembering too much."

Cesare said nothing. He took a large mouthful of grappa.

"Do you remember the man from the crash who had no head?" asked Adolfo.

"Of course."

"I always wondered where the head went," said Adolfo. "And his money. I was surprised he didn't have more."

"You saw what we took from him," said Cesare, his voice almost calm. "And I found the head the next morning, it had rolled down the hill, almost to the path. Why are you thinking about all this?"

Adolfo shook his head. "I keep seeing their faces," he said. The grappa had loosened his tongue.

"Well, stop," said Cesare. "This kind of talk will do nothing but cause trouble. We did what we did, we have the money, now let's get on with things. I'll finish my hotel, then fix up your restaurant. Keep busy, that's the thing."

Adolfo looked morosely into his glass.

"You've got to stop worrying," Cesare said. Adolfo raised his head, surprised that Cesare was being so assertive. Maybe running the hotel project had finally toughened him up.

"I don't think of that night at all," Cesare went on, and this time Adolfo could hear the doubt, the lack of self-confidence. He wondered why Cesare should have any anxieties at all about that night. He was only along for the ride, after all.

Cesare drank the last of his grappa.

"I'd better go and see what Rosabella has made for supper," he said.

Adolfo raised a hand as Cesare hurried out, then refilled his glass again. He hadn't meant to tell Cesare that he was seeing faces, it just slipped out, but it was true. He had seen them on the mountain during the Mass when the cross went up and now he was seeing them in the middle of the night. He wondered what he'd have to do before they left him in peace.

At least the man from the plane who looked like a priest had died quickly, something denied to Father Giovanni. Earlier in the day, Adolfo would have rejoiced in knowing that the older man was suffering a prolonged and painful death, terrified of spending eternity in Hell. But now he wasn't so sure. Perhaps he should have said something to ease his mind, not tried to play God.

No, it was asking too much for him to forgive what Giovanni had done to him. I'm no saint, he thought, I can't do it. I'll be angry, instead, nurture the flame, keep it alive. That's the only way to honour the pain. The thought was reassuring for a moment, a return to what he knew and understood.

And then he realized that he didn't want to be angry all his life, that he had to do whatever it took to free himself, to cut the rope that bound him to Father Giovanni. But he didn't know if forgiving the priest would be enough. There was only one way to find out and that was to see Giovanni one more time.

Soon, he thought. There was much to do in the shop, and he wanted time to think this through.

Chapter Nineteen

BROTHER RENATO SAT BY FATHER GIOVANNI'S BED, trying to keep his mind clear. Breathing slowly and evenly, he focused his attention on the heavy wooden crucifix hanging on the wall above Giovanni's head. His hands lay in his lap, one resting gently in the other.

Watching Father Giovanni's decline, he knew the end was near. In the last few days, Giovanni had stopped eating, taking only an occasional sip of water to moisten his mouth. He spent more time asleep than awake, a blessing, really, since he was restless when awake. He didn't seem to be in pain any more, he just couldn't stop moving when he was not sleeping. And his hands were ice-cold, something that surprised Renato when he held them.

Renato did what he could to make Giovanni comfortable in spite of his abhorrence of what the priest had done to the altar boys. If Jesus could heal sinners, he thought, the least I can do is sit beside Father Giovanni's bed for his last few days on this earth. He even found a peace of his own in sitting with the dying man, as he always did whenever he cared for the sick or the dying. He had learned to pause before entering a sick room, to carefully leave his own worries and needs at the door; only then could he devote his entire being to supporting whoever was lying in the bed.

He still remembered the first time he'd done this, how anxious he'd been to get it right. He'd asked a much older priest for advice.

"We enter the world alone," the priest had said, "and we leave it the same way. Just as it's a privilege to help a baby leave the safety of its mother's womb to join us, it's a privilege to support someone as they depart this life. You don't need me or the Church's teachings. Let human decency guide you and you'll know what to do."

And so he had. He was working in a small village at the time, high in the mountains that lie a day's journey south of Siena. It was bitterly cold, with new snow thick on the ground and covering the rooftops, swallowing the sounds that would normally echo along the stone streets. The young man in the bed was dying of some dreadful disease that had made him blind. But he could smell the fresh snow and hear the silence, and when Renato entered the room after climbing several flights of narrow stairs, he demanded to be taken out into the open air. "I know I'm dying," he said, "I want to be in the snow one more time."

Renato's heart sank. There was no way to help the weakened boy down the stairs and none to get him back up. He opened the window instead and helped the boy sit at the end of the bed so he could lean out. Breathing deeply of the hushed, cold air, the boy said, "It's clean. So clean." After a few minutes he shivered, so Renato helped him back into bed, closed the window, and held his hand until he'd fallen asleep. The young man died the next day, slipping softly away.

Since then, Renato had helped many people die. Some deaths were like the young man's, peaceful and quiet; others were difficult. He never could tell which it would be. Some good people died well, some ended their days terrified that an insignificant or imagined sin would condemn them to burn in Hell. Some desperately hung onto life despite being in terrible agony, preferring the pain they knew to the mysteries of death. Some sinners found it in their heart to truly repent of their sins, large or small, and died secure in the knowledge that God had forgiven them and would welcome them to Heaven; others refused to confess or even acknowledge their sins and, Renato knew with complete certainty, would spent eternity suffering the torments of Hell. But every time, he did the best he could to calm and reassure, to mediate with God, to ease someone's way to whatever inevitable destiny awaited them. He thought it the most profound part of his calling.

Now he wondered what kind of death awaited Father Giovanni. Would he repent and be saved in God's infinite forgiveness, or would he end up in Hell? Renato's revulsion at what the priest had done made him tense, his hands clenching in his lap. This was the only time he'd ever felt like this beside a deathbed, and he didn't know if he could reconcile his personal feelings with his duty as a priest. Or how.

His thoughts must have disturbed Father Giovanni, who chose that moment to wake up. Renato leaned forward.

"How are you feeling?" he asked.

"The Bishop has asked me to go to Napoli, you know." Giovanni's voice was surprisingly clear.

"Really? Why is that?"

"He wants me to meet the Pope. I've been a priest for so many years and I don't know what he looks like. I've never seen him, never been in his presence, not once. The Bishop thought it was time we met."

Renato had heard variations of this many times. Death is a journey, after all.

"That's good," he said. "We'll have to pack your bags for the trip. You'll want to look your best for His Holiness."

Giovanni smiled, and the two men sat quietly.

"I'm going to die, you know." Calm and matter of fact. "Very soon, I think."

"Yes, I know. Are you ready?" Renato kept his voice as calm as Giovanni's.

"I would ask that you administer the Last Rites. Then the Lord can summon me whenever He wishes."

Taking a deep breath, Renato said, "Very well. We start with confession, as you know. I ask you again, are you ready?"

Giovanni nodded. "I am."

"Have trust in God, my son. Be open and honest, confess and truly repent your sins, and He will extend His forgiveness."

Giovanni sketched a shaky sign of the cross. He rested his hands on the crucifix lying on his chest.

"Forgive me, Father, for I have sinned," he started.

Five minutes later, Renato was feeling sick and angry, unable to speak. The supposed sins that Giovanni had confessed were trivial, inconsequential, nowhere near venal. There was nothing about the abuse, the degradation of so many innocent boys. No recognition of lives wrecked. And now this monster, this unrepentant sinner was looking expectantly at him, expecting absolution and a clear path to Heaven. Renato wanted nothing more than to throw things at Giovanni and storm out of the room. Let him spend eternity in Hell!

For a moment, he savoured the feeling of righteousness, the knowledge that he could condemn Giovanni's soul to everlasting torment by doing nothing, by letting him die alone, without absolution. Was this how God felt, wielding such power?

The thought brought him up short. What was he doing? The decision on what to do with Giovanni's soul belonged to God, not to him, however tempting that might be. How could he have been so arrogant to think, even for a second, that he could assume God's role?

Shaken, he realized that he had no choice in the matter. He was just a lowly priest, not God. He must do the work required of a priest and leave God's work to Him. Help Father Giovanni truly confess his sins, so that he might repent before God and be forgiven. His revulsion at what Giovanni had done didn't come into it.

He leaned forward and cleared his throat. Giovanni shifted his gaze to him from the ceiling.

"My son," Renato said, "what about the boys?"

Giovanni could not meet Renato's intense look. He turned his head and looked at the light coming through a gap in the heavy curtains.

"What about the boys? Which boys?" His voice was querulous.

"Adolfo, Guido, all the others. You know who they are and you know what you did to them. My son, I beg you to confess the sins you committed with them. Your soul depends on it."

"What sins? I committed no sins with them." But Giovanni sounded uncertain, wavering.

"You and I both know that to be untrue. Giovanni, you are not long for this world. If you will not confess and repent of all your sins, I can do nothing. You will go before God with this stain on your soul and He will do what He will. This is your only chance, if you wish to avoid spending eternity in Hell. Your only chance. After this, I cannot help you, it will be too late."

Renato pulled his chair closer to the bed and reached out to hold Giovanni's frozen hand. Giovanni made to jerk his hand away, but left it in Renato's warm embrace. Slowly, he turned back to look at Renato. The sadness on his face was almost more than Renato could bear.

"Giovanni, confess. Confess, repent before God." Renato managed to keep his voice quiet and calm.

"I meant no harm." Giovanni seemed to have retreated inside himself, looking at memories from long ago. His voice was almost inaudible. "Truly, I meant no harm. Truly…"

Renato held his breath, willing Giovanni to come out from behind his walls, built high and strong.

"Graziano was the first. He was such a beautiful child, and loved being an altar boy. One day, he asked for help. He had been working hard in the fields and his back and shoulders hurt. He was too young for such heavy work. I offered to rub his sore muscles and he accepted. I was good at that, you know, I had strong hands. The other novitiates in the seminary all enjoyed my massages."

Giovanni paused, licking his dry lips. "May I have some water?" he asked.

Renato held the glass to his mouth, letting Giovanni drink as much as he needed. He put the glass back on the table and took Giovanni's hand between both of his. Leaning forward, with his elbows on the bed, he might have been praying.

"And then?"

"And then… and then I found that I liked giving the massages. Too much, in fact. I started doing it for myself, not because the boys asked for it. To my shame, I could not stop. I would say whatever was needed to make them submit. Eventually, I came to believe that it was their duty to give me the pleasure of massaging them. How else could I justify it?"

"My son, you know you must tell me about each and every one of these."

"Yes, I know." Such a simple thing to say, yet so hard.

Painfully, slowly, Giovanni gave Renato chapter and verse of what he had done over the years. The names of the boys, what he did. Every now and again, he'd pause for a dab of water to moisten his lips before resuming his account. Adolfo's was just one name of many.

By the end, Renato felt as if he was swimming in a cesspit. The number of boys and the degradation they had experienced was almost more than he could bear. It had taken all his self control to calmly hold Giovanni's hands in his and remain as still as possible to give the other man the strength to finish what he had started.

Eventually, Giovanni's voice tailed off. Renato waited to see if there was any more. When the silence had lasted long enough, he asked, "My son, have you told me everything? Do you repent of your sins?"

"This is all I can remember. I am truly sorry for these and all my sins. I am so sorry..." Giovanni's voice was an agonized whisper as he recited the required words. His cheeks glistened.

"My son, I can think of no penance that is suitable at this time for these sins. And yet you must pay some penance."

"Look at my will. I changed it after Adolfo came to see me the first time, a few weeks ago. I have left such money as I have to the Church, with instructions that it be used to pay for the education of boys from this parish. I leave it to you to decide how best to do that."

Renato nodded. "That seems appropriate," he said.

There was an awkward silence. Renato knew very well what came next and he also knew that it was irrevocable. Giovanni's hand trembled in his, while his other hand picked nervously at a loose thread on the bedspread. But his confession had stripped the last vestiges of pride and denial from him and he merely watched Renato's face with exhausted resignation, knowing that his fate now lay in Renato's hands.

Renato was reluctant to complete the ritual, his disgust with Giovanni forming a lump in his throat. Who was he to act *in persona Christi*, to ensure that this abuser of children received God's forgiveness, despite what he felt was genuine remorse? Adolfo had refused to forgive Giovanni, according to Viviana, so why should he?

Because it was his job, and because Giovanni had done what he had to do by confessing and repenting before God. As with every other step along this stony path, Renato had no choice.

Letting go of Giovanni's hand, he made the sign of the Cross over his body and said, "I absolve you from your sins in the name of the Father, and of the Son, and of the Holy Spirit."

There, it was done.

Giovanni sagged with relief.

"Thank you, Renato," he said. "I can die in peace now, knowing that the good Lord accepts my repentance and will welcome me to Heaven."

God might forgive Giovanni, thought Renato, but I wonder if those boys can ever forgive him? And will they forgive me for what I've just done? What will Adolfo do when he finds out?

The rest of the Sacrament went quickly. The two priests said the Lord's Prayer together, then Giovanni received the Eucharist. He couldn't handle the wafer and only just managed to swallow a small sip of communion wine, barely sufficient *viaticum* for his final journey. Finally, Renato anointed Giovanni, tracing the shape of the Cross on his forehead with holy oil.

Moments after the end of the ritual, Giovanni fell into a deep sleep, his gaunt face more peaceful than Renato had seen it for weeks. Renato tidied up around the bed, more to occupy his hands than because of any mess.

Some time later, Giovanni's eyes flickered open again. He looked toward the heavy curtain blocking the bright sunlight from entering the room.

"Did you see the shepherd?"

"The shepherd?"

"The boy who threw himself off the cliff, Paolo. He was outside the window. He wanted a glass of milk, but I had none to give him."

Renato thought Giovanni was raving. The window was fifteen feet off the ground and Paolo was dead and buried, in no position to hover outside Giovanni's window. Or anywhere else, for that matter.

He said, "I'll take him something."

Giovanni nodded, apparently satisfied with this solution. He closed his eyes again, his breathing uneven and fretful. His hand feebly waved away some imagined pest, drawing Renato's attention to the ring he always wore on his wedding finger. It carried a simple cross and was, Renato knew, a present from his parents when he joined the priesthood. Was he depraved even then?

The sight of the ring took Renato back to his conversation with the English officer in the cemetery. What was it the man had said after discovering the missing rings and fingers? "Anger is the only thing we have in the face of great wrong. If we lose the anger, evil will be all that's left." And he had replied, "If God in his infinite wisdom can forgive great wrongs, who are we to deny that forgiveness?"

What good would it have done anyone if he had denied Giovanni the forgiveness he craved? What was done to those boys was done and punishing Giovanni by sending him to Hell could never undo the harm. If God understood that forgiveness was preferable to anger, to retribution and revenge, should we not take heed?

Another groan came from the bed. Giovanni was in some distress, so Renato leaned forward and took his hand between his.

Holding Giovanni's hand against his forehead, Renato began to feel pity for the pathetic creature lying before him. This was no way for a man to die, mewling with pain and reduced to a helpless, whimpering shell, terrified of crossing the final threshold. At least Giovanni had found it within himself to confront his sins, say out loud before God that he had done great wrong, and express his remorse. It was done at the last minute, but it was done, and had to be respected. If he could not help the boys, at least he had spared Giovanni the pain of a very bad death.

Worn out by his emotional turmoil and the effort of getting Father Giovanni through his confession, Renato dozed. Viviana looked in to see if they needed anything and saw the two priests asleep, one in the bed, the other in his chair. She quietly closed the door again, careful not to disturb them. The afternoon wore on and dissolved into evening, the already dim light in the room fading to near darkness.

When Renato woke up, he was disoriented by the gloom and the stiffness in his neck. For a moment, he thought he was back in Siena, sitting beside his father's bed in the last few days of his life. He remembered how his mother had retreated to her room and refused to come out except to eat, sometimes not even then. She was raddled with pain from arthritis and couldn't even start to imagine life by herself, her husband dead and her only son a priest living at the other end of Italy. Renato had hurried home after getting the telegram from a neighbour telling him that his father's time had come, and quickly realized that he had two people to care for, even if his father was the one who was dying.

Two mornings after he arrived home, the nurse came to change his father's dressings and give him his medications. Renato had left the room after listening to his father make sounds like a wounded animal, something no son should ever have to hear. The nurse was apologetic, saying that she was doing her best but that the bedsores were getting worse.

"I don't think this will take long," she said, looking at him with pity and sorrow. Renato had fled, unable to bear it.

Then his mother wanted him in her room so she could complain about the arthritis, how she couldn't even walk down the street to sit with her oldest friend, how last night's pasta was overcooked and tasteless, how could his father leave her like this... Renato stood it as long as he could, then ran from the room with its old woman smells, out to the street, to fresh air and sunlight.

Greatly distressed by the state in which he found his parents, he walked. Soon he was in the Piazza del Campo, which bustled with life, young couples shyly holding hands and older people enjoying an expresso together in the outdoor cafes. A young woman walked past him, flirting outrageously with some young male friends, delighted by a suggestive and totally inappropriate remark from one of them. He knew he should disapprove of such behaviour but it was so innocent, so full of life, that he couldn't help but smile, watching as she swayed her hip against her companion.

He sat on one of the bollards separating the centre of the Piazza from the periphery where the horses raced, his face raised to the sun, and tried to forget the sounds, and the smells, and the sights in his parents' house. Comforted by the warmth and familiarity of the Piazza, he lost track of time. The sun's shadow had moved some distance along the wall beside him when he was startled by a small boy who was playing tag with his older brother and, not seeing him, ran into his leg.

"Mario, be careful! Father, I am so sorry, children these days…" Their mother was harried and hot. Renato raised his hand, it's nothing, it said, and smiled at her. Better the careless exuberance of the young than the travails at the other end of life's winding trail, he thought. Relieved, she moved on, trying to keep her energetic young sons under some kind of control.

Renato realized that he'd been away from the house for far too long. Holding his cassock up to avoid tripping on it, he hurried back along the streets he knew so well from playing in them as a child. The house was silent when he entered the cool, dark hall. He hung his hat on the rack inside the front door and walked as quietly as he could up the stairs to his father's room.

He knew as soon as he went in.

Death filled the room, a tangible presence that left little room for the living. Renato pushed against it to get to the bed, feeling that he was wading through treacle.

His father lay with his eyes staring at the ceiling, his mouth open. He looked a bit surprised and as if he wanted to make some mildly witty remark about whatever he was seeing. The kind of remark he liked to make over dinner, making his wife smile tolerantly and his son squirm with embarrassment. There was not even the flicker of a pulse and his forehead was cool, almost cold.

Renato had anticipated this moment ever since he'd heard that his father was very ill. He'd seen many people grieve after a loved one died and was curious about how he'd feel when it was his turn. Now that it was here, he was surprised to discover that he felt nothing,

nothing at all. He was completely numb as he bent over to kiss that forehead for the last time.

He went along the corridor to see his mother. She looked up as he entered her room, ready to resume her complaints.

"Mama, he's gone," he said without any preamble. His capacity to be gentle, to prepare people for bad news, had deserted him.

"Oh, no," she cried and put her hand to her mouth. When she took it away, there was bright red lipstick on her fingers and smeared beside her mouth. He found that he could say nothing, so he sat beside her and held her hand while she noisily wept. A small woman, she was normally composed, neat, correct, a good lawyer's wife. But grief and rage stripped away her natural dignity, leaving only a raw, ugly anguish.

When he knelt beside his bed much later that night, he prayed for his father's soul, that it might have found its way to God's embrace in Heaven, that his father was finally at peace after a long and hard journey. Turning out the light, he climbed into bed, completely drained after dealing with the doctor and the undertaker. And with his mother, who had wept continuously, especially as the undertaker and his assistants carried his father's body along the long passage, down the stairs and out of the front door for the last time. At last, after an endless, difficult evening, his mother had taken a sedative and was now fast asleep.

Despite his exhaustion, he could not sleep. He had loved his father and knew that he would miss his bad jokes as much as his wisdom and warmth. He should be grieving, not as messily as his mother, perhaps, more as a man should grieve, but grieving nonetheless. Instead, he just felt empty, drained of all feeling.

Without warning, the guilt crashed in on him out of the dark. It lay heavy and massive on his chest, pinning him to his bed, a weight that nearly suffocated him. My father was dying today, he thought, and where was I? Looking at pretty girls in the Piazza like a lovelorn young calf, instead of being with him. It was wrong, wrong, wrong, that his father should die alone, no one with him to hold his hand, to share or even mark the time of his death. He should have been beside the bed so his father could be comforted by knowing that he was not by himself at this most final, most intimate, most lonely moment. No one should die alone, and in his selfishness, he'd let his father do just that. The gap between what he'd done and what he knew he should have done was unbridgeable, a chasm carved into his conscience by guilt.

There was no way to wind back the clock and there was no way to recover the one and only chance he'd been given to do the right thing. No way to honour the man who had given him so much, no way to make him proud by telling him about the Bishop's hints of promotion.

Since then, he thought about his lapse almost every day, feeling the familiar twinge of guilt each time. And he still had not grieved his father's death.

Sitting beside Father Giovanni's bed, the memory was more vivid than ever. It was all the same. The dark room, the figure in the bed struggling for breath, the unmistakable smell of impending death, the sure knowledge that there was only one end to the vigil. But this time, Renato would have crawled over broken glass before leaving Giovanni alone. Renato had long ago decided that he owed it to his father to never let anyone else die by themselves and, despite his personal feelings about the priest, he must stay with Giovanni to the bitter end. If he could not go back and do what he failed to do in Siena, he could at least atone for his lapse. And what was sitting beside the deathbed of a man he despised if not a form of penance?

Viviana must have heard him stirring, because she stuck her head around the door again.

"Father, would you like something to eat? You need something to keep your strength up."

Renato was not accustomed to being addressed as Father, so he didn't reply at first. Feeling stupid, he asked for a plate of pasta. Something simple, and could he perhaps have a small glass of wine with it?

The room was very dark, so he lit a lantern on the far side from the bed. The light was enough to see Giovanni's sleeping face, but not enough to read by. He made himself comfortable in the chair again, settling in for a wait of uncertain length.

He ate the pasta without tasting a thing. Time slowly passed.

Shortly after the clock in the hall outside the room struck nine, Giovanni stirred slightly.

Renato said, "Would you like some water?"

The merest hint of a nod. Renato held the cup to his lips as carefully and gently as he'd feed milk to a baby.

"I'm sorry, so sorry." The voice was as quiet as the breeze in long grass.

"I know you are," he said. "You must rest before your journey."

"Journey?"

"To meet the Pope, in Napoli. Remember, the Bishop invited you. It's a great honour, to meet the Pope. Your bags are packed, so you can go whenever you're ready."

"Oh, yes."

Giovanni turned his head back to the ceiling, exhausted by the effort of talking. His chest moved fitfully, each slight movement followed, after a long pause, by another. His faint breath rasped at the back of his throat. Renato leaned forward once more to hold Giovanni's hand, as if the physical contact would help him take that last, final step. He could feel a faint, fluttering pulse in Giovanni's wrist.

"I never meant to hurt people. Oh, the damage I've done…"

Renato didn't trust himself to speak. He pressed Giovanni's hand, just the slightest possible pressure. You can let go now, the squeeze said, there's nothing left for you to do on this earth. Go, go and meet your fate.

Was that a squeeze in return?

Giovanni's breathing gradually slowed even further, each ragged breath coming after an agonising delay when his chest didn't move at all. Renato sat quietly, holding Giovanni's hand, wondering if each breath would be the last.

It was close to midnight when Giovanni took a shallow breath, his chest barely rising. After an interminable pause, he gently exhaled, a long, sighing release of air. Renato waited, holding his own breath, but Giovanni lay unmoving, his face empty, and his pulse was quiet.

Renato gently crossed Giovanni's hands on his chest, over the crucifix he always wore. He closed Giovanni's eyes and mouth. Then he sat down, made the sign of the cross, and said prayers for the newly dead. "Come to his assistance, all you Saints of God: meet him, all you Angels of God: receiving his soul, offering it in the sight of the Most High…"

After a long, long while, he went out to find Viviana and summon the undertaker.

Father Renato returned to the house early the next morning. There was much to be done, starting with a telegram to the Bishop with the news that Father Giovanni had died.

He had just finished drafting the telegram in the office when there was a knock at the door, followed by Viviana.

"The butcher is here," she said. "He wants to see Father Giovanni."

Renato could see Adolfo standing behind her in the passage and waved him into the room.

"Please take a seat," he said, pointing at a chair beside the desk. "I understand you came to see Father Giovanni?"

Adolfo nodded. His hands were clenched tight.

"I'm afraid he died last night. May God have mercy on his soul."

Adolfo sagged in his chair. "I wanted to see him before he died," he said.

"I'm sorry," Renato said. "Perhaps I could be of assistance instead?"

"I don't think so." Adolfo got up to go.

"Adolfo, I know that Father Giovanni hurt you. And I know that you were not the only one."

Adolfo quickly sat down again. "How do you know that?" he asked. There was no surprise in his voice, just resignation and shame.

"I learned of it recently," Renato said. "What he did was deeply wrong and sinful. I wish with all my heart that it could be undone, but we both know that's impossible. If there's anything I can do to help, you have only to ask."

Adolfo laughed bitterly. "That's what Father Giovanni told me. You'll understand if I refuse your offer."

"I'm ashamed of what a fellow priest did," Renato said. "And I'm ashamed that the Church allowed it to happen. On behalf of all the good priests in this world, I can only apologize to you."

"That's all I wanted from him," Adolfo said. "I wanted him to look me in the eye as a man should, tell me that he knew he did wrong, that he was sorry for it."

"And then?"

"And then perhaps I could forgive him for what he did, and cut him out of my life." Adolfo's eyes filled with tears. "He lives on, you know, in my heart. I can't help thinking about him, what he did. The anger… it's like poison…"

He paused, then said, almost to himself, "I wonder if I will ever be rid of him."

Only you can decide that, thought Renato. Giovanni will live in your heart as long as you let him. But he could not tell Adolfo that. Adolfo had suffered enough and there was no point in making him a victim twice over.

Instead, he said, "At the very end, he told me that he was sorry. He knew he had committed great sins, and repented of them."

"Truly? He said that?"

"He did, and not just to me. I cannot tell you precisely what he said, but you should know that he confessed his sins, all of them, before God. It was not easy for him, not easy at all. And then he sincerely repented."

"Did he receive absolution?"

"Of course. He had confessed and repented, I could not withhold it."

"So the people he wronged have not forgiven him. And yet, because he repents before God, he goes to Heaven? That doesn't seem right, He should be in Hell."

"It is for God to decide who goes to Heaven, not us. We do not have His infinite capacity for forgiveness, and should not try to do His work for Him."

"The last time I was here, I told him I wanted him to suffer for all eternity. I knew he was suffering great pain and was glad of it. I wonder now if I should been more generous, even though it would have been very difficult."

"It's too late now for you to forgive him yourself. But it's never too late to rejoice that God has forgiven him and that his soul is on its way to Heaven. Be glad of that, my son, and perhaps you will free yourself of his presence."

That was as far as Renato could go. The rest was up to Adolfo.

Chapter Twenty

DESPITE HER BEST INTENTIONS, Serafina found herself going over to see Rosabella more and more often. Looking after Adolfo's house left her with plenty of spare time, which she frequently used by wandering over to see Rosabella, just a few streets away. Rosabella might be cooking or, more likely, sitting in the comfortable chair under the window, knitting for the baby she was expecting.

Serafina was attracted less by the prospect of overhearing their all too active sex life (which had fallen off lately, now that Rosabella was pregnant) than by the opportunity of looking through a window into a life she'd never have. It was something to feed her fantasies late at night when she was alone in bed. Talking with Rosabella across the kitchen table, she heard what it was like to have a husband, to be proud of what he was doing, to look forward to having the first of many children in the house. She couldn't help coming back for a story so compelling, so different to her own, a discarded spinster squandering her life by housekeeping for a cousin who no one liked.

At the same time, the resentment and jealousy she felt as a result provided their own perverse pleasure. What right did Rosabella have to all the things missing in her own life? Who did Rosabella think she was, taking Cesare, her favourite brother, away from her? Serafina had adored Cesare ever since he was a baby, always eager to please, the best companion a young girl could ask for, so much more rewarding than a doll. When Baldassare arrived, she had tried to play with him the same way. But Baldassare was more reserved and kept both her and Cesare at a slight distance, as if he found things to disapprove of in both of them.

Serafina did not think that Rosabella was good enough for her brilliant Cesare. Look what he was doing, starting a new business (building a hotel, already!), and Rosabella just cooking and making babies. She could see through Cesare's extravagant praise for his wife at Sunday lunch as window-dressing and was certain that he secretly regretted marrying an over-sexed, blousy, money-grubbing whore with hair the colour of red paint. She could also tell when Rosabella was making an effort to be nice to her, welcoming her into the kitchen as if her arrival was the best treat imaginable. Oh, the hypocrisy of it all! Cesare deserved much better.

So Serafina's trips to Rosabella's kitchen always combined sweet and sour, like the grilled sausages she prepared for Adolfo with both sugar and apple cider vinegar in the sauce. Truth to tell, she quite enjoyed listening to Rosabella's twaddle and storing away more and more details about their life together, some salacious and some unutterably domestic and dull. Walking home later, she'd examine what she'd learned, savouring the sharp pains of anger and jealousy. Her rage was an intense but dormant volcano that dominated and gave meaning to the otherwise flat landscape of her life.

The cobblestones were still damp from a brief February rain shower as Serafina walked to Rosabella's house one morning. Turning into Rosabella's street, she caught a glimpse of a brightly-coloured skirt as her sister-in-law disappeared around a corner ahead of her. This had happened before, usually when Rosabella had forgotten or run out of some important ingredient for Cesare's lunch. On these occasions, Serafina was free to let herself in, make some coffee, and wait for Rosabella's return.

Going into the kitchen, Serafina saw the preparations for coffee already laid out. At the end of the counter, the door to Cesare's workshop was slightly ajar. Normally closed and locked, this was so unusual that she noticed it at once. Unable to resist the temptation, she opened the door and went in.

Light poured in through the tall windows of uneven glass that filled most of the back wall. A large door at one side led out to the alley that ran behind the house. A rack on the right-hand wall held a bewildering array of tools—saws at one end, chisels next, then hammers and mallets, some planes, strange things that she couldn't identify. Below the rack, a thick bench sat heavily, its surface pockmarked by gouges left from many years of slipping tools. Another bench occupied the middle of the room, with space to walk around it on all sides. It also bore the scars of honest work. An almost-finished crib rested in the middle of the bench. The sweet aroma of fresh wood shavings filled the room.

Serafina hadn't been in the workshop since she was a girl, occasionally allowed by her younger brother to sit in the corner while he made things, learning his craft. The smell of shavings brought back a memory from long ago, when life was uncomplicated by adult matters. They had been chatting in the easy way of two siblings who spend a lot of time with each other. Cesare was using a plane to carefully smooth out the join between two pieces of wood. He'd been working on it for hours.

"Do you have secrets?" she'd asked, out of the blue.

Cesare paused his planing and gave her a quick, sly look.

"Well, do you?"

"Do you promise not to tell?"

"Of course I do!"

She could still taste the delicious, illicit thrill of learning something that no one else knew.

Cesare made a big show of locking both doors to the workshop, then beckoned Serafina to kneel beside him, next to the bench in the middle of the room. At his urging, she looked under the bench and saw a small box resting on a ledge attached high up the side corners, completely invisible to anyone standing nearby.

"Pull it out," he said. She carefully slid the box off the shelf and put it on the bench. Cesare looked very serious. The box was as long as Serafina's forearm, as deep as her hand was long, and the thickness of her hand from side to side.

"I made this as an exercise," Cesare said, his pride showing. "No one else knows about it, only you."

Beautifully made, the box was locked.

"Where's the key?" Serafina asked.

Cesare didn't seem to hear the repressed excitement in her voice. "That's the second secret," he said. "It's over here." He went to the post in the corner of the room, beside the door to the kitchen. Reaching up, he put his hand beside the post where the shadow was deepest. When he pulled it out again, a small key rested in the palm of his hand.

Carefully, so carefully, knowing what a privilege he was offering, Serafina took the key and went back to the box, which seemed to be waiting for her. The key slid easily into the lock, turned. She slowly opened the lid, wanting to prolong the moment for as long as possible.

When she saw what was in the box, she shrieked, putting her hand over her mouth. The lid dropped shut.

"What's wrong?" asked Cesare. "It's only my rabbit foot." He seemed offended by Serafina's reaction.

"I... I... didn't expect this," she said. "Is this from the rabbit you shot last month?"

"A rabbit foot is lucky, you know," said Cesare, sounding grown up. "Remember, you promised you wouldn't tell anyone. A promise is forever, you understand?" He was as fierce as a boy could when talking to his older sister.

Standing again in front of the bench, she did remember, and had kept her promise all these years. But she'd never promised to forget that he had a secret box, or how to find and open it. Now she wondered if the box was still there and what secrets it might contain.

Bending over low beside the bench, she saw the box in the corner, exactly where it was supposed to be. She reached under to retrieve the box and put it on the bench, just as she had so many years ago. The key was in the same small recess beside the post, and opened the lock as easily as when they were both young and innocent.

When she saw what was inside and realized what she was looking at, her fragile world collapsed. Like the little girl she once was, she made a small noise, and put her hand over her mouth.

A booklet with strange writing on it, a wad of paper money with the same writing, a watch and chain, several heavy rings, a long thin box that only just fit inside Cesare's box, an envelope with lumps of something inside.

There was only one place this treasure could have come from, she knew. But that meant that her beautiful Cesare, the only man she truly loved, had been with Adolfo's group that night, looting and mutilating. Even when confronted with solid evidence like this, she wanted to deny it. Then she wondered how she could have been so blind, ignoring the awkward silences whenever the subject of the crash came up. And she'd heard him specifically deny being up there that night, although Tifeo had given him a strange look at the time. She never knew what to make of Tifeo.

She'd wasted no time in giving any credence to Father Giovanni's tortuous defence of the looting. She knew all too well how uncaring priests could be and how removed they were from the concerns of ordinary people, and recognised his homily as a way to launder the stained souls of the looters for his own reasons. She believed that what they did was deeply wrong and had no patience for anyone who pretended otherwise. Now she had to recognise Cesare as one of the worst looters. And change how she thought of him.

She stared at the contents of the box for a long moment, then closed the lid and locked it before putting the box back under the bench. Stretching up beside the post, she was startled by the sound of the front door banging shut.

There was no time to retrieve the key from where it fell or even run into the kitchen and pretend she'd been there all the time, so she quickly went to the back door, opened it as quietly as she could, and slipped out into the alley. The latch made a small click as she closed the door behind her. Hurrying as fast as her long skirt would allow, she half-ran to the corner, just making it to safety as she heard the workshop door open behind her.

Cesare whistled as he walked home, enjoying the fresh air. His bank account was healthy and growing, always a good thing for a builder, and the hotel was coming along nicely, reaching a significant milestone that afternoon when they got the electricity working for the first time. This was all very new, so the electrician had needed some time to make the connections, with much trial and error and increasingly colourful invective. When Cesare was confident it would work, he invited the whole crew down to the foyer.

"Today is a special day," he said. "You are helping to build a great hotel, one that will bring many visitors to Ischia. This is a modern hotel, with all the luxuries that our guests will expect. Including something new to Ischia–electricity!"

With an elaborate flourish, he flicked the switch and turned on the electric light hanging by itself from the centre of the ceiling. When the applause died down, he said, "You should all be proud of what you are building here. This is an occasion to celebrate, so there is much refreshment next door. Enjoy it, we'll see you in the morning!"

The men rushed into the dining room, where they found one trestle table sagging under a mountain of food and another with glasses and many bottles of prosecco. The foreman had tut-tutted when Cesare told him about his plans for the celebration. "You'll spoil them, Signor Cesare," he grumbled.

"They've earned it," replied Cesare. "Besides, word will get around, and people will want to work with us. Then we can choose the best workers on the island. That'll make our lives easier, I think."

Watching a plasterer load his plate to precarious levels, Cesare felt a glow of self-satisfaction. These were his people, working on his project in a company that he had built. To his own surprise–and his family's considerable astonishment–he was rather good at this. He liked working out the best way to get something done and, because of his own humble origins, he had an easy way with the men that they appreciated. He knew good work when he saw it and was more than willing to let his workers do their job without looking over their shoulders all the time. This was his world, somewhere he was capable and respected, not looked down on and patronised.

Despite his sunny good mood, there were clouds in Cesare's sky. He was still troubled by Adolfo's loose talk after Christmas about money and seeing faces. Adolfo was excitable, always saying whatever was on his mind–if he couldn't keep his big mouth shut, Rosabella would learn that he was one of the looters. He could feel his testicles contract at the mere thought of her fury.

Rosabella was nowhere to be seen when he got home. He called upstairs but heard only the silence of an empty house. Shrugging, he decided to relax in his workshop, sanding the crib he was making for the new baby.

The crib sat on the workbench in the centre of the room, waiting for a final sand on some rough spots before receiving its first coat of oil. Cesare liked what he'd built after working on it for much of his spare time over several weeks and was looking forward to seeing the finished result. He picked out the finest sandpaper from the pile at the end of the workbench against the wall. He was about to turn back to the crib when a glint on the floor caught his eye. Bending down, he saw that it was the key to his secret box.

Shocked, he grabbed the key. Someone's been in here, he thought, trying not to panic. Rosabella had told him about hearing someone a few days earlier, but the room had been empty when she went in. That was one of the few occasions he'd left the room unlocked; since then, he made sure that the door was properly locked at all times. Serafina? No, Rosabella was always here when she dropped in. So who was it?

And what about the box?

He quickly ducked beneath the table and relaxed when he saw that the box was still there. Then he saw that someone had moved the box; he always left one corner exactly on the edge of the shelf and now it was displaced. Had they taken anything? If so, he had lost a considerable amount of money. And someone knew that he was one of the looters. He didn't know which was worse.

Holding his breath, he put the box on the table beside the crib as gently as if it was an unexploded bomb. He carefully unlocked it. He paused for a moment, knowing with complete certainty that his life had irreversibly changed because of this intrusion, then quickly opened it.

Everything was still there, seemingly undisturbed. He let out his breath in relief. But still, someone knew…

He locked the box and replaced it on the shelf, meticulously lining up one corner with the edge as he had done since he was a

boy, a secret he'd never shared with anyone. By the time he'd put the
key back where it belonged, he knew what he had to do.

A week later, he was back at Gasparo's. The ride over was as rough
as it had been the first time, but he'd made the journey so many
times since then that he barely noticed. Lost in his thoughts, he
ignored the shoreline as they passed, rousing himself and paying
attention only as they entered the port.

Walking into the city, he could feel the weight of the bag in the
inside pocket of his jacket. After much thought, he'd decided that he
should only bring some of the treasure in the box. It was dangerous
to carry all of it at once, even more dangerous to carry a large
amount of cash in the streets around the port, and he thought he'd
get a better price by selling pieces in small quantities. He'd wanted to
hide the box with the remaining pieces somewhere different, but
hadn't been able to think of a good place. That was something to
take care of when he got back.

Gasparo didn't seem to have changed a bit–the same thick white
hair, same white shirt under red suspenders, same generous face. He
beamed as he saw Cesare walk up the alley.

"Signor Ischia," he cried with apparently unfeigned delight.
"What a pleasure, to see you again. I thought you had forgotten poor
Gasparo."

"Not at all," replied Cesare politely. "But you have to work hard
on Ischia just to get by. Unfortunately, we cannot come to Napoli as
often as we'd like."

"I hope you will find your trip worthwhile," Gasparo said,
responding to the opening of negotiations. "Business here is very
slow at this time of year."

Cesare said, "I have some unusual things to show you. Perhaps
they will be of interest to your customers."

"Let's go inside, then," said Gasparo. "But tell me, where are your
friends?"

"One could not come from Ischia," replied Cesare, "and the

other is now working in Napoli."

Gasparo nodded knowingly and invited Cesare to precede him into the dark recess of the shop.

 Cesare was content with the result of his negotiating when he left. Gasparo had liked the two gold necklaces, which could be easily melted down and recast. The single diamond was more valuable, but also more difficult and costly to get to Antwerp and one of the less scrupulous diamond-cutters.

"I would like to see more of those necklaces, if you have any," Gasparo said after handing over a substantial amount of cash.

"Perhaps when business is better for you," replied Cesare. He produced his most guileless smile.

"Don't be a stranger," said Gasparo, with an equally innocent look. "You are always welcome here. And your friends."

Cesare left Gasparo sitting at his desk looking unhappily at several high, chaotic piles of paper, his hand resting casually on an antique telephone. Following the pawnbroker's suggestion, he turned right at the end of the alley, away from the port. A few streets up, Gasparo had assured him, was a tailor where Signor Ischia could be sure of getting a beautiful suit at a most reasonable price. And a few doors beyond that was another shop where he would undoubtedly find a suitable gift to adorn the lady of the house.

The headline at the top of page one screamed the whole story: FONTANA WOMAN HAS TERRIBLE MISFORTUNE TO BE STRUCK BY MOTOR CAR, NARROWLY AVERTS DEATH. The huge block letters were designed to be legible across the street and to appeal to those who had neither the ability nor the desire to read the actual article.

"It seems you're famous," Rosabella said, putting the newspaper on the bed. Serafina groaned, feebly waving the paper away. Her room was almost monastic in its plainness; the only decoration was a cheap statue of the Madonna with her child, probably bought at a street market in Napoli. The curtains were drawn after she complained about the bright light, making the room too dark for comfortable reading.

"I brought you some soup," said Rosabella. "Let's get you sitting up."

That was easier said than done. Serafina was most comfortable when leaning back against cushions brought from every part of the house. An improvised wooden frame extended from the foot of the bed to her waist, holding the weight of bedclothes away from her broken leg. The leg, fractured in several places, was encased in thick plaster from ankle to hip; whenever she had to move it, Serafina found the pain excruciating. This made taking care of normal bodily functions something to be delayed as long as possible, and sitting up became a carefully choreographed ballet between the two of them.

Rosabella brought more cushions over and put a hand behind Serafina's back. "Ready?" she asked.

"Do we have to?" Serafina sounded querulous. "I'm really not hungry." Her voice sounded tired, still a bit slurred.

"You need to build up your strength." Rosabella was firm. Serafina didn't know whether to hate being so dependent on her despised sister-in-law or be grateful that someone was taking care of her for the first time in many years. Sighing, she nodded and gritted her teeth. Moments later, she was sitting bolt upright, holding a steaming mug of sausage and lentil soup in one hand and a spoon in the other.

"Adolfo made the sausages especially for you," Rosabella told her. "He said they were your favourite."

"Mmmfrg," said Serafina, her mouth full.

"How are you feeling today?" Rosabella asked, watching the soup disappear with remarkable speed.

Serafina waited until the bowl was empty before she responded. "Stupid," she said. That's a remarkable admission, thought Rosabella, she must be even more shaken up than I realized. Maybe it's the blow to her head?

The accident wasn't exactly stupid, more a sign of changing times.

Three days earlier, Serafina had started the day with her usual routine. Get up, prepare breakfast for Adolfo, make the beds and

clean the already spotless house. Look in the larder and decide what
to buy for dinner. The things that any good wife did for her husband
and family, that Serafina, now a confirmed spinster, did for her also
unmarriageable cousin in return for bed and board. And if that was
as close as she could get to a normal married life, it was surely better
than nothing.

Her visits to Rosabella's house had fallen off lately. She was still
intensely jealous and resentful of Rosabella, who had everything
Serafina craved, but she was confused by her discovery of Cesare's
involvement in the looting. How could her precious little brother
have been involved in something so wicked?

Lost in her thoughts, Serafina had left the house in the middle of
the morning. Instead of dropping in on Rosabella, she began walking
to the middle of town, where she could buy some fresh pasta and
vegetables, something special for Adolfo's dinner. Turning the
corner on to Via Andrea Mattera, she started crossing the street. She
had played, run and walked on the streets of Fontana her entire life,
and had seen exactly one motorised vehicle there in all those years,
the jeep with the two English officers who came after the crash. The
biggest risks to someone walking in Fontana were running children
and random piles of mule dung; you'd hear the sound of hooves on
cobblestones long before a mule and cart posed any danger. In her
innocence, the notion that she should look before walking into the
middle of the road from behind a wall never even crossed her mind.
And so it was that she walked straight into the path of a motor car
being driven by a wealthy young man from Forio who was inspired
by the glorious motorcar brought to Ischia by the English milord
and wanted to show off his new pride and joy to his uncle.

She had enough time to realise she was in terrible trouble but not
enough to scream before the car hit her, breaking her leg and
throwing her sideways. She hit her head on the stone wall and fell
unconscious to the ground.

Within moments, the previously empty street was full. Some
people attended to Serafina, lying inert between the car and the wall.
Some began crowding around the terrified young man, who began

fearing for his life, and some merely wanted to look at the strange sight of a motor car in their streets.

Before long, a neighbour recognized Serafina and two strong men were assigned to carry her home. Someone went to summon the doctor and an older child was sent up the hill to tell Adolfo what had happened. This was how people handled those rare occasions when someone was foolish enough to be hit by a cart and no one thought to do anything different.

The doctor arrived at the house commendably quickly, delighted that for once he had a patient who was suffering from something he both understood and could treat. Giving Serafina enough chloroform to drop a horse, he got Adolfo to hold her shoulders while he manipulated the broken bones back into alignment. When the cast was on, he stepped back to admire his work. "She'll need that on for several weeks," he said.

"What about her head?" asked Adolfo, looking at the blood congealing in Serafina's scalp.

"Well, let's clean it up," the doctor said. "Scalp wounds always bleed a lot. I'll put a bandage on it while the cut heals, but she'll be fine. Her leg is the main thing."

In the days since the accident, Serafina's leg hurt less, although her head still ached and she was troubled by strong light. Rosabella and Amedea took it in turns to nurse her. Neither of them particularly liked their patient, but it was their duty to help a family member, so they put their feelings to one side and provided the care she needed. Adolfo couldn't help with the more intimate aspects of this, but sat with her in the evening. Neither of them knew what to say to the other.

"There's more soup where that came from," said Rosabella, holding up the empty mug. "Would you like some?"

Serafina shook her head, then winced. "My head," she said. "Can I have some laudanum?"

Once Serafina was sedated and comfortable, Rosabella had some of the soup herself, washed up the mugs, and went back into Serafina's room. She and Amedea had agreed that one of them should be in the house at all times during the day in case Serafina needed help with anything. Making herself at home in a chair by the window, she settled down to finish knitting a blanket for the baby that would soon arrive.

Her own dozing was interrupted when Serafina moved her leg and cried out in pain. Rosabella went over to the bed, leaned over and gently stroked Serafina's hair.

"Hush," she said, "go back to sleep."

Serafina turned her head away from the light and Rosabella's swollen belly.

"What a fool I was," she said, "so foolish…" She sounded confused, disoriented. Rosabella wondered if that was the laudanum, or perhaps the blow to the head.

"No, no," she said, "none of us is used to having motor cars drive in town like that. That could have happened to anyone."

"That's not what I meant," said Serafina, and began to cry.

"What's the matter, Serafina?" Rosabella was quite alarmed. She only knew Serafina as hard and tart-tongued and couldn't imagine what would make her get weepy like this.

"It was nothing. Nothing." Serafina began retreating back into her shell, hugging herself tightly under the bedcover.

"Nothing? I've never seen you like this. Serafina, tell me what happened, what made you so unhappy. You'll feel better for it."

Serafina looked at her miserably, tears damp on her cheeks.

Rosabella said, "We're family, Serafina."

"You promise not to tell anyone?"

Rosabella could see that Serafina's story was struggling to break free. What could it be? Serafina was unnaturally closed and private, and Rosabella knew nothing of her earlier life.

"Of course," she said. "You can trust me with anything."

Serafina took a deep breath.

"He was so beautiful," she said, and started crying again.

Rosabella was dumbfounded. Serafina talking about a man that way?

"Who?" she asked, careful to be very gentle. "Who was so

beautiful?"

"You know I went to work in Napoli during the war?" Serafina said. Rosabella shook her head.

"In 1943. Several of us went to work at the Bishop's palace. His regular servants had run away because of the war. Father Giovanni told the Bishop that he could send over some replacements. He came to us one day and told us to pack."

"He didn't ask if you wanted to go?"

"Oh, no, why would he?" Serafina seemed genuinely surprised at the question.

"What was it like, working for the Bishop?"

"We never saw him, of course, but it was nice. We had good clothes to wear, nicer than we could get here, and the work wasn't too hard. And we got plenty of time off, enough that we could leave the palace and explore Napoli. Even in wartime, we could have fun there, going to nightclubs. Us girls from Fontana, we stuck together, being in Napoli was so exciting after growing up here."

"What happened?"

"I met Franklin."

"Franklin?" Rosabella rolled the unfamiliar syllables around on her tongue. They tasted strange, exotic.

"We were at a nightclub one evening. He came over and offered to buy us drinks. The American soldiers had lots of money to spend, you know. Of course, we said yes. By the end of the evening, it was obvious that I was the one he liked."

Now Rosabella knew how this story would end.

"When did you find out?" she asked, hoping to spare Serafina some of the pain.

"We had such a good time." Serafina sounded proud, and defiant, and desolate. "His family was originally Italian, from the north, so he spoke quite good Italian. He told me that he loved me, that he'd take me to meet his grandparents in Lucca when the war was over. He loved me, he really did."

Serafina sniffed and wiped her eyes with the corner of the sheet.

"His leave was over at the end of the summer and he had to

rejoin his unit. Two months later, one of his friends was at the nightclub we used to go to. He told me that Franklin was dead, killed at Monte Cassino. His friend was nice, he offered to buy me a drink, but I said no, I wanted to be alone.

"A week or two later, I went to a doctor that one of the other girls told me about. I'd missed my bleeding twice, you see. He told me I was carrying a baby. I only went with Franklin once, the night before he left. I thought it was safe, that you had to lie with a man many times before anything happened. That's what I was told, anyway, and I was too young to know better."

And too innocent, thought Rosabella, to know when she was being taken advantage of.

"I always wanted a baby," cried Serafina. "When I was growing up, it's all I ever thought of. I would have been a good mother, I know. I wanted a baby so badly, but not like that."

"What happened to the child?" asked Rosabella.

"I was sent to the convent at Camaldoli. One of the nuns was nice but the others were horrible. They told me that I had sinned, that I was going to go to Hell and burn in everlasting fires, that God turned His back on loose women like me. I had to do everything they told me. They'd hit me if I was too slow or did things wrong."

"What about your parents? Did they know what had happened?"

"My aunt came over once. She told me that I'd disgraced the family. I was brought up to be a good girl, she said, so I could find a good husband and give my mother lots of grandchildren. Mama said nothing, but I don't think she ever forgave me.

"The nice nun helped me when the baby was born. It took a very long time. When they finally cut the cord, one of the other nuns came and washed him. 'So this is baby Salvatore,' she said. 'I want to call him Franklin,' I said, but she looked straight at me, eyes like daggers, and said I had no right to give him a name after what I'd done, especially not the name of the man who'd led me into sin and depravity. 'I want to hold him,' I said, 'please, let me hold my son, please, just once,' but she said no, that he was gone from me forever, and then she took him away. The afterbirth was still inside me and they took my beautiful baby away from me."

Finally, Serafina's grief overflowed in great, wracking sobs. Rosabella tried to hold her hand but Serafina snatched it away angrily.

Rosabella could do nothing but sit there until the tumult passed. How quick we are to judge people, she thought, how little we really understand why they act as they do. Like everyone else, she had just assumed that Serafina was born bitter and unhappy, had never tried to look past the surface to find the real person underneath, never tried to understand why she behaved the way she did.

"Serafina, I'm so sorry," she said. She meant, for not giving you a chance.

"Why are you sorry?" asked Serafina. "The fault is mine, not yours." It seemed to Rosabella that she wanted to hoard the guilt, make it hers alone, that her suffering would somehow be less noble if shared.

Rosabella said, "You made a mistake. But can you not take some comfort from knowing that your baby was welcomed into a new family?"

"He was dead," Serafina wailed. "He was born dead. He never opened his eyes, never took even a single breath. My beautiful Franklin, already dead before he lived…" Her voice fell away into bottomless sadness.

Rosabella had wondered with Amedea why Serafina disappeared so suddenly when they found the dead baby after the crash. Now she understood.

"God knew I had sinned," Serafina said after a long silence. "and this is my punishment." She sounded quite matter of fact, the waves of grief seemingly behind her. "I must carry the shame for the rest of my life, knowing that I disgraced my family, that I will never have a family of my own, that my only child died, all because I did one bad thing. How can I ever forgive myself? I don't need to wait before going to Hell, I'm already there."

"Hush," said Rosabella. "You're still young, I'm sure you can find a husband, start a family." She didn't really believe this, but needed to say something encouraging, anything that might deflect Serafina from whipping herself.

"Look at me," Serafina replied angrily. "Who would take a whore like me for his wife? Besides, I'm not sure I want to get married any more. How can I rely on a man after what Franklin did? He got himself killed, didn't he? He should have been there to take care of me after the baby died. Instead, he abandoned me."

"I doubt he wanted to get killed," Rosabella said. Her patience with Serafina was starting to wear thin, in spite of all her best intentions.

"He should have been more careful," Serafina snapped. "One thing I'm sure of, you can't trust men."

Rosabella thought that Serafina had every right to be angry with the long-dead Franklin for seducing a naïve country girl and leaving her pregnant. But blaming him for being killed in battle was unreasonable, unless this was how she dealt with her grief and guilt.

She said, "Well, I know I can trust my Cesare," surprising herself by how prim she sounded.

Serafina turned to look directly at her, careful not to move her leg. One side of her face had been badly bruised when she hit her head and the puffy, discoloured skin closed her eye to a slit. Her other eye, malevolent and unblinking, was fixed on Rosabella.

"Really?" she asked. "Are you sure?"

"Of course, why should I not be?"

Serafina's small pink tongue flickered across thin, dry lips.

"All men have secrets," she said in a sly voice. "All of them, even your precious Cesare. I grew up with him and I know more about him than anyone, even you. Believe me, he has secrets hidden away."

"What secrets?" Rosabella was getting annoyed. "You have to tell me."

"Oh, no. His secrets are his, and not mine to share. You have to find them out for yourself."

Despite herself, Rosabella could feel the tug of curiosity, the temptation to know more. What kind of secrets could Cesare possibly have? How could she find out? She always felt she could trust Cesare because she thought she knew him, but she could feel the uncertainty starting to gnaw away at the edges. Would she feel differently about him if she really knew his innermost thoughts?

Troubled by her doubts and unfamiliar thirst to learn things, Rosabella suddenly felt chilly. The sun no longer warmed the room, which had seemed so welcoming when she arrived earlier. A draft of cool air blew across her bare shoulders. Shivering, she rummaged in her bag, found her shawl with its pattern of green leaves, and pulled it around herself.

As she sat down again, she heard Amedea arriving downstairs. Greatly relieved, she collected her things and prepared to leave.

"My story is safe with you, I hope," said Serafina from the bed. "There is no need to burden anyone else with my troubles. Perhaps you should just forget what I told you."

"Once something is known," replied Rosabella, "it cannot be made unknown again. But yes, your secret is safe with me. I hope you feel better for showing it the light of day, some memories thrive best when kept hidden away."

After Rosabella had left, Serafina thought about Cesare's locked box, tucked away under his workbench. How long would it be before Rosabella ferreted the secret from him? Would knowing that her faith in him was misplaced drive a wedge between them? Serafina hoped so; she shouldn't have confessed her darkest secret to Rosabella when her discretion was dulled by pain and laudanum. She wished she could untell her story and keep it for herself, her own crown of thorns, the only thing that was hers and hers alone.

That and the shame, the acid that ate at her soul. She was a good person when she went to Napoli, she knew that. Obedient and God-fearing, an example to the other girls. But she'd done something bad, just once, and now she'd be punished for it for the rest of her life. Well, other people did bad things as well. It was only right that they be punished as she was.

The idea of forgiving other people for their misdeeds, let alone forgiving herself, never came close to entering her head.

SEVERAL WEEKS AFTER FATHER GIOVANNI'S DEATH, Adolfo arrived early at the shop one morning. He'd made a fresh batch of sausages the evening before and wanted to lay them out before the first customers of the day arrived. The sausages were milder than their predecessors; not all his customers had appreciated the heat of recent batches, and it was clear that they expected a return to a more conventional taste, slightly spicy on occasion, but not enough to deter the children.

The first batch he'd made after Giovanni's funeral was hot enough to make people sweat and reach quickly for a drink of water. Later batches weren't as volcanic but they were definitely on the hot side of normal. It was time to reassure his customers that he hadn't lost his touch.

He hadn't been able to bring himself to attend the funeral itself. The thought of being trapped in church, forced to listen to hypocritical praise being lavished on Father Giovanni, was more than he could stomach. He was afraid that people would be watching him, and he didn't think he could hide his loathing and anger.

Or the shame. Shame for what he'd allowed the dead priest to do to him, for being so powerless, for not fighting harder. And the humiliation and loss of self-respect from what had been done to him.

Despite what he'd said to Father Renato, he didn't know if he had it in him to forgive Giovanni or even if he wanted to. There was something pure and powerful in withholding forgiveness, even after Giovanni was in his grave. And although he didn't want to be this angry all his life, he still had the satisfaction of knowing that his anger was justified, that he had every right to feel like this.

So he stayed away from the funeral service, contenting himself with watching people entering the church and then, after he'd waited in the warm sun, seeing them leave again. The Bishop led the procession for the short distance down the hill to the cemetery, Father Renato by his side. Six members of the congregation—fine, upstanding citizens all–carried the ornate coffin, which was draped with an exuberant coat of flowers. An altar boy, looking clean and innocent in his white robe, carried a cross in front of the coffin. Another swung a thurible, a trail of incense floating away from it. Adolfo wondered if they realized how lucky they were to be burying Father Giovanni instead of having his rough hands pawing at them.

He followed the procession and found a place on the wall overlooking the cemetery where he could watch and hear the actual burial.

By the Madonna, you'd think they were burying a saint, the way the Bishop went on. As everyone knew, Father Giovanni possessed all the virtues known to man with none of the vices. The world was poorer for his passing but we could all take solace in knowing that he had gone to a better place, that he was resting in the bosom of God, that the angels and even the archangels were celebrating his arrival in Heaven. Yes, it was proper and right to mourn the passing of a good man, a great man, but we must also remember and rejoice that he is now with God.

Adolfo listened to this self-serving claptrap with growing disgust. Clearly, the Bishop had no idea what kind of man he was talking about.

At last, the pallbearers lowered the coffin into the waiting hole in the ground. Mourners took it in turns to drop handfuls of earth onto the coffin. Adolfo thought that some of them tossed the earth in with perhaps a little too much enthusiasm.

One last prayer and it was done. The mourners drifted away like leaves being scattered by the wind, and the sexton began filling in the grave. Adolfo waited until he was finished, wanting to be certain that there was enough earth holding down the coffin that Giovanni could not possibly emerge to reclaim his place among the living. Once he was satisfied that the world was safe, he went back to the shop and tried to resume a normal life.

He wanted today's batch of sausages to be a bit of a peace offering to his customers. He realized that his emotions were getting the better of him and compromising the artistry he was proud of bringing to his work. It was time to regain his customers' trust.

Working on the fresh batch the previous evening, he'd used all the love and skill he could. He liked the result but now it was up to his customers to decide if they agreed with him. He arranged the sausages in the display case to show them at their best, then put a hand-written sign beside them. EXELENT, it said, in loud block letters. NORMAL.

The first customer was the widow Agresta, who lived with her son, daughter-in-law, and an indeterminate number of ragamuffin grandchildren in a small, crumbling house on the edge of town. The family was very poor and sausages were an occasional treat for their Sunday lunch. Adolfo knew that the daughter-in-law had a new winter coat that was retrieved from the mountain the morning after the crash. The widow Agresta studied the sausages closely, then looked at Adolfo's crude sign.

"Normal?" she asked suspiciously. "Not like the last lot? They were far too hot."

"These are exactly as you like them, Signora," he said. "And because you were disappointed last time, they are at a very modest price."

"I'll take eight." There were no thanks for his consideration, just the resigned acceptance that the truly poverty-stricken generally show for whatever the gods throw their way.

Adolfo took his father's knife from the counter, carefully wiped the blade clean, cut off eight sausages, and laid them on a sheet of paper for wrapping. They looked exactly like fingers.

He took a deep breath, pushed his hands onto the counter so they wouldn't shake. They're only sausages, he told himself. But he couldn't avoid the image of a hand outstretched on stony ground, palm up, an expensive ring on one finger. Nor could he ignore the sharp memory of four severed fingers wrapped in a cigar box in his secret crevice high up the mountain.

It was a long day. But he had the satisfaction of seeing that all the sausages were gone as he cleaned up after the last customer had left. He'd done his grovelling, apologised countless times for making the sausages too hot, offered extravagant promises about the excellence of this batch, made no profit on the day's sales, and felt completely spent.

There was nothing left to do in the shop once he'd washed his hands. He could have an aperitivo on his own, since Cesare rarely came these days, but he didn't enjoy drinking by himself in the empty shop. Or he could go home. Either way, he'd be alone.

After closing up, he decided not to go home just yet. Instead, he locked the door and headed through town and the growing darkness, down the hill, towards the cemetery.

Somewhat to his surprise, Adolfo had found after Giovanni's funeral that he was drawn to the cemetery. He'd go down there every few days, find a seat in the shade under one of the umbrella pines, and sit there for an hour or so. The cemetery was quiet and peaceful, undisturbed by the bustle of town up the hill behind him. He could see Father Giovanni's grave from his seat, and watched as the flowers placed there after the funeral gradually wilted and faded. He liked the calm and the solitude, and always left feeling a little better, even if the anger and bitterness never went away.

By the time he got to the cemetery and took his usual seat, a full moon rested just above the horizon, casting a cold white light across the graves. Headstones glowed as if they had lanterns inside, and the shadows were pitch black.

Not for the first time, Adolfo thought about Tifeo. By what right did his little brother appoint himself the family's conscience? Didn't Tifeo appreciate how hard he made things?

Since his encounter with the spirits on the mountain, Adolfo had found it increasingly difficult to reassure himself about what he'd done after the crash, and Tifeo's ice-cold contempt just made things worse. Adolfo's first and strongest instinct was to reject Tifeo's criticism, but now he was starting to worry that maybe–just maybe– his brother had been right all along.

So why had Tifeo extended the invitation to Christmas dinner? Adolfo still hadn't decided if the offer was real. But he was starting to wonder if perhaps he had been too quick to reject the invitation.

In a grudging truth he admitted only to himself, he was lonely. Ulisse was in Napoli, Cesare hardly ever came to the shop any more, and Serafina could hardly be described as lively company; she said little, and what she did say tasted like spoiled vinegar. Adolfo was forced to the unwelcome conclusion that he might have to find a way, to use Rosabella's words, to close the gap with his brother.

The cemetery was hushed and calm. A soft wind blew and the fig tree on the other side of the path swayed gently from side to side. Adolfo closed his eyes and leaned his head against the stone wall behind him, and listened to the pines whispering their secrets to each other.

When he opened his eyes some time later, Father Giovanni was sitting in the fig tree, watching him.

"You," Adolfo said, unsurprised. He knew that this encounter was inevitable.

"I cannot leave," Giovanni's spirit said sadly. "The thread that binds us together is altogether too strong. Try as I might, I cannot break it."

"And what does that have to do with me? Is that my fault?"

"No, no, none of this is your fault, that is all mine. Adolfo, I betrayed your trust and hurt you. I cannot tell you how much I regret what I did to you. How ashamed I am, how much I despise myself, that I could do such things. When I was dying, the guilt was all I could think of. I confessed my sins and repented of them before God, but not to you. It was too hard. Even now, it is almost more than I have strength for. But I would do now what I could not do before, to acknowledge the harm. Apologise to you. I am so, so sorry."

Adolfo could not speak. After all this time, after all the hurt, after all the denial, he finally had the apology he craved. His eyes filled and his throat ached.

The spirit said, "I could not apologize when I still lived. It was too much for me. I could not accept that I could cause such harm. That was more than I could bear; something else to regret. But I did not think that an apology would be so hard to receive."

At last, Adolfo found his voice.

"This is more difficult than I expected," he said. "It has been part of my life for so long. What happens now?"

"Only you can answer that. All I know is that the thread has two ends, and there is but one connected to me."

"And if I forgive you, will that untie the thread? Will that release us?"

The spirit said again, "Only you can answer that. I have apologised, that is all I can do. You were unable to forgive me before, I cannot fault you for that. God may have forgiven me, but I am tied to this place as long as I live in your heart. Adolfo, I beg you to forgive me. It will set me free."

"I've waited so long for this," said Adolfo, "I have lain awake at night, wondering if you would ever apologise, and what you might say. Sometimes I thought I should throw your words back in your face, thinking that no apology could ever make up for what you did to me. And now the moment is here, I don't know what to do."

The spirit looked stricken. "But God has already forgiven me," he said. "How can you not do the same?"

"Because I'm just a simple butcher, not God."

Adolfo and the spirit were silent for a long time. The moon climbed in the sky, shortening the shadows beside the headstones. Its reflection glittered on the waters of the Bay far below them, a shimmering carpet of light.

Adolfo said, "You have done me such harm, made so many things wrong with my life. There is no one who loves me, no one who would truly mourn if I died tomorrow. My family despise me. I have no control over my life, have done terrible things, all because of you…"

Startled by his outburst, the spirit interrupted. "Do you want to be a victim forever?" he asked.

"You, of all people, have no right to ask me that question!"

"Perhaps not. But who else will? And I have more interest than most in helping you. I placed this burden on you, I would do what I can to lift it. This is the only way left to me to atone for what I did."

Adolfo said, "I have been angry with you for so long, the anger has become part of me. I don't know if I want to lose it."

"Does being angry with me help you live the life you long for?" the spirit asked. "Does it bring you love? Or the warmth of your family? And how does blaming me for all your problems help you deal with them?"

Adolfo was shocked into silence. Once again, he became lost in his thoughts. The fig tree continued to sway in the breeze, its branches carrying Giovanni's spirit back and forth in a slow, endless dance.

Eventually, Adolfo said, "You told me that you were tied to this place as long as you lived in my heart. I think the opposite is also true, that I will never be free of you as long as I allow you to occupy my heart, controlling what I feel. So yes, I will forgive you. But understand that this is to free myself, to untie my end of the thread and cast it as far away as I can. What you do with your end is for you to decide."

He sat up straight.

"Giovanni, I forgive you for what you did to me. I hope that if the other boys were here, they would extend their forgiveness as well."

As he said the words, Adolfo could feel just the slightest easing of the tightness around his heart. Forgiving was not a single act, he realized, but an ongoing, gradual process that would take time. But it felt wonderfully good to untie the first knot, to know that more would follow.

Giovanni's spirit had listened with anticipation. When Adolfo finished speaking, his expression gradually turned to dismay.

"You have done what I asked," he said. "But I feel no different. I am still tethered and cannot leave. What else must I do?"

Adolfo said, "I cannot say. All I know is that only I can untie my end of the thread, and only you can undo yours. Until you can do that, you will be tangled in the thread, tied to this place."

"But God has forgiven me, and I would go to Heaven!"

"I have forgiven you, Giovanni, and cannot do more. It seems you have more work to do on this earth before you can leave."

For the first time, Adolfo felt sorry for Giovanni, something he could only do once he'd forgiven him. The desolation on the spirit's face was almost more than he could bear. Giovanni had apologised, probably the hardest thing he had ever done, and yet it was not enough.

"I would help you," Adolfo said, "if I knew how."

The spirit winced on hearing the pity in his voice.

"I don't know what to do," he said.

Adolfo was about to speak when he heard footsteps on the gravel path at the cemetery entrance nearest to the town. It was a young couple, looking for somewhere quiet and private. He turned back to the spirit but the fig tree was quite empty. He had no wish to deter the lovers, so he walked quickly along the grass verge to the other entrance and slipped away.

Walking home, Adolfo felt better than he had in a long time. The hurt and pain would always be part of who he was, like the scar on his leg, a permanent reminder of trying to crawl through a barbed wire fence when he was a boy. But by saying 'I forgive you', he had somehow unlocked the anger, opening the sluice gates that would eventually allow the pus to drain away.

After the very public execution of Giordano Bruno, Ulisse found that he was treated with considerably higher levels of respect. His brothers within the Camorra knew what he had done, and admired both his loyalty to the family and the ruthlessness and inventiveness with which he handled a tricky problem. Cutolo even praised him publicly at a meeting of the clan bosses. It was like seeing the Inquisition in action, he'd said, publicly burning a heretic to punish him and provide a salutary example to anyone else who might think of abandoning the one true faith. And he'd made sure that Ulisse was given a bigger and more comfortable flat.

All of Napoli were both horrified and fascinated by the spectacular immolation in the heart of Camorra territory. The police were faced by a wall of stony silence from everyone they talked to and had given up trying to identify the perpetrator. In fact, they were secretly relieved; they knew about the threat posed by the 'Ndrangheta, and did not like the potential for a lengthy, all-out war between the two rivals.

As much as the Camorra bosses enjoyed the Neapolitan flamboyance of Bruno's death 'at the stake', as one of them put it after hearing Cutolo's comment, they were especially pleased by the results. The 'Ndrangheta were shocked by the speed and decisiveness of the Camorra response to their challenge, and withdrew to consider their options. Anyone with lingering 'Ndrangheta sympathies went deep underground, furtively meeting in private to avoid persecution and the same fate meted out to Bruno. And the people under Camorra protection were quick to appreciate that unwavering and visible adherence to the Camorra way of doing things was much wiser than questioning their authority. There was peace on the streets, and shopkeepers stopped grumbling publicly about paying one tenth of their revenue for protection and guidance on how to conduct their business.

Ulisse's new flat was even closer to the Pizzeria San Gennaro. The staff there were quick to recognize Ulisse's new status, even if they didn't know the exact cause, so he enjoyed an better table, with better wine, and paid less. He generally ate alone and in peace; the white-coated waiters took care that the tables nearest to his were the last to be filled. He no longer had to chase the soccer-playing boys away; whenever they saw him, they flowed like quicksilver to the other side of the square, followed by the inevitable small dogs.

Ulisse enjoyed the attention, but thought little of what he'd done. He'd learned to kill as a soldier when it was kill or be killed, and the rights and wrongs of killing a man seemed more distant each time he did it. Now it was just an occasional part of the job. Unpleasant, perhaps, but necessary. Certainly nothing to lose sleep over.

Two days after Cesare visited Gasparo, Raffaele Cutolo joined Ulisse at his table. A waiter saw him arrive and a fresh bottle of Lacryma Christi appeared with commendable speed. Cutolo took an appreciative sip of the wine before sitting back with a satisfied sigh. Ulisse watched, wondering what problem Cutolo was going to dump into his lap. As always, Cutolo took his time, talking about inconsequential matters, not allowing the pressures of business to interfere with the pleasures of life. After a while, he poured another glass of wine for himself and for Ulisse, the signal that the time had come for serious conversation.

"I need you to go to Ischia," he said.

Ulisse was surprised. "Not to Fontana, I hope. I'm too well known there."

"We have a small problem there," Cutolo said, "and you're the best person to deal with it."

Ulisse waited.

Cutolo said, "You know that we have several business partners on Ischia. They're all building for the tourists we expect to start coming soon. One of them has become greedy. We tolerate a certain amount of this from any of our partners, they're only human, but this one has gone too far and needs a warning."

"A warning?"

"No more for now, no more."

"How did we learn of this greed?" Ulisse had no experience in business and was genuinely curious.

"Many suppliers to the construction business are friends of ours. One of them told us that our partner is padding invoices; when we looked into it, we found that he was doing the same thing with others. He is being exceptionally stupid, thinking we would not find out."

"How strong a warning should he get?"

"He just needs to be told that we're aware of what he's doing, that we don't like it, and that we'll know if he continues in this foolishness. No more than that, Ulisse, just a warning. Now he's shown us he can build, we need him for another project, even larger and much more profitable. He should also know that he must pay us the money he has stolen from us plus ten percent as punishment, and that this will be the only warning he gets—we can forgive a single transgression, but he must reform or we will terminate our relationship in a way that he will not like."

All this made sense to Ulisse. The Camorra understood only too well that people were fallible and imperfect, and, if it suited their purposes, could be remarkably forgiving when someone acknowledged their mistakes and promised not to make them again. But they could be equally merciless when dealing with people who consistently violated the Camorra code of conduct.

"And who is to receive this warning?"

Cutolo hesitated before answering.

"It's your cousin, Cesare," he said. "I think he'll listen to you more than someone he doesn't know."

Ulisse felt sick. I should have seen that coming, he thought. Cesare may have shown he was a good builder, but he was still weak and easily tempted. And stupid, evidently.

"So this is why you think I'm the best person for the job?"

"Indeed. He's your family. You can have a quiet word with him, emphasise that he is making a big mistake, say that no one but you two will know what he's done. There's no need for him to lose face."

"When do you need this done?"

"Sometime in the next few weeks," Cutolo replied. "It's not like the situation with Bruno, where we had to act quickly."

They finished the wine together over more small talk, although Cutolo did most of the talking; Ulisse was wondering how best to get Cesare on his own, and then thinking, how can he be so stupid?

Once the wine was gone, Cutolo got up to leave. Standing beside the table, he said, "By the way, I understand that Cesare went to see the pawnbroker down by the port not long ago. Gasparo said he brought a rough diamond and some quite good pieces, unusual ones he hadn't seen before. They looked Middle Eastern, he said. Is anything going on I should know about?"

"I don't know where they came from," said Ulisse, quite truthfully. With a colossal effort, he kept his face and voice quite expressionless. "I expect he bought them cheap from one of the tourists, some of them come from there."

Cutolo nodded. "That's probably it," he said, and left.

Ulisse put his usual very generous tip on the table and headed home. Walking through the narrow alleys, his mind raced like a dog chasing its own tail. What on earth was Cesare doing with more loot from the plane? When did he find it and why hadn't he told him and Adolfo about it when they divided up the spoils? What the fuck was going on?

Chapter Twenty-two

FATHER RENATO WAS BUSIER THAN BROTHER RENATO ever was. Until the Bishop saw fit to send an assistant, he was the only priest in the parish, with the workload of two. Despite this, he still made time to go up to the forge as often as possible to sit with Tifeo and Amedea.

He found their friendship as refreshing as the clean air up the mountain. If they were in the middle of something when he arrived, he'd sit and watch while they finished; otherwise, they were quite happy to put down whatever they were doing and pull out a bottle of wine. Sometimes their talk would be utterly inconsequential, or they would talk of events in town. Tifeo had a habit of pulling a question out of thin air like the magician Renato saw once when he was a child in Siena, who produced brightly coloured marbles for the boys, ribbons for the girls. The questions always made him think hard about something entirely unexpected. Then the conversation might go anywhere, something that Renato thoroughly enjoyed.

On this occasion, the three friends sat comfortably and quietly on the terrace, looking down the hill. Amedea had prepared some cutlets of breaded zucchini and *scamorza*, which disappeared with remarkable speed, washed down by a bottle of crisp white wine from the Casa D'Ambra.

"Amedea, you cook like an angel," said Renato. "If we ever get to Heaven, this is what it will be like."

"Unfortunately, there is no more zucchini," she said, "so that's all you get. There's rationing, even in Heaven."

"She might cook like an angel," Renato said to Tifeo, "but she tempts like Satan."

Tifeo had been studying Renato. "You look tired," he said. "Is everything alright?"

Renato rubbed his eyes. "I have come to realize that there is not just one Church, but many. Today, I refereed a soccer match between the schools in Fontana and Forio that took weeks to organize. When I recovered my breath and my legs, I held Mass. I took confession. I visited several elderly widows who live on their own to make sure they were being looked after properly and were getting enough to eat. I met with Mayor Artigiani to ensure that the town takes proper care of the cemetery. I spoke to Tommaso Masaccio about painting the statue of our Lord Jesus in the main square."

He paused for breath.

"There is a Church that does social work, one that maintains buildings and property, there is a Church that teaches and celebrates our faith in God, and one that disciplines the wayward."

"And do you find one of these Churches more rewarding than the others?" A classic Tifeo question.

"That's easy. I'm a shepherd at heart, so helping people find their way to God is a joy for me. A close second, though, is just looking after people. If the Church did not care for the unfortunate in our community, I don't know who would. It's good going to bed knowing that someone's life is just a little better because you helped them."

"And your least favourite?"

"Tifeo, you know the answer to that."

"One of the most remarkable things about your Church to me is its capacity for doing both great good and great harm. Soccer games, looking out for little old ladies, helping people think about or even believe in something larger than themselves, that is all admirable. Punishing and threatening people for not following your rules, less so."

"Enough, Tifeo," said Amedea. "Let the poor man enjoy his wine."

Renato said, "Let me say one thing. I never thought I should have to choose between my conscience and what the Church requires of me. The choice seemed exquisitely painful and difficult. And yet…"

His voice trailed off as he looked over the Bay. Tifeo and Amedea waited for him to recover himself.

"…and yet," he went on, "It was not so difficult in the end. I realized that I must do what I think right. It seems sometimes that some of my fellow priests rely too much on doctrine instead of trusting their own conscience. I will say this to no one else, but I have more confidence in God than I do in the Church."

"I'm glad you're here," said Amedea. "Fontana needs a man like you. We should not speak ill of the dead, but I never liked Father Giovanni. He was too rigid, too wedded to doctrine."

"I agree," said Tifeo. "But it will be difficult for you, I think, continuing as a priest."

"Not really," said Renato. "I can do more for my community inside the Church than outside. If I must be a touch more flexible than the Church, that is the price I must pay."

"I have rabbit in the pot and must tend to it," said Amedea. "Renato, you're more than welcome to stay and enjoy it with us. I'm sure Tifeo can find a suitable wine to go with it."

She disappeared into the kitchen. Tifeo was about to go inside when Renato stopped him.

"I have my own question of you," he said. "It concerns your brother Adolfo."

Tifeo sat down, his face darkening.

Renato said, "You seem very angry with Adolfo, something that goes well beyond what you think he did after the crash. What did he do, that you find it so hard to forgive him?"

"And what business is that of yours?" Tifeo sounded wary but not yet hostile.

"A friend's business. It grieves me to see brothers estranged."

Tifeo said, "I invited him to dinner with us, you know. He made it very clear that he wanted nothing to do with us. With his family."

Renato said, "I think that perhaps he was just protecting himself."

"What do you mean?"

Before Renato could respond, Amedea came out to the terrace.

"Dinner is ready," she said. "Tifeo, where's the wine? Renato, come on through."

Tifeo was uncharacteristically quiet through the meal. He could usually be relied on to keep a conversation rolling along, but not this time. Renato thought the rabbit was delicious and said so, but Tifeo picked away at his without paying it the attention it deserved. To fill the silence, Renato gossiped shamelessly with Amedea, comparing scandalous notes on the high and mighty of Fontana.

At the end of an excellent meal, Amedea began clearing away the plates. "You two have more to talk about, I can tell," she said. "I'll take care of this and leave you to it."

Tifeo refilled their glasses, and they went out to the terrace again. The sun had just dropped below the horizon and the west sky glowed salmon-pink.

The two men sat quietly for a long time. Renato was calm, enjoying the evening, knowing that Tifeo would break the silence when he was ready.

"You said that he was protecting himself. What did you mean?" Tifeo eventually asked.

Renato said, "Normally I wouldn't do this. But one of the people involved in this is now dead, and there's something about Adolfo you need to know."

"You know more about Adolfo than I do?"

"I talked with Adolfo himself. And with the other person. And learned things I wish were not there to be learned."

Tifeo had the good sense to wait. Whatever Renato had to say could not be good, and he had to say it in his own way.

"We talked earlier about the Church," Renato went on, "and how it can be fallible by relying too much on doctrine. In this case, the Church was more than fallible, it was complicit in a great sin. I'm deeply ashamed of what was done to Adolfo. And also to you, Tifeo. Because of what happened, Adolfo was badly hurt, and lost his relationship with you. So you, too, are a victim."

"What on earth are you talking about? Renato, you speak in riddles."

So Renato told him the whole sorry story.

A day later, Tifeo stood outside Adolfo's shop, hesitating before going in. Fontana bustled with people going home after a long day in the fields, heading out for an early dinner, or just enjoying a casual drink with friends. A group of four men were playing Briscola together outside Ampelio's bar, the tone and volume of their ribald comments and teasing shifting with the fortunes of each pair of players. A waitress brought them a fresh round of drinks, making a tart but good-natured retort to a particularly suggestive remark from one of the men. It was all completely innocent, and perfectly normal.

How could we not know, wondered Tifeo. He grew up in Fontana, knew many people there, and there had been no indication of the evil being done right under their noses. According to Renato, Adolfo was not the only person to suffer from Giovanni's attentions. Tifeo knew many of the other altar boys and had never suspected that any of them could have been treated the same way. Some of them seemed a bit withdrawn after they became too old to be altar boys, but he'd never thought about asking why, and no one he knew had shown any signs of seeing that something was wrong. Now he wished he'd been more perceptive, more caring. Not just himself, the whole community. How could none of us know, or did we just not see what we did not want to acknowledge?

And was this also how the community suppressed the knowledge of evil done after the crash?

A customer came out of the shop and Tifeo moved sideways to let her by. Adolfo had come to the door to see her out—when he saw Tifeo outside, he froze. Recovering quickly, he flipped the sign from *Aperto* to *Chiuso* and held the door open for him, saying, "Come in."

Entering the shop, Tifeo looked around.

"You've made some changes since I was last here," he said. "The place looks good."

Adolfo nodded and waved Tifeo to the table in the corner.

"I brought some grappa," Tifeo said, putting a bottle on the table. "The best."

Another nod, and Adolfo brought two glasses over. He sat down, silent and cautious.

Tifeo poured two generous helpings of grappa. He held his glass up in a silent toast to Adolfo, who paused for a second before holding his glass up in return. In silence, they both took a sip.

"That *is* good," Tifeo said appreciatively, taking another sip. Adolfo put his glass on the table, and waited. His hands lay still on the table, but Tifeo could see the strain around his eyes.

"I had a long talk with Father Renato last night," he said.

"He's a priest," Adolfo said, dismissing anything a priest might say.

"Of course. But he's a good man, I think. Not like Father Giovanni."

"And what do you know about Father Giovanni?" Tifeo could almost hear the doors to Adolfo's heart being slammed shut and padlocked.

"I know now what he did to you. And the other altar boys."

"He did nothing."

"Adolfo, Father Renato told me everything."

"He did nothing." But Adolfo now sounded uncertain.

"Adolfo, we both know he did."

"You heard this from that priest?" A last sign of defiance. "What right does he have to talk about such things?"

"Father Renato is deeply shamed by what a priest of his Church did. He understands only too well that such deeds cannot be undone, but he wants to help repair some of the damage. Last night, he told me everything he knows. I said I wanted to talk to you about it, and he gave me his permission."

"I care nothing for his shame. But why are you doing this to me? Nothing that happened has anything to do with you, it's none of your fucking business. I keep trying to put it out of my mind, and now you want to drag me through it all over again?" Adolfo sounded increasingly desperate.

"Oh, but it did affect me. I lost my older brother because of what Giovanni did. I miss him, have always missed him, and would have him back."

"You've done a very good job of telling me you want nothing to do with me. That's a curious way of missing me, don't you think?"

"You abandoned me!"

"What?" Adolfo was shocked.

The words had flown out of Tifeo's mouth before he could hold them back. He tried to collect himself; but now he'd said it, he had to continue.

"In the schoolyard. I was being bullied by those older boys, you saw what was happening, and instead of breaking it up as you normally did, you just ignored me. Left me alone. They watched you go away not caring, and hit me even harder. I had bruises for weeks."

Tifeo had tears in his eyes, of remembered humiliation, of being bullied, and of being abandoned.

"When I was small, you were my big brother, my hero, someone to look up to. You were Poppa's favourite, he loved how you'd make sausages just the way he did. I wanted to be like you, have him love me like he loved you. I tried to make sausages, but they never turned out right. He praised your sausages at the dinner table, but he never talked about mine. I wanted to be like you. Loved like you."

He paused to take a deep breath.

"And you were my protector at school. I relied on you to keep me safe. When you went away that day, it was not long after you became an altar boy, I thought you'd turned your back on me, abandoned me. So I did a childish thing, deciding that if you did not want me in your life, I did not want you in mine. That might be understandable for a child, if stupid, but it's really stupid for an adult."

Adolfo fiddled with his glass, turning it around and around, looking intently at something fascinating inside it. Eventually, he looked up, and now his eyes were wet.

"Tifeo, this very hard for me, to talk of… what happened. It has been my shame for so long…" His voice trailed off. "I thought that if I never spoke of it, the pain would go away. But it doesn't, you know. It just sits there, eating you from the inside."

Adolfo paused, seeming to prepare himself for what had to be said.

"What happened in the schoolyard was the day after I told

Momma about—about Father Giovanni. She hit me, told me that he was a good man and that I should respect him as I did Poppa. I was abandoned as well, not by you, but by Momma. And Poppa wasn't there to help."

He wiped his eyes.

"I didn't know how to take care of anyone except myself. Even that was difficult. And when I did eventually look for you, you had turned your back on me. Oh, I tried for a while, but gave up when you didn't respond. Things had changed between us, and it was easier to accept that than it was to keep trying. I thought I had done something to offend you, but did not know what. Perhaps I should have tried harder, I don't know."

"When you left me alone that day," said Tifeo, "I was too young to understand that something had happened to you, that you had been hurt much more than I ever was. As I got older, I would wonder what I had done to make you abandon me. I thought it was my fault, that I had done something to offend you. I never realized until last night that neither of us has ever been at fault."

For the first time in years, the two brothers smiled at each other, blinking back their tears. Simultaneously, they both reached out for the grappa.

Tifeo laughed and pulled his hand back. He said, "After you, brother. You're the eldest."

Adolfo took the bottle, leaned across the table, refilled Tifeo's glass, and put the bottle down again midway between them. Tifeo laughed and refilled Adolfo's glass with a flourish. The two brothers toasted each other again, this time with real feeling, instead of forced politeness.

"We did have fun together, didn't we?"

"Yes, we did. Those were good times."

For the next several glasses, they swapped stories of their childhood together, the long summer days when they'd go down and spend the whole day on the beach at Sant' Angelo, watching the fishermen and catching crabs, the evenings spent chasing each other though the streets, the thrill of grabbing oranges from the trees lining the track out of town and sucking every drop of sweet juice from them. Like all the other children their age, they were feral, sent outside to look after themselves by parents who were too busy trying to survive to do anything else.

But a dragon was in the room with them, one that would steal all the air if they let it, one they both knew had to be dealt with before they parted company. Reluctant to acknowledge the beast too soon, they agreed by silent consent to ignore it for as long as possible. Instead, they began, slowly and carefully, to build a bridge across the chasm that had separated them for so long.

At one point, Adolfo said, "I'm sorry I didn't spend Christmas with you and Amedea. It was good of you to ask."

"There's always next Christmas," said Tifeo. "And plenty of opportunity before."

When their reminiscing had run its course, they sat in comfortable silence for a while. Eventually, Adolfo cleared his throat.

He said, "There is another thing."

"Yes, I know."

"But first," said Adolfo, "I must tell you something about Father Giovanni."

Tifeo was surprised. He thought he knew what was coming, and it did not concern Father Giovanni.

Adolfo said, "You know that Father Renato sat by Giovanni's bed as he died."

"Yes."

"At the very end, when Giovanni was moments from his death, Renato administered the Last Rites."

"Yes, he told me this."

"Then you'll know that Giovanni, at long last, confessed his sins, including those involving me and the others. That he repented of those sins. Sincerely repented, Renato said. And that because of that, Renato gave him absolution. Meaning that Giovanni's path to Heaven is open, despite what he did to so many people."

"When Renato told me this," said Tifeo, "I told him that I

thought it more important that people on earth should forgive the person who did them harm. He said that if God could forgive sinners, who was he to deny it?"

"After Giovanni died," said Adolfo, "I started going to the cemetery. It was calm there and I liked the peace. I was there late one evening not so long ago, it was almost dark, and I talked with his spirit."

Tifeo said, "Go on." He knew that spirits often find it difficult to leave this world behind.

"He apologised to me. I wanted that apology so much… And I forgave him. I finally realized that I had to free myself of him, and that forgiveness was the first step."

"Why are you telling me this, Adolfo?"

"Because he still found it impossible to leave. God had forgiven him, I had forgiven him, and yet he was still tied to the cemetery and, he thought, to me, to us. He did not know what else he had to do before he could depart this world."

"Tell him that now he must forgive himself."

"What?"

Tifeo said, "Renato told me that, before he died, Giovanni grieved for what he had done. He hated himself, hated what he did."

"His spirit told me the same thing. 'Despise' was the word he used."

"Then tell me, what kind of place is Heaven if it is filled with people who despise themselves? It's all very well for God to forgive the sinner, but the sinner cannot be free of the wrongs he has done until he forgives himself. Otherwise, he would carry his guilt to Heaven. I cannot see how a soul can enjoy love and eternal happiness in Heaven, if there is such a place, while still burdened by guilt and self-loathing. Giovanni must forgive himself before he can leave the cemetery."

Tifeo paused. Adolfo looked ashen, shifting uncomfortably, playing with his glass. Are we only talking of Giovanni's guilt here, Tifeo wondered. He said, "There is another thing, you said."

"This is difficult for me," Adolfo began, then stopped. The

dragon in the room stirred, knowing that its name was about to be called. Adolfo stared into space, unsure of how best to proceed now that he'd started.

He said, "This concerns the crash. Of the airplane. On the mountain."

He ran his fingers through his hair.

"You think I had something to do with… with taking things. From the crash. I know I denied it to you, to everyone, but you're right. After you left us, we went up and found them. At the time, it seemed alright. They were dead, didn't need anything any more, and then Father Giovanni said that it was all God's will. I didn't really understand why he did that, but it was a good thing to hide behind. You know that Demonte blames me for Paolo's death, don't you?"

"Yes, he told me that Paolo saw what was happening, that it broke his mind. He thinks Paolo did what he did to stop the pain. He blames you, but mostly himself, for not looking after Paolo better."

Adolfo winced.

"I started to doubt what we'd done when Paolo died. Now I wish with all my heart that we never went up the mountain. That one night, the things we did—I did—will shape the rest of my life."

Tifeo said, "Ulisse and Cesare were here with you when I left. Did you all go up?"

"Yes, all three of us."

Tifeo could see a burden lift from Adolfo's shoulders as the truth finally came out. Dangerous truths kept hidden in the dark will hold you hostage, he thought. Speaking the truth out loud is the only way to be set free, hard as that might be.

"Now I have no secrets from you," Adolfo said. "Tifeo, I regret what I did, and would ask for your forgiveness."

"Mine?" Tifeo was surprised. "You don't need my forgiveness, you have done me no harm by this. It is I who should beg for your forgiveness instead. I have said harsh things about you, brother, words I should not have used, especially outside the family. I'm sorry I said those things. I promised you I would stop and I have. You can be sure I will never do it again."

Adolfo said, "It's good to have my brother back. When you're ready, ask me to dinner again. Before Christmas, that's too far away. I would be glad to accept."

Tifeo smiled and nodded. "Let me speak with Amedea," he said.

Adolfo said, "You and I can be brothers once more, but I still feel the guilt of what I did on the mountain. I don't know how to deal with that."

Tifeo said, "There are restless spirits on the mountain because of that night, I can feel them whenever I go up there. I think you must make your peace with them. Then you can deal with your guilt."

Adolfo said, "Can you help with that?"

"Of course," Tifeo said, putting down his empty glass. "But not tonight. It's getting late and I should be getting home. Adolfo, I rejoice that we can be brothers again."

On his way home, Tifeo thought of the gods on the mountain. Normally, they were unconcerned about human affairs. But if Adolfo was lucky and if they felt merciful, they would shine a light into the darker corners of his soul, so he might understand himself better, that he might heal himself of both the harm suffered at the hands of that priest and his guilt for what he did after the crash.

Chapter Twenty-three

ADOLFO CURSED AS HE STUMBLED OVER A ROOT that seemed to reach out from the ground to trip him. He kicked angrily at the root and stubbed his toe, and cursed again. The offending root lay across the path, ancient and gnarled, pushed up by a half-buried piece of tufa. Furious, Adolfo kicked it again and again until his breath and frustration were exhausted.

He sat on a nearby rock and looked around to see if anyone had seen his foolishness. This was highly unlikely; people did not come so high up the mountain at the end of the day, preferring to relax at home or at Ampelio's with friends or family. But Adolfo liked the solitude and had taken to closing the shop as soon as he could so he could climb the mountain to be by himself.

Soon after his encounter with Father Giovanni's spirit at the cemetery, he stopped going there to find peace. He spoke to the spirit just once, when he repeated Tifeo's suggestion about the need to forgive oneself (the spirit seemed to not like the idea). Even after that, he could still feel the spirit's presence, a nagging reminder of his anger at the priest. After a while, he understood that Father Giovanni would continue to rule his emotions as long as he allowed it and that the visits to the cemetery weren't helping.

And he didn't like the resurgence of humiliation and guilt every time he went there. The humiliation was just a dull ache, but the guilt stabbed him afresh each time. How could he possibly have found even a tiny sliver of enjoyment from what Giovanni did? Why did he not protest sooner?

Now, when he left the shop at the end of the day, Adolfo turned right to head high up the mountain instead of left, down the hill to the cemetery.

Breathing heavily after his futile admonishment of the root, he rubbed his sore toe, enjoying the view and the clean air, as fresh on his tongue as shaved ice. The silence was palpable, substantial, something he could reach out and touch. The sky was clear except for some clouds far off to the south. This was his favourite spot to sit, high enough to escape from Fontana and be alone but not so high that he could see the crash site.

He went up there once and retreated almost immediately, beaten back by the strong feeling of being watched and, even worse, being accused. Confessing his involvement in the looting to Tifeo had been like lancing a boil, and Adolfo was glad to have done it. But saying it out loud meant that he could no longer deny to himself what he'd grown to fear, that what he had done on the mountain was terribly wrong. Thinking over and over again about Father Giovanni's homily eventually left him with no escape—why would the priest have gone to such lengths to justify something that needed no justification? Looting dead bodies, hacking out their teeth to get at the gold fillings… how could that possibly be God's will?

Demonte was also on the mountain that afternoon. Once or twice a week, he'd go and sit beside Paolo's unmarked grave in the small hollow under the low, stunted chestnut tree. Demonte couldn't imagine how the tree found its way to the arid heights high on the mountain from the more fertile slopes lower down, but he could sit there for hours, looking out over the Bay. He liked the tree for more than its shade—it was welcome reassurance that nature is strong and resilient, that living things can survive much adversity.

Sitting where Paolo was buried, he was sure that Paolo was nearby. This gave him some comfort, although not enough to offset the troubling knowledge that he'd failed to protect his brother, failed to keep the promise he'd made to his parents. Demonte had no one else he could talk to about any of this, so he came to the hollow and talked to Paolo. Being a shepherd who spent many hours alone, he was a taciturn man, unused to long conversations or to revealing his innermost thoughts. But he found it easy to talk to Paolo about the small events of his days and, every now and again, to express his remorse about letting him down. He thought Paolo was listening, but there was never any reply.

Like Adolfo and Demonte, Father Renato was pulled to the mountain as a place to reflect, stealing time from his pastoral duties whenever possible. He couldn't find any particularly convincing excuses for this; he just knew that he found easier to meditate on the mountain than he did in the church, and was drawn to spend as much time there as he could.

Every step he took on the track up the mountain brought him closer to Heaven and to God. He could have reached the very top of Mount Epomeo, the highest point on the island, by clambering up through the jumble of tufa boulders coughed out aeons ago by the mountain, but that required walking along the track that went right past the crash site.

Each time he saw the cross standing above the site, he turned off the main path to walk carefully along the side trail, threading his way between the huge rocks on either side until he reached the flat, open area below the cross. Once there, he'd sit beside a large rock where he could be in the sun but out of the wind on a cool day, or in shade if it was warm. Protected by the rock, the same boulder that had sheltered Paolo from the cold wind and fog two years earlier, he could look up to where the cross stood proudly outlined against the sky. Then he could kneel and ask God for help in placing his wandering feet back on the path to renewing his faith.

Renato felt the weather start to change. The wind moved around to the south and suddenly seemed much warmer. Distracted from his devotions, he looked over his shoulder. The sky overhead was as blue as when he arrived. But now a bank of cloud lay over the Bay, the dark purple of a fresh bruise, its edge as sharp as if cut with one of Adolfo's knives. Heavy, swirling curtains of rain fell from the cloud, obscuring Capri and half the Bay. It was moving rapidly towards him; Renato had no doubt that he was about to get very wet.

He decided to surrender to the inevitable and watch the storm from the heights. There was nowhere near enough time to get home before it struck and he was going to get soaked anyway. But the air was getting warmer by the minute, so he didn't think he'd die of cold, and he might even dry out quickly once the rain ended. There was a certain grace in accepting what could not be changed, was there not, and he thought it would be interesting to experience seeing the Sirocco from close up.

Moments later, he wondered if he'd made the right decision. The wind arrived first, hitting him as hard as an angry mule and pressing him back against the rock. The light was sucked out of the air and day turned to twilight. Clutching his hat, Renato sidled sideways so he could get behind the rock but was knocked flat by the wind as soon as the rock was no longer there to support him. His flat hat flew from his head and flung itself against a bush, where it hung as securely as if it had been pinned there. Crawling over to the bush, he rescued the hat, then forced his way back through the wind to the shelter behind the boulder.

The rain struck. Its ferocity stunned Renato. Driven by the wind, huge drops of water flew sideways a few feet in front of him like bullets, making a deafening hissing noise as they hit rocks and vegetation. Within seconds, puddles formed in hollows where the ground was too hard to absorb so much water. Gingerly, Renato stuck his hand into the rain; it felt like being stung by a swarm of hornets and he quickly pulled his arm back. Sitting in the shadow of the rock, he was warm and relatively dry as the rain blew several feet past him. But he still pulled his knees hard against his chest, his head down and his arms tight around his shins, as if that would protect him from the appalling violence around him.

The sound of the rain altered slightly, a deeper sound, even louder. Renato raised his head and looked out into the storm. To his horror, he saw that the rain had turned red, as red and dark as dried blood. By all the saints, what kind of sign was this?

A bolt of lightning hit the cross, the blinding flash illuminating the hillside for what seemed like seconds. The instantaneous crash of thunder knocked Renato sideways. It was the loudest sound he'd ever heard and he lay on his side for several minutes wondering if he was going to die alone in the storm.

He sat up again and was immediately punished by another bolt of lightning striking the cross like a spear hurled down by angry gods, with the same percussive thunder. Terrified for his life, Renato put his hands over his ears and squeezed his eyes shut as if this childish gesture would make the storm go away.

It didn't.

Eventually he firmly told himself to find a little more courage, and sat up again.

The wind picked up even more, howling through the bushes like lost souls. He shivered with superstitious dread and fingered his crucifix for reassurance. How much longer can this go on, he wondered, feeling overwhelmed by the ceaseless onslaught. Indifferent to his suffering, torrents of rain poured down in great sheets of driving water and the wind blew hard enough to peel the vegetation from the hillside.

Renato stood up, needing to stretch and get off the hard, stony ground. Much to his surprise, he was getting used to the tumult. Once he'd decided the storm was not going to kill him, his terror subsided and, *miraculum miraculorum*, he started to enjoy himself. Holding his hat by his side, he stood at the corner of the rock with the rain flying by just inches in front of his nose. And when the wind shifted a bit and blew the warm rain straight into his face, soaking him as thoroughly as if he was swimming off the beach at Sant' Angelo, he laughed out loud for the sheer joy of it.

For a man who spent most of his working life in the quiet, measured calm of the church, the storm was like a wild animal; unpredictable, noisy, elemental, violent, exhilarating. When he prayed by himself in the church, he felt as if he was floating, suspended in an immense sea of silence, a vast space in which he might hear the voice of God if he could only listen carefully enough. The tempest provided no such support. It filled him to overflowing with pure sensation, leaving no room for contemplation.

And now that he was no longer petrified by the tempest, he marvelled at it. The storm and the battered mountain spoke to him as directly as God ever had, but telling instead of ancient gods that roamed the hills long before there were men, of mountains that vomited fire, of how Typhon, trapped beneath the mountain, would make the ground shake in his futile attempts to break free. Silence and serene contemplation were not necessary for this understanding; all he had to do was open his heart and his skin. Standing by the rock and immersed in the rain, he rejoiced, knowing deep in his soul that he was as one with the mountain and all that lived on it, that he was a small part of something far bigger than he was.

Eventually, the rain eased up a little, but the storm was not yet done. The wind gusted even more strongly and another bolt of lightning hit, followed after the slightest of pauses by the same immense, rumbling roll of thunder. The flash lit up the hillside as brightly as before and Renato could see the whole scene as clearly as if it was midday in summer.

The cross was gone.

Demonte saw the cloud racing across the Bay and knew exactly what it meant. Muttering a quick goodbye to Paolo, he hurried down to his hut, slamming the door behind him just as the building shook with the onset of the wind. He'd brought the sheep in before going to Paolo's grave, so they were safe and he wouldn't have to spend the next day criss-crossing the mountain trying to find them.

Adolfo wasn't so lucky. Lost in his thoughts, he'd been facing west and didn't see the approaching storm until it was almost on him. Feeling the change in the wind, he casually glanced over to his left, toward Capri, and was startled to see the cloud and rain racing up the mountain toward him.

He looked around in vain for somewhere to take shelter. This part of the mountain was barren, covered only by the low shrubs and rocks that were all that grew here, and there was nowhere he could escape from what was coming. The emptiness and beautiful desolation were what attracted him to this spot in the first place, but now he felt very exposed on the open hillside with the mother and father of all storms about to hit.

Then he remembered the old caves set into the side of the valley opposite the crash site. He managed to resist the urge to run down the hill to the distant safety of Fontana and turned instead onto the narrow, twisting side path that led up and across the valley to the caves. He half-ran, half-walked up the steep track as fast as he could, trying to not trip on rocks or any more roots.

The wind struck him on the side without warning, knocking him over. As he fell, he could see that he was about to impale himself on the broken-off stump of a small sapling. Just in time, he put his hands out and broke his fall, the stiletto point of the sapling lightly touching his chest, right over his heart. He pushed off the ground and struggled back to his feet, fighting the wind that was trying to force him over again.

The downpour started when he was within sight of the nearest cave. Within seconds, he was drenched. Water began coursing down the steep path, coating the packed earth with slick mud and making the many rocks as slippery as ice.

By the time he got to the cave, he was waterlogged, muddy and exhausted. His squelching shoes were full of water. Panting, he threw himself into the cave, which was little more than an indentation in the cliff. Still, it was enough to provide the slightest of shelters from the wind and rain. He tried leaning back against the wall, but a sharp outcrop of rock dug into his back. Clearly, the ancient hermits were unconcerned with their physical comfort. He had no choice but to sit uncomfortably upright on the cave floor, his legs crossed in front of him. Still, he had an excellent view of the valley and the storm.

Like Father Renato on the other side of the shallow valley but hidden behind his rock, Adolfo saw the rain turn red. Unlike Renato, Adolfo had seen Sahara sand like this every time the Sirocco blew and was not alarmed. But the sudden flash of lightning made him jump. Even through the rain, he could see the cross illuminated by the lightning, standing proud against the dark, swirling clouds.

The storm stalled at the mountain top, seemingly unable to pass over to the other side. The rain teemed down and bolt after lightning bolt hit the peak, each with its own deafening roll of thunder, sounding like the gods waging war. Every time the valley lit up, he saw the cross, fixed and reassuring despite the violence churning around it.

After a while, Adolfo was beaten into submission by the ceaseless assault on his senses. He sank into the dazed acceptance that he was powerless against the forces of nature and that, while the mountain could absorb everything that was thrown at it, he could not.

Another flash of lightning, another fleeting impression of the cross. The image persisted but in reverse, a white cross glowing bright against a black, Satanic background. Another image came into his mind—himself as a small boy, awed by the solemn majesty of the church and wanting desperately to share whatever mystical experience the adults were enjoying. Perhaps the white cross was God's way of telling him it was time to rediscover his faith. Perhaps it was time to confess his sins to Father Renato, show his repentance, and set his feet once more on the one true path to God's forgiveness, to redemption.

The wind gusted even more for a moment, the strongest wind he'd ever experienced, then shifted direction slightly and eased a little. At the same time, the rain seemed less intense. It was as if the storm could read his mind and wanted to reward him for finally realising that he had to find his way back to God. He could feel his consciousness spread out from his body, flowing out of the hermit's cave and across the valley towards the cross, and he silently thanked the good Lord for sending him such a clear message.

The next bolt of lightning hit the ground beyond the peak on the far side of the crash site. For the first time, there was a slight delay before the thunder clap. At last, Adolfo thought, the storm is finally moving on, maybe I can get home soon, have some hot soup, crusty bread, wine.

Then he sank back, crushed by what his eyes had seen but his mind refused to accept—the small peak where the cross stood was now empty, as bare as it was the night of the crash.

The thunder still rumbled down the mountain, as if the gods were taunting him. You gullible, arrogant fool, they seemed to say, who are you to think we care about you and your petty problems? We were here long before you and will be here long after you are gone. Your life is less than an eyeblink for us, and utterly insignificant.

He cried out with the cruelty of it all. He had thought that the cross might offer the promise of redemption and now that faint hope was stolen from him. By allowing the cross to fall, God had shown that He had abandoned him. And the gods on the mountain were equally clear about their indifference.

He was completely alone, and had to find his way by himself.

Early the next morning, Tifeo and Amedea sat outside, enjoying a cup of coffee before starting work. The sun shone through a gap in the trees, warming a place where they could sit comfortably.

Amedea said, "Adolfo got caught in the storm last night. He came into his house all wet and muddy, looking like he'd slid all the way down the mountain on his arse."

Tifeo laughed at the image. He and Amedea had enjoyed the storm from the safety of the covered patio on the north side of the house. Well protected and with glasses of wine in hand, they'd watched the lightning display above them. Tifeo thought it was like a wonderful fireworks display, especially when seen through the Sahara-red rain. Amedea had gone into town after the storm to take her turn looking after Serafina, who was still bed-bound, although she seemed a bit less sour as her broken leg healed.

"Poor man," Amedea went on, "he looked like death warmed over. I wondered if he'd seen a ghost. He didn't say anything to me, just went to his room. I had some soup waiting for him, too. You don't suppose the Linchetti were out in the storm as well?"

Amedea's tone was light-hearted, but Tifeo turned serious. "I don't think he saw the Linchetti," he said, "but there are other spirits besides them and they have no reason to be well-disposed towards him."

Amedea nodded. "Well, he saw something," she said. "Or someone."

Tifeo decided seeing Adolfo right away was more important than firing up the forge. But when he got to the shop, the door was locked, and the sign in the window still said *Chiuso*, even though it was well past Adolfo's normal opening time.

He knocked hard. After a few moments, Adolfo came to the door, saw who it was and unlocked the door to let Tifeo enter. He looked terrible, haggard and uncombed, dark rings under his eyes.

Tifeo said, "I heard you were on the mountain last night. That was a big storm, so I came to see how you were."

Adolfo just grunted. He waved Tifeo to a seat at the table in the corner and sat down himself.

Tifeo was surprised to see a huge bunch of flowers on the counter. Violets, cyclamen, blue rosemary, the flowers looked as if Adolfo had picked them on the mountain.

"Those are beautiful flowers," he said. "They brighten the place up."

"They're for Serafina," Adolfo said. "I was going to take them down yesterday, but I got caught in the storm."

"So I heard."

"The cross came down," Adolfo said. "One minute it was there, the next…"

Tifeo was shocked. "How in the name of all the gods did that happen?" he asked. "Are you sure?"

"Of course I'm sure. The wind was stronger than anything I've seen before. Just before the cross disappeared, there was a really big gust, I suppose it just blew down."

Tifeo could hardly speak. After all the effort in building the cross and putting it up, getting the Bishop to consecrate it… the cross couldn't just fall down, something must have happened to it.

"Did you go and look at it?" he asked.

"Of course not," Adolfo replied. "I was soaked to the skin, all I wanted to do was get home. Besides, I don't like going there, it makes me uncomfortable."

Tifeo sat silently, shaking his head. He knew as well as anyone how hard the winds could blow at the top of the mountain, but thought the bolts he used would anchor the cross securely enough to withstand anything the elements could throw at it.

Adolfo said, "It was a sign, you know."

"What? What kind of sign? Who from?"

"From God. When I saw the cross standing up in the storm, I thought God was inviting me back. But He wasn't."

Adolfo hadn't slept at all during the night and was exhausted. He began crying.

"I've thought so much about what we did," he said, furiously wiping his cheek. "It felt alright at the time, but now I wish we'd stayed down here. I can't live with myself any more, knowing what we did. I want God to forgive me, tell me that my sins have been washed away, give me peace, and what did He do? He tore His cross down in front of me. Why? So He could tell me instead that He wants nothing to do with me."

"It's not for me to say whether or not God's forgiveness will open your path to Heaven," said Tifeo, as gently as he could. "You should speak to Father Renato about that. But any such forgiveness will do nothing to change your knowledge that what you did was wrong. How can it? The deed was done, cannot be undone, and you know it was wrong. Being forgiven–by God, or by anyone else– cannot erase either the deed or the knowledge."

"I wonder if this is how Father Giovanni felt. I know he craved my forgiveness at the end, but I think he also feared it."

"Feared?"

"Because once I forgave him, he could no longer hide from what he did."

"But you cannot hide from your deeds forever."

"I'm learning that," Adolfo said, sounding forlorn.

Tifeo thought that if there was an elixir Adolfo could take to make the pain go away, he'd drink deeply of it and ask for more, hoping for relief in the morning.

"We are all a mosaic," he said, "with light pieces and dark pieces, and some in between. You cannot love the whole mosaic if you only see the white pieces. Once you allow that there is dark as well as light in your soul, you must learn to keep it under control, not let it run rampant. That does not mean pretending the dark is not there–you cannot control what you deny. But control it you must."

"The spirits," Adolfo said. "I see them on the mountain, you know. They're all around me when I go to where the plane crashed. They come out when I'm there, I can feel them accusing me. How can I forgive myself when the ones I harmed have not?"

"You must first make your peace with them, atone for what you did. Until then, you cannot be free of them, and cannot take care of yourself."

"Forgiving Father Giovanni was the hardest thing I've ever done. I don't know if I can forgive myself."

"You'll know when you are ready," Tifeo said. "But perhaps there is something we can do together that will help."

For the first time, Adolfo looked hopeful.

"Come by tonight, if you can," he said. "I'd like to hear more about that."

When Tifeo had left, Adolfo went to the door and turned the sign from *Chiuso* to *Aprire*. Then he went to the back to freshen up before any customers arrived.

Renato was by himself in the church, kneeling under the huge crucifix that dominated the altar, when he heard someone come in through the door at the back, which was still unoiled. Footsteps came echoing down the aisle before stopping as his visitor sat down. Renato waited for a few moments to collect himself in the renewed silence, then stood up and turned to see Tifeo sitting a few pews from the front. He went over to sit beside his friend.

"I was on the mountain yesterday," Renato said, "when the storm hit. Did you know the cross came down?"

"Yes, Adolfo told me."

Renato nodded, as if sharing the storm with Adolfo was the most natural thing in the world.

"And now I am filled with doubt," he said. "Uncertainty. They cloud my mind and challenge my faith. I feel sure that God was sending me a message by letting me see the cross fall, but I cannot tell what it is He wants me to know."

"Doubt and uncertainty can be unsettling," said Tifeo. "But they are less foolish than unshakeable belief in the face of great mysteries. Perhaps your God is inviting you to explore your faith so you might understand it better."

Renato looked around the church, so familiar to him after only a few years.

"I love being here," he said. "The calm, the sanctity, they bring me closer to God. And yet last night, I experienced something completely different. Being in the storm was a mystical experience– different than in here, but mystical just the same. I sensed that I was surrounded by spirits and ancient gods. But in spite of the strangeness of it all, I could also feel the presence of God. I am here, He told me, and these are part of who I am."

"Mountains are powerful places," Tifeo said, "and not for the faint-hearted."

"I have been taught all my life that there is but one God. And yet I felt joy in knowing these other gods were there, feeling that the mountain, the rocks, the storm, were all alive. I could almost believe in the old myth that Typhon is buried beneath the mountain. But I cannot reconcile any of this with my faith in God."

"The biggest difference between us is the number of gods we believe in," Tifeo said. "I am glad if our little mountain could show you how the gods are everywhere. But I'm surprised you are not more worried by the cross falling down. Adolfo thought it meant that God had abandoned him. I talked with Demonte on the way here; he thought that we paid insufficient respect to the mountain and the gods who live there when we put it up, so they brought it down at the first opportunity."

"The cross is but a symbol, not to be worshipped for itself," said Renato, "and men will read into it what they will. Why do you think it fell down?"

"I didn't fasten it well enough," Tifeo said. "I used only two rods to hold it to the ground; we'll find that the wind simply blew it down across those rods. The fault is all mine. We Ischians have a saying: Trust in God, but first tie up your mule. I should have fastened it more securely. There is no deeper meaning than that."

"So what do we do?"

"We'll put it up again but with more rods to hold it down."

"And what about poor Adolfo? I cannot believe that God has abandoned him."

"Maybe not. But I have told him that he cannot depend on God to remove his guilt. He knows now—and has confessed to me, at least—that what he did after the crash was wrong. He must make his peace with the spirits of the people he harmed and then with himself. After that, he can come to you and seek God's forgiveness."

Renato nodded, remembering how Father Giovanni was tormented on his deathbed by his guilt, even after receiving absolution and God's forgiveness.

"God lives within each of us," he said. "Perhaps making peace with himself, as you put it, will be how he finds his way back to God."

"The spirits must be part of this," Tifeo said. "Adolfo has to sever the thread that connects him to them."

How strange, Renato thought, all this talk about spirits. If my teachers at the seminary could hear this, they'd be wearing their knees out with their praying, when they weren't looking for a way to burn this heretic. And yet here I am, accepting the presence of spirits on the mountain as a simple matter of fact.

"This will require a ceremony on the mountain," Tifeo said. "Rather a strange one compared to the ones you have here, nothing like what you were taught. I would not have offered this to Father Giovanni but you would be welcome to join us."

Renato didn't have to think hard about the invitation. The Bishop would have a fit if he knew, but Renato thought that this was a subject about which it would be kinder to shield the Very Reverend Ottavio Acquaviva d'Aragona from a surfeit of information. The same went for those of his parishioners whose beliefs were aligned with a more classic Catholic faith. And if, as he suspected, there were quite a few parishioners who managed to accommodate both Catholic and pagan beliefs, he hoped they would appreciate his efforts to do the same.

"I would be honoured to join you," he said.

"Good," Tifeo said. "I will reattach the cross as soon as possible. More securely, this time, I assure you. We don't want anyone else to draw wrong conclusions from the failure of their blacksmith to tie up his mule."

Chapter Twenty-four

ROSABELLA STOOD IN CESARE'S WORKSHOP, one hand resting on the workbench in the centre, the other on her swollen belly. The baby stirred restlessly as she looked around. She didn't normally come into this room; Cesare had made it very clear that this was his domain, and generally kept it locked. But Serafina's sly insinuations about secrets had been festering since she heard them and she had finally succumbed to her curiosity.

She knew she'd have the rest of the day to herself after Cesare left to meet Ulisse at the hotel. He'd been in high spirits over lunch; she thought he was like a small child wanting to show off a precious possession to a visiting uncle. She'd waved at him from the door as he headed down the hill, looking very smart in his new suit. She didn't have the heart to tell him that his tie pin clashed with the tie.

"I'll be back tomorrow night," he said before leaving. "Ulisse and I will spend the night in Forio."

In some whore's bed, no doubt, she thought, both angry and sad that he could be so casual about sex. She knew she looked like a galleon under full sail at her advanced state, but he'd been like this ever since she'd known him. Even after they were married, she knew that he occasionally slept with loose women, just as other men did. It was a commonplace that all the married women she knew had to accept without feeling betrayed. And so they did, as long as their husbands did their job as head of the household and didn't let it affect the marriage too much.

She waited for a few minutes after he left to make sure he didn't return for something important but forgotten, then went upstairs and retrieved the key to the workshop. Cesare being who he was, she had always known where he kept it–apparently he'd never considered the possibility that, since she washed his socks and put them away, she'd know there was a key in the corner of the drawer.

She'd already searched every other room in the house for whatever secrets Serafina was hinting at. 'Hidden away', Serafina had said, so Rosabella assumed there was an object of some kind to find. The workshop was the last room to investigate.

Standing beside the workbench, she felt that this was the only room in the house that was distinctly his. All the other rooms bore the stamp of her personality and taste but none of his. How strange, she thought, he could leave tomorrow and no one would ever know that he'd lived there. She tucked the idea away somewhere safe so she could pull it out later and consider it more carefully, what his lack of presence meant, what it said about their marriage.

Looking at the mess in the workshop, she decided that finding anything in there was going to be like locating a particular sheep in the middle of a large flock. She knew that Cesare made sporadic attempts to sort things out, but he always left tools wherever he put them down last, ruining any order he might have had. She shook her head, thinking of how she liked to keep her kitchen well organized and tidy.

And the boxes! There were boxes everywhere, boxes of all shapes and sizes, unlabelled except for their original purpose. Opening a tin with the label 'Farfalloni' superimposed on a picture of the fan-shaped pasta, she found a collection of mixed screws, ranging from small ones made of brass to much larger steel screws. Cesare was a skilled woodworker, but Rosabella could not understand how he could make beautiful things in such a disorganized mess.

Starting at one end of the workbench against the wall, she methodically searched every box, every drawer, every shelf, and found nothing. Sighing, she started again on the workbench in the middle of the room. This one was quicker, since it was clearly Cesare's primary work area and there was less to search. Her back was aching by now, so she sat down on the only chair in the workshop to consider a pile of odd pieces of wood stacked in a corner, raw material for one of his projects. How likely was it that he would hide something important behind a stack like that? And if not there, where else was there to look?

She leaned forward to ease her back, the baby protesting at being squeezed against her thighs. Hanging her head down, she gazed at the floor, her eyes unfocused and her mind blank. Gradually, she realized that there was a faint mark leading under the workbench, the slightest scuffing on the stone floor. She knelt on all fours beside the bench. The baby immediately stopped its complaints. She looked under the bench, and there it was.

By the time she'd retrieved the box and clambered back to her feet, Rosabella was breathing heavily. She hefted the box, feeling its weight, wondering what made it so heavy. The box was locked. She cast her mind back over her searches through the house, thinking that she hadn't seen any keys other than the one to this room. Nor had she found a key in any of the boxes in the workshop.

The ledge above the door was an obvious place to look, so she pulled the chair over to the door and climbed onto it. Holding the post beside the door for balance, she immediately found the small recess, carefully cut to be invisible from the room. She pushed her fingers further into the recess, and found the key.

Rosabella hesitated before unlocking and opening the box, uncertain if she was doing the right thing. She knew that opening the box would be irreversible, that once she saw whatever lay inside, she'd be drawn irresistibly to learn more about her husband, the soon-to-be-father of her child, and what made him who he was.

Chewing her lip, she decided that it was more important to know than remain ignorant. Now she knew there were things to learn, she could never be content unless she pursued her curiosity.

She turned the key, opened the box.

A large wad of cash lay on top of whatever else was in the box. Rosabella's first reaction was one of disappointment–was this the big secret that Serafina had made so much of? If Cesare wanted to hide his own money in this box, so what? She picked up the cash and counted it, and was surprised by the amount. No wonder he could pay so much for a new suit, she thought.

She turned her attention to what else was in the box. Puzzled, she picked up a strange document with strange writing she'd never seen before. The rings certainly looked expensive, but why were they so special? She shook the contents of the small envelope onto the bench; the rough diamonds looked like small lumps of misshapen glass. Finally, she opened the long box, and gasped at three beautiful gold necklaces, neatly arranged beside each other.

Where had all this come from, she wondered. She tried out various explanations, pushing away what she knew must be true but did not want to accept. None of them worked. Finally, she was forced to concede that the contents of the box could only have come from one place. Cesare was one of the looters. And had lied to her and everyone else in the family, not just once, but over and over again. And if he'd lied about this, what else about him was false? How could she believe anything he said to her?

Her faith in her husband shattered, she fled from the workshop and up to her bedroom, where she threw herself on the bed, sobbing, not knowing which was worse: that Cesare was one of the people who had robbed and mutilated dead bodies, or that he had consistently lied about it all and she could no longer trust him.

Cesare couldn't help strutting a little as he showed Ulisse around the hotel. He was proud of what he and his crew had built and could see that Ulisse was impressed, despite the mess. The place was still a construction site, with tools scattered haphazardly throughout the building, pails of paint stacked just inside the main entrance, small piles of waste material everywhere. But it was nearly finished, enough to show how impressive it would be when it opened.

A large dust cloth covered the newly-installed reception desk. Ulisse lifted one corner, exposing the creamy marble of the counter.

"We brought that all the way down from the quarries at Carrara," said Cesare. "It cost a fortune. But it's the first thing that a guest will see and it's important to create the right impression."

Ulisse had no idea where Carrara was or why their marble was any better than somewhere closer, but he managed to look suitably approving. Following Cesare down a corridor, he carefully brushed some dust from the sleeve of his immaculate suit.

"This is one of the bedrooms. The bed will go here, a closet there, a chair in that corner. You'll be able to lie in bed and see Capri through the window." Cesare waved his arms as he spoke, conjuring a vision of sybaritic luxury out of thin air. The plaster in the room was still very fresh and Ulisse's nose wrinkled with the pungent, distinctive smell.

Retracing their steps, they passed through the reception area and went out onto the terrace. A stone balustrade ran the entire length, high enough to stop small children falling over the cliff below but low enough that adults enjoying a quiet sit down could appreciate the spectacular view. Stone statues and tall clay urns broke the long expanse. The cliff fell thirty feet or more from the terrace to thick forest; beyond that, vineyards and small fields led down to the coast.

Standing by the balustrade, Ulisse could see Sant' Angelo to the right, with its jumble of roofs and the narrow causeway leading to the pimple of rock, covered in wild flowers, growing out of the sea. Small fishing vessels, as brightly coloured as the flowers, rocked gently in the shelter of the causeway and the warm light of the setting sun. Capri was to the left, silhouetted against the sky in the gathering dusk. The terrace was peaceful and private, hidden from the road by the hotel building, yet completely open to the waters of the Bay, stretching to the horizon.

"Where is everyone?" Ulisse asked. The official opening was only three weeks away and he expected to see more activity.

"I gave them the day off," replied Cesare. "It's been a long week, they needed a break. Men cannot do their best work when they are tired. Besides, it's been a long time since we saw each other, and I thought some peace and quiet would be good."

Ulisse nodded. He could feel the irritation scratching at his veneer of polite interest, mostly because of the Sirocco wind that was still blowing several days after the huge storm. Cesare was chattering away, something about people coming in the summer to make a film; 'The Cliff of Sin', it was to be called, a stupid name if ever he heard one, and the crew would be staying at the hotel.

Ulisse thought that Cesare was trying too hard to impress, a country chicken striving to be a royal peacock. A gold ring with a huge red stone adorned his right hand, and his suit was too loud and just a bit too expensive. The stone in the tiepin matched the ring, but clashed with the darker purple of the tie. The ostentatious display of new wealth troubled Ulisse as being in bad taste.

He realized that Cesare had stopped talking and was looking at him expectantly. What was the last thing he said? Looking for approval, by the expression on his face.

"This all seems very impressive," he said. "I'll tell Signor Cutolo when I see him. And you'll be ready for the opening day, you say?"

Cesare relaxed a bit. "Yes, we've allowed several days to take care of last minute problems, but we'll be ready. No question."

"Good," Ulisse said. "But there is something else I must explain to Signor Cutolo, and that is how you could be so fucking stupid as to steal from him."

The profanity hit Cesare like a slap on the face. He took a quick step back. "I've stolen nothing," he said. "What are you talking about, cousin?"

Ulisse heard the appeal to family solidarity but ignored it.

"You stole from him," he repeated. He kept calm and quiet, the way he'd talked to the wayward soccer players beside the Pizzeria San Gennaro, managing to control his irritation. He allowed just the slightest menace to enter his voice. "You have taken money that belongs to him. Not surprisingly, he regards that as theft. As I would, in his place."

"And how did I do that?" asked Cesare. "Go to Napoli, break into his home?"

Ulisse ignored the feeble attempt to deflect him.

"Signor Cutolo is financing this project, is he not?"

Cesare nodded, getting cautious.

"When you pad invoices a little," Ulisse continued, "and submit your requests for money to him, he ends up paying too much. The extra money ends up in your pocket. And that, cousin, is theft."

Cesare laughed, clearly relieved, but missing the slight emphasis that Ulisse placed on 'cousin'. "But everyone does that," he exclaimed. "It's expected. I think he would be disappointed if I did not do a little of this. Who can trust an honest man, after all?"

Ulisse did not share in the laughter. My cousin is a moron, he thought. Can he not tell the difference between a little that can be tolerated and too much that cannot?

"You have gone much too far," he said. "Far beyond the little that Signor Cutolo can understand and overlook."

"No, no," protested Cesare. "No more than any reasonable man in my position."

"Cesare, I warned you to be careful when you accepted his offer. Being careful does not include getting greedy."

"I was not greedy." Now Cesare sounded indignant.

"I would call this greedy, wouldn't you?" Ulisse asked, and named a specific and substantial amount of money.

Cesare was shocked. "Where did you get that number from?" he asked.

"From Signor Cutolo. And don't ask me where he got it from, because I don't know."

"This is a difficult business," Cesare complained. "Everyone tries to rob me blind, and there are always unexpected costs. I need a cushion of cash on hand, that's all I was doing."

"In that case," said Ulisse, "you won't mind returning the money, all of it, to Signor Cutolo, with a penalty. After all, the project is almost complete, you won't be needing your cushion any more."

"But there goes my profit," cried Cesare. "Surely he doesn't expect me to work for nothing?"

"He assures me that your profit without your so-called cushion is more than adequate. Enough of this, Cesare. You must pay the money back at once and you must promise never to do this again. Signor Cutolo told me that he can forgive you once, but once only. If you are foolish enough to try this again, there will be consequences and, I can assure you, they will be extremely unpleasant."

Cesare was defeated. "Very well," he said. "You can tell your precious Signor Cutolo that I will give him the money when he comes for the hotel opening."

Ulisse said, "You must remember, Cesare, that the Camorra see and know everything. They have agents working everywhere, acting as intermediaries between the clans and ordinary people. They don't wear special clothing or badges, they're not like priests, so you'll never be able to identify them. But they know who you are, and they're watching. So don't be such an idiot again."

Cesare said, "Enough, Ulisse, enough. I've promised to return the money, perhaps now we can enjoy this beautiful evening before we go down to Forio."

But Ulisse had lost his appetite for appreciating the view or anything else about the evening. Cesare's feeble attempts to deny his thievery annoyed him and it was all he could do to not pick his disaster of a cousin up and shake some sense into him.

He said, "There is something else that Signor Cutolo told me that concerns you. Perhaps you could tell me what you sold to Gasparo the pawnbroker."

Cesare scratched his head, seeming to misunderstand the question. "Why," he said, "we all went there together. You know exactly what we sold."

Ulisse could feel his control over his temper starting to slip. His cousin must have mule shit for brains, he thought, first trying to steal from Cutolo, then thinking I'd fall for something as pathetic as that.

"A couple of months ago, when you bought that suit. Which, by the way, doesn't fit properly," he said, getting impatient. "You went to Gasparo and sold him things. What were they?"

"Oh, then," said Cesare, sulky as a small child. "Just a few trinkets."

"A diamond is a trinket?" Now Ulisse let his anger show. "A gold necklace is a trinket?"

"Who told you that? They're mistaken, all I sold him were a few small things, I wanted some quick cash to buy Rosabella a present."

"Cesare, try telling the truth for once. You know and I know what you sold Gasparo. Where did these things come from?"

"Oh, give it a rest, can't you," Cesare said. "It's been a bitch of a week, what with all the work here and everyone getting pissed off with everyone else because of the Sirocco, I had to break up more fights than I have fingers. Anyway, we all kept some stuff from the crash, what I do with my share is for me to worry about."

"There were no diamonds or gold necklaces in what we shared between us. Did you keep them from us all this time?"

"Fuck off, Ulisse," Cesare shouted. "Get off your high horse for once. Who do you think you are, coming back in your fancy suit, lording it over us poor Ischians? Just because you work for the God-forsaken Camorra, you think you're so much better than us."

"Where did you get the diamonds and necklaces?" Ulisse shouted back. "Are there anything else that we don't know about? Where is your honour?"

"Don't tell me you didn't keep some stuff back as well. Adolfo, too."

"No, we didn't. But you did, apparently. You really are a miserable little shit."

"Well, look at you," said Cesare contemptuously. "A hit man for the Camorra, a street bully thinking a fancy suit makes him someone special. I'm here trying to do something useful–look around you, this hotel wouldn't be here if it wasn't for me. And what are you doing? You're just a thug, working for even bigger thugs. So don't talk to me about honour. You lost yours when you went to Napoli."

Ulisse's temper finally snapped. The two men had moved closer and closer as they argued until they were shouting in each other's faces. Now Cesare had insulted Ulisse in the worst possible way. In a blind rage, Ulisse hit Cesare hard in the face, breaking his nose. Blood spurted out and Cesare staggered back. Ulisse hit him again and again, as Cesare raised his arms in a futile attempt to ward off the blows.

Ulisse hit his cousin one last time, hard, on the side of his head. Cesare spun around and lurched heavily towards the balustrade. Tripping over his own feet, he lost his balance and fell heavily across the low barrier, looking straight down the sheer face of the cliff. For a very brief moment, Ulisse could see that he was at a fork in the road, that he had a choice of what to do next. Then the blood lust took over again. He grasped Cesare's ankles and heaved his cousin over the edge. A second later, he heard a crash as the body landed in the trees below the cliff, followed by complete silence.

Adolfo had been glad when Tifeo re-entered his life, but he'd also been apprehensive. Years of muddy water had flowed under the bridge since they'd fallen out as boys, and Adolfo found it difficult to forget Tifeo's disdain. Knowing that the disapproval was justified didn't make reconciliation any easier, although Tifeo's promise not to be publicly critical was helping.

He was learning instead that it took time, and patience, and tolerance. He had to find the good will to overlook the occasions when one of them would say something that made the fading embers of their mutual enmity glow warm again. But as they continued to meet at the end of the day in the shop, he was starting to find those occasions rarer and easier to cope with.

"You should come up to the forge sometimes," Tifeo was saying, cradling a drink in his huge hands. "Sit with us, enjoy a glass of wine, watch the sun go down… it would be good to see you up there."

Adolfo opened his mouth to reply but closed it abruptly as Ulisse entered the shop. He usually found it difficult to know what his brother was thinking or feeling, but not this time. Ulisse looked distraught and Adolfo could see several spots of blood on his otherwise white shirt.

"I thought you were at the hotel with Cesare," he said.

Ulisse pointed at Tifeo. "Why is he here?" he asked.

"We were just having a quiet drink together," said Adolfo.

Ulisse said, "He's a little prick." Tifeo glanced at Adolfo, a question on his face. Adolfo shrugged.

Tifeo pushed his drink away and stood up, towering over Ulisse. "I'll be on my way," he said to Adolfo. "It seems you two have other things to talk about."

"Wait a moment," Adolfo said. To Ulisse, he said, "Tifeo and I have agreed to set aside our differences. I have no secrets from him any more. None." The emphasis on the last word spoke volumes to

Ulisse. "For our little brother," Adolfo continued, "he is surprisingly wise, and I have learned to value his advice. You would do well to do the same."

"I don't want him to hear what I have to tell you."

"Oh, for God's sake, Ulisse. He's family, isn't he? He knows what we did on the mountain and he's still here, having a sociable drink with me. He's stopped criticizing us to anyone who'll listen. I trust him absolutely and so should you."

Ulisse said, "He doesn't know everything. And neither do you."

"What do you mean?"

"Let me get a drink first."

When all three of them were sitting around the table, Adolfo said, "I didn't expect to see you this evening, I thought you'd be with Cesare, carousing in Forio and getting laid. Where is he, anyway?"

"Dead. He's dead." Ulisse's voice was flat.

Adolfo found his voice first. "What on earth happened?" he asked.

"I killed him. By accident," said Ulisse.

"Sweet Jesus on the Cross," said Adolfo. "What have you done?"

Ulisse said, "It was all Cesare's fault."

Adolfo shouted, "I don't give a shit whose fault it was! If you killed him, people will want to know why. That goddam crash was two years ago, people have forgotten all about it. Now they'll get nosy again, we won't be able to stop it."

Ulisse shouted back, "He cheated us, Adolfo. He took things and didn't tell us. Didn't share them."

"What? What things?"

"Diamonds, necklaces, things like that."

"But we didn't get any diamonds or necklaces from the crash." Adolfo seized on the detail, which seemed less alarming than the threat of public exposure. Or his cousin's violent death.

"You and I didn't," Ulisse said, regaining some self control. "He must have found them on one of the bodies when we weren't looking, and kept them for himself. He cheated us, Adolfo." Ulisse's voice rose again, fuelled by outrage.

"He doesn't have the balls for that."

"I didn't think so, either. But he sold them to Gasparo, according to Signor Cutolo."

"So you killed him," Adolfo said. "What happened?"

"We were at the hotel, outside on the terrace," said Ulisse, "beside that low wall. He insulted me, so I hit him, and he fell over the wall, down the cliff. It was an accident." Ulisse had told himself it was an accident several times on the way back to Fontana. The repetition had worked, blurring his memory of pushing Cesare over the wall and seeing his brightly-coloured socks disappear from sight.

Tifeo watched him tell the lie with complete conviction, and didn't believe a word of it. He'd seen the wall, and, while it was quite low, he thought it too high and too broad for anyone to fall over it by accident. But so far, this was none of his business, and he said nothing.

"You and your temper," Adolfo said. "For the love of God, why can't you control it? Now look at the trouble we're in."

"I didn't mean to," Ulisse said. "But he tried to cheat Cutolo, how stupid was that? He cheated us, he insulted me, and that was too much, I lost my temper and hit him." He took a deep drink. "How he ever managed to build that hotel, I'll never know."

"Where is Cesare now?" Tifeo asked.

"At the bottom of the cliff below the terrace. I heard him fall into the trees."

"You idiot," Adolfo said, "you've got a fucking cabbage for brains…"

"Enough, Adolfo, enough," Tifeo cut in. "What are we going to do about this mess?"

"What do you mean, 'we'? You don't have to get involved."

"Of course I do. You're my brothers and Cesare was my cousin. What affects you affects me."

Ulisse said, "You've been quiet all this time. If you're so wise, what do you suggest?"

Tifeo said, "I should be halfway to the police by now, so they can come and arrest you for killing Cesare. And what good would that do? You'll end up in prison, of course, but Rosabella's family will still come looking for revenge, they'll never forgive you. We'd end up with family killing family, innocent people dying just because you lost your temper."

"God, someone will have to tell Rosabella," Adolfo said.

"Not tonight," Tifeo said. "No one will miss Cesare until tomorrow. Let her have one more night of peace."

"I like her," said Ulisse. "I wish I had not done this to her."

"It's too late for that," Tifeo said. "The question is, what are you going to do?"

Ulisse's shoulders sagged. He said. "I cannot return to Napoli or my job with Cutolo after this."

"Why is that?" Tifeo was surprised, but kept his voice neutral, calm.

"Cutolo had other projects in mind for Cesare. I was to stop him getting so greedy, no more. Now Cutolo will have to find someone else, and he does not take kindly to having his plans changed for him."

"That hardly seems enough…"

"When he finds out what happened, he will realize that I put family concerns ahead of his. You are my birth brothers and Cesare was my cousin, but I swore an oath when I joined that my new family in Napoli would always come first, always. I broke my promise to him. He will not easily forgive me for betraying his trust."

"So what will he do?"

"He will either banish me from Napoli or have me executed. He must punish what I did, people have to see what happens when our oath is broken."

"Neither of those sound attractive," Tifeo said drily.

"I do not want to risk him making the wrong choice," said Ulisse. "I have an old army friend who went to Australia after the war. He tells me that life there is good, even though there is no wine worth drinking and they cannot make proper pizza. I will go to him and he will help me start a new life."

"I will miss you," said Adolfo.

"As will I," said Tifeo. "I have just rediscovered one brother, and now I must lose the other."

"I do not think you would ever approve of what I did in Napoli," Ulisse said to Tifeo.

"Perhaps not," Tifeo replied, "but you are my brother, and I am learning that this is more important than I thought. If we cannot live with what our family does, then where would we be?"

"I'm sorry to leave you with this mess," said Ulisse. "And I'm sorry I lost my temper with that idiot Cesare. I should have known better."

"You can catch the last ferry to Napoli if you hurry. Collect whatever you need tomorrow and then disappear. We'll worry about what to do here."

The three men stood up. Ulisse hugged Adolfo, kissing him on both cheeks. "Farewell, brother," he said. "I'll send word to you when I'm safe in Australia."

He turned to Tifeo and put his hands on both shoulders.

"You've changed," he said. "I'm sorry not to see more of you. Take care of Adolfo, he needs someone to look after him." He hugged Tifeo abruptly and gave him the same kiss on both cheeks before turning and hurrying out of the shop.

"*Porco Dio*," said Adolfo as he sat down again. "We've always known Ulisse had a short temper, but I never imagined he'd do anything this stupid."

Tifeo nodded, deciding not to say anything about his belief that this was no accident. Nothing he could say would bring Cesare back to life; a fatal accident was bad enough, and how would it help anyone if he made things worse?

Chapter Twenty-five

CESARE'S COFFIN RESTED ON ITS STAND in front of the altar, covered with an immense carpet of white chrysanthemums. The coffin was magnificent, nothing like the plain boxes that the poorer dead of Fontana lay in for eternity. Only the best oak was used, the coffin maker had explained, cut at the base of Mount Epomeo, finished with six coats of French polish.

Scenes of Christ performing miracles were carved with meticulous detail into the sides. Turning water into wine and feeding the multitude were on one side, casting demons into a herd of pigs on the other. Very helpful, Tifeo had thought when he saw them, food and drink provided for the dead, and protection from evil spirits. At least there was nothing about Christ raising Lazarus from the dead, that was probably one promise too many.

Inside the coffin, Cesare rested on a bed of white satin, his hands holding a crucifix over his second-best suit; his best suit was no longer wearable after being shredded when he fell through the trees below the terrace. Several small bells lay conveniently close to his hands, in case the crucifix or carvings were insufficient to scare off spirits who would do him harm.

The undertaker didn't even try to restore Cesare's good looks; there was considerable damage from Ulisse's fists and from the trees, and feral dogs had found the body before the searchers located it at the end of the day after he was tossed off the terrace. With great reluctance, Rosabella had accepted that her last memory of her husband should be watching him walk jauntily down the street rather than the painful experience of seeing his ruined face. And one quiet mention of the dogs was enough to explain to the curious few why the coffin was not open at the viewing before the funeral.

A great sea of faces watched Father Renato as he came to the end of his eulogy. The church was full. Family and friends were there, of course, together with many people who cared for Rosabella and wanted to support her in this, the most difficult day of her life.

Cesare's business associates and his construction crew were there, some out of duty, some because they genuinely liked him, some wondering if and when their outstanding bills would be paid. At the very back were the casually curious with nothing else to do and those who went to every funeral they could, emotional vampires feasting on the blood of other people's grief.

The only person not there was Ulisse, an absence that several people noticed, although no one was ill-mannered or indiscreet enough to ask where he was.

"… and although we all grieve at seeing this fine young man taken from us far too soon," Renato said to the crowd, "we can at least take comfort from knowing that he has gone to Heaven, that he will rest in the arms of the Lord, and that we shall be joyfully reunited with him there one day. Amen."

Rosabella sat in the front pew, staring at the coffin with unseeing eyes. Behind the frozen mask of her face, her fury roiled, stirred by Renato's well-meaning but empty words. Fine young man, indeed! By getting himself killed like that, Cesare had abandoned her, just when she needed him most. How was she going to cope with a brand new baby and no husband? Cesare had fed her a good line about how he'd be a great father and where was he now? Dead and about to be buried, that's where, and unlikely to be of much help from the confines of the grave.

Thinking about his treachery led Rosabella to what she'd discovered by opening his secret box, that he had comprehensively lied to her and everyone else about his involvement in the looting. She'd always known that he was easily led and tempted, but had never imagined that he was capable of robbing dead bodies. And what about the mutilation? She shuddered to think that his hands, which gave her such pleasure in bed, had also cut off fingers or pried teeth from the mouths of dead people. Had he lied about that, as well?

And if he deceived her about the crash, what other deceptions might there be? Were there other women in his life besides the occasional whore? The Cesare lying in the coffin and awaiting his appointment with the grave was not the man she trusted and thought she knew. Her faith in him lay in tatters around her feet, replaced by this unremitting resentment and anger.

Her fine young man? The words echoed in her mind, a bitter reminder of what might have been. Because not only had he stolen from dead people, he'd robbed her of her future. Like every other girl on Ischia, she'd grown up with the expectation of finding a good husband, having lots of babies, keeping house for her growing family, cooking good food for them, and finding her fulfillment in nurturing them until they grew up and could repeat the cycle. All the women she knew lived their lives like that and her aspirations were no more and no less than theirs. And now Cesare, the treacherous little thief, had betrayed her and stolen her dreams as well. His betrayal was all the more bitter because she had loved and trusted him. And thought that he loved her in return.

Unable to forgive him, her fury left no room in her heart for grief. She might have wept for the Cesare she thought she knew and loved, but not for the stranger who betrayed her. So she sat in her pew, staring at the coffin with absolutely no expression on her face, seeing nothing at all.

Some of the people who saw the look on her face marvelled that she could confront tragedy with such courage; others, more traditional in their expectations, found her stoicism unseemly and thought that she should be sobbing as loudly and extravagantly as a new widow should. But she shed no tears for her dead husband, then or ever.

A few days after the funeral, Rosabella starting to go to Cesare's workshop, trying to regain some fragments of her love for him. Drawn there by echoes of his presence, she'd pick up one tool after another, wondering if they held any memory of his hands to pass on to her. This was the only place she could feel him; the rest of the house was empty, silent, and lonely. Even though she had spent her days by herself when he was working, the knowledge that he'd be back at the end of the day was a comforting companion, and the house had never felt as vacant as it did now.

But she couldn't stay in the workshop for long. The tools held their secrets tight and she always ended up frustrated because she couldn't understand him or why he'd done the things he had. And angry with herself for being so trusting; hadn't the signs been there all along? The evasiveness, the sudden willingness to spend cash, the closeness with Adolfo, who everyone knew had been on the mountain that night, even though no one except Tifeo was prepared to come out and say so. Then she'd leave the room to get away from her thoughts, wander through the house, and wonder what else to do with the long day until she was drawn back to the workshop for another futile attempt to understand.

Sitting in the chair under the huge window, she turned a mallet over and over in her hands. How strange it is, she thought, that the people we love above all can cause us the most suffering. She was coming to love Amedea as a sister and Tifeo as brother-in-law, but now she felt reluctant to get too close to them for fear of being hurt again. She knew in her head that this was nonsense but her bruised heart refused to listen. So when Amedea came around, which she did often, Rosabella found herself keeping a little distance between them, and their conversations took on a slightly formal nature, as if they were new neighbours talking over a fence. Baldassare dropped in every day to see how she was doing and to keep her company, but she had little to say to him, either.

Lost in her reflections, it took her a few moments to realize that the doorbell was ringing. Putting the mallet on the bench, she hurried to the front door and opened it. Tifeo was standing there with someone she had never seen before. Tall for an Italian, the stranger wore an pin-striped suit and carried an enormous bouquet of flowers. She knew immediately that this was a very dangerous man.

Tifeo said, "Rosabella, this is Signor Raffaele Cutolo. He has come from Napoli to speak with you. May we come in?"

Flustered, she led them to the parlour and left them there while she went to make coffee. When they were all settled, Cutolo leaned forward and put the bouquet in her hands.

"Signora," he said, "I am desolated by your loss. Please accept these flowers as a small sign of my condolences."

Rosabella looked at the flowers, at Cutolo, at Tifeo.

Tifeo said, "Cesare is—was—a business associate of Signor Cutolo. In fact, Signor Cutolo provided the financing that Cesare needed for the hotel."

Rosabella nodded, wondering where this was going.

Tifeo shifted in his seat, evidently uncomfortable. Oh no, thought Rosabella, suddenly alarmed. What now?

Tifeo said, "Rosabella, there are some things you must know about Cesare. But I must warn you, they will not be easy for you to hear."

She felt her face redden, resenting being talked to like a little girl. "Say what you have to say," she said. "Let me decide what's easy or not."

Cutolo said, "Signora, your husband was doing a good job of building the hotel. We were pleased, and were considering other projects that we might ask him to undertake with us."

Rosabella didn't bother asking who 'we' were; she knew all about the Camorra, and mentally kicked herself for not realizing who Cesare's business partners in Napoli were. In retrospect, it was all very obvious.

"It pains me to say this," Cutolo continued, "but I learned recently that your husband had, shall we say, unfortunately sticky fingers. He found a way to inflate his costs, so I sent considerably more money to him than I should have."

Oh, Cesare, thought Rosabella, you innocent fool. How did you ever think you could get away with something like that, with a man like this?

Cutolo said, "I sent one of my men to talk with him, show him the error of his ways, and persuade him that it would be in his best interests to pay the money back." He spoke with silky smoothness, but Rosabella could hear the menace below the surface.

She said, "What happened?"

"He agreed to pay Signor Cutolo what he was owed." This was Tifeo, picking up the story. How does he know this, Rosabella wondered, sitting calmly on her hard, upright chair, the only place she could be comfortable.

"But there's more to this, isn't there?" she said. "Tifeo, tell me what happened."

"The man that Signor Cutolo sent over to talk with Cesare was Ulisse," Tifeo said. "He thought that Cesare would find it easier to have this conversation with his cousin, someone he knew well and trusted."

Cutolo said, "I told Ulisse to warn Cesare and get the money back. Warn him, no more than that, I assure you." Rosabella could see how important it was that she believe him.

"Rosabella, did you know that Cesare was with Adolfo and Ulisse the night of the crash?" Tifeo spoke with great care.

Rosabella felt the room start to close in on her. "Yes. I found out the day he died."

"Ulisse discovered that Cesare kept back some of what they found up there. He didn't share it with the others. You know that Ulisse has always had a short temper. Cesare denied everything, and Ulisse killed Cesare in a rage. I'm sorry, but that's what happened."

Rosabella could hardly breathe. The air in the small room seemed thick and fetid, and she thought she would drown in the swamp of Cesare's weakness and greed. She gasped for air and wiped the sudden dampness from her brow.

Tifeo leapt up and brought back a glass of water.

"How did you learn all this?" she asked when she had drunk it.

"Ulisse told me and Adolfo before he left. He's gone to America, Rosabella, you'll never see him again."

Rosabella said sadly, "I found a box with what he'd taken from the crash. I knew what it meant, but I never imagined that he kept it from the others."

"After what he did, Ulisse wants no part of it," said Tifeo. "Neither does Adolfo. What you found is yours to keep."

"I don't want it!" The words exploded from her mouth before she had a chance to think. "It's all tainted, taken from those poor dead people. How could I possibly take it?"

"No one else wants it," Tifeo said. "I urge you to take it, if only for your baby."

"Your reluctance is admirable," added Cutolo. "Taking valuables from dead people is, indeed, deplorable." He spoke with great sincerity. "But I agree with Tifeo. You must think of how to support yourself and a new child on your own."

Rosabella glared at him. "Why is that any of your business?" she demanded.

"Signora, Ulisse was working for me when he came to see your husband," he replied. "Please believe me, I feel personally responsible for you being in this situation, something I deeply regret. Because of that, I will not ask you for the money that Cesare said he would return to me."

"That's dirty money as well," said Rosabella. "I can't possibly accept it."

"People seem to think the Camorra exploit the people in our care," Cutolo said sadly. "I don't know why. But in truth, our first concern is for their protection and welfare. I ask you, what would people think if they knew that a woman was widowed and cast into poverty because one of our men made a terrible mistake? How can a flock rely on the shepherd who fails to protect them?"

He looked pained at the thought, and answered his own question. "They would no longer trust us. And how then could we do our work?"

Rosabella said nothing, unable to cope with his brazen hypocrisy.

"Money is money," Cutolo continued after a pause. "It has no memory of where it came from and cares not where it goes. Neither does whatever is in that box. Signora, you cannot live on charity. This money will make the difference between living in poverty and being able to take care of your child. I assure you, it is enough to make your life considerably easier."

Rosabella looked around the parlour, at the sepia photographs of her parents and their parents, all of them looking stiffly but proudly at the camera, secure in the knowledge that they had made a good life for themselves and their descendants. She couldn't ignore that, and she could not bring herself to let them down by raising her child as a pauper, dependent on the unreliable good will of other people. Cesare had stolen from his cousins and from the man sitting opposite her–if his victims all told her to take the money, surely she should accept it and be grateful.

"But I don't know where the money is," she said, a last attempt to delay what she now knew to be inevitable, if not desirable.

"I will ask Cesare's book-keeper to get you the money," Cutolo said. "He knows where it is."

That answered one of Tifeo's many questions.

"Signora, this tragic affair cannot be unwound and we cannot bring Cesare back to you. All I can do is apologise from the bottom of my heart for what has happened, and hope that you can forgive me."

"Ulisse needs my forgiveness, not you," said Rosabella. "Cesare died by his hand, not yours."

"Nevertheless," said Cutolo, "I cannot help but feel responsible. I would like to do what I can to help you in this difficult time. For example, if you would trust me with Cesare's box, I will ensure that you get the best possible price for its contents."

Once Cutolo had left, carrying the box with its key, Rosabella returned to the parlour. Tifeo was still sitting where she'd left him. He said, "Would you like Amedea to come down and keep you company? She told me to ask you."

"How could Cesare be so stupid?" she asked. "And so greedy. He stole from his cousins, he stole from the dead people after the crash, he stole from that man…"

Tifeo put his hands up in defeat. "I don't know…" he started.

"And you know what the worst thing is?" she asked, rolling over whatever he was about to say. Her voice rose with her fury. "He betrayed his family. He betrayed his cousins by stealing from them, and he betrayed me and my baby by putting us at risk. How did he ever think he could get away with taking money from the Camorra? He lied to me, you know, he told me he wasn't part of the looting, that he hated the mutilation. Tell me, did he cut fingers off dead men? Did he cut teeth from their mouths? Did he lie about that as well?"

"I don't know," said Tifeo. "I honestly don't know."

"He lied to me," shouted Rosabella, "and now I doubt everything about him. What else did he lie to me about? How can I trust anything he said? I don't think he ever really loved me. If he did, how could he do this to me? How can I possibly forgive him for what he did?"

Tifeo said, "I'm sure he loved you," but his words were lost in a storm of sobbing. An overwhelming wave of sorrow surged through the dam of her self-control, and Rosabella cried her broken heart out as she grieved, not for her dead husband, but for everything else she'd lost. Her future, her dreams, her illusions.

Chapter Twenty-six

THE LIGHT WAS FAILING as the small group made its way up the track out of Fontana. It was a warm, clear April evening and the sky was a deep indigo over their heads. The sun had just passed beyond the horizon and the warm glow of the light reflected off the waters of the Bay like burnished copper.

Tifeo and Amedea walked on either side of Father Renato, who was dressed in the rough clothes of an Ischian farm labourer. This was the first time Amedea had seen him without his cassock and white priest's collar and she thoroughly approved of the transformation. She liked Renato but found his normal uniform to be a barrier. He must be lonely, she thought, always separate from the people around him.

She'd had to work hard to dissuade Rosabella from joining them.

"I want to come," Rosabella had said. "Maybe Cesare will be up there, I can tell him what I think of him."

"It's far too risky," Amedea had insisted. "You're due in only a few days."

Rosabella had reluctantly agreed to stay behind with Baldassare, who'd seemed glad of the chance to keep her company. But Amedea wondered how her friend would ever get over Cesare's many betrayals.

Adolfo brought up the rear, carrying a small box and lost in his thoughts. Despite his ready acceptance of Tifeo's offer of help, he was scared. Sharing his darkest secrets with Tifeo in private was one thing, publicly confessing his sins was something else entirely. He knew very well what people thought he'd done, and he dreaded the moment when he said out loud what they all believed anyway. And why had they invited that damned priest to come along?

His feet seemed heavier with every step up the mountain. Nothing good had ever happened to him where they were going and, as they got higher up the mountain, his doubts about what they were doing only grew stronger. But turning back would be even more humiliating, so he kept going, head down so he wouldn't have to talk with anyone.

This was the third time in three days that Renato had made this trip and his legs were starting to feel the strain. The first trip had been to help Tifeo re-erect the cross. As the blacksmith had thought, the high winds of the storm had simply blown the cross over, the two bolts acting as a hinge. There was no damage to the cross itself so they drilled another pair of holes in the rock, put the cross back up and anchored two more bolts across the foot, cemented securely into the holes.

"That cross should still be standing there when you and I are no longer here to see it," Tifeo said. "Having four bolts there will keep it up regardless of what the wind might do."

The two of them returned the next day for a quiet Mass.

"This isn't really necessary," Renato had said, "but I'll feel better for doing it."

The small, private service was one of the most satisfying celebrations of his faith that he ever experienced. Being so high on the mountain, he felt he could reach up and touch Heaven, and there was a solemn hush in the air–it was as if God, his angels, and all the saints paused in what they were doing to be part of their celebration. And he could feel ancient divinities paying attention to and approving of what he was saying and doing.

By the end of Mass, Renato had arrived at a state of exultation unlike anything he'd known since he first officiated as a new priest. Tifeo had waited until his friend collected himself. "That was beautiful," he said. "I could feel their presence all around us."

Renato wasn't sure if Tifeo was talking about the Heavenly host or the mountain gods, but it didn't really matter any more, and he just nodded in agreement.

His new-found acceptance that his God and the mountain gods could co-exist seemed entirely natural. Long ago, people worshipped gods who represented all that was virtuous, something that didn't seem all that different from the small army of saints celebrated by the Church, some martyred and some not, but all demonstrating one or more of the very same virtues. And if his faith focused on his individual God, that did not have to mean he had to deny the others.

On the way back to Fontana after the Mass, he told Tifeo that the Bishop had offered him a position at Sorrento, a prestigious role in a much larger parish. "It would be a significant promotion for me," he said, "exactly what I was hoping for."

"Congratulations," Tifeo said. "When do you leave?"

"I don't."

"What?"

"I told him I was very happy here," Renato said, enjoying Tifeo's surprise. "That I felt fully satisfied doing God's work in a smaller community. That I liked my volcanos to be asleep and that working at the foot of Mount Vesuvius, always smoking, would be a constant distraction. That I valued his approval and hoped I could continue to earn it by staying on Ischia."

"And what did he say to that?"

"Oh, I don't think he understood it at all. He was showing me a path to become Bishop one day, the same path that he travelled with such energy. He must have been very disappointed that I turned down something that he valued so highly, something he thought I wanted. Something *I* thought I wanted. But I would be a very poor Bishop, you know. The Church is better off with me here."

"As are we, Renato," Tifeo said. "The town needs you."

Renato smiled. He said, "I didn't tell the Bishop this, but I also like being a bit further away from his watchful eye. I can be a touch more flexible here in how I interpret some of the stricter demands placed on me as a priest of the Church. Being so easily overlooked is a mixed blessing, isn't it? "

Tifeo thought of Paolo, and said nothing.

"And I would suffocate in a large town," Renato said, sounding a little surprised at himself, having grown up in one. "I've come to love this mountain, and I've learned that I can find God out here as easily as in our church, as beautiful as it is. Perhaps even more easily."

As Tifeo walked up the track with Renato and Amedea, he

breathed in the scent of the warm air, a rich mixture of rosemary, pine and traces of lemon brought up from further down the mountain. Of course Renato finds his God out here, he thought. What he calls God, I call the gods, and they are all around us. Why would they consent to be trapped in the stone walls of a man-made building? Their real home is out here, roaming freely over the mountains and hills as they have since the beginning of time. And when they see fit to honour you with their attention, they will make their presence felt and, if you are very lucky, tell you the things they think you should know.

Turning a corner and arriving at the small side track that led to the crash site, they found Demonte resting against a rock. A small lamb was tethered to his ankle by an old piece of rope. The lamb had found a patch of grass where it could graze without pulling on the tether and waking Demonte, who appeared to be dozing. It raised its head from the grass and looked at them suspiciously. It didn't seem to like what it saw, for it tossed its head and tugged on the rope. Demonte opened his eyes.

"You're finally here," he said. "I thought you'd never arrive."

He'd been waiting there for some time. But before going to wait for Tifeo and the others, he'd gone to visit Paolo. The grave was just off the path between his hut and the crash site; it was easy to take the lamb there, tie it up to the chestnut tree, and sit in his usual spot in the shade. It wasn't long before he felt Paolo's presence.

"Hello, Paolo," he'd said, not expecting any reply. His conversations with Paolo were always one way.

"Hello, brother."

Startled, he sat up and looked around, feeling very stupid.

"I'm here with you, Demonte," said Paolo. "I always have been."

"Paolo, my little brother," said Demonte fondly. "How I've missed you."

"I'm here," Paolo said again. "I always know when you come to be with me."

"I'm glad," said Demonte. "But I wish you were still with me in the house, that we might talk and eat together as we used to."

"Do not wish for what you do not and cannot have," said Paolo's spirit. "It is better by far to enjoy what you already have."

"But I miss you," Demonte said again. "And it feels worse because it was all my fault."

"All what?"

"I was too hard on you. I thought your troubles were a sign of weakness, that I had to make you stronger, tougher. I loved you so much and did not want to see you hurt."

Paolo said, "It is not your fault that I was broken by forces I could not withstand."

"Paolo, please forgive me," whispered Demonte through his tears. "I go to bed each night with the bitter regret of knowing that I let you down. I promised our father I would look after you, and I failed."

"There is nothing to forgive. I knew you loved me, that you did your best for me."

"But I still feel the guilt. I have often thought I should throw myself off the cliff and join you."

"Don't do that," the spirit said, quite alarmed. "You are one of the few people who knows what happened after the crash, both the bad and the good. I tell you again, you have no reason for guilt. But if that is not enough, then live long enough that you can tell the story of all that happened here."

"But how can I live with myself?"

"Go to bed each night comforted that you did your best for me. Guilt is for people who know they did wrong. You did no wrong and have no reason to feel guilty. You did your best, and no one can ask for more than that."

"My best wasn't good enough. That is my burden."

"You can never go back and use the wisdom of today to solve the problems of yesterday," said the spirit. "What's done is done, can never be undone or redone. All anyone can do is live with it."

"That's a hard lesson," said Demonte.

"Indeed."

"Will you still be here?" Demonte asked. "I would like to visit you and feel your presence."

"When I became one of them," Paolo said, "the spirits promised me I would be here until you joined me."

"I will be by myself until then."

"Keep my memory alive," Paolo's spirit said, "and I will always be with you."

A moment later, Demonte realized that he was alone again except for the lamb, who was placidly chewing the lush grass beside the grave. He sat for a while trying to gather himself. Then, seeing the sun sink towards the horizon, he went up the path and found a place to sit comfortably while he waited for Tifeo and the others.

Now they'd arrived, it was time to stand up and stretch.

"Are you all here?" Demonte asked as Adolfo arrived. Without waiting for an answer, he started along the track to the crash site. leading the lamb by its rope.

The rocks on either side of the path glowed in the last light as they threaded their way in single file along the narrow path. The site was empty when they arrived except for a large circle of stones with a small conical pile of wood stacked up in the middle. More firewood had been placed beside one of the stones. On the other side of the site, the cross stood proud on its small peak, outlined against the deep rose-pink of the sky.

"Baldassare and I came up this morning to get things ready," Tifeo said in answer to Renato's questioning look. To the group, he said, "Take a seat anywhere around the circle. Sit on a rock if you wish, or on the ground leaning against a rock. But whatever happens, do not go outside the circle."

Amedea sat opposite Renato, leaving room for Tifeo between them. Demonte pounded a small stake into the ground beside the entrance, tied the lamb to the stake, and settled down on the ground beside it. Adolfo sat on the other side of the opening.

Tifeo opened a large bag he'd been carrying and pulled out five small earthenware plates and a loaf of fresh bread. He put the plates down around the outside of the stone circle, making sure they were equally spaced from each other, forming a perfect star with a point on either side of the entrance. He went around again and put a torn-off piece of bread on each plate. Returning to his bag, he took out five clay goblets and a bottle of wine. Going around the circle a last time, he put a goblet beside each plate, pouring a little wine into each one. Renato watched all this with a radiant face.

When Tifeo was satisfied with the offerings, he came back into the circle. Kneeling in front of the pile of wood, he pulled out a box of matches and lit the wood shavings and dried grasses at the base. Within seconds, the fire leapt up and began licking hungrily at the heavier wood.

His preparations complete, he went and sat between Amedea and Renato.

"Now we wait," he said. "The spirits and the gods know we are here and our gifts show that we welcome them. When they are ready, they will speak to us. Perhaps to all or some of us, perhaps to just one. When they speak to you, you will know what to do."

Adolfo could sense the spirits from the moment the group arrived at the crash site. They knew we were coming, he thought. They knew that *I* was coming. The idea was not reassuring. It was bad enough seeing Amedea, Tifeo and the others all trying hard not to look at him, but feeling the spirits all around him was exquisite agony. They did not seem angry or hostile, but more… intense. It seemed they had unfinished business with him and were determined to get it done. He felt very vulnerable, and very exposed, and very afraid.

The fire roared higher and higher, sparks flying up into the sky. Adolfo could not bring himself to look back into the gathering darkness beyond the circle, so he focused on the fire. Very quickly, he became mesmerised by the flickering flames, curling lasciviously around pieces of wood, the tongues of fire weaving an intricate, timeless dance.

He was entirely unsurprised when he saw a face looking at him from the fire. It was only a matter of time before the spirits revealed themselves. But which one was this?

Your brother killed me, the spirit said. I was at death's door already, but he pushed me through and took away the little time left to me.

I'm sorry, said Adolfo. This was the soldier in the plane, sitting next to the small boy with his crayon. Adolfo remembered the blood and brains spattered on the soldier's uniform and Ulisse's trousers, and Ulisse screaming incoherently. He shook his head to clear the images away.

Why should you be sorry? asked the spirit. You didn't kill me. That was your brother.

I should have stopped him. I regret not doing that.

Regret for things not done is futile, said the spirit. There are so many paths not taken, you could spend the rest of your life lost in regret. Your brother, on the other hand, has much to be sorry for. Where is he?

He has gone far away. But he feels no regret or guilt for what he has done, and your forgiveness would mean nothing to him.

Nevertheless, I have forgiven him. Not for his sake, but for mine. He must live with what he did, but he no longer lives in my thoughts. I was tied to this place by anger and sorrow, but by forgiving him, I have freed myself of him. And now I can leave.

Across the fire, Tifeo had been watching Adolfo. He didn't know which spirit had occupied Adolfo's mind and it didn't really matter. It was enough that the spirits had come out and that the healing had begun. He could see that Demonte, being of the mountain, knew what was happening, but the shepherd sat calmly, the lamb quiet beside him. Judging by their faces, it seemed that none of the others had experienced anything out of the ordinary.

Adolfo watched as Tifeo got up and put more wood on the fire. Strange, shifting shadows flickered across the stone wall and the bushes beyond the circle.

"Oh, no," Adolfo cried out as the shadows took shape. Spirits from the crash surrounded the circle, staring accusingly at him. In desperation, he tried looking into the fire, but was confronted by the spirit of the man he'd killed. Guilt crashed in on him from all directions—guilt for stealing from dead people, guilt for mutilating them, and the worst of them all from being denied for so long, guilt for killing a helpless man. So much guilt, so much evil, so much to be bitterly ashamed of–the weight of it all filled him with horror. He was a good man, he knew he was, but he had done these things, and did not know if he could ever live with himself again with this dark, indelible stain on his soul.

The spirit in the fire looked hard at Adolfo as the other spirits moved closer to the stone walls. Adolfo sank to the ground, holding his head, unable to look at any of them. His mind was a violent whirlpool of pain and the agonised loss of all that might have been, for him and for them. No, he howled, no, get away from me, let me be.

The spirits moved in even closer. Adolfo clambered clumsily to his feet and backed away from the fire and the spirit there, but the stone wall was right behind him. Panicked, he climbed over it and ran into the darkness. Behind him, he dimly heard Tifeo shouting his name but paid it no heed.

Just a few yards from the stone circle, he was forced to stop by shrubs as high as his waist. Without more light, he could not see a path away from the circle and the spirits. He turned to go back to the circle but stopped when he realized the spirits had moved with him and now surrounded him. The priest from the plane, the man who lost his head, a woman holding a tiny baby in one arm, a very small boy, the pilots, the soldier that Ulisse killed, they were all there, looking at him.

He said, You were already dead, I did you no harm.

Do not mock us, a spirit said. Desecrating the dead is the act of an animal, not a decent man.

I'm not an animal, he shouted back. And it's not my fault that you crashed up here, that was your doing. Why blame me for what anyone would have done?

He knew that anyone else on Ischia would have done what he did, had they the opportunity. Besides, his outrage was a welcome relief from the guilt, something that might deflect these spirits from their course.

If someone else had done what you did, they would be standing here instead of you, a spirit said calmly, and we would be saying the same things to them.

It was the middle-aged man from the back of the plane.

Adolfo sank to his knees again, defeated by his inability to defend himself. He said, What would you have me do? Should I give all the money away? Perhaps I should find your families and give it to them. Is that what you want?

Oh, no, said another spirit. You cannot buy your way out of this.

Then what must I do so you will leave me in peace?

A last, pathetic attempt to retain a little dignity.

He did not hear the answer, because Tifeo and Renato ran up behind him and, seizing him under each arm, lifted him to his feet.

"No," he cried, "I have to finish."

"Finish inside the circle," said Tifeo. "I told you not to leave the circle, didn't I? It's not safe out here."

They hustled him back to the circle, through the small entrance, and returned him to his place. The others looked at him in astonishment, wondering why he'd rushed away and what had happened out there.

After he climbed over the wall, they could just see him in the light from the fire, standing in front of the bushes waving his arms in silence like a madman. There was no sound except the sighing of the wind. When he sank to his knees, Tifeo said to Renato, "You and I must go out there and get him. They will not harm us."

It was a measure of how much Renato trusted Tifeo that he did not hesitate. The two men rushed out from the circle, grabbed Adolfo and brought him back.

Now he sat sobbing on his rock, his head in his hands.

Amedea came and sat beside him.

"Are you alright, Adolfo?" she asked. "What happened?"

"The spirits," whispered Adolfo. "They were all there."

"What spirits? Who are they?"

Adolfo raised his head to respond, but froze. "They're out there," he said. "Waiting for me." Just over Amedea's shoulder, he could see the spirits huddled together on the other side of the open entrance to the circle. The spirit of the man he killed stood at one end of the group, an indecipherable look on his face.

Amedea followed his gaze but saw nothing except the darkness. Even though Tifeo had warned her of what might happen, a cold trickle of fear slid down her back.

Renato crossed himself. He could not see the spirits but he could feel them. And beyond them, he knew the mountain gods were watching and waiting.

Tifeo coughed to get everyone's attention. He said, "Much has happened on the mountain since the gods were last at peace here. They do not often think of us, but we have troubled them and they are disturbed. It is time to appease them in the way that people here have done since days beyond memory. Demonte, will you bring the lamb, that we might offer his life to the gods?"

The lamb had been waiting placidly beside the entrance, but once Demonte untied him from the stake, seemed to know the fate that awaited him. He began to bleat frantically, pulling against the rope around his neck and struggling to get loose. Renato went over to help Demonte and between them they wrestled the lamb to the ground. Renato held it pinned down while Demonte pulled some pieces of old twine from his pocket and lashed its feet together. Breathing heavily from their exertions, the two men stood up. The lamb lay on its side at their feet, kicking feebly and looking up at them with an accusing eye.

"We sacrifice this lamb to wash away our sins," Tifeo said. "By watering the ground with its blood, we seek redemption from the gods who live here. And the lamb is also an offering to them, to show that we honour them and to ask them to restore peace to this place."

Adolfo listened to Tifeo while still looking through the entrance at the spirit of the priest. Remember me, the spirit said, and what you did to me.

Tifeo's words faded into the background as Adolfo fell into the memories of that dreadful night. The damp, freezing fog, the plane lying across the hillside, the bodies lying on the ground like broken dolls… and the sickening, wet sound of his rock crashing into this man's forehead. The shuddering of his legs as he died from the blow.

"No," he cried, "no!" He turned around as Tifeo raised the lamb's head and prepared to draw his knife across the neck. "No," he cried out again, "you can't. There's been enough killing here already."

Tifeo hesitated, annoyed that the solemnity of the sacrifice had been disturbed. It was important that the lamb died quickly and cleanly, with dignity. The interruption was unseemly, disrespectful. Then he looked up as Adolfo's words sank in.

"Enough killing?" he asked. "What do you mean?"

"Put the knife down," Adolfo said. "Put it down, there's something I must say."

Reluctantly, Tifeo put the knife on the ground. Whatever was troubling Adolfo had to be serious, he was the last person in the group to be squeamish about killing a sheep.

Adolfo said, "Tifeo, the gods are disturbed because of all the wrongs done here. One more killing will not appease them."

"One more *killing*? What are you talking about?"

"Sacrificing a lamb and shedding his blood will not undo the wrongs done here, and cannot remove my guilt. How can slaying innocence possibly purify sin? Our sins live within us, and cannot be discarded so easily."

Tifeo said, "The gods…"

"…demand blood, I know. But this lamb has done nothing wrong and we should not ask it to carry the burden of our sins. If the gods need blood, I will give them mine, so they know I truly repent of the harm I have done."

He took out his father's knife.

Amedea cried, "Adolfo, don't do it!"

Renato crossed himself and put his hand inside his shirt to hold the crucifix that lay against his chest. Tifeo and Demonte gentled the lamb, which now lay quietly as they stroked it.

Adolfo looked at her sadly, tears in his eyes. "I must," he said.

"There will be no peace on the mountain until the gods taste my blood."

He stepped through the gap in the stone wall and turned to face the fire. Tifeo made no move to stop him leaving the safety of the circle.

Slowly and carefully, Adolfo drew the razor edge of the knife from one end of his forearm to the other. Blood quickly welled up along the cut, running down to his hand and glistening red in the light of the fire. He held his hand just above the ground beside the nearest goblet, allowing generous drops of blood to fall to the dry earth. Going around the fire, he offered his blood beside each of the other goblets. The earth drank the blood within seconds, leaving only the slightest of stains.

By the time he got back to the entrance, Adolfo felt light-headed with relief. At last, he knew what he had to do.

He faced the group inside the circle. He had no choice but to trust himself to them.

"This is very hard for me," he said, "but it must be done. I have said this to Tifeo, but I must now say out loud what you know already. To my shame, I took things from the people who died in the crash. Worse, I...I..." The words caught in his throat. Unable to continue, he breathed deeply while the others waited. When he recovered, he said, "I cut them, to get things I could not take otherwise. I wish I had not."

Tifeo began to speak but Adolfo stopped him. "There's more," he said. "One of the English was thrown from the plane. He was still alive when we found him, just. He was wearing a cloak, with a hood that covered his head. It must have been cold in the airplane, I suppose."

He looked over at Father Renato, who was watching him with a growing look of horror.

"Forgive me, Father," Adolfo said. "I thought he was a priest." He laughed, without a trace of humour. "But that's no excuse, is it? For killing him, I mean."

Oh, Giovanni, thought Father Renato, look at what you did.

Look at how violence begets violence, how abusing a young boy shaped someone capable of killing a helpless man, how victims can, when the circumstances are just so, create more victims. This is one face of evil, when Satan conspires to make good people do terrible things by exploiting their flaws. And we're all flawed, so who can tell what evil we might do in different circumstances?

"This was my greatest sin," Adolfo said to the group, his voice shaking, "killing a helpless man because I could not control my anger and shame."

He looked at Tifeo. "Killing an innocent lamb could never undo the sin of killing an innocent man, could it? How could the gods possibly demand such a sacrifice before they forgive us?"

In complete silence, he turned and walked out to the waiting spirits.

He said, The gods have drunk their fill. They know that I truly repent of what I have done. Now I am here in front of you. What would you have me do?

One of the spirits said, Adolfo, we are tied together by your deeds. You know this as well as anyone. We ask for no more than what you asked of Father Giovanni.

Adolfo swallowed several times, trying to lose the tightness in his throat. His wet cheeks reflected the light of the fire.

Spirits, he managed to say. I am here.

He stopped, looking at the ground.

The spirits waited with the patience of beings with all eternity ahead of them.

Adolfo took a deep breath and raised his head to look directly at them. Another deep breath, as he visibly prepared himself.

Spirits, he said, I did you great wrong. I stole from you. I desecrated your bodies. I killed one of you. I wish with all my heart I had not done these things, but I did. I am deeply sorry that I harmed you so, and beg your forgiveness.

The spirit of the middle-aged man said, Have you learned nothing? When you forgave Father Giovanni, that was for your benefit, not his. So it is with us. We can forgive you, but that will not help you.

I don't know what to do, cried Adolfo.

You will live the rest of your life knowing that you stole from us, replied the spirit, that you killed a helpless man. Our forgiveness will not undo what you did, will not take away the knowledge. Stop looking to others for forgiveness, Adolfo. The only person who must forgive you is you.

The other spirits nodded in agreement.

Adolfo said, Now I know how Father Giovanni felt when he begged me for forgiveness.

For the first time, he saw compassion on the faces before him.

You have acknowledged what you did, said another spirit. Adolfo, we forgive you for what you did, and hope you can find peace within yourself. For our part, we can start to unravel the threads that tie us to you and to this place. We have no wish to take anger with us where we are going. Soon we will be gone, leaving only memories behind.

Memories are short and fragile, said Adolfo. It will not be long before people forget who died here.

That is the way things are. We all die, and the most we can hope for is to live on for a short time in the memories of people who knew and loved us.

Adolfo said, I cannot undo the things I have done. But I can atone for them.

How? asked the spirit.

What is more permanent than stone? Adolfo said. I will make a memorial to you in granite, a stone with all your names on it, and will place it under the cross. When people see the cross, they will wonder why it is there and will come to find out. The stone will tell them of the crash and who died in this place. That is my promise to you all, to keep your memory alive. There is a kind of immortality in that.

Adolfo walked back to the entrance to the circle. Standing in the gap, he turned to the spirits to say goodbye and wish them well.

Some are ready to leave, said one of the spirits. But some of us are still held back.

Why? asked Adolfo, I have done all I can. What else must I do?

In response, four of the spirits held up a hand. All of them were missing a finger.

You took part of our bodies, the spirit said, and we were buried incomplete. We can feel them nearby and cannot leave while you hold them.

What must I do with them? asked Adolfo.

Send them to Heaven, for that is where we are going.

Adolfo turned to Tifeo.

"Build up the fire," he said, "there is one last thing I must do."

When the fire was roaring high, Adolfo retrieved the small box from where he had placed it next to his seat. Looking through the entrance, he could see the spirits watching. He opened the box. Inside, four fingers lay side by side, brown and shrivelled. He was never quite sure why he'd kept them, but had taken great care to hide them safely in the secret crevice. Now he knew.

He closed the box. He took the two longest sticks left in the pile and held them out so Tifeo could balance the box across them at the end, then carefully placed the box at the very top of the fire.

Within seconds, the box burst into flames. The group stood around the fire, fixated by the flames and heat, watching the box get consumed. No one said a word.

The fire suddenly collapsed, releasing a huge shower of sparks that flew high up into the air before being blown sideways out of the circle into the darkness. Startled, everyone stepped back and then looked at each other, slightly embarrassed by their reaction. They all sat down on their rock, except for Adolfo.

He went back to the entrance and looked out. The hillside was bare except for some rocks, the bushes waving gently in the breeze that always blew at the top of the mountain, and the cross on its peak, standing strong in the light of the fire.

His remorse at everything he'd done up here still sat heavy in his heart and he knew it would be a long time before he learned how to live with it. But as he took his place with the others, he also felt more at peace than any time he could remember.

They stayed there long into the night, until the moon rose behind Mount Epomeo and the fire burned down, leaving only a few glowing embers. When it was time, they left without looking back, walking carefully back to the main track under the gentle light of the moon.

The townsfolk took the track down to Fontana, Amedea as always with Tifeo, Adolfo at Renato's side. Demonte watched them leave, then took his lamb and led it past Paolo's grave, down the path to his hut and his quiet, solitary life as a shepherd.

Behind them, the mountain was silent, and peaceful, and empty.

www.ingramcontent.com/pod-product-compliance
Lightning Source LLC
Chambersburg PA
CBHW030358030726
47497CB00002B/388